Humphry Ward

I0592264

Sir George Tressady by Mrs. Humphry Ward

Third edition

Humphry Ward

Sir George Tressady by Mrs. Humphry Ward
Third edition

ISBN/EAN: 9783743333192

Manufactured in Europe, USA, Canada, Australia, Japa

Cover: Foto ©Andreas Hilbeck / pixelio.de

Manufactured and distributed by brebook publishing software
(www.brebook.com)

Humphry Ward

Sir George Tressady by Mrs. Humphry Ward

SIR GEORGE TRESSADY

BY

MRS HUMPHRY WARD

AUTHOR OF

'ROBERT ELSMERE' 'DAVID GRIEVE' 'MARCELLA' ETC.

THIRD EDITION

LONDON

SMITH, ELDER, & CO., 15 WATERLOO PLACE

1897

SIR GEORGE TRESSADY

PART I

CHAPTER I

' WELL, that's over, thank Heaven ! '

The young man speaking drew in his head from the carriage-window. But instead of sitting down he turned with a joyous, excited gesture and lifted the flap over the little window in the back of the landau, supporting himself, as he stooped to look, by a hand on his companion's shoulder. Through this peephole he saw, as the horses trotted away, the crowd in the main street of Market Malford, still huzzaing and waving, the wild glare of half a dozen torches on the faces and the moving forms, the closed shops on either hand, the irregular roofs and chimneys sharp-cut against a wintry sky, and in the far distance the little lantern belfry and taller mass of the new town-hall.

'I'm much astonished the horses didn't bolt ! ' said the man addressed. ' That bay mare would have lost all the temper she's got in another moment. It's a good thing we made them shut the carriage—it has turned abominably cold. Hadn't you better sit down ? '

And Lord Fontenoy made a movement as though to withdraw from the hand on his shoulder.

The owner of the hand flung himself down on the

B

seat, with a word of apology, took off his hat, and drew a
long breath of fatigue. At the same moment a sudden
look of disgust effaced the smile with which he had taken
his last glimpse at the crowd.

'All very well!—but what one wants after this business is *a moral tub!* The lies I've told during the last
three weeks—the bunkum I've talked!—it's a feeling
of positive dirt! And the worst of it is, however
you may scrub your mind afterwards, some of it must
stick.'

He took out a cigarette, and lit it at his companion's
with a rather unsteady hand. He had a thin, long face,
and fair hair; and one would have guessed him some
ten years younger than the man beside him.

'Certainly—it will stick,' said the other. 'Election
promises nowadays are sharply looked after. I heard no
bunkum. As far as I know, our party doesn't talk any.
We leave that to the Government!'

Sir George Tressady, the young man addressed,
shrugged his shoulders. His mouth was still twitching
under the influence of nervous excitement. But as they
rolled along between the dark hedges, the carriage-lamps
shining on their wet branches, green yet, in spite of
November, he began to recover a half-cynical self-control.
The poll for the Market Malford Division of West Mercia
had been declared that afternoon, between two and three
o'clock, after a hotly contested election; he, as the
successful candidate by a very narrow majority, had since
addressed a shouting mob from the balcony of the Grey-
hound Hotel, had suffered the usual taking out of horses
and triumphal dragging through the town, and was now
returning with his supporter and party-leader, Lord
Fontenoy, to the great Tory mansion which had sent
them forth in the morning, and had been Tressady's headquarters during the greater part of the fight.

'Did you ever see anyone so down as Bewick?' he said presently, with a little leap of laughter. 'By George! it *is* hard lines. I suppose he thought himself safe, what with the work he'd done in the division and the hold he had on the miners. Then a confounded stranger turns up, and the chance of seventeen ignorant voters kicks you out! He could hardly bring himself to shake hands with me. I had come rather to admire him, hadn't you?'

Lord Fontenoy nodded.

'I thought his speeches showed ability,' he said, indifferently, 'only of a kind that must be kept out of Parliament—that's all. Sorry you have qualms—quite unnecessary, I assure you! At the present moment, either Bewick and his like knock under, or you and your like. This time—by seventeen votes—Bewick knocks under. Thank the Lord! say I'—and the speaker opened the window an instant to knock off the end of his cigar.

Tressady made no reply. But again a look, half-chagrined, half-reflective, puckered his brow, which was smooth, white, and boyish under his straight, fair hair; whereas the rest of the face was subtly lined, and browned as though by travel and varied living. The nose and mouth, though not handsome, were small and delicately cut, while the long, pointed chin, slightly protruding, made those who disliked him say that he was like those innumerable portraits of Philip IV., by and after Velasquez, which bestrew the collections of Europe. But if the Hapsburg chin had to be admitted, nothing could be more modern, intelligent, alert than the rest of him.

The two rolled along a while in silence. They were passing through an undulating midland country, dimly seen under the stars. At frequent intervals rose high mounds, with tall chimneys and huddled buildings beside

them or upon them which marked the sites of collieries;
while the lights also, which had begun to twinkle
over the face of the land, showed that it was thickly
inhabited.

Suddenly the carriage rattled into a village, and Tressady looked out.

'I say, Fontenoy, here's a crowd! Do you suppose
they know? Why, Gregson's taken us another way round!'

Lord Fontenoy let down his window, and identified
the small mining village of Battage.

'Why did you bring us this way, Gregson?' he said
to the coachman.

The man, a Londoner, turned, and spoke in a low
voice. 'I thought we might find some rioting going on
in Marraby, my Lord. And now I see there's lots o them
out here!'

Indeed, with the words he had to check his horses.
The village street was full from end to end with miners
just come up from work. Fontenoy at once perceived
that the news of the election had arrived. The men
were massed in large groups, talking and discussing, with
evident and angry excitement, and as soon as the well-
known liveries on the box of the new member's carriage
were identified there was an instant rush towards it.
Some of the men had already gone into their houses on
either hand, but at the sound of the wheels and the
uproar they came pouring out again. A howling hubbub
arose, a confused sound of booing and groaning, and the
carriage was soon surrounded by grimed men, gesticulating and shouting.

'Yer bloated parasites, yer!' cried a young fellow,
catching at the door-handle on Lord Fontenoy's side;
'we'll make a d——d end o yer afore we've done wi
yer. Who asked yer to come meddlin in Malford—
d——n yer!'

'Whativer do we want wi the loikes o yo representin us!' shouted another man, pointing at Tressady. 'Look at im; ee can't walk, ee can't; mus be druv, poor hinnercent! When did yo iver do a day's work, eh? Look at my ands! Them's the ands for honest men—ain't they, you fellers?'

There was a roar of laughter and approval from the crowd, and up went a forest of begrimed hands, flourishing and waving.

George calmly put down the carriage-window, and, leaning his arms upon it, put his head out. He flung some good-humoured banter at some of the nearest men, and two or three responded. But the majority of the faces were lowering and fierce, and the horses were becoming inconveniently crowded.

'Get on, Gregson,' said Fontenoy, opening the front window of the brougham.

'If they'll let me, your lordship,' said Gregson, rather pale, raising his whip.

The horses made a sudden start forward. There was a yell from the crowd, and three or four men had just dashed for the horses' heads, when a shout of a different kind ascended.

'Bewick! Ere's Bewick! Three cheers for Bewick!'

And some distance behind them, at the corner of the village street, Tressady suddenly perceived a tall dog-cart drawing up with two men in it. It was already surrounded by a cheering and tumultuous assembly, and one of the men in the cart was shaking hands right and left.

George drew in his head, with a laugh. 'This is dramatic. They've stopped the horses, and here's Bewick!'

Fontenoy shrugged his shoulders. 'They'll blackguard us a bit, I suppose, and let us go. Bewick 'll keep them in order.'

'What d'yer mean by it, heh, dash yer!' shouted a huge man, as he sprang on the step of the carriage and shook a black fist in Tressady's face—'thrustin yer d——d carkiss where yer ain't wanted? We wanted *im*, and we've worked for im. This is a workin-class district, an we've a *right* to im. Do yer ear?'

'Then you should have given him seventeen more votes,' said George composedly, as he thrust his hands into his pockets. 'It's the fortunes of war—your turn next time. I say, suppose you tell your fellows to let our man get on. We've had a long day, and we're hungry. Ah '—to Fontenoy—'here's Bewick coming!'

Fontenoy turned, and saw that the dogcart had drawn up alongside them, and that one of the men was standing on the step of it, holding on to the rail of the cart.

He was a tall, finely built man, and as he looked down on the carriage, and on Tressady leaning over the window, the light from a street-lamp near showed a handsome face blanched with excitement and fatigue.

'Now, my friends,' he said, raising his arm, and addressing the crowd, 'you let Sir George go home to his dinner. He's beaten us, and so far as I know *he's* fought fair, whatever some of his friends may have done for him. I'm going home to have a bite of something and a wash. I'm done. But if any of you like to come round to the club—eight o'clock—I'll tell you a thing or two about this election. Now good-night to you, Sir George. We'll beat you yet, trust us. Fall back there!'

He pointed peremptorily to the men holding the horses. They and the crowd instantly obeyed him.

The carriage swept on, followed by the hooting and groans of the whole community, men, women, and children, who were now massed along the street on either hand.

'It's easy to see this man Gregson's a new hand,' said Fontenoy, with an accent of annoyance, as they got clear of the village. 'I believe the Wattons have only just imported him, otherwise he'd never have avoided Marraby, and come round by Battage.'

'Battage has some special connection with Bewick, hasn't it? I had forgotten.'

'Of course. He was check-weigher at the Acme pit here for years, before they made him district secretary of the union.'

'That's why they gave me such a hot meeting here a fortnight ago!—I remember now; but one thing drives another out of one's head. Well, I daresay you and I'll have plenty more to do with Bewick before we've done.'

Tressady threw himself back in his corner with a yawn.

Fontenoy laughed.

'There'll be another big strike some time next year,' he said drily—'bound to be, as far as I can see. We shall all have plenty to do with Bewick then.'

'All right,' said Tressady indistinctly, pulling his hat over his eyes. 'Bewick or anybody else may blow me up next year, so long as they let me go to sleep now.'

However, he did not find it so easy to go to sleep. His pulses were still tingling under the emotions of the day and the stimulus of the hubbub they had just passed through. His mind raced backwards and forwards over the incidents and excitements of the last six months, over the scenes of his canvass—and over some other scenes of a different kind which had taken place in the country-house whither he and Fontenoy were returning.

But he did his best to feign sleep. His one desire was that Fontenoy should not talk to him. Fontenoy, however, was not easily taken in, and no sooner did George make his first restless movement under the rug he had drawn over him, than his companion broke silence.

'By the way, what did you think of that memorandum of mine on Maxwell's bill?'

George fidgeted and mumbled. Fontenoy, undaunted, began to harangue on certain minutiæ of factory law with a monotonous zest of voice and gesture which seemed to Tressady nothing short of amazing.

He watched the speaker a minute or two through his half-shut eyes. So this was his leader to be—the man who had made him member for Market Malford.

Eight years before, when George Tressady had first entered Christchurch, he had found that place of tempered learning alive with traditions on the subject of 'Dicky Fontenoy.' And such traditions—good Heavens! Subsequently, at most race-meetings, large and small, and at various clubs, theatres, and places of public resort, the younger man had had his opportunities of observing the elder, and had used them always with relish, and sometimes with admiration. He himself had no desire to follow in Fontenoy's footsteps. Other elements ruled in him, which drew him other ways. But there was a magnificence about the impetuosity, or rather the doggedness with which Fontenoy had plunged into the business of ruining himself, which stirred the imagination. On the last occasion, some three and a half years before this Market Malford election, when Tressady had seen Fontenoy before starting himself on a long Eastern tour, he had been conscious of a lively curiosity as to what might have happened to 'Dicky' by the time he came back again. The eldest sons of peers do not generally come to the workhouse; but there are aristocratic substitutes which, relatively, are not much less disagreeable; and George hardly saw how they were to be escaped.

And now—not four years!—and here sat Dicky Fontenoy, haranguing on the dull clauses of a technical Act, throat hoarse with the speaking of the last three weeks, eyes cavernous with anxiety and overwork, the creator and leader of a political party which did not exist when Tressady left England, and now bade fair to hold the balance of power in English government! The surprises of fate and character! Tressady pondered them a little in a sleepy way; but the fatigue of many days asserted itself. Even his companion was soon obliged to give him up as a listener. Lord Fontenoy ceased to talk; yet every now and then, as some jolt of the carriage made George open his eyes, he saw the broad-shouldered figure beside him, sitting in the same attitude, erect and tireless, the same half-peevish pugnacity giving expression to mouth and eye.

'Come, wake up, Tressady! Here we are!'

There was a vindictive eagerness in Fontenoy's voice. Ease was no longer welcome to him, whether in himself or as a spectacle in other men. George, startled from a momentary profundity of sleep, staggered to his feet, and clutched at various bags and rugs.

The carriage was standing under the pillared porch of Malford House, and the great house-doors, thrown back upon an inner flight of marble steps, gave passage to a blaze of light. George, descending, had just shaken himself awake, and handed the things he held to a footman, when there was a sudden uproar from within. A crowd of figures—men and women, the men cheering, the women clapping and laughing—ran down the inner steps towards him. He was surrounded, embraced, slapped on the back, and finally carried triumphantly into the hall.

'Bring him in!' said an exultant voice; 'and stand back, please, and let his mother get at him.'

The laughing group fell back, and George, blinking,
radiant, and abashed, found himself in the arms of an
exceedingly sprightly and youthful dame, with pale,
frizzled hair, and the figure of seventeen.

'Oh, you dear, great, foolish thing!' said the lady,
with the voice and the fervour, moreover, of seventeen.
'So you've got in—you've done it! Well, I should never
have spoken to you again if you hadn't! And I suppose
you'd have minded that a little—from your own mother.
Goodness! how cold he is!'

And she flew at him with little pecking kisses, retreating every now and again to look at him, and then
closing upon him again in ecstasy, till George, at the end
of his patience, held her off with a strong arm.

'Now, mother, that's enough. Have the others been
home long?' he asked, addressing a smiling young man
in knickerbockers who, with his hands in his pockets,
was standing beside the hero of the occasion surveying
the scene.

'Oh! about half an hour. They reported you'd have
some difficulty in getting out of the clutches of the crowd.
We hardly expected you so soon.'

'How's Miss Sewell's headache? Does she know?'

The expression of the young man's eye, which was
bent on Tressady, changed ever so slightly as he replied:

'Oh yes, she knows. As soon as the others got back
Mrs. Watton went up to tell her. She didn't show at
lunch.'

'Mrs. Watton came to tell *me*—naughty man!' said
the lady whom George had addressed as his mother,
tapping the speaker on the arm with her fan. 'Mothers
first, if you please, especially when they're cripples like
me, and can't go and see their dear darlings' triumphs
with their own eyes. And *I* told Miss Sewell.'

She put her head on one side, and looked archly at

her son. Her high gown, a work of the most approved
Parisian art, was so cut as to show much more throat
than usual, and, in addition, a row of very fine pearls.
Her very elegant waist and bust were defined by a
sort of Empire sash ; her complexion did her maid and,
indeed, her years, infinite credit.

George flushed slightly at his mother's words, and
was turning away from her when he was gripped by the
owner of the house, Squire Watton, an eloquent and
soft-hearted old gentleman who, having in George's
opinion already overdone it greatly at the town-hall in
the way of hand-shaking and congratulations, was now
most unreasonably prepared to overdo it again. Lady
Tressady joined in with little shrieks and sallies, the
other guests of the house gathered round, and the hero
of the day was once more lost to sight and hearing amid
the general hubbub of talk and laughter—for the young
man in knickerbockers, at any rate, who stood a little way
off from the rest.

'I wonder when she'll condescend to come down,' he
said to himself, examining his boots with a speculative
smile. 'Of course it was mere caprice that she didn't
go to Malford; she meant it to annoy.'

'I say, do let me get warm,' said Tressady at last,
breaking from his tormentors, and coming up to the open
log fire, in front of which the young man stood. 'Where's
Fontenoy vanished to ?'

'Went up to write letters directly he had swallowed a
cup of tea,' said the young man, whose name was Bayle ;
'and called Marks to go with him.' (Marks was Lord
Fontenoy's private secretary.)

George Tressady threw up his hands in disgust.

'It's absurd. He never allows himself an hour's
peace. If he expects me to grind as he does, he'll soon
regret that he lent a hand to put me into Parliament.

Well, I'm stiff all over, and as tired as a rat.   I'll go and have a warm bath before dinner.'

But still he lingered, warming his hands over the blaze, and every now and then scanning the gallery which ran round the big hall.   Bayle chatted to him about some of the incidents of the day.   George answered at random.   He did, indeed, look tired out, and his expression was restless and discontented.

Suddenly there was a cry from the group of young men and maidens who were amusing themselves in the centre of the hall.

' Why, there's Letty ! and as fresh as paint.'

George turned abruptly.   Bayle saw his manner stiffen and his eye kindle.

A young girl was slowly coming down the great staircase which led to the hall.   She was in a soft black dress with a blue sash, and a knot of blue at her throat—a childish slip of a dress, which answered to her small rounded form, her curly head, and the hand gliding along the marble rail.   She came down silently smiling, taking each step with great deliberation, in spite of the outbreak of half-derisive sympathy with which she was greeted from her friends below.   Her bright eyes glanced from face to face—from the mocking inquirers immediately beneath her to George Tressady standing by the fire.

At the moment when she reached the last step Tressady found it necessary to put another log on a fire already piled to repletion.

Meanwhile Miss Sewell went straight towards the new member and held out her hand.

' I am so glad, Sir George ; let me congratulate you.'

George put down his log, and then looked at his fingers critically.

' I am very sorry, Miss Sewell, but I am not fit to touch.   I hope your headache is better.'

Miss Sewell, dropped her hand meekly, shot him a glance which was not meek, and said demurely:

'Oh! my headaches do what they're told. You see, I was determined to come down and congratulate you.'

'I see,' he repeated, making her a little bow. 'I hope my ailments, when I get them, will be as docile. So my mother told you?'

'I didn't want telling,' she said placidly. 'I knew it was all safe.'

'Then you knew what only the gods knew—for I only got in by seventeen votes.'

'Yes, so I heard. I was very sorry for Bewick.'

She put one foot on the stone fender, raised her pretty dress with one hand, and leant the other lightly against the mantelpiece. The attitude was full of grace, and the little sighing voice fitted the curves of a mouth which seemed always ready to laugh, yet seldom laughed frankly.

As she made her remark about Bewick Tressady smiled.

'My prophetic soul was right,' he said deliberately; 'I knew you would be sorry for Bewick.'

'Well, it is hard on him, isn't it? You can't deny you're a carpet-bagger, can you?'

'Why should I? I'm proud of it.'

Then he looked round him. The rest of the party—not without whispers and smothered laughter—had withdrawn from them. Some of the ladies had already gone up to dress. The men had wandered away into a little library and smoking-room which opened on the hall. Only the squire, safe in a capacious armchair a little way off, was absorbed in a local paper and the last humours of the election.

Satisfied with his glance, Tressady put his hands into his pockets, and leant back against the fireplace, in a way to give himself fuller command of Miss Sewell's countenance.

'Do you never give your friends any better sympathy than you have given me in this affair, Miss Sewell?' he said suddenly, as their eyes met.

She made a little face.

'Why, I've been an angel!' she said, poking at a prominent log with her foot.

George laughed.

'Then our ideas of angels agree no better than the rest. Why didn't you come and hear the poll declared, after promising me you would be there?'

'Because I had a headache, Sir George.'

He responded with a little inclination, as though ceremoniously accepting her statement.

'May I ask at what time your headache began?'

'Let me see,' she said, laughing; 'I think it was directly after breakfast.'

'Yes. It declared itself, if I remember right, immediately after certain remarks of mine about a Captain Addison?'

He looked straight before him, with a detached air.

'Yes,' said Letty, thoughtfully; 'it was a curious coincidence, wasn't it?'

There was a moment's silence. Then she broke into infectious laughter.

'Don't you know,' she said, laying her hand on his shoulder—'don't you know that you're a most foolish and wasteful person? We get along capitally, you and I—we've had a rattling time all this week—and then you will go and make uncivil remarks about my friends—in public, too! You actually think I'm going to let you tell Aunt Watton how to manage me! You get me into no end of a fuss—it'll take me weeks to undo the mischief you've been making—and then you expect me to take it like a lamb! Now do I look like a lamb?'

All this time she was holding him tight by the arm, and her dimpled face, alive with mirth and malice, was so close to his that a moment's wild impulse flashed through him to kiss her there and then. But the impulse passed. He and Letty Sewell had known each other for about three weeks. They were not engaged—far from it. And these— the hand on the arm, and the rest—were Letty Sewell's ways.

Instead of kissing her, then, he scanned her deliberately.

'I never saw anyone more plainly given over to obstinacy and pride,' he said, quietly; 'I told you some plain facts about the character of a man whom I know, and you don't, whereupon you sulk all day, you break all your promises about coming to Malford, and when I come back you call me names.'

She raised her eyebrows and withdrew her hand.

'Well, it's plain, isn't it? that I must have been in a great rage. It was very dull upstairs, though I did write reams to my best friend all about you—a very candid account—I shall have to soften it down. By the way, are you ever going to dress for dinner?'

George started, and looked at his watch.

'Are we alone? Is anyone coming from outside?'

'Only a few "locals," just to celebrate the occasion. I know the clergyman's wife's coming, for she told me she had been copying one of my frocks, and wanted me to tell her what I thought.'

George laughed.

'Poor lady!',

'I don't *think* I shall be nice to her,' said Letty, playing with a flower on the mantelpiece. 'Dowdy people make me feel wicked. Well, *I* must dress.'

It was now his turn to lay a detaining hand.

'Are you sorry?' he said, bending over to her. His bright grey eyes had shaken off fatigue.

'For what? Because you got in?'

Her face overflowed with laughter. He let her go. She linked her arm in that of the daughter of the house —Miss Florence Watton—who was crossing the hall at the moment, and the two went upstairs together, she throwing back one triumphant glance at him from the landing.

George stood watching them till they disappeared. His expression was neither soft nor angry. There was in it a mocking self-possession which showed that he too had been playing a part—mingled, perhaps, with a certain perplexity.

CHAPTER II

GEORGE TRESSADY came down very late for dinner, and found his hostess on the verge of annoyance. Mrs. Watton was a large, commanding woman, who seldom thought it worth while to disguise any disapproval she might feel—and she had a great deal of that commodity to expend, both on persons and institutions.

George hastened to propitiate her with the usual futilities: he had supposed that he was in excellent time, his watch had been playing tricks, and so on.

Mrs. Watton, who, after all, on this great day beheld in the new member the visible triumph of her dearest principles, received these excuses at first with stiffness, but soon thawed.

'Oh, you *naughty* boy, you naughty, mendacious boy!' said a sprightly voice in Tressady's ear. '" Excellent time," indeed! I saw you—for shame!'

And Lady Tressady flounced away from her son, laughing over her shoulder in one of her accustomed poses. She wore white muslin over cherry-coloured silk. The display of neck and shoulders could hardly have been more lavish ; and the rouge on her cheeks had been overdone, which rarely happened. George turned from her hurriedly to speak to Lord Fontenoy.

'What a fool that woman is!' thought Mrs. Watton to herself, as her sharp eye followed her guest. 'She will make George positively dislike her soon—and all the time she is bound to get him to pay her debts, or there

o

will be a smash. What! dinner? John, will you please
take Lady Tressady; Harding, will you take Mrs.
Hawkins'—pointing her second son towards a lady in
black sitting stiffly on the edge of an ottoman; 'Mr.
Hawkins takes Florence; Sir George'—she waved her
hand towards Miss Sewell. 'Now, Lord Fontenoy, you
must take me; and the rest of you sort yourselves.'

As the young people, mostly cousins, laughingly
did what they were told, Sir George held out his arm to
Miss Sewell.

'I am very sorry for you,' he said, as they passed into
the dining-room.

'Oh! I knew it would be my turn,' said Letty with
resignation. 'You see, you took Florrie last night, and
Aunt Watton the night before.'

George settled himself deliberately in his chair, and
turned to study his companion.

'Do you mind warning me, to begin with, how I can
avoid giving you a headache? Since this morning my
nerve has gone—I want directions.'

'Well—' said Letty, pondering, 'let us lay down the
subjects we *may* talk about first. For instance, you may
talk of Mrs. Hawkins.'

She gave an imperceptible nod which directed his
eyes to the thin woman sitting opposite, to whom Harding
Watton, a fashionable ·and fastidious youth, was paying
but scant attention.

George examined her.

'I don't want to,' he said shortly; 'besides, she would
last us no time at all.'

'Oh!—on the contrary,' said Letty, with malice
sparkling in her brown eye, 'she would last me a good
twenty minutes. She has got on my gown.'

'I didn't recognise it,' said George, studying the thin
lady again.

'I wouldn't mind,' said Letty, in the same tone of reflection, 'if Mrs. Hawkins didn't think it her duty to lecture me in the intervals of copying my frocks. If I disapproved of anybody, I don't think I should send my nurse to ask their maid for patterns.'

'I notice you take disapproval very calmly.'

'Callously, you mean. Well, it is my misfortune. I always feel myself so much more reasonable than the people who disapprove.'

'This morning, then, you thought me a fool?'

'Oh no! Only—well—I *knew*, you see, that I knew better. *I* was reasonable, and——'

'Oh! don't finish,' said George, hastily; 'and don't suppose that I shall ever give you any more good advice.'

'Won't you?'

Her mocking look sent a challenge, which he met with outward firmness. Meanwhile he was inwardly haunted by a phrase he had once heard a woman apply to the mental capacities of her best friend. 'Her *mind?*—her mind, my dear, is a shallow chaos!' The words made a neat label, he scoffingly thought, for his own present sensations. For he could not persuade himself that there was much profundity in his feelings towards Miss Sewell, whatever reckless possibilities life might seem to hold at times; when, for instance, she wore that particular pink gown in which she was attired to-night, or when her little impertinent airs suited her as well as they were suiting her just now. Something cool and critical in him was judging her all the time. Ten years hence, he made himself reflect, she would probably have no prettiness left. Whereas now, what with bloom and grace, what with small proportions and movements light as air, what with an inventive refinement in dress and personal adornment that never failed, all Letty Sewell's defects of feature or

c 2

expression were easily lost in a general aspect which most
men found dazzling and perturbing enough. Letty, at
any rate within her own circle, had never yet been without partners, or lovers, or any other form of girlish
excitement that she desired, and had been generally
supposed—though she herself was aware of some strong
evidence to the contrary—to be capable of getting anything she had set her mind upon. She had set her mind,
as the spectators in this particular case had speedily
divined, upon enslaving young George Tressady. And
she had not failed. For even during these last stirring
days it had been tolerably clear that she and his election
had divided Tressady's mind between them, with a
balance, perhaps, to her side. As to the *measure* of her
success, however, that was still doubtful—to herself and
him most of all.

To-night, at any rate, he could not detach himself from
her. He tried repeatedly to talk to the girl on his left, a
noble-faced child fresh out of the schoolroom, who in three
years' time would be as much Letty Sewell's superior in
beauty as in other things. But the effort was too great.
The strenuous business of the day had but left him—in
fatigue and reaction—the more athirst for amusement
and the gratification of another set of powers. He turned
back to Letty, and through course after course they
chattered and sparred, discussing people, plays and books,
or rather, under cover of these, a number of those topics
on the borderland of passion whereby men and women
make their first snatches at intimacy—till Mrs. Watton's
sharp grey eyes smiled behind her fan, and the attention
of her neighbour, Lord Fontenoy—an uneasy attention—
was again and again drawn to the pair.

Meanwhile, during the first half of dinner, a chair
immediately opposite to Tressady's place remained vacant.
It was being kept for the eldest son of the house, his

mother explaining carelessly to Lord Fontenoy that she
believed he was ' Out parish-ing somewhere, as usual.'

However, with the appearance of the pheasants the
door from the drawing-room opened, and a slim dark-
haired man slipped in. He took his place noiselessly,
with a smile of greeting to George and his neighbour,
and bade the butler in a whisper aside bring him any
course that might be going.

'Nonsense, Edward!' said his mother's loud voice
from the head of the table ; ' don't be ridiculous. Morris,
bring back that hare *entrée* and the mutton for Mr.
Edward.'

The newcomer raised his eyebrows mildly, smiled,
and submitted.

'Where have you been, Edward?' said Tressady; 'I
haven't seen you since the town-hall.'

'I have been at a rehearsal. There is a parish concert next week, and I conduct these functions.'

'The concerts are always bad,' said Mrs. Watton,
curtly.

Edward Watton shrugged his shoulder. He had
a charming timid air, contradicted now and then by a
look of enthusiastic resolution in the eyes.

'All the more reason for rehearsal,' he said. 'However, really, they won't do badly this time.'

'Edward is one of the persons,' said Mrs. Watton in a
low aside to Lord Fontenoy, 'who think you can make
friends with people—the lower orders—by shaking hands
with them, showing them Burne-Jones's pictures, and
singing "The Messiah" with them. I had the same idea
once. Everybody had. It was like the measles. But
the sensible persons have got over it.'

'Thank you, mamma,' said Watton, making her a
smiling bow.

Lady Tressady interrupted her talk with the squire

at the other end of the table to observe what was going
on. She had been chattering very fast in a shrill,
affected voice, with a gesticulation so free and French,
and a face so close to his, that the nervous and finicking
squire had been every moment afraid lest the next should
find her white fingers in his very eyes. He felt an
inward spasm of relief when he saw her attention
diverted.

'Is that Mr. Edward talking his Radicalism?' she
asked, putting up a gold eyeglass—'his dear, wicked
Radicalism? Ah! we all know where Mr. Edward got it.'

The table laughed. Harding Watton looked particularly amused.

'Egeria was in this neighbourhood last week,' he said,
addressing Lady Tressady. 'Edward rode over to see
her. Since then he has joined two new societies, and
ordered six new books on the Labour Question.'

Edward flushed a little, but went on eating his dinner
without any other sign of disturbance.

'If you mean Lady Maxwell,' he said good-humouredly,
'I can only be sorry for the rest of you that you don't
know her.'

He raised his handsome head with a bright air of
challenge that became him, but at the same time exasperated his mother.

'That *woman!*' said Mrs. Watton with ponderous
force, throwing up her hands as she spoke. Then she
turned to Lord Fontenoy. 'Don't *you* regard her as the
source of half the mischievous work done by this precious
Government in the last two years?' she asked him imperiously.

A half-contemptuous smile crossed Lord Fontenoy's
worn face.

'Well, really, I am not inclined to make Lady Maxwell
the scapegoat. Let them bear their own misdeeds.'

'Besides, what worse can you say of English Ministers than that they should be led by a woman?' said Mr. Watton, from the bottom of the table, in a piping voice. 'In my young days such a state of things would have been unheard of. No offence, my dear, no offence,' he added hastily, glancing at his wife.

Letty glanced at George, and put up a handkerchief to hide her own merriment.

Mrs. Watton looked impatient.

'Plenty of English Cabinet Ministers have been led by women before now,' she said drily; 'and no blame to them or anybody else. Only in the old days you knew where you were. Women were corrupt—as they were meant to be—for their husbands and brothers and sons. They wanted something for somebody—and got it. Now they are corrupt—like Lady Maxwell—for what they are pleased to call "causes," and it is that which will take the nation to ruin.'

At this there was an incautious protest from Edward Watton against the word 'corrupt,' followed by a confirmatory clamour from his mother and brother which seemed to fill the dining-room. Lady Tressady threw in affected comments from time to time, trying hard to hold her own in the conversation by a liberal use of fan and Christian names, and little personal audacities applied to each speaker in turn. Only Edward Watton, however, occasionally took civil or smiling notice of her; the others ignored her. They were engaged in a congenial task, the hunting of the one disaffected and insubordinate member of their pack, and had for the moment no attention to spare for other people.

'I shall see the great lady, I suppose, in a week or two,' said George to Miss Sewell, under cover of the noise. 'It is curious that I should never have seen her.'

'Who? Lady Maxwell?'

'Yes. You remember I have been four years out of England. She was in town, I suppose, the year before I left, but I never came across her.'

'I prophesy you will like her enormously,' said Letty, with decision. 'At least, I know that's what happens to me when Aunt Watton abuses anybody. I couldn't dislike them afterwards if I tried.'

'That, allow me to impress upon you, is *not* my disposition! I am a human being—I am influenced by my friends.'

He turned round towards her so as to appropriate her again.

'Oh! you are not at all the poor creature you paint yourself!' said Letty, shaking her head. 'In reality, you are the most obstinate person I know—you can never let a subject alone—you never know when you're beaten.'

'Beaten?' said George reflectively; 'by a headache? Well, there is no disgrace in that. One will probably "live to fight another day." Do you mean to say that you will take no notice—no notice—of all that array of facts I laid before you this morning on the subject of Captain Addison?'

'I shall be kind to you, and forget them. Now, do listen to Aunt Watton! It is your duty. Aunt Watton is accustomed to be listened to, and you haven't heard it all a hundred times before, as I have.'

Mrs. Watton, indeed, was haranguing her end of the table on a subject that clearly excited her. Contempt and antagonism gave a fine energy to a head and face already sufficiently expressive. Both were on a large scale, but without commonness. The old-lace coif she wore suited her waved and grizzled hair, and was carried with conscious dignity; the hand, which lay beside her on the table, though long and bony, was full of nervous distinction. Mrs. Watton was, and looked, a tyrant—but a tyrant of ability.

'A neighbour of theirs in Brookshire,' she was saying, 'was giving me last week the most extraordinary account of the doings at Mellor. She was the heiress of that house at Mellor'—here she addressed young Bayle, who, as a comparative stranger in the house, might be supposed to be ignorant of facts which everybody else knew—'a tumbledown place with an income of about two thousand a year. Directly she married she put a Socialist of the most unscrupulous type—so they tell me—into possession. The man has established what they call a " standard rate " of wages for the estate —practically double the normal rate—coerced all the farmers, and made the neighbours furious. They say the whole district is in a ferment. It used to be the quietest part of the world imaginable, and now she has set it all by the ears. *She*, having married thirty thousand a year, can afford her little amusements ; other people, who must live by their land, have their lives worried out of them.'

'She tells me that the system works on the whole extremely well,' said Edward Watton, whose heightened colour alone betrayed the irritation of his mother's chronic aggression, 'and that Maxwell is not at all unlikely to adopt it on his own estate.'

Mrs. Watton threw up her hands again.

'The *idiocy* of that man ! Till he married her he was a man of sense. And now she leads him by the nose, and whatever tune he calls, the Government must dance to, because of his power in the House of Lords.'

'And the worst of it is,' said Harding Watton, with an unpleasant laugh, 'that if she were not a handsome woman, her influence would not be half what it is. She uses her beauty in the most unscrupulous way.'

'I believe that to be *entirely* untrue,' said Edward Watton with emphasis, looking at his brother with hostility.

George Tressady interrupted. He had an affection for Edward Watton, and cordially disliked Harding. 'Is she really so handsome?' he asked, bending forward and addressing his hostess.

Mrs. Watton scornfully took no notice.

'Well, an old diplomat told me the other day,' said Lord Fontenoy—but with a cold unwillingness, as though he disliked the subject—' that she was the most beautiful woman, he thought, that had been seen in London since Lady Blessington's time.'

'Lady Blessington! dear, dear!—Lady Blessington!' said Lady Tressady with malicious emphasis—'an unfortunate comparison, don't you think? Not many people would like to be regarded as Lady Blessington's successor.'

'In any other respect than beauty,' said Edward Watton, haughtily, with the same tension as before, 'the comparison, of course, would be ridiculous.'

Harding shrugged his shoulders, and, tilting his chair back, said in the ear of a shy young man who sat next him:

'In my opinion, the Count d'Orsay is only a question of time! However, one mustn't say that to Edward.'

Harding read memoirs, and considered himself a man of general cultivation. The young man addressed, who read no printed matter outside the sporting papers that he could help, and had no idea as to who Lady Blessington and Count d'Orsay might be, smiled vaguely, and said nothing.

'My dear,' said the squire plaintively, 'isn't this room extremely hot?'

There was a ripple of meaning laughter from all the

young people, to many of whom this particular quarrel was already tiresomely familiar. Mr. Watton, who never understood anything, looked round with an inquiring air. Mrs. Watton condescended to take the hint and retire.

In the drawing-room afterwards Mrs. Watton first allotted a duty-conversation of some ten minutes in length, and dealing strictly with the affairs of the parish, to Mrs. Hawkins, who, as clergyman's wife, had a definite official place in the Malford House circle, quite irrespective of any individuality she might happen to possess. Mrs. Hawkins was plain, self-conscious, and in no way interesting to Mrs. Watton, who never took the smallest trouble to approach her in any other capacity than that upon which she ·had entered by marrying the incumbent of the squire's home living. But the civilities and respects that were recognised as belonging to her station she received.

This however, alas ! was not enough for Mrs. Hawkins, who was full of ambitions, which a bad manner, a plague of shyness, and a narrow income, were perpetually thwarting. As soon as the ten minutes were over, and Mrs. Watton, who was nothing if not political, and saw no occasion to make a stranger of the vicar's wife, had plunged into the evening papers brought her by the footman, Mrs. Hawkins threw herself on Letty Sewell. She was effusively grateful—too grateful—for the patterns lent her by Miss Sewell's maid.

'Did she lend you some patterns?' said Letty, raising her brows. 'Dear me ; I didn't know.'

And her eyes ran coolly over Mrs. Hawkins's attire, which did, indeed, present a village imitation of the delicate gown in which Miss Sewell had robed herself for the evening.

Mrs. Hawkins coloured.

'I specially told my nurse,' she said hastily, 'that of course your leave must be asked. But my nurse and your maid seem to have made friends. Of course my nurse has plenty of time for dressmaking with only one child of four to look after, and—and—one really gets no new ideas in a poky place like this. But I would not have taken a liberty for the world.'

Her pride and *mauvaise honte* together made both voice and manner particularly unattractive. Letty was seized with the same temper that little boys show towards flies.

'Of course I am delighted!' she said indifferently. 'It's so nice and good to have one's things made at home. Your nurse must be a treasure.'

All the time her gaze was diligently inspecting every ill-cut seam and tortured trimming of the home-made triumph before her. The ear of the vicar's wife, always morbidly sensitive in that particular drawing-room, caught a tone of insult in every light word. A passionate resentment flamed up in her, and she determined to hold her own.

'Are you going in for more visits when you leave here?' she inquired.

'Yes, two or three,' said Letty, turning her delicate head unwittingly. She had been throwing blandishments to Mrs. Watton's dog, a grey Aberdeen terrier, who stood on the rug quietly regarding her.

'You spend most of the year in visits, don't you?'

'Well, a good deal of it,' said Letty.

'Don't you find it dreadfully time-wasting? Does it leave you leisure for *any* serious occupations at all? I am afraid it would make *me* terribly idle!'

Mrs. Hawkins laughed, attempting a tone of banter.

Letty put up a small hand to hide a sudden yawn, which, however, was visible enough.

Would it?' she said, with an impertinence which hardly tried to conceal itself. 'Evelyn, do look at that dog. Doesn't he remind you of Mr. Bayley?'

She beckoned to the handsome child of sixteen who had sat on George 'Tressady's left hand at dinner, and, taking up a pinch of rose-leaves that had dropped from a vase beside her, she flung them at the dog, calling him to her. Instead of going to her, however, the dog slowly curled himself up on the rug, and, laying his nose along his front paws, stared at her steadily with the expression of one mounting guard.

'He never will make friends with you, Letty. Isn't it odd?' said Evelyn, laughing, and stooping to stroke the creature.

'Never mind; other dogs will. Did you see that adorable black Spitz of Lady Arthur's? She has promised to give me one.'

The two cousins fell into a chatter about their county neighbours, mostly rich and aristocratic people, of whom Mrs. Hawkins knew little or nothing. Evelyn Watton, whose instincts were quick and generous, tried again and again to draw the vicar's wife into the conversation. Letty was determined to exclude her. She lay back against the sofa, chatting her liveliest, the whiteness of her neck and cheek shining against the red of the damask behind, one foot lightly crossed over the other, showing her costly little slippers with their paste buckles. She sparkled with jewels as much as a girl may—more, indeed, in Mrs. Hawkins's opinion, than a girl should. From head to foot she breathed affluence, seduction, success—only the seduction was not for Mrs. Hawkins and her like.

The vicar's wife sat flushed and erect on her chair, disdaining after a time to make any further effort, but inwardly intolerably sore. She could not despise Letty

Sewell, unfortunately, since Letty's advantages were just those that she herself most desired. But there was something else in her mind than small jealousy. When Letty had been a brilliant child in short frocks, the vicar's wife, who was scarcely six years older, had opened her heart, had tried to make herself loved by Mrs. Watton's niece. There had been a moment when they had been 'Madge' and 'Letty' to each other, even since Letty had 'come out.' Now, whenever Mrs. Hawkins attempted the Christian name, it stuck in her throat; it seemed, even to herself, a familiarity that had nothing to go upon; while with every succeeding visit to Malford, Letty had dropped her former friend more decidedly, and 'Madge' was heard no more.

The gentlemen, deep in election incident and gossip, were, in the view chiefly of the successful candidate, unreasonably long in leaving the dining-room. When they appeared at last, George Tressady once more made an attempt to talk to some one else than Letty Sewell, and once more failed.

'I want you to tell me something about Miss Sewell,' said Lord Fontenoy presently in Mrs. Watton's ear. He had been sitting silent beside her on the sofa for some little time, apparently toying with the evening papers, which Mrs. Watton had relinquished to him.

Mrs. Watton looked up, followed the direction of his eyes towards a settee in a distant corner of the room, and showed a half-impatient amusement.

'Letty? Oh! Letty's my niece—the daughter of my brother, Walter Sewell, of Helbeck. They live in Yorkshire. My brother has my father's place—a small estate, and rents very irregular. I often wonder how they manage to dress that child as they do. However, she has always had her own way since she was a foot high. As for my poor brother, he has been an invalid for the last ten years, and neither he nor his wife—oh! such a stupid woman!'—Mrs. Watton's energetic hands and eyes once more called Heaven to witness—' have ever counted for much, I should say, in Letty's career. There is another sister, a little delicate, silent thing, that looks after them. Oh! Letty isn't stupid; I should think not. I suppose you're alarmed about Sir George. You needn't be. She does it with everybody.'

The candid aunt pursued the conversation a little further, in the same tone of a half-caustic indulgence. At the end of it, however, Lord Fontenoy was still uneasy. He had only migrated to Malford House for the declaration of the poll, having spent the canvassing weeks mainly in another part of the division. And now, on this triumphant evening, he was conscious of a sudden sense of defective information, which was disagreeable and damping.

When bedtime came, Letty lingered in the drawing-room a little behind the other ladies, on the plea of gathering up some trifles that belonged to her. So that when George Tressady went out with her to light her candle for her in the gallery, they found themselves alone.

He had fallen into a sudden silence, which made her sweep him a look of scrutiny as she took her candle-stick. The slim yet virile figure drawn to its full height the significant, long-chinned face, pleased her senses. He might be plain — she supposed he was — but he was, nevertheless, distinguished, and extraordinarily alive.

'I believe you are tired to death,' she said to him. 'Why don't you go to bed?'

She spoke with the freedom of one accustomed to

advise all her male acquaintance for their good.   George
laughed.

'Tired?   Not I.   I was before dinner.   Look here,
Miss Sewell, I've got a question to ask.'

'Ask it.'

'You don't want to spoil my great day, do you?   You
do repent that headache?'

They looked at each other, dancing laughter in
each pair of eyes, combined in his with an excited in-
sistence.

'Good-night, Sir George,' she said, holding out her
hand.

He retained it.

'You do?' he said, bending over her.

She liked the situation, and made no immediate effort
to change it.

'Ask me a month hence, when I have proved your
statements.'

'Then you admit it was all pretence?'

'I admit nothing,' she said, joyously.   'I protected
my friend.'

'Yes, by injuring and offending another friend.   Would
it please you if I said I missed you *very* much at Malford
to-day?'

'I will tell you to-morrow—it is so late!   Please let
me have my hand.'

He took no notice, and they went hand-in-hand, she
drawing him, to the foot of the stairs.

'George!' said a shrill, hesitating voice from overhead.

George looked up, and saw his mother.   He and Letty
started apart, and in another second Letty had glided
upstairs and disappeared.

'Yes, mother,' said George, impatiently.

'Will you come here?'

He mounted, and found Lady Tressady a little discomposed, but as affected as usual.

'Oh, George! it was so dark—I didn't see—I didn't know. George, will you have half an hour's talk with me after breakfast to-morrow? Oh, George, my dear boy, my *dear* boy! Your poor mammy understands!'

She laid one hand on his shoulder and, lifting her feather fan in the other, shook it with playful meaning in the direction whither Letty had departed.

George hastily withdrew himself. 'Of course I will have a talk with you, mother. As for anything else, I don't know what you mean. But you really must let me go to bed; I am much too tired to talk now. Good-night.'

Lady Tressady went back to her room, smiling but anxious.

'She has caught him!' she said to herself; 'barefaced little flirt! It is not altogether the best thing for me. But it may dispose him to be generous, if—if I can play my cards.'

Letty Sewell meanwhile had reached the quiet of a luxurious bedroom, and summoned her maid to her assistance. When the maid departed, the mistress held long counsel with herself over the fire: the general position of her affairs; what she desired; what other people intended; her will, and the chances of getting it. Her thoughts dealt with these various problems in a skilled and business-like way. To a particular form of self-examination Letty was well accustomed, and it had become by now a strong agent in the development of individuality, as self-examination of another sort is said to be by other kinds of people.

She herself was pleasantly conscious of real agitation. George Tressady had touched her feelings, thrilled her nerves, more than—— Yes! she said to herself decidedly,

more than anybody else, more than 'the rest.' She
thought of 'the rest,' one after the other—thought of
them contemptuously. Yet, certainly few girls in her
own set and part of the country had enjoyed a better
time—few, perhaps, had dared so many adventures.
Her mother had never interfered with her; and she
herself had not been afraid to be 'talked about.' Dances,
picnics, moonlight walks; the joys of outrageous 'sitting-
out,' and hot rivalries with prettier girls; of impertinences
towards the men who didn't matter, and pretty flatteries
towards the men who did—it was all pleasant enough to
think of. She could not reproach herself with having
missed any chances, any opportunities her own will might
have given her.

And yet—well, she was tired of it!—out of love
altogether with her maiden state and its opportunities.
She had come to Malford House in a state of soreness,
which partly accounted, perhaps, for such airs as she had
been showing to poor Mrs. Hawkins. During the past year
a particular marriage—the marriage of her neighbourhood
—had seemed intermittently within her reach. She had
played every card she knew—and she had failed! Failed,
too, in the most humiliating way. For the bride, indeed,
was chosen; but it was not Letty Sewell, but one of
Letty's girl-neighbours.

To-night, almost for the first time, she could bear to
think of it; she could even smile at it. Vanity and
ambition alone had been concerned, and to-night these
wild beasts of the heart were soothed and placable.

Well, it was no great match, of course—if it came off.
All that Aunt Watton knew about the Tressadys had
been long since extracted from her by her niece. And
with Tressady himself Letty's artless questions had been
very effective. She knew almost all that she wished to
know. No doubt Ferth was a very second-rate 'place';
and, since those horrid miners had become so trouble-

some, his income as a coalowner could not be what his father's had been—three or four thousand a year, she supposed—more, perhaps, in good years. It was not much.

Still—she pressed her hands on her eyes—he was *distinguished*; she saw that plainly already. He would be welcome anywhere.

'And we are *not* distinguished—that is just it. We are small people, in a rather dull set. And I have had hard work to make anything of it. Aunt Watton was very lucky to marry as she did. Of course, she *made* Uncle Watton marry her; but that was a chance—and papa always says nobody else could have done it!'

She fell happily thinking of Tressady's skirmishes with her, her face dimpling with amusement. Captain Addison! How amazed he would be could he know the use to which she had put his name and his very hesitating attentions. But he would never know; and meanwhile Sir George had been really pricked—really jealous! She laughed to herself—a low laugh of pure pleasure.

Yes—she had made up her mind. With a sigh, she put away from her all other and loftier ambitions. She supposed that she had not money or family enough. One must face the facts. George Tressady would take her socially into another *milieu* than her own, and a higher one. She told herself that she had always pined for Parliament, politics, and eminent people. Why should she not succeed in that world as well as in the Helbeck world? Of course she would succeed!

There was his mother—silly, painted old lady! She was naturally the *great* drawback; and Aunt Watton said she was absurdly extravagant, and would ruin Tressady if it went on. All the more reason why he should be protected. Letty drew herself sharply together in her pretty white dressing-gown, with the feeling that mothers of that kind must and could be kept in their place.

A house in town, of course—and *not* in Warwick Square, where, apparently, the Tressadys owned a house, which had been let, and was now once more in Sir George's hands. That might do for Lady Tressady—if, indeed, she could afford it when her son had married and taken other claims upon him.

Letty allowed her thoughts to wander dreamily on, imagining the London life that was to be : the young member, Lord Fontenoy's special friend and *protégé*— the young member's wife making her way among great people, giving charming little parties at Ferth—

All very well ! But what, please, were the facts on his side ? She buried her small chin deep in her hands as she tried, frowning, to think it out. Certainly he was very much drawn, very much taken. She had watched him, sometimes, trying to keep away from her—and her lips parted in a broad smile as she recalled the triumph of his sudden returns and submissions. She believed he had a curious temper—easily depressed, for all his coolness. But he had never been depressed in her company.

Still, *nothing* was certain. All that had happened might melt away into nothingness with the greatest ease if—well ! if the right steps were not taken. He was no novice, any more than she ; he must have had scores of ' affairs ' by now, with that manner of his. Such men were always capable of second thoughts, of tardy retreats —and especially if there were the smallest thought of persecution, of pursuit.

She believed—she was nearly certain—he would have a reaction to-morrow, perhaps because his mother had caught them together. Next morning he would be just a little bored by the thought of it—a little bored by having to begin again where he had left off. Without great tact and skill the whole edifice might tumble together like a house of cards. Had she the courage

to make difficulties—to put a water-ditch across his
path?

It was close on midnight when Letty at last raised
her little chin from the hands that held it and rang the bell
that communicated with her maid's room, but cautiously,
so as not to disturb the rest of the sleeping house.

'If Grier *is* asleep, she must wake up, that's all!'

Two or three minutes afterwards a dishevelled maid
startled out of her first slumber appeared, to ask whether
her mistress was ill.

'No, Grier, but I wanted to tell you that I have
changed my mind about staying here till Saturday. I am
going to-morrow morning by the 9.30 train. You can
order a fly first thing, and bring me my breakfast early.'

The maid, groaning at the thought of the boxes that
would have to be packed in this inconceivable hurry,
ventured to protest.

'Never mind, you can get the housemaid to help you,'
said Miss Sewell, decidedly. 'I don't mind what you
give her. Now go to bed, Grier. I'm sorry I woke you
up; you look as tired as an owl.'

Then she stood still, looking at herself—hands clasped
lightly before her—in the long glass.

'"Letty went by the nine o'clock train,"' she said aloud,
smiling, and mocking her own white reflection. '"Dear
me! How sudden! how extraordinary!' Yes, but that's
like her. H'm—" Then he must write to me, for I shall
write *him* a civil little note asking for that book I lent
him. Oh! I *hope* Aunt Watton and his mother will bore
him to death!'

She broke out into a merry laugh; then, sweeping
her mass of pretty hair to one side, she began rapidly to
coil it up for the night, her fingers working as fast as her
thoughts, which were busy with one ingenious plan after
another for her next meeting with George Tressady.

CHAPTER III

DURING this same space of time, which for Miss Sewell's maid ended so disagreeably, George Tressady was engaged in a curious conversation.

He had excused himself from smoking, on the ground of fatigue, immediately after his parting from Letty. But he had only nominally gone to bed. He too found it difficult to tear himself from thinking and the fire, and had not begun to undress when he heard a knock at his door. On his reply, Lord Fontenoy entered.

'May I come in, Tressady?'

'By all means.'

George, however, stared at his invader in some astonishment. His relations with Fontenoy were not personally intimate.

'Well, I'm glad to find you still up, for I had a few words on my mind to say to you before I go off to-morrow. Can you spare me ten minutes?'

'Certainly; do sit down. Only—well, I'm afraid I'm pretty well done. If it's anything important, I can't promise to take it in.'

Lord Fontenoy for a moment made no reply. He stood by the fire, looking at the cigarette he still held, in silence. George watched him with repressed annoyance.

'It's been a very hot fight, this,' said Fontenoy at last, slowly, 'and you've won it well. All our band have prospered in the matter of elections. But this contest of yours has been, I think, the most conspicuous that any

of us have fought. Your speeches have made a mark—
one can see that from the way in which the Press has
begun to take them, political beginner though you are.
In the House you will be, I think, our best speaker—of
course with time and experience. As for me, if you give
me a fortnight to prepare in, I can make out something.
Otherwise I am no use. *You* will take a good debating
place from the beginning. Well, it is only what I expected.'

The speaker stopped. George, fidgeting in his chair,
said nothing ; and presently Fontenoy resumed :

' I trust you will not think what I am going to say
an intrusion, but—you remember my letters to you in
India ? '

George nodded.

' They put the case strongly, I think,' Fontenoy
went on, ' but, in my opinion, not strongly enough.
This wretched Government is in power by the help of a
tyranny—a tyranny of Labour. They call themselves
Conservatives—they are really State Socialists, and the
mere catspaws of the revolutionary Socialists. You and
I are in Parliament to break down that tyranny, if we can.
This year and next will be all-important. If we can hold
Maxwell and his friends in check for a time—if we can
put some backbone into the party of freedom—if we can
rally and call up the forces we have in the country, the
thing will be done. We shall have established the
counterpoise—we shall very likely turn the next election,
and liberty—or what still remains of it !—will be saved
for a generation. But to succeed, the effort, the sacrifice, from each one of us, will have to be *enormous*.'

Fontenoy paused, and looked at his companion.
George was lying back in an armchair with his eyes shut.
Why on earth—so he was thinking—should Fontenoy
have chosen this particular hour and this particular night

to *débiter* these very stale things, that he had already
served up in innumerable speeches and almost every
letter that George had received from him?

'I don't suppose it will be child's-play,' he said,
stifling a yawn—'hope I shall feel keener after a night's
rest!' He looked up with a smile.

Fontenoy dropped his cigarette into the fender and
stood silent a moment, his hands clasped behind his
back.

'Look here, Tressady!' he said at last, turning to his
companion; 'you remember how affairs stood with me
when you left England? I didn't know much of you,
but I believe, like many of my juniors, you knew a
great deal about me?'

George made the sign of assent expected of him.

'I knew something about you, certainly,' he said,
smiling; 'it was not difficult.'

Fontenoy smiled too, though without geniality. Geniality had become impossible to a man always overworked
and on edge.

'I was a fool,' he said quickly—'an open and notorious
fool. But I enjoyed my life. I don't suppose anyone ever
enjoyed life more. Every day of my former existence
gave the lie to the good people who tell you that to be
happy you must be virtuous. I was idle, extravagant, and
vicious, and I was one of the happiest of men. As to my
racing and my horses, they were a constant delight to
me. I can't think now of those mornings on the Heath
—the gallops of my colts—the change and excitement of it all, without longing for it to come back
again. Yet I have never owned a horse, or seen a race,
or made a bet, for the last three years. I never go into
society, except for political purposes; and I scarcely ever
touch wine. In fact, I have thrown overboard everything
that once gave *me* pleasure and amusement so com-

pletely that I have, perhaps, some right to press upon the party that follows me my conviction that unless each and all of us give up private ease and comfort as I have done—unless we are contented, as the Parnellites were, to be bores in the House and nuisances to ourselves —to peg away in season and out of season—to give up everything for the cause, we may just as well not go into the fight at all—for we shall do nothing with it.'

George clasped his hands round his knee, and stared stubbornly into the fire. Sermonising was all very well, but Fontenoy did too much of it; nobody need suppose that he would have done what he had done, unless, on the whole, it had given him more pleasure to do it than not to do it.

'Well,' he said, looking up at last with a laugh, 'I wonder what you *mean*—really. Do you mean, for instance, that I oughtn't to get myself married?'

His offhand manner covered a good deal of irritation. He made a shrewd guess at the idea in Fontenoy's mind, and meant to show that he would not be dictated to.

Fontenoy also laughed, with as little geniality as before. Then he applied himself to a deliberate answer.

'*This* is what I mean. If you, just elected—at the beginning of this critical session—were to give your best mind to anything else in the world than the fight before us, I should regard you as, for the time, at any rate, lost to us—as, so far, betraying us.'

The colour rushed into George's cheeks.

'Upon my word!' he said, springing up—'upon my word, you are a taskmaster!'

Fontenoy hastened to reply, in a different tone, 'I only want to keep the machine in order.'

George paced up and down for a few moments without speaking. Presently he paused.

'Look here, Fontenoy! I cannot look at the matter

politician he had now pledged himself to follow—the quality of intensity. Dicky Fontenoy in his follies had been neither gay nor lovable, but his fierce will, his extravagant and reckless force, had given him the command of men softer than himself. That will and that force were still there, steeled and concentrated. But George Tressady was sometimes restlessly doubtful as to how far he himself was prepared to submit to them.

His personal acquaintance with Fontenoy was of comparatively recent date. He himself had been for some four years away from England, to which he had only returned about three months before the Market Malford election. A letter from Fontenoy had been the immediate cause of his return; but before it arrived the two men had been in no direct communication.

The circumstances of Tressady's long absence concern his later story, and were on this wise. His father, Sir William, the owner of Ferth Place, in West Mercia, died in the year that George, his only surviving child and the son of his old age, left college. The son, finding his father's debts considerable and his own distaste for the law, to which he had been destined, amazingly increased by his newly acquired freedom to do what he liked with himself, turned his mind at once towards travelling. Travel he must if he was ever to take up public and Parliamentary life, and for no other profession—so he announced—did he feel the smallest vocation. Moreover economy was absolutely necessary. During his absence the London house could be let, and Lady Tressady could live quietly at Ferth upon an allowance, while his uncles looked after the colliery property.

Lady Tressady made no difficulty, except as to the figure first named for the proposed allowance, which she declared was absurd. The uncles, elderly business men, could not understand why the younger generation should not go into harness at once without indulgences, as they themselves had done; but George got his way, and had much reason to show for it. He had not been idle at college, though perhaps at no time industrious enough. Influenced by natural ambition and an able tutor, he had won some distinction, and he was now a man full of odds and ends of ideas, of nascent interests, curiosities, and opinions, strongly influenced moreover already, though he said less about it than about other things, by the desire for political distinction. While still at college he had been especially attracted—owing mainly to the chances of an undergraduate friendship—by a group of Eastern problems bearing upon England's future in Asia; and he was no sooner free to govern himself and his moderate income than there flamed up in him the Englishman's passion to see, to touch, to handle, coupled with the young man's natural desire to go where it was dangerous to go, and where other men were not going. His friend—the son of an eminent geographer, possessed by inheritance of the explorer's instincts—was just leaving England for Asia Minor, Armenia, and Persia. George made up his mind, hastily but firmly, to go with him, and his family had to put up with it.

The year, however, for which the young fellow had stipulated went by; two others were added to it; and a fourth began to run its course—still George showed but faint signs of returning. According to his letters home, he had wandered through Persia, India, and Ceylon; had found friends and amusement everywhere; and in the latter colony had even served eight months as private secretary to the Governor, who had taken a fancy to him, and had been suddenly bereft by a boating accident of the indispensable young man who was accustomed to direct the hospitalities of Government House before Tressady's advent. Thence he went to China and Japan, made

a trip from Pekin into Mongolia, landed on Formosa, fell in
with some French naval officers at Saigon, spending with
them some of the gayest and maddest weeks of his life ;
explored Siam, and finally returned by way of Burmah to
Calcutta, with the dim intention this time of some day,
before long, taking ship for home.

Meanwhile during the last months of his stay in
Ceylon he had written some signed articles for an important English newspaper, which, together with the natural
liking felt by the many important persons he had come
to know in the East for an intelligent and promising
young fellow, endowed with brains, family, and good
manners, served to bring him considerably into notice.
The tone of the articles was strongly English and Imperialist. The first of them came out immediately before his
visit to Saigon, and Tressady thanked his lucky stars that
the foreign reading of his French friends was, perhaps, not
so extensive as their practical acquaintance with life. He
was, however, proud of his first literary achievement, and
it served to crystallise in him a number of ideas and sentiments which had previously represented rather the prejudices of a traveller accustomed to find his race in the
ascendant, and to be well received by its official class,
than any reasoned political theory. As he went on writing, conviction grew with statement, became a faith,
ultimately a passion—till, as he turned homewards, he
seemed to himself to have attained a philosophy sufficient
to steer the rest of life by. It was the common philosophy
of the educated and fastidious observer ; and it rested
on ideas of the greatness of England and the infinity of
England's mission, on the rights of ability to govern as
contrasted with the squalid possibilities of democracy, on
the natural kingship of the higher races, and on a profound
personal admiration for the virtues of the administrator
and the soldier.

Now, no man in whom these perceptions take strong root early, need expect to love popular government. Tressady read his English newspapers with increasing disgust. On that little England in those far seas all depended, and England meant the English working-man with his flatterers of either party. He blundered and blustered at home, while the Empire, its services and its defences, by which alone all this pullulating 'street folk' existed for a day, were in danger of starvation and hindrance abroad, to meet the unreasonable fancies of a degenerate race. A deep hatred of mob-rule rooted itself in Tressady, passing gradually, during his last three months in India, into a growing inclination to return and take his place in the fight—to have his say. 'Government to the competent—*not* to the many,' might have been the summary of his three years' experience.

Nor were private influences wanting. He was a West Mercian landowner in a coal-mining district, and owned a group of pits on the borders of his estate. His uncles, who had shares in the property, reported to him periodically during his absence. With every quarter it seemed to Tressady that the reports grew worse and the dividends less. His uncles' letters, indeed, were full of anxieties and complaints. After a long period of peace in the coal-trade, it looked as though a time of hot war between masters and men was approaching. 'We have to thrash them every fifteen years,' wrote one of the uncles, ' and the time is nearly up.'

The unreason, brutality, and extravagance of the men ; the tyranny of the Union ; the growing insolence of the Union officials—Tressady's letters from home after a time spoke of little else. And Tressady's bank-book meanwhile formed a disagreeable comment on the correspondence. The pits were almost running at a loss ;

yet neither party had made up their minds to the trial of
strength.

Tressady was still lingering in Bombay—though
supposed to be on his way home—when Lord Fontenoy's letter reached him.

The writer referred slightly to their previous acquaintance, and to a remote family connection between himself
and Tressady; dwelt in flattering terms on the reports
which had reached him from many quarters of Tressady's opinions and abilities; described the genesis and
aims of the new Parliamentary party, of which the writer
was the founder and head; and finally urged him to come
home at once, and to stand for Parliament as a candidate
for the Market Malford division, where the influence of
Fontenoy's family was considerable. Since the general
election, which had taken place in June, and had returned a moderate Conservative Government to power,
the member for Market Malford had become incur-
ably ill. The seat might be vacant at any moment.
Fontenoy asked for a telegram, and urged the next
steamer.

Tressady had already—partly from private talk, partly
from the newspapers—learnt the main outlines of Lord
Fontenoy's later story. The first political speech of
Fontenoy's he had ever read made a half-farcical impression on him—let Dicky stick to his two-year-olds!
The second he read twice over, and alike in it, in certain
party manifestoes from the same hand printed in the
newspapers, and in the letter he had now received, there
spoke something for which it seemed to him he had been
waiting. The style was rough and halting, but Tressady
felt in it the note and power of a leader.

He took an hour's walk through the streets of
Bombay to think it over, then sent his telegram, and
booked his passage on his way home to luncheon.

Such, in brief outline, had been the origin of the two men's acquaintance. Since George's return they had been constantly together. Fontenoy had thrown his whole colossal power of work into the struggle for the Market Malford seat, and George owed him much.

After he was left to himself on this particular night, Tressady was for long restless and wakeful. In spite of resistance, Fontenoy's talk and Fontenoy's personality had nevertheless restored for the moment an earlier balance of mind. The interests of ambition and the intellect returned in force. Letty Sewell had, no doubt, made life very agreeable to him during the past three weeks; but, after all—was it worth while?

Her little figure danced before the inward eye as his fire sank into darkness; fragments of her chatter ran through his mind. He began to be rather ashamed of himself. Fontenoy was right. It was not the moment. No doubt he must marry some day; he had come home, indeed, with the vague intention of marrying; but the world was wide, and women many. That he had very little romance in his temperament was probably due to his mother. His childish experiences of her character, and of her relations to his father, had left him no room, alas! for the natural childish opinion that all grown-ups, and especially all mothers, are saints. In India he had amused himself a good deal; but his adventures had, on the whole, confirmed his boyish bias. If he had been forced to put his inmost opinions about women into words, the result would have been crude—perhaps brutal; which did not prevent him from holding a very strong and vivid conviction of the pleasure to be got from their society.

Accordingly, he woke up next morning precisely in the mood that Letty, for her own reasons, had foreseen. It

E

worried him to think that for two or three days more he and Letty Sewell must still be thrown together in close relations. He and his mother were waiting on at Malford for a day or two till some workmen should be out of his own house, which lay twenty miles away, at the farther edge of the Market Malford division. Meanwhile a couple of shooting-parties had been arranged, mainly for his entertainment. Still, was there no urgent business that required him in town?

He sauntered in to breakfast a little before ten. Only Evelyn Watton and her mother were visible, most of the men having already gone off to a distant meet.

'Now sit down and entertain us, Sir George,' said Mrs. Watton, holding out her hand to him with an odd expression. 'We're as dull as ditchwater—the men have all gone—Florrie's in bed with a chill—and Letty departed by the 9.30 train.'

George's start, as he took his coffee from her, did not escape her.

'Miss Sewell gone? But why this suddenness?' he inquired. 'I thought Miss Letty was to be here to the end of the week.'

Mrs. Watton raised her shoulders. 'She sent a note in to me at half-past eight to say her mother wasn't well, and she was wanted at home. She just rushed in to say good-bye to me, chattered a great deal, kissed everybody a great deal—and I know no more. I hear she had breakfast and a fly, which is all I troubled myself about. I never interfere with the modern young woman.'

Then she raised her eyeglass, and looked hard and curiously at Tressady. His face told her nothing, however, and as she was the least sympathetic of women, she soon forgot her own curiosity.

Evelyn Watton, a vision of fresh girlhood in her morning frock, glanced shyly at him once or twice as she

gave him scones and mustard. She was passing through
a moment of poetry and happy dreams. All human
beings walked glorified in her eyes, especially if they were
young. Letty was not wholly to her taste, and had never
been a particular friend. But she thought ill of no one,
and her little heart must needs flutter tenderly in the
presence of anything that suggested love and marriage.
It had delighted her to watch George and Letty together.
Now, why had Letty rushed away like this? *She* thought
with concern, thrilling all the time, that Sir George
looked grave and depressed.

George, however, was not depressed—or thought he
was not. He walked into the library after breakfast,
whistling, and quoting to himself:

> And there be they
> Who kissed his wings which brought him yesterday,
> And thank his wings to-day that he is flown.

He prided himself on his memory of some. modern
poets, and the lines pleased him particularly.

He had no sooner done quoting, however, than his
mother peered into the room, claiming the business talk
that had been promised. From that talk George emerged
irritable and silent. His mother's extravagance was really
preposterous!—not to be borne. For four years now he
had been free from the constant daily friction of money
troubles which had spoilt his youth and robbed him of
all power of respecting his mother. And he had hugged
his freedom. But all the time it seemed he had been
hugging illusion, and the troubles had been merely piling
up for his return! Her present claims—and he knew
very well that they were not the whole—would exhaust
all his available balance at his bankers'.

Lady Tressady, for her part, thought, with indignant
despair, that he had not behaved at all as an only son

should—especially an only son just returned to a widowed
mother after four years' absence. How could anyone
suppose that in four years there would be no debts—on
such a pittance of an income? Some money, indeed, he
had promised her; but not nearly enough, and not immediately. He 'must look into things at home.' Lady
Tressady was enraged with herself and him that she had
not succeeded better in making him understand how
pressing, how *urgent*, matters were.

She *must*, indeed, bring it home to him that there
might be a scandal at any moment. That odious livery-
stable man, two or three dressmakers—in these directions
every phase and shift of the debtor's long *finesse* had
been exhausted long ago. Even *she* was at her wits' end.

As for other matters—— But from these her thoughts
turned hurriedly away. Luck would change, of course,
sometime; it must change! No need to say anything
about *that* just yet, especially while George's temper was
in such a queer state.

It was very odd—most annoying! As a baby even
he had never been caressing or sweet like other people's
babies. And now, really!—why *her* son should have
such unattractive ways!

But, manœuvre as she would, George would not be
drawn into further discussion. She could only show him
offended airs, and rack her brains morning and night as
to how best to help herself.

Meanwhile George had never been so little pleased
with living as during these few days. He was overwhelmed with congratulations; and, to judge from the
newspapers, 'all England,' as Lady Tressady said, 'was
talking of him.' It seemed to him ridiculous that a man
should derive so little entertainment from such a fact.
Nevertheless, his dulness remained, and refused to be
got rid of. He discussed with himself, of course, for a

new set of reasons, the possibility of evading the shooting parties, and departing. But he was deeply pledged to stay; and he was under considerable obligations to the Wattons. So he stayed ; but he shot so as to increase his own dissatisfaction with the universe, and to make the other men in the house wonder what might be the general value of an Indian sporting reputation when it came to dealing with the British pheasant.

Then he turned to business. He tried to read some Parliamentary reports bearing on a coming measure, and full of notes by Fontenoy, which Fontenoy had left with him. But it only ended in his putting them hastily aside, lest in the mood of obscure contradiction that possessed him he should destroy his opinions before he had taken his seat.

On the day before the last 'shoot,' among the letters his servant brought him in the early morning, was one that he tore open in a hurry, tossing the rest aside.

It was from Miss Sewell, requesting, prettily, in as few words as possible, that he would return her a book she had lent him.

'My mother,' she wrote, 'has almost recovered from her sudden attack of chill. I trust the shooting-parties have amused you, and that you have read *all* Lord Fontenoy's Blue Books.'

George wrote a reply before he went down to breakfast —a piece of ordinary small-talk, that seemed to him the most wretched stuff conceivable. But he pulled two pens to pieces before he achieved it.

Then he went out for a long walk alone, pondering what was the matter with him. Had that little witch dropped the old familiar poison into his veins after all ? Certainly some women made life vivacity and pleasure, while others—his mother or Mrs, Watton, for instance —made it fatigue or tedium,

Ever since his boyhood Tressady had been conscious of intermittent assaults of melancholy, fits of some inner disgust, which hung the world in black, crippled his will, made him hate himself and despise his neighbours. It was, possibly, some half-conscious dread lest this morbid speck in his nature should gain upon the rest that made him so hungry for travel and change of scene after he left college. It explained many surprises, many apparent ficklenesses in his life. During the three weeks that he had spent in the same house with Letty Sewell he had never once been conscious of this lurking element of his life. And now, after four days, he found himself positively pining for her voice, the rustle of her delicate dress, her defiant, provocative ways that kept a man on the alert—still more, her smiling silences that seemed to challenge all his powers, the touch of her small cool hand that crushed so easily in his.

What had she left the house for in that wilful way? He did not believe her excuses. Yet he was mystified. Did she realise that things were becoming serious, and did she not mean them to be serious? If so, who or what hindered?

As for Fontenoy——

Tressady quickened his step impatiently as he recalled that harassed and toiling figure. Politics or no politics, *he* would live his life! Besides, it was obviously to his profit to marry. How could he ever make a common household with his mother? He meant to do his duty by her, but she annoyed and abashed him twenty times a day. He would be far happier married, far better able to do his work. He was not passionately in love—not at all. But—for it was no good fencing with himself any longer—he desired Letty Sewell's companionship more than he had desired anything for a long time. He wanted the right to carry off the little musical box, with all its tunes,

and set it playing in his own house, to keep him gay.
Why not? He could house it prettily, and reward it well.

As for the rest, he decided, without thinking about it,
that Letty Sewell was well born and bred. She had,
of course, all the little refinements a fastidious taste
might desire in a woman. She would never discredit a
man in society. On the contrary, she would be a great
strength to him there. And she must be sweet-tempered,
or that pretty child Evelyn Watton would not be so fond
of her.

That pretty child, meanwhile, was absorbed in the
excitement of her own small *rôle*. Tressady, who had only
made duty-conversation with her before, had found out
somehow that she was sympathetic—that she would talk
to him charmingly about Letty. After a very little pretending, he let himself go; and Evelyn dreamt at night
of his confidences, her heart, without knowing it, leaping
forward to the time when a man would look at her so,
for her own sake—not another's. She forgot that she
had ever criticised Letty, thought her vain or selfish.
Nay, she made a heroine of her forthwith; she remembered all sorts of delightful things to say of her, simply
that she might keep the young member talking in a
corner, that she might still enjoy the delicious pride of
feeling that she knew—she was helping it on.

After the big 'shoot,' for instance, when all the other
gentlemen were stiff and sleepy, George spent the whole
evening in chattering to Evelyn, or, rather, in making her
chatter. Lady Tressady loitered near them once or
twice. She heard the names 'Letty,' 'Miss Sewell,'
passing and repassing—one talker catching up the other.
Over any topic that included Miss Sewell they lingered;
when anything was begun that did not concern her, it
dropped at once, like a ball ill thrown. The mother went
away smiling rather sourly.

She watched her son, indeed, cat-like all these days, trying to discover what had happened—what his real mind was. She did not wish for a daughter-in-law at all, and she had even a secret fear of Letty Sewell in that capacity. But somehow George must be managed, her own needs must be met. She felt that she might be undoing the future ; but the present drove her on.

On the following morning, from one of Mrs. Watton's numerous letters there dropped out the fact that Letty Sewell was expected immediately at a country house in North Mercia whereof a certain Mrs. Corfield was mistress —a house only distant some twenty miles from the Tressadys' estate of Ferth Place.

'My sister-in-law has recovered with remarkable rapidity,' said Mrs. Watton, raising a sarcastic eye. 'Do you know anything of the Corfields, Sir George?'

'Nothing at all,' said George. 'One hears of them sometimes from neighbours. They are said to be very lively folk. Miss Sewell will have a gay time.'

'Corfield?' said Lady Tressady, her head on one side and her cup balanced in two jewelled hands. 'What! *Aspasia Corfield!* Why, my dear George—one of my oldest friends!'

George laughed—the short, grating laugh his mother so often evoked.

'Beg pardon, mother; I can only answer for myself. To the best of my belief I never saw her, either at Ferth or anywhere else.'

'Why, Aspasia Corfield and I,' said Lady Tressady with languid reflectiveness—'Aspasia Corfield and I copied each other's dresses, and bought our hats at the same place, when we were eighteen. I haven't seen her for an eternity. But Aspasia used to be a *dear* girl—and so fond of me!'

She put down her cup with a sigh, intended as a

reproach to George. George only buried himself the deeper in his morning's letters.

Mrs. Watton, behind her newspaper, glanced grimly from the mother to the son.

'I wonder if that woman has a single real old friend in the world. How is George Tressady going to put up with her?'

The Wattons themselves had been on friendly terms with Tressady's father for many years. Since Sir William's death and George's absence, however, Mrs. Watton had not troubled herself much about Lady Tressady, in which she believed she was only following suit with the rest of West Mercia. But now that George had reappeared as a promising politician, his mother—till he married—had to be to some extent accepted along with him. Mrs. Watton accordingly had thought it her duty to invite her for the election, not without an active sense of martyrdom. 'She always has bored me to tears since I first saw Sir William trailing her about,' she would remark to Letty. 'Where did he pick her up? The marvel is that she has kept respectable. She has never looked it. I always feel inclined to ask her at breakfast why she dresses for dinner twelve hours too soon!'

Very soon after the little conversation about the Corfields Lady Tressady withdrew to her room, sat thoughtful for a while, with her writing-block on her knee, then wrote a letter. She was perfectly aware of the fact that since George had come back to her she was likely to be welcome once more in many houses that for years had shown no particular desire to receive her. She took the situation very easily. It was seldom her way to be bitter. She was only determined to amuse herself, to enjoy her life in her own way. If people disapproved of her, she thought them fools, but it did not prevent her from trying to make it up with them next day, if she saw an opening and it seemed worth while.

'There!' she said to herself as she sealed the letter, and looked at it with admiration, 'I really have a knack for doing those things. I should think Aspasia Corfield would ask him by return—me, too, if she has any decency, though she *has* dropped me for fifteen years. She has a tribe of daughters.—*Why* I should play Miss Sewell's game like this I don't know! Well, one must try something.'

That same afternoon mother and son took their departure for Ferth Place.

George, who had only spent a few weeks at Ferth since his return from India, should have found plenty to do both indoors and out. The house struck him as singularly dingy and out of order. Changes were imperatively demanded in the garden and in the estate. His business as a colliery-owner was in a tangled and critical condition. And meanwhile Fontenoy plied him incessantly with a political correspondence which of itself made large demands upon intelligence and energy.

Nevertheless he shuffled out of everything, unless it were the correspondence with Fontenoy. As to the notion that all the languor could be due merely to an unsatisfied craving for Letty Sewell's society, when it presented itself he still fought with it. The Indian climate might have somehow affected him. An English winter is soon forgotten, and has to be re-learnt like a distasteful lesson.

About a week after their arrival at Ferth George was sitting at his solitary breakfast when his mother came floating into the room, preceded by a rattle of bangles, a flutter of streamers, and the barking of little dogs.

She held various newly opened letters, and, running up to him, she laid her hands on his shoulders.

'Now'—thought George to himself with annoyance, 'she is going to be arch!'

'Oh! you silly boy!' she said, holding him, with her head on one side. 'Who's been cross and nasty to his poor old mammy? Who wants cheering up a bit before he settles down to his horrid work? Who would take his mammy to a nice party at a nice house, if he were prettily asked—eh? who would?'

She pinched his cheek before he could escape.

'Well, mother, of course you will do what you like,' said George, walking off to supply himself with ham. 'I shall not leave home again, just yet.'

Lady Tressady smiled.

'Well, anyhow, you can read Aspasia Corfield's letter,' she said, holding it out to him. 'You know, really, that house isn't bad. They took over the Dryburghs' *chef*, and Aspasia knows how to pick her people.'

'Aspasia!' The tone of patronising intimacy! George blushed, if his mother did not.

Yet he took the letter. He read it, then put it down, and walked to the window to look at a crowd of birds that had been collecting round a plate of food he had just put out upon the snow.

'Well, will you go?' said his mother.

'If you particularly wish it,' he said, after a pause, in an embarrassed voice.

Lady Tressady's dimples were in full play as she settled herself into her seat and began to gather a supply of provisions. But as he returned to his place, and she glanced at him, she saw that he was not in a mood to be bantered, and understood that he was not going to let her force his confidence, however shrewdly she might guess at his affairs. So she controlled herself, and began to chatter about the Corfields and their party. He responded, and by the end of breakfast they were on much better terms than they had been for some weeks.

That morning also he wrote a cheque for her immediate necessities, which made her—for the time—a happy woman; and she overwhelmed him with grateful tears and embraces, which he did his best to bear.

Early in December he and she became the Corfields' guests. They found a large party collected, and Letty Sewell happily established as the spoilt child of the house. At the first touch of her hand, the first glance of her eyes, George's cloud dispersed.

'Why did you run away?' George asked her on the first possible occasion.

Letty laughed, fenced with the question for four days, during which George was never dull for a single instant, and then capitulated. She allowed him to propose to her, and was graciously pleased to accept him.

The following week Tressady went down with Letty to her home at Helbeck. He found an invalid father, a remarkably foolish, inconsequent mother, and a younger sister, Elsie, on whom, as it seemed to him, the burdens of the house mainly rested.

The father, who was suffering from a slow but incurable disease, had the remains of much natural ability and acuteness. He was well content with Tressady as a son-in-law; though in the few interviews that Tressady was able to have with him on the question of settlements the young man took pains to state his money affairs as carefully and modestly as possible. Letty was not often in her father's room, and Mr. Sewell treated her, when she did come, rather like an agreeable guest than a daughter. But he was evidently extremely proud of her —as also was the mother—and he would talk much to

George, when his health allowed it, of her good looks and her social success.

With the younger sister Tressady did not find it easy to make friends.

She was plain, sickly, and rather silent. She seemed to have scientific tastes and to be a great reader. And, so far as he could judge, the two sisters were not intimate.

'Don't hate me for taking her away!' he said, as he was bidding good-bye to Elsie, and glancing over her shoulder at Letty on the stairs.

The girl's quiet eyes were crossed by a momentary look of amusement. Then she controlled herself, and said gently:

'We didn't expect to keep her! Good-bye.'

CHAPTER IV

'Oh, Tully, look at my cloak! You've let it fall! Hold my fan, please, and give me the opera-glasses.'

The speaker was Miss Sewell. She and an elderly lady were sitting side by side in the stalls, about half way down St. James's Hall. The occasion was a popular concert, and, as Joachim was to play, every seat in the hall was rapidly filling up.

Letty rose as she asked for the opera-glasses, and scanned the crowds streaming in through the side-doors.

'No—no signs of him! He must have been kept at the House, after all,' she said, with annoyance. 'Really, Tully, I do think you might have got a programme all this time! Why do you leave everything to me?'

'My dear!' said her companion, protesting, 'you didn't tell me to.'

'Well, I don't see why I should *tell* you everything. Of course I want a programme. Is that he? No! What a nuisance!'

'Sir George must have been detained,' murmured her companion timidly.

'What a very original thing to say, wasn't it, Tully?' remarked Miss Sewell, with sarcasm, as she sat down again.

The lady addressed was silent, instinctively waiting till Letty's nerves should have quieted down. She was a

Miss Tulloch, a former governess of the Sewells, and now often employed by Letty, when she was in town, as a convenient chaperon. Letty was accustomed to stay with an aunt in Cavendish Square, an old lady who did not go out in the evenings. A chaperon therefore was indispensable, and Maria Tulloch could always be had. She existed somewhere in West Kensington, on an income of seventy pounds a year. Letty took her freely to the opera and the theatre, to concerts and galleries, and occasionally gave her a dress she did not want. Miss Tulloch clung to the connection as her only chance of relief from the boarding-house routine she detested, and was always abjectly ready to do as she was told. She saw nothing she was not meant to see, and she could be shaken off at a moment's notice. For the rest, she came of a stock of gentlefolk; and her invariable black dress, her bits of carefully treasured lace, the weak refinement of her face, and her timid manner did no discredit to the brilliant creature beside her.

When the first number of the programme was over, Letty got up once more, opera-glass in hand, to search among the late-comers for her missing lover. She nodded to many acquaintances, but George Tressady was not to be seen; and she sat down finally in no mood either to listen or to enjoy, though the magician of the evening was already at work.

'There's something very special, isn't there, you want to see Sir George about to-night?' Tully inquired humbly when the next pause occurred.

'Of course there is!' said Letty crossly. 'You do ask such foolish questions, Tully. If I don't see him to-night, he may let that house in Brook Street slip. There are several people after it—the agents told me.'

'And he thinks it too expensive?'

'Only because of *her*. If she makes him pay her that

preposterous allowance, of course it will be too expensive. But I don't mean him to pay it.'

'Lady Tressady is terribly extravagant,' murmured
Miss Tulloch.

'Well, so long as she isn't extravagant with his money
—*our* money—I don't care a rap,' said Letty; 'only she
sha'n't spend all her own and all ours too, which is what
she has been doing. When George was away he let her
live at Ferth, and spend almost all the income, except five
hundred a year that he kept for himself. And *then* she
got so shamefully into debt that he doesn't know when
he shall ever clear her. He gave her money at Christmas,
and again, I am *sure*, just lately. Well! all I know is
that it must be *stopped*. I don't know that I shall be
able to do much till I'm married, but I mean to make
him take this house.'

'Is Lady Tressady nice to you? She is in town, isn't
she?'

'Oh yes! she's in town. Nice?' said Letty, with a
little laugh. 'She can't bear me, of course; but we're
quite civil.'

'I thought she tried to bring it on?' said the con-
fidante, anxious, above all things, to be sympathetic.

'Well, she brought him to the Corfields, and let me
know she had. I don't know why she did it. I suppose
she wanted to get something out of him. Ah! *there* he
is!'

And Letty stood up, smiling and beckoning, while
Tressady's tall thin figure made its way along the central
passage.

'Horrid House! What made you so late?' she said,
as he sat down between her and Miss Tulloch.

George Tressady looked at her with delight. The
shrewish contractions in the face, which had been very
evident to Tully a few minutes before, had all disappeared,

and the sharp slight lines of it seemed to George the height of delicacy. At sight of him colour and eyes had brightened. Yet at the same time there was not a trace of the raw girl about her. She knew very well that he had no taste for *ingénues*, and she was neither nervous nor sentimental in his company.

'Do you suppose I should have stayed a second longer than I was obliged?' he asked her, smiling, pressing her little hand under pretence of taking her programme.

The first notes of a new Brahms quartette mounted, thin and sweet, into the air. The musical portion of the audience, having come for this particular morsel, prepared themselves eagerly for the tasting and trying of it. George and Letty tried to say a few things more to each other before yielding to the general silence, but an old gentleman in front turned upon them a face of such disdain and fury they must needs laugh and desist.

Not that George was unwilling. He was tired; and silence with Letty beside him was not only repose, but pleasure. Moreover, he derived a certain honest pleasure of a mixed sort from music. It suggested literary or pictorial ideas to him which stirred him, and gave him a sense of enjoyment. Now, as the playing flowed on, it called up delightful images in his brain : of woody places of whirling forms, of quiet rivers, of thin trees Corot-like against the sky—scenes of pleading, of frolic, reproachful pain, dissolving joy. With it all mingled his own story, his own feeling ; his pride of possession in this white creature touching him ; his sense of youth, of opening life, of a crowded stage whereon his 'cue' had just been given, his 'call' sounded. He listened with eagerness, welcoming each fancy as it floated past, conscious of a grain of self-abandonment even—a rare mood with him.

F

He was not absorbed in love by any means ; the music spoke to him of a hundred other kindling or enchanting things. Nevertheless it made it doubly pleasant to be there, with Letty beside him. He was quite satisfied with himself and her; quite certain that he had done everything for the best. All this the music in some way emphasised—made clear.

When it was over, and the applause was subsiding, Letty said in his ear : 'Have you settled about the house ? '

He smiled down upon her, not hearing what she said, but admiring her dress, its little complication and subtleties, the violets that perfumed every movement, the slim fingers holding the fan. Her mere ways of personal adornment were to him like pleasant talk. They surprised and amused him — stood between him and ennui.

She repeated her question.

A frown crossed his brow, and the face changed wholly.

'Ah !—it is so difficult to see one's way,' he said, with a little sigh of annoyance.

Letty played with her fan, and was silent.

'Do you so much prefer it to the others ? ' he asked her.

Letty looked up with astonishment.

'Why, it is a house ! ' she said, lifting her eyebrows ; ' and the others—— '

'Hovels ? Well, you are about right. The small London house is an abomination. Perhaps I can make them take less premium.'

Letty shook her head.

' It is not at all a dear house,' she said, decidedly.

He still frowned, with the look of one recalled to an annoyance he had shaken off.

' Well, darling, if you wish it so much, that settles it. Promise to be still nice to me when we go through the Bankruptcy Court ! '

' We will let lodgings, and I will do the waiting,' said Letty, just laying her hand lightly against his for an instant. 'Just think! That house would draw like anything. Of course, we will only take the eldest sons of peers. By the way, do you see Lord Fontenoy ? '

They were in the middle of the ' interval,' and almost everyone about them, including Miss Tulloch, was standing up, talking or examining their neighbours.

George craned his neck round Miss Tulloch, and saw Fontenoy sitting beside a lady, on the other side of the middle gangway.

' Who is the lady ? ' Letty inquired. ' I saw her with him the other night at the Foreign Office.'

George smiled.

' *That*—if you want to know—is Fontenoy's story ! '

' Oh, but tell me at once ! ' said Letty, imperiously. ' But he hasn't got a story, or a heart. He's only stuffed with blue-book.'

' So I thought till a few weeks ago. But I know a good deal more now about Master Fontenoy than I did.'

' But who is she ? '

' She is a Mrs. Allison. Isn't that white hair beautiful? And her face—half saint, I always think—you might take her for a mother-abbess—and half princess. Did you ever see such diamonds ? '

George pulled his moustaches, and grinned as he looked across at Fontenoy.

' Tell me quick ! ' said Letty, tapping him on the arm—' Is she a widow ?—and is he going to marry her ? Why didn't you tell me before ?—why didn't you tell me at Malford ? '

' Because I didn't know,' said George, laughing.

F 2

' Oh ! it's a strange story—too long to tell now. She is a widow, but he is not going to marry her, apparently. She has a grown-up son, who hasn't yet found himself a wife, and she thinks it isn't fair to him. If Fontenoy wants to introduce her, don't refuse. She is the mistress of Castle Luton, and has delightful parties. Yes !—if I'd known at Malford what I know now ! '

And he laughed again, remembering Fontenoy's nocturnal incursion upon him, and its apparent object. Who would have imagined that the preacher of that occasion had ever given one serious thought to woman and woman's arts—least of all that he was the creation and slave of a woman !

Letty's curiosity was piqued, and she would have plied George with questions, but that she suddenly perceived that Fontenoy had risen, and was coming across to them.

' Gracious ! ' she said ; ' here he comes. I can't think why ; he doesn't like me.'

Fontenoy, however, when he had made his way to them, greeted Miss Sewell with as much apparent cordiality as he showed to anyone else. He had received George's news of the marriage with all decorum, and had since sent a handsome wedding-present to the bride-elect. Letty, however, was never at ease with him, which, indeed, was the case with most women.

He stood beside the *fiancés* for a minute or two, exchanging a few commonplaces with Letty on the performers and the audience ; then he turned to George with a change of look.

' No need for us to go back to-night, I think ? '

' What, to the House ? Dear, no ! Grooby and Havershon may be trusted to drone the evening out, I should hope, with no trouble to anybody but themselves. The Government are just keeping a house, that's all. Have you been grinding at your speech all day ? '

Fontenoy shrugged his shoulders.

'I sha'n't get anything out that I want to say. Are you coming to the House on Friday, Miss Sewell?'

'Friday?' said Letty, looking puzzled.

George laughed.

'I told you. You must plead trousseau if you want to save yourself!'

Amusement shone in his blue eyes as they passed from Letty to Fontenoy. He had long ago discovered that Letty was incapable of any serious interest in his public life. It did not disturb him at all. But it tickled his sense of humour that Letty would have to talk politics all the same, and to talk them with people like Fontenoy.

'Oh! you mean your Resolution!' cried Letty. 'Isn't it a Resolution? Yes, of course I'm coming. It's very absurd, for I don't know anything about it. But George says I must, and till I promise to obey, you see, I don't mind being obedient!'

Archness, however, was thrown away on Fontenoy. He stood beside her, awkward and irresponsive. Not being allowed to be womanish, she could only try once more to be political.

'It's to be a great attack on Mr. Dowson, isn't it?' she asked him. 'You and George are mad about some things he has been doing? He's Home Secretary, isn't he? Yes, of *course!* And he's been driving trade away, and tyrannising over the manufacturers? I *wish* you'd explain it to me! I ask George, and he tells me not to talk shop.'

'Oh, for goodness sake,' groaned George, 'let it alone! I came to meet you and hear Joachim. However, I may as well warn you, Letty, that I sha'n't have time to be married once Fontenoy's anti-Maxwell campaign begins; and it will go on till the Day of Judgment.'

'Why anti-Maxwell?' said Letty, puzzled. 'I thought it was Mr. Dowson you are going to attack?'

George, a little vexed that she should require it, began to explain that as Maxwell was 'only a miserable peer,' he could have nothing to do with the House of Commons, and that Dowson was the official mouthpiece of the Maxwell group and policy in the Lower House. 'The hands were the hands of Esau,' &c. Letty meanwhile, conscious that she was not showing to advantage, flushed, began to play nervously with her fan, and wished that George would leave off.

Fontenoy did nothing to assist George's political lesson. He stood impassive, till suddenly he tried to look across his immediate neighbours, and then said, turning to Letty:

'The Maxwells, I see, are here to-night.' He nodded towards a group on the left, some two or three benches behind them. 'Are you an admirer of Lady Maxwell's, Miss Sewell?—you've seen her, of course?'

'Oh yes, *often!*' said Letty, annoyed by the question, standing, however, eagerly on tiptoe. 'I know her, too, a little; but she never remembers me. She was at the Foreign Office on Saturday, with such a *hideous* dress on —it spoilt her completely.'

'Hideous!' said Fontenoy, with a puzzled look. 'Some artist—I forget who—came and raved to me about it; said it was like some Florentine picture—I forget what —don't think I ever heard of it.'

Letty looked contemptuous. Her expression said that in this matter, at any rate, she knew what she was talking about. Nevertheless her eyes followed the dark head Fontenoy had pointed out to her.

Lady Maxwell was at the moment the centre of a large group of people, mostly men, all of whom seemed to be eager to get a word with her, and she was talking with great animation, appealing from time to time to a tall, broad-shouldered gentleman, with greyish hair, who stood, smiling and silent, at the edge of the group. Letty noticed that many glasses from the balcony were directed to this particular knot of persons; that everybody near them, or rather every woman, was watching Lady Maxwell, or trying to get a better view of her. The girl felt a secret pang of envy and dislike.

The figure of a well-known accompanist appeared suddenly at the head of the staircase leading from the artists' room. The interval was over, and the audience began to subside into attention.

Fontenoy bowed and took his leave.

'You see, he *didn't* introduce me,' said Letty, not without chagrin, as she settled down. 'And how plain he is! I think him uglier every time I see him.'

George made a vague sound of assent, but did not really agree with her in the least. Fontenoy's air of overwork was more decided than ever; his eyes had almost sunk out of sight; the complexion of his broad strong face had reddened and coarsened from lack of exercise and sleep; his brown hair was thinning and grizzling fast. Nevertheless a man saw much to admire in the ungainly head and long-limbed frame, and did not think any the better of a woman's intelligence for failing to perceive it.

After the concert, as George and Letty stood together in the crowded vestibule, he said to her, with a smile:

'So I take that house?'

'If you want to do anything disagreeable,' she retorted, quickly, 'don't *ask* me. Do it, and then wait till I am good-tempered again!'

'What a tempting prospect! Do you know when you put on that particular hood that I would take Buckingham Palace to please you? Do you know also that my mother will think us very extravagant?'

'Ah, we can't all be economical!' said Letty.

He saw the little toss of the head and sharpening of the lips. They only amused him. Though he had never, so far, discussed his mother and her affairs with Letty in any detail, he understood perfectly well that her feeling about this particular house in some way concerned his mother, and that Letty and Lady Tressady were rapidly coming to dislike each other. Well, why should Letty pretend? He liked her the better for not pretending.

There was a movement in the crowd about them, and Letty, looking up, suddenly found herself close to a tall lady, whose dark eyes were bent upon her.

'How do you do, Miss Sewell?'

Letty, a little fluttered, gave her hand and replied. Lady Maxwell glanced across her at the tall young man, with the fair, irregular face. George bowed involuntarily, and she slightly responded. Then she was swept on by her own party.

'Have you sent for your carriage?' George heard some one say to her.

'No; I am going home in a hansom. I've tired out both the horses to-day. Aldous is going down to the club to see if he can hear anything about Devizes.'

'Oh! the election?'

She nodded, then caught sight of her husband at the door beckoning, and hurried on.

'What a head!' said George, looking after her with admiration.

'Yes,' said Letty, unwillingly. 'It's the hair that's so splendid, the long black waves of it. How ridiculous to talk of tiring out her horses—that's just like her! As though she mightn't have fifty horses if she liked! Oh, George, there's our man! Quick, Tully!'

They made their way out. In the press George put his arm half round Letty, shielding her. The touch of her light form, the nearness of her delicate face, enchanted him. When their carriage had rolled away, and he turned homewards along Piccadilly, he walked absently for a time, conscious only of pulsing pleasure.

It was a mild February night. After a long frost, and a grudging thaw, westerly winds were setting in, and Spring could be foreseen. It had been pouring with rain during the concert, but was now fair, the rushing clouds leaving behind them, as they passed, great torn spaces of blue, where the stars shone.

Gusts of warm moist air swept through the street. As George's moment of intoxication gradually subsided, he felt the physical charm of the soft buffeting wind. How good seemed all living!—youth and capacity—this roaring multitudinous London—the future with its chances! This common pleasant chance of marriage amongst them—he was glad he had put out his hand to it. His wife that was to be was no saint and no philosopher. He thanked the fates! He at least asked for neither—on the hearth. 'Praise, blame, love, kisses'—for all of those, life with Letty would give scope; yet for none of them in excess. There would be plenty of room left for other things, other passions—the passion of political power, for instance, the art of dealing with and commanding other men. He, the novice, the beginner, to talk of 'commanding!' Yet already he felt his foot upon the ladder. Fontenoy consulted him, and confided in him more and more. In spite of his engagement, he was informing himself rapidly on a hundred questions, and the mental wrestle of every day was exhilarating. Their small group in the House, compact, tireless, audacious, was growing in importance and in the attention it extorted from the public. Never had the whole tribe of factory inspectors shown a more hawk-like, a more inquisitorial, a more intolerable vigilance than during the past twelve months. All the persons concerned with matches and white-lead, with certain chemical or metal-working industries, with 'season' dressmaking or tailoring, were up in arms, rallying to Fontenoy's support with loud wrath and lamentations, claiming to speak not only for themselves, but for their 'hands,' in the angry protest that things had gone and were going a great deal too far, that trade was simply being harassed out of the country. A Whiggish group of manufacturers on the Liberal side were all with Fontenoy; while the Socialists, on whom the Government should have been able in such a matter to count to the death, had a special grievance against the Cabinet at the moment, and were sulking in their tents. The attack and defence would probably take two nights; for the Government, admitting the gravity of the assault, had agreed, in case the debate should not be concluded on Friday, to give up Monday to it. Altogether the affair would make a noise. George would probably get in his maiden speech on the second night, and was, in truth, devoting a great deal of his mind to the prospect; though to Letty he had persistently laughed at it and belittled it, refusing altogether to let her come and hear him.

Then, after Easter would come Maxwell's Bill, and the fat in the fire! Poor little Letty!—she would get but few of the bridal observances due to her when *that* struggle began. But first would come Easter and their wedding; that one short fortnight, when he would carry her off—soft, willing prey!—to the country, draw a 'wind-warm space' about himself and her, and minister to all her whims.

He turned down St. James's Street, passed Marlborough House, and entered the Mall, on the way to Warwick Square, where he was living with his mother.

Suddenly he became aware of a crowd, immediately

in front of him, in the direction of Buckingham Palace. A hansom and horse were standing in the roadway ; the driver, crimson and hatless, was bandying words with one of the policemen, who had his notebook open, and from the middle of the crowd came a sound of wailing.

He walked up to the edge of the circle.

'Anybody hurt?' he said to the policeman, as the man shut his notebook.

'Little girl run over, sir.'

'Can I be of any assistance? Is there an ambulance coming?'

'No, sir. There was a lady in the hansom. She's just now bandaging the child's leg, and says she'll take it to the hospital.'

George mounted on one of the seats under the trees that stood handy, and looked over the heads of the crowd to the space in the centre which the other policeman was keeping clear. A little girl lay on the ground, or rather on a heap of coats ; another girl, apparently about sixteen, stood near her, crying bitterly, and a lady——

'Goodness!' said Tressady ; and, jumping down, he touched the policeman on the shoulder.

'Can you get me through? I think I could be some help. That lady'—he spoke a word in the policeman's ear.

The man touched his hat.

'Stand back, please!' he said, addressing the crowd, 'and let this gentleman through.'

The crowd divided unwillingly. But at the same moment it parted from the inside, and a little procession came through, both policemen joining their energies to make a free passage for it. In front walked the policeman carrying the little girl, a child apparently of about twelve years old. Her right foot lay stiffly across his arm, held straight and still in an impromptu splint of umbrellas and handkerchiefs. Immediately behind came the lady whom George had caught sight of, holding the other girl's hand in hers. She was bareheaded and in evening dress. Her opera-cloak, with its heavy sable collar, showed beneath it a dress of some light-coloured satin, which had already suffered deplorably from the puddles of the road, and, as she neared the lamp beneath which the cab had stopped, the diamonds on her wrists sparkled in the light. During her passage through the crowd, George perceived that one or two people recognised her, and that a murmur ran from mouth to mouth.

Of anything of the sort she herself was totally unconscious. George saw at once that she, not the policeman, was in command. She gave him directions, as they approached the cab, in a quick, imperative voice which left no room for hesitation.

'The driver is drunk,' he heard her say; 'who will drive?'

'One of us will drive, ma'am.'

'What—the other man? Ask him to take the reins at once, please, before I get in. The horse is fresh, and might start. That's right. Now, when I say the word, give me the child.'

She settled herself in the cab. George saw the policeman somewhat embarrassed, for a moment, with his burden. He came forward to his help, and between them they handed in the child, placing her carefully on her protector's knee.

Then, standing at the open door of the cab, George raised his hat. 'Can I be of any further assistance to you, Lady Maxwell? I saw you just now at the concert.'

She turned in some astonishment as she heard her name, and looked at the speaker. Then, very quickly, she seemed to understand.

'I don't know,' she said, pondering. 'Yes! you could

help me. I am going to take the child to hospital. But there is this other girl. Could you take her home—she is very much upset? No!—first, could you bring her after me to St. George's? She wants to see where we put her sister.'

'I will call another cab, and be there as soon as you.'

'Thank you. Just let me speak to the sister a moment, please.'

He put the weeping girl forward, and Lady Maxwell bent across the burden on her knee to say a few words to her—soft, quick words in another voice. The girl understood, her face cleared a little, and she let Tressady take charge of her.

One of the policemen mounted the box of the hansom, amid the 'chaff' of the crowd, and the cab started. A few hats were raised in George's neighbourhood, and there was something of a cheer.

'I tell yer,' said a voice, 'I knowed her fust sight— seed her picture lots o' times in the papers, and in the winders too. My word, ain't she good-lookin! And did yer see all them diamonds?'

'Come along!' said George impatiently, hurrying his charge into the four-wheeler the other policeman had just stopped for them.

In a few more seconds he, the girl, and the policeman were pursuing Lady Maxwell's hansom at the best speed of an indifferent horse. George tried to say a few consoling things to his neighbour; and the girl, reassured by his kind manner, found her tongue, and began to chatter in a tearful voice about the how and when of the accident: about the elder sister in a lodging in Crawford Street, Tottenham Court Road, whom she and the little one had been visiting; the grandmother in Westminster with whom they lived; poor Lizzie's place in a laundry, which now she must lose; how the lady had begged handkerchiefs and umbrellas from the crowd to tie up Lizzie's leg with—and so on through a number of other details incoherent or plaintive.

George heard her absently. His mind all the time was absorbed in the dramatic or ironic aspects of what he had just seen. For dramatic they were—though perhaps a little cheap. Could he, could anyone, have made acquaintance with this particular woman in more characteristic fashion? He laughed to think how he would tell the story to Fontenoy. The beautiful creature in her diamonds, kneeling on her satin dress in the mud, to bind up a little laundrymaid's leg—it was so extravagantly in keeping with Marcella Maxwell that it amused one like an overdone coincidence in a clumsy play.

What made her so beautiful? The face had marked defects; but in colour, expression, subtlety of line—incomparable! On the other hand, the manner—no!—he shrugged his shoulders. The remembrance of its mannish —or should it be, rather, boyish?—energy and assurance somehow set him on edge.

In the end, they were not much behind the hansom; for the hospital porter was only just in the act of taking the injured child from Lady Maxwell as Tressady dismounted and went forward again to see what he could do.

But, somewhat to his chagrin, he was not wanted. Lady Maxwell and the porter did everything. As they went into the hospital, George caught a few of the things she was saying to the porter as she supported the child's leg. She spoke in a rapid, professional way, and the man answered, as the policeman had done, with a deference and understanding which were clearly not due only to her 'grand air' and her evening dress. George was puzzled.

He and the elder sister followed her into the waiting-room. The house-surgeon and a nurse were summoned, and the injured leg was put into a splint there and then.

The patient moaned and cried most of the time, and Tressady had hard work to keep the sister quiet. Then nurse and doctor lifted the child.

'They are going to put her to bed,' said Lady Maxwell, turning to George. 'I am going up with them. Would you kindly wait? The sister'—she dropped her business tone, and, smiling, touched the elder girl on the arm—'can come up when the little one is undressed.'

The little procession swept away, and George was left with his charge. As soon as the small sister was out of sight, the elder one began to chatter again out of sheer excitement, crying at intervals. George did not heed her much. He walked up and down, with his hands in his pockets, conscious of a curious irritability. He did not think a woman should take a strange man's service quite so coolly.

At the end of another quarter of an hour a nurse appeared to summon the sister. Tressady was told he might come too if he would, and his charge threw him a quick, timid look, as though asking him not to desert her in this unknown and formidable place. So they followed the nurse up white stone stairs, and through half-lit corridors, where all was silent, save that once a sound of delirious shrieking and talking reached them through a closed door, and made the sister's consumptive little face turn whiter still.

At last the nurse, putting her finger on her lip, turned a handle, and George was conscious of a sudden feeling of pleasure.

They were standing on the threshold of a children's ward. On either hand was a range of beds, bluish-white between the yellow picture-covered walls and the middle-way of spotless floor. Far away, at the other end, a great fire glowed. On a bare table in the centre, laden with bottles and various surgical necessaries, stood a shaded

lamp, and beside it the chair where the night-nurse
had been sitting. In the beds were sleeping children
of various ages, some burrowing, face downward, animal-
like, into their pillows; others lying on their backs,
painfully straight and still. The air was warm, yet light,
and there was the inevitable smell of antiseptics.
Something in the fire-lit space and comfort of the great
room, its ordered lines and colours, the gentleness of the
shaded light as contrasted with the dim figures in the
beds, seemed to make a poem of it—a poem of human
tenderness.

Two or three beds away to the right, Lady Maxwell
was standing with the night-nurse of the ward. The
little girl had been undressed, and was lying quiet, with
a drawn, piteous face that turned eagerly as her sister
came in. The whole scene was new and touching to
Tressady. Yet, after the first impression, his attention
was perforce held by Lady Maxwell, and he saw the rest
only in relation to her. She had slipped off her heavy
cloak, in order, perhaps, that she might help in the undressing of the child. Beneath, she wore a little shawl
or cape of some delicate lace over her low dress. The
dress itself was of a pale shade of green; the mire and
mud with which it was bedabbled no longer showed in
the half light; and the satin folds glistened dimly as she
moved. The poetic dignity of the head, so finely
wreathed with its black hair, of the full throat and
falling shoulders, received a sort of special emphasis
from the wide spaces, the pale colours and level lines of
the ward. Tressady was conscious again of the dramatic
significant note as he watched her, yet without any
softening of his nascent feeling of antagonism.

She turned and beckoned to the sister as they entered:

'Come and see how comfortable she is! And then
you must give this lady your name and address.'

The girl timidly approached. Whilst she was occupied with her sister and with the nurse, Lady Maxwell suddenly looked round, and saw Tressady standing by the table a yard or two from her.

A momentary expression of astonishment crossed her face. He saw that, in her absorption with the case and the two sisters, she had clean forgotten all about him. But in a flash she remembered, and smiled.

' So you are really going to take her home ? That is very kind of you. It will make all the difference to the grandmother that somebody should go and explain. You see, they leave her in the splint for the night, and to-morrow they will put the leg in plaster. Probably they won't keep her in hospital more than about three weeks, for they are very full.'

' You seem to know all about it !

' I was a nurse myself once, for a time,' she said, but with a certain stiffness which seemed to mark the transition from the professional to the great lady.

' Ah ! I should have remembered that. I had heard it from Edward Watton.'

She looked up quickly. He felt that for the first time she took notice of him as an individual.

' You know Mr. Watton ? I think you are Sir George Tressady, are you not ? You got in for Market Malford in November ? I recollect. I didn't like your speeches.'

She laughed. So did he.

' Yes, I got in just in time for a fighting session.'

Her laugh disappeared.

' An odious fight ! ' she said gravely.

' I am not so sure. That depends on whether you like fighting, and how certain you are of your cause ! '

She hesitated a moment ; then she said :

' How can Lord Fontenoy be certain of his cause ! '

The slight note of scorn roused him.

G

'Isn't that what all parties say of their opponents?'

She glanced at him again, curiously. He was evidently quite young—younger than herself, she guessed. But his careless ease and experience of bearing, contrasted with his thin boy's figure, attracted her. Her lip softened reluctantly into a smile.

'Perhaps,' she said. 'Only sometimes, you know, it must be true! Well, evidently we can't discuss it here at one o'clock-in the morning—and there is the nurse making signs to me. It is really very good of you. If you are in our neighbourhood on Sunday, will you report?'

'Certainly—with the greatest pleasure. I will come and give you a full account of my mission.'

She held out a slim hand. The sister, red-eyed with crying, was handed over to him, and he and she were soon in a cab, speeding towards the Westminster mews whither she directed him.

Well, was Maxwell to be so greatly envied? Tressady was not sure. Such a woman, he thought, for all her beauty, would not have greatly stirred his own pulses.

CHAPTER V

THE week which had opened thus for Tressady promised to be one of lively interest for such persons as were either concerned in or took notice of the House of Commons and its doings. Fontenoy's onslaught upon the administration of the Home Office, and, through the Home Secretary, on the Maxwell group and influence, had been long expected, and was known to have been ably prepared. Its possible results were already keenly discussed. Even if it were a damaging attack, it was not supposed that it could have any immediate effect on the state of parties or the strength of the Government. But after Easter, Maxwell's factory Bill—a special Factory Act for East London, touching the grown man for the first time, and absolutely prohibiting home-work in certain specified industries—was to be brought forward, and could not fail to provide Maxwell's adversaries with many chances of red and glorious battle. It was disputable from end to end; it had already broken up one Government; it was strongly pressed and fiercely opposed; and on the fate of each clause in Committee might hang the life or death of the Ministry—not so much because of the intrinsic importance of the matter, as because Maxwell was indispensable to the Cabinet, and it was known or believed that neither Maxwell nor his close friend and henchman, Dowson, the Home Secretary, would accept defeat on any of the really vital points of the Bill.

The general situation was a curious one. Some two years before this time a strong and long-lived Tory Government had come to an end. Since then all had been confusion in English politics. A weak Liberal Government, undermined by Socialist rebellion, had lasted but a short time, to be followed by an equally precarious Tory Ministry, in which Lord Maxwell—after an absence from politics of some four years or so—returned to his party, only to break it up. For he succeeded in imposing upon them a measure in which his own deepest convictions and feelings were concerned, and which had behind it the support of all the more important trade unions. Upon that measure the Ministry fell; but during their short administration Maxwell had made so great an impression upon his own side that when they returned, as they did return, with an enlarged majority, the Maxwell Bill retained one of the foremost places in their programme, and might be said, indeed, at the present moment to hold the centre of the political field.

That field, in the eyes of any middle-aged observer, was in strange disarray. The old Liberal party had been almost swept away; only a few waifs and strays remained, the exponents of a programme that nobody wanted, and of cries that stirred nobody's blood. A large Independent Labour and Socialist party filled the empty benches of the Liberals—a revolutionary, enthusiastic crew, of whom the country was a little frightened, and who were, if the truth were known, a little frightened at themselves. They had a coherent programme, and represented a formidable ' domination ' in English life. And that English life itself, in all that concerned the advance and transformation of labour, was in a singularly tossed and troubled state. After a long period of stagnation and comparative industrial peace, storms at home, answering to storms on the Continent, had been let loose, and forces both of reaction and of revolution were making themselves felt in new forms and under the command of new masters.

At the head of the party of reaction stood Fontenoy. Some four years before the present session the circumstances of a great strike in the Midlands—together, no doubt, with some other influence—had first drawn him into public life, had cut him off from racing and all his natural pleasures. The strike affected his father's vast domain in North Mercia; it was marked by an unusual violence on the part of the men and their leaders; and Fontenoy, driven, sorely against his will, to take a part by the fact that his father, the hard and competent administrator of an enormous fortune, happened at the moment to be struck down by illness, found himself before many weeks were over taking it with passion, and emerged from the struggle a changed man. Property must be upheld; low-born disorder and greed must be put down. He sold his race-horses, and proceeded forthwith to throw into the formation of a new party all the doggedness, the astuteness, and the audacity he had been accustomed to lavish upon the intrigues and the triumphs of the Turf.

And now in this new Parliament his immense labour was beginning to tell. The men who followed him had grown in number and improved in quality. They abhorred equally a temporising conservatism and a plundering democracy. They stood frankly for birth and wealth, the Church and the expert. They were the apostles of resistance and negation; they were sworn to oppose any further meddling with trade and the personal liberty of master and workman, and to undo, if they could, some of the meddling that had been already carried through. A certain academic quality prevailed among them, which made them peculiarly sensitive to the absurdities of men who had not been to Oxford or Cambridge; while some, like Tressady, had·been travellers, and wore an Imperialist heart upon their sleeve. The group possessed an unusual share of debating and oratorical ability, and they had never attracted so much attention as now that they were about to make the Maxwell Bill their prey.

Meanwhile, for the initiated, the situation possessed one or two points of special interest. Lady Maxwell, indeed, was by this time scarcely less of a political force than her husband. Was her position an illustration of some new power in women's hands, or was it merely an example of something as well known to the Pharaohs as to the nineteenth century—the ability of any woman with a certain physique to get her way? That this particular woman's way happened to be also her husband's way made the case less interesting for some observers. On the other hand, her obvious wifely devotion attracted simple souls to whom the meddling of women in politics would have been nothing but repellent had it not been recommended to them by the facts that Marcella Maxwell was held to be good as well as beautiful; that she loved her husband; and was the excellent mother of a fine son.

Of her devotion, in the case of this particular Bill, there was neither concealment nor doubt. She was known to have given her husband every assistance in the final drafting of the measure: she had seen for herself the working of every trade that it affected; she had innumerable friends among wage-earners of all sorts, to whom she gave half her social life; and both among them and in the drawing-rooms of the rich she fought her husband's cause unceasingly, by the help of beauty, wits, and something else—a broad impulsiveness and charm—which might be vilified or scorned, but could hardly be matched, by the enemy.

Meanwhile Lord Maxwell was a comparatively ineffective speaker, and passed in social life for a reserved and difficult personality. His friends put no one else beside him ; and his colleagues in the Cabinet were well aware that he represented the keystone in their arch. But the man in the street, whether of the aristocratic or plebeian sort, knew comparatively little about him. All of which, combined with the special knowledge of an inner circle, helped still more to concentrate public attention on the convictions, the temperament, and the beauty of his wife.

Amid a situation charged with these personal or dramatic elements the Friday so keenly awaited by Fontenoy and his party arrived.

Immediately after question-time Fontenoy made his speech. In reply, the Home Secretary, suave, statistical, and conciliatory, poured a stream of facts and reports upon the House. The more repulsive they were, the softer and more mincing grew his voice in dealing with them. Fontenoy had excited his audience, Dowson succeeded in making it shudder. Nevertheless, the effect of the evening lay with Fontenoy.

George stayed to hear the official defence to its end. Then he hurried upstairs in search of Letty, who, with Miss Tulloch, was in the Speaker's private gallery. As he went he thought of Fontenoy's speech, its halting opening, the savage force of its peroration. His pulses tingled : ' Magnificent ! ' he said to himself; ' *magnificent !* We have found a man ! '

Letty was eagerly waiting for him, and they walked down the corridor together. ' Well ? ' he said, thrusting his hands deep into his pockets, and looking down upon her with a smile. ' Well ? '

Letty saw that she was expected to praise, and she did her best, his smile still bent upon her. He was perfectly aware all the time of the fatuity of what she was saying.

She had caught up since her engagement a certain number of political phrases, and it amused him to note the cheap and tinkling use she made of them. Nevertheless she was chatting, smiling, gesticulating, for his pleasure. She was posing for him, using her grey eyes in these expressive ways, all for him. He thought her the most entertaining plaything; though it did occur to him some-times that when they were married he would give her instruction.

'Ah, well, you liked it—that's good!' he said at last, interrupting her. 'We've begun well, any way. It'll be rather hard, though, to have to speak after that on Monday!'

'As if you need be afraid! You're not, you know—it's only mock modesty. Do you know that Lady Max-well was sitting two from me?'

'No! Well, how did she like Fontenoy?'

'She never moved after he got up. She pressed her face against that horrid grating, and stared at him all the time. I thought she was very flushed—but that may have been the heat—and in a very bad temper,' added Letty maliciously. 'I talked to her a little about your adven-ture.'

'Did she remember my existence?'

'Oh dear yes! She said she expected you on Sunday. She never asked *me* to come.' Letty looked arch. 'But then one doesn't expect her to have pretty manners. People say she is shy. But, of course, that is only your friends' way of saying that you're rude.'

'She wasn't rude to you?' said George, outwardly eager, inwardly sceptical. 'Shall I not go on Sunday?'

'But of course you must go. We shall have to know them. She's not a woman's woman—that's all. Now, are we going to get some dinner, for Tully and I are famishing?'

'Come along, then, and I'll collect the party.'

George had asked a few of his acquaintance in the House to meet his betrothed, together with an old General Tressady and his wife who were his distant cousins. The party were to assemble in the room of an under-secretary much given to such hospitable functions; and thither accordingly George led the way.

The room, when they reached it, was already fairly full of people, and alive with talk.

'Another party!' said George, looking round him. 'Benson is great at this sort of thing.'

'Do you see Lady Maxwell?' said Letty in his ear.

George looked to his right, and perceived the lady in question. She also recognised him at once, and bowed, but without rising. She was the centre of a group of people, who were gathered round her and the small table on which she was leaning, and they were so deeply absorbed in the conversation that had been going on that they hardly noticed the entrance of Tressady and his companion.

'Leven has a party, you see,' said the under-secretary. 'Blaythwaite was to have taken them in—couldn't at the last moment; so they had to come in here. This is *your* side of the room! But none of your guests have come yet. Dinner at the House in the winter is a poor sort of business, Miss Sewell. We want the Terrace for these occasions.'

He led the young girl to a sofa at the further end of the room, and made himself agreeable, to him the easiest process in the world. He was a fashionable and charming person, in the most irreproachable of frock-coats, and Letty was soon at her ease with him, and mistress of all her usual arts and graces.

'You know Lady Maxwell?' he said to her, with a slight motion of the head towards the distant group.

Letty replied; and while she and her companion

chattered, George, who was standing behind them, watched the other party.

They were apparently in the thick of an argument, and Lady Maxwell, whose hands were lightly clasped on the table in front of her, was leaning forward with the look of one who had just shot her bolt, and was waiting to see how it would strike.

It struck apparently in the direction of her *vis-à-vis* Sir Frank Leven, for he bent over to her, making a quick reply in a half-petulant boy's voice. He had been three years in the House, but had still the air of an Eton ' swell' in his last half.

Lady Maxwell listened to what he had to say, a sort of silent passion in her face all the time—a noble passion, nobly restrained.

When he stopped, George caught her reply.

' He has neither *seen* nor *felt*—every sentence showed it—that is all one can say. How can one take his judgment ? '

George's mouth twitched. He slipped, smiling, into a place beside Letty. ' Did you hear that ? ' he inquired.

'Fontenoy's speech, of course,' said the under-secretary, looking round. ' She's pitching into Leven, I suppose. He's as cranky and unsound as he can be. Shouldn't wonder if you got him before long.'

He nodded good-temperedly to Tressady, then got up to speak to a man on the edge of the further group.

' How amusing ! ' said George, his satirical eyes still watching Lady Maxwell. ' How much that set has " seen and felt " of sweaters, and white-lead workers, and the like ! Don't they look like it ? '

' Who are they ? '

Letty was now using all her eyes to find out, and

especially for the purpose of carrying away a mental photograph of Lady Maxwell's black hat and dress.

'Oh ! the Maxwells' particular friends in the House—most of them as well provided with family and goods as they make 'em : a philanthropic, idealist lot, that yearns for the people, and will be the first to be kicked downstairs when the people gets its own. However, they aren't all quite happy in their minds. Frank Leven there, as Benson says, is decidedly shaky. He is the member for the Maxwells' division—Maxwell, of course, put him in. He has a house there, I believe, and he married Lady Maxwell's great friend, Miss Macdonald—an ambitious little party, they say, who simply insisted on his going into Parliament. Oh, then, Bennett is there—do you see ? —the little dark man with a frock-coat and spectacles ? He's Lady Maxwell's link with the Independents—oldest workman member—been in the House a long time, so that by now he isn't quite as one-eyed and one-eared as the rest of them. I suppose she hopes to make use of him at critical moments—she takes care to have tools of all sorts. Gracious—listen !'

There was, indeed, a very storm of discussion sweeping through the rival party. Lady Maxwell's penetrating but not loud voice seemed to pervade it, and her eyes and face, as she glanced from one speaker to another, drew alternately the shafts and the sympathy of the rest.

Tressady made a face.

'I say, Letty, promise me one thing !' His hand stole towards hers. Tully discreetly looked the other way. 'Promise me not to be a political woman, there's a dear !'

Letty hastily withdrew her fingers, having no mind at all for caresses in public.

'But I *must* be a political woman—I shall have to be ! I know heaps of girls and married women who get up everything in the papers—all the stupidest things—not because they know anything about it, or because they care a rap, but because some of their men friends happen to be members ; and when they come to see you, you must know what to talk to them about.'

'Must you?' said George. 'How odd! As though one went to tea with a woman for the sake of talking about the very same things you have been doing all day, and are probably sick to death of already.'

'Never mind,' said Letty, with her little air of sharp wisdom. 'I *know* they do it, and I shall have to do it too. I shall pick it up.'

'Will you? Of course you will! Only, when I've got a big Bill on, let me do a little of it for myself—give me some of the credit!'

Letty laughed maliciously.

'I don't know why you've taken such a dislike to her,' she said, but in rather a contented tone, as her eye once more travelled across to Lady Maxwell. 'Does she trample on her husband, after all?'

Tressady gave an impatient shrug.

'Trample on him? Goodness, no! That's all part of the play, too—wifely affection and the rest of it. Why can't she keep out of sight a little? We don't want the women meddling.'

'Thank you, my domestic tyrant!' said Letty, making him a little bow.

'How much tyranny will you want before you accept those sentiments?' he asked her, smiling tenderly into her eyes. Both had a moment's pleasant thrill ; then George sprang up.

'Ah, here they are at last!—the General, and all the lot. Now, I hope, we shall get some dinner.'

Tressady had, of course, to introduce his elderly

cousins and his three or four political friends to his future
wife; and, amid the small flutter of the performance, the
break-up and disappearance of the rival party passed
unnoticed. When Tressady's guests entered the dining-
room which looks on the Terrace, and made their way to
the top table reserved for them, the Leven dinner, near
the door, was already half through.

George's little banquet passed merrily enough. The
grey-haired General and his wife turned out to be agreeable and well-bred people, quite able to repay George's
hospitality by the dropping of little compliments on the
subject of Letty into his half-yielded ear. For his way
of taking such things was always a trifle cynical. He
believed that people say habitually twice what they mean,
whether in praise or blame; and he did not feel that his
own view of Letty was much affected by what other
people thought of her.

So, at least, he would have said. In reality, he got a
good deal of pleasure out of his *fiancée's* success. Letty,
indeed, was enjoying herself greatly. This political
world, as she had expected, satisfied her instinct for
social importance better than any world she had yet
known. She was determined to get on in it; nor, apparently, was there likely to be any difficulty in the matter.
George's friends thought her a pretty, lively creature, and
showed the usual inclination of the male sex to linger
in her society. She mostly wanted to be informed as
to the House and its ways. It was all so new to her!
—she said. But her ignorance was not insipid; her questions had flavour. There was much talk and laughter;
Letty felt herself the mistress of the table, and her social
ambitions swelled within her.

Suddenly George's attention was recalled to the
Maxwell table by the break up of the group around it.
He saw Lady Maxwell rise and look round her as though

in search of some one. Her eyes fell upon him, and he involuntarily rose at the same instant to meet the step she made towards him.

'I must say another word of thanks to you'—she held out her hand. 'That girl and her grandmother were most grateful to you.'

'Ah, well!—I must come and make my report. Sunday, I think you said?'

She assented. Then her expression altered:

'When do you speak?'

The question fell out abruptly, and took George by surprise.

'I? On Monday, I believe, if I get my turn. But I fear the British Empire will go on if I don't!'

She threw a glance of scrutiny at his thin, whimsical face, with its fair moustache and sunburnt skin.

'I hear you are a good speaker,' she said simply. 'And you are entirely with Lord Fontenoy?'

He bowed lightly, his hands on his sides. ·

'You'll agree our case was well put? The worst of it——'

Then he stopped. He saw that Lady Maxwell had ceased to listen to him. She turned her head towards the door, and, without even saying good-bye to him, she hurried away from him towards the further end of the room.

'Maxwell, I see!' said Tressady to himself, with a shrug, as he returned to his seat. 'Not flattering—but rather pretty, all the same!'

He was thinking of the quick change that had re-made the face while he was talking to her—a change as lovely as it was unconscious.

Lord Maxwell, indeed, had just entered the dining-room in search of his wife, and he and she now left it together, while the rest of the Leven party gradually dispersed. Letty also announced that she must go home.

'Let me just go back into the House and see what is going on,' said George. 'Ten to one I sha'n't be wanted, and I could see you home.'

He hurried off, only to return in a minute with the news that the debate was given up to a succession of superfluous people, and he was free, at any rate for an hour. Letty, Miss Tulloch, and he accordingly made their way to Palace Yard. A bright moon shone in their faces as they emerged into the open air, which was still mild and spring-like, as it had been all the week.

'I say—send Miss Tulloch home in a cab!' George pleaded in Letty's ear, 'and walk with me a bit. Come and look at the moon over the river. I will bring you back to the bridge and put you in a cab.'

Letty looked astonished and demure. 'Aunt Charlotte would be shocked,' she said.

George grew impatient, and Letty, pleased with his impatience, at last yielded. Tully, the most complaisant of chaperons, was put into a hansom and despatched.

As the pair reached the entrance of Palace Yard they were overtaken by a brougham, which drew up an instant in the gateway itself, till it should find an opening in the traffic outside.

'Look!' said George, pressing Letty's arm.

She looked round hurriedly, and, as the lamps of the gateway shone into the carriage, she caught a vivid glimpse of the people inside it. Their faces were turned towards each other as though in intimate conversation—that was all. The lady's hands were crossed on her knee; the man held a despatch-box. In a minute they were gone; but both Letty and George were left with the same impression—the sense of something exquisite surprised. It had already visited George that evening, only a few minutes earlier, in connection with the same woman's face.

Letty laughed, rather consciously.

George looked down upon her as he guided her through the gate.

'Some people seem to find it pleasant to be together!' he said, with a vibration in his voice. 'But why did we look?' he added, discontentedly.

'How could we help it, you silly boy?'

They walked towards the bridge and down the steps, happy in each other, and freshened by the night breeze. Over the river the moon hung full and white, and beneath it everything—the silver tracks on the water, the blaze of light at Charing Cross Station, the lamps on Westminster Bridge and in the passing steamers, a train of barges, even the darkness of the Surrey shore—had a gentle and poetic air. The vast city had, as it were, veiled her greatness and her tragedy; she offered herself kindly and protectingly to these two—to their happiness and their youth.

George made his companion wait beside the parapet and look, while he himself drew in the air with a sort of hunger.

'To think of the hours we spend in this climate,' he said, 'caged up in abominable places like the House of Commons!'

The traveller's distaste for the monotony of town and indoor life spoke in his vehemence. Letty raised her eyebrows.

'I am very glad of my furs, thank you! You seem to forget that it is February.'

'Never mind!—since Monday it has had the feel of April. Did you see my mother to-day?'

'Yes. She caught me just after luncheon, and we talked for an hour.'

'Poor darling! I ought to have been there to protect you. But she vowed she would have her say about that house.'

He looked down upon her, trying to see her expression in the shifting light. He had gone through a disagreeable little scene with his mother at breakfast. She had actually lectured him on the rashness of taking the Brook Street house!—he understanding the whole time that what the odd performance really meant was, that, if he took it, he would have a smaller margin of income wherefrom to supplement her allowance.

'Oh, it was all right!' said Letty, composedly. 'She declared we should get into difficulties at once, that I could have no idea of the value of money, that you always *had* been extravagant, that everybody would be astonished at our doing such a thing, etcetera, etcetera. I *think*—you don't mind?—I think she cried a little. But she wasn't really very unhappy.'

'What did you say?'

'Well, I suggested that when we were married, we and she should both set up account-books; and I promised faithfully that if she would let us see hers, we would let her see ours.'

George threw back his head with a gurgle of laughter.

'Well?'

'She was afraid,' said Letty, demurely, 'that I didn't take things seriously enough. Then I asked her to come and see my gowns.'

'And that, I suppose, appeased her?'

'Not at all. She turned up her nose at everything, by way of punishing me. You see, she had on a new Worth—the third since Christmas. My poor little trousseau rags had no chance.'

'H'm!' said George, meditatively. 'I wonder how

H

my mamma is going to manage when we are married,'
he added, after a pause.

Letty made no reply. She was walking firmly and
briskly; her eyes, full of a sparkling decision, looked
straight before her; her little mouth was close set.
Meanwhile through George's mind there passed a number of fragmentary answers to his own question. His
feeling towards his mother was wholly abnormal; he had
no sense of any unseemliness in the conversation about
her which was gradually growing common between himself and Letty; and he meant to draw strict lines in the
future. At the same time, there was the tie of old habit,
and of that uneasy and unwelcome responsibility with
regard to her which had descended upon him at the time
of his father's death. He could not honestly regard himself as an affectionate son; but the filial relationship,
even in its most imperfect aspect, has a way of imposing
itself.

'Ah, well! I daresay we shall pull through,' he said,
dismissing the familiar worry with a long breath. 'Why,
how far we have come!' he added, looking back at
Charing Cross and the Westminster towers. 'And how
extraordinarily mild it is! We can't turn back yet, and
you'll be tired if I race you on in this way. Look, Letty,
there's a seat! Would you be afraid—just five minutes?'

Letty looked doubtful.

'It's so absurdly late. George, you *are* funny! Suppose somebody came by who knew us?'

He opened his eyes.

'And why not? But see! there isn't a carriage, and
hardly a person, in sight. Just a minute!'

Most unwillingly Letty let herself be persuaded. It
seemed to her a foolish and extravagant thing to do; and
there was now no need for either folly or extravagance.
Since her engagement she had dropped a good many of

the small audacities of the social sort she had so freely allowed herself before it. It was as though, indeed, now that these audacities had served their purpose, some stronger and perhaps inherited instincts emerged in her, obscuring the earlier self. George was sometimes astonished by an ultra-conventional note, of which certainly he had heard nothing in their first days of intimacy at Malford.

However, she sat down beside him, protesting. But he had no sooner stolen her hand, than the moonlight showed her a dark absent look creeping over his face. And to her amazement he began to talk about the House of Commons, about the Home Secretary's speech, of all things in the world! He seemed to be harking back to Mr. Dowson's arguments, to some of the stories the Home Secretary had told of those wretched people who apparently enjoy dying of over-work and phosphorus and white-lead, who positively will die of them, unless the inspectors are always harrying them. He still held her hand, but she saw he was not thinking of her ; and a sudden pique rose in her small mind. Generally, she accepted his love-making very coolly—just as it came, or did not come. But to-night she asked herself with irritation—for what had he led her into his silly escapade, but to make love to her? And now here were her fingers slipping out of his, while he harangued her on things she knew and cared nothing about, in a voice and manner he might have addressed to anybody!

' Well, I don't understand—I really *don't !*' she interrupted sharply. 'I thought you were all against the Government—I thought you didn't believe a word they say !'

He laughed.

' The difference between them and us, darling, is only that *they* think the world can be mended by Act of Parlia-

ment, and *we* think it can't. Do what you will, *we* say
the world is, and must be, a wretched hole for the
majority of those that live in it; *they* suppose they
can cure it by quack meddlings and tyrannies.'

He looked straight before him, absorbed, and she was
struck with the harsh melancholy of his face.

What on earth had he kept her here for to talk this
kind of talk!

'George, I really *must* go!' she began, flushing, and
drawing her hand away.

Instantly he turned to her, his look brightening and
melting.

'Must you? Well, the world sha'n't be a wretched
hole for us, shall it, darling? We'll make a little nest
in it—we'll forget what we can't help—we'll be happy as
long as the fates let us—won't we, Letty?'

His arm slipped round behind her. He caught her
hands.

He had recollected himself. Nevertheless Letty was
keenly conscious that it was all most absurd, this sitting
on a seat in a public thoroughfare late at night, and
behaving like any 'Arry and 'Arriet.

'Why, of course we shall be happy,' she said, rising
with decision as she spoke; 'only somehow I don't always
understand you, George. I wish I knew what you were
really thinking about.'

'*You!*' he said, laughing, and drawing her hand
within his arm, as they turned backwards towards the
bridge.

She shook her head doubtfully. Whereupon he awoke
fully to the situation, and during the short remainder of
their walk, he wooed and flattered her as usual. But
when he had put her safely into a hansom at the
corner of the bridge, and smiled good-bye to her, he
turned to walk back to the House in much sudden flatness

of mood.   Her little restless egotisms of mind and manner
had chilled him unawares.   Had Fontenoy's speech been
so fine, after all?   Were politics—was anything—quite
worth while?   It seemed to him that all emotions were
small, all crises disappointing.

CHAPTER VI

THE following Sunday, somewhere towards five o'clock,
George rang the bell of the Maxwells' house in St. James's
Square.   It was a very fine house, and George's eye, as
he stood waiting, ran over the façade with an amused,
investigating look.

He allowed himself the same expression once or twice
in the hall, as one mute and splendid person relieved him
of his coat, and another, equally mute and equally un-
surpassable, waited for him on the stairs, while across a
passage beyond the hall he saw two red-liveried footmen
carrying tea.

'When one is a friend of the people,' he pondered as
he went upstairs, 'is one limited in horses but not in
flunkeys ?   These things are obscure.'

He was ushered first into a stately outer drawing-
room, filled with old French furniture and fine pictures ;
then the butler lifted a velvet curtain, pronounced the
visitor's name with a voice and emphasis as perfectly
trained as the rest of him, and stood aside for George to
enter.

He found himself on the threshold of a charming
room looking west, and lit by some last beams of February
sun.   The pale-green walls were covered with a medley
of prints and sketches.   A large writing-table, untidily
heaped with papers, stood conspicuous on the blue self-
coloured carpet, which over a great part of the floor was

pleasantly void and bare. Flat earthenware pans, planted
with hyacinths and narcissus, stood here and there, and
filled the air with spring scents. Books ran round the
lower walls, or lay piled wherever there was a space for
them; while about the fire at the further end was
gathered a circle of chintz-covered chairs—chairs of all
shapes and sizes, meant for talking. The whole impression of the pretty, disorderly place, compared with
the stately drawing-room behind it, was one of intimity
and freedom ; the room made a friend of you as you
entered.

Half a dozen people were sitting with Lady Maxwell
when Tressady was announced. She rose to meet him
with great cordiality, introduced him to little Lady Leven,
an elfish creature in a cloud of fair hair, and with a
pleasant 'You know all the rest,' offered him a chair
beside herself and the tea-table.

'The rest' were Frank Leven, Edward Watton,
Bayle, the Foreign Office private secretary who had
been staying at Malford House at the time of Tressady's
election, and Bennett, the 'small, dark man' whom George
had pointed out to Letty in the House as a Labour
member, and one of the Maxwells' particular friends.

'Well?' said Lady Maxwell, turning to her new
visitor as she handed him some tea, 'were you as much
taken with the grandmother as the grandmother was
taken with you? She told me she had never seen a
"more haffable gentleman, nor one as she'd a been more
willin to ha done for"!'

George laughed. 'I see,' he said, 'that my report
has been anticipated.'

'Yes—I have been there. I have found a "case" in
them indeed—alack! The granny—I am afraid she is
an unseemly old woman—and the elder girl both work for
the Jew son-in-law on the first floor—home-work of the

most abominable kind—that girl will be dead in a year if it goes on.'

George was rapidly conscious of two contradictory impressions—one of pleasure, one of annoyance—pleasure in her tall slim presence, her white hand, and all the other flashing points of a beauty not to be denied—and irritation that she should have talked ' shop ' to him with her first breath. Could one never escape this altruistic chatter?

But he was not left to grapple with it alone, for Lady Leven looked up quickly.

' Mr. Watton, will you please take Lady Maxwell's tea away if she mentions the word " case " again? We gave her fair warning.'

Lady Maxwell hastily clasped both her hands round her tea-cup.

' Betty, we have discussed the opera for at least twenty minutes.'

' Yes—at peril of our lives !' said Lady Leven. ' I never talked so fast before. One felt as though one *must* say everything one had to say about Melba and the de Reszkes, all in one breath—before one's poor little subject was torn from one—one would never have such a chance again.'

Lady Maxwell laughed, but coloured too.

' Am I such a nuisance ?' she said, dropping her hands on her knee with a little sigh. Then she turned to Tressady.

' But Lady Leven really makes it out worse than it is. We haven't even *approached* a Factory Act all the afternoon.'

Lady Leven sprang forward in her chair. ' Because ! *because*, my dear, we simply declined to let you. We made a league—didn't we, Mr. Bennett ?—even you joined it.'

Bennett smiled.

'Lady Maxwell overworks herself—we all know that,' he said, his look, at once kind, honest, and perennially embarrassed, passing from Lady Leven to his hostess.

'Oh, don't sympathise, for Heaven's sake!' cried Betty. 'Wage war upon her—it's our only hope.'

'Don't you think Sunday at least ought to be frivolous?' said Tressady, smiling, to Lady Maxwell.

'Well, personally, I like to talk about what interests me on Sunday as well as on other days,' she said with a frank simplicity; 'but I know I ought to be kept in order —I become a terrible bore.'

Frank Leven roused himself from the sofa on which he had languidly subsided.

'Bores?' he said indignantly, 'we're all bores. We all have been bores since people began to think about what they're pleased to call "social work." Why should I love my neighbour?—I'd much rather hate him. I generally do.'

'Doesn't it all depend,' said Tressady, 'on whether he happens to be able to make it disagreeable for you in return?'

'That's just it,' said Betty Leven, eagerly. 'I agree with Frank—it's all so stupid, this "loving" everybody. It makes one positively hot. We sit under a clergyman, Frank and I, who talks of nothing every Sunday but love —*love*—like that, long drawn-out—how our politics should be "love," and our shopping should be "love"—till we long simply to bastinado somebody. I want to have a little real nice cruelty—something sharp and interesting. I should like to stick pins into my maid, only unfortunately, as she has more than once pointed out to me, it would be so much easier for her to stick them into me!'

'You want the time of Miss Austen's novels back again,' said young Bayle, stooping to her, with his measured and agreeable smile—'before even the clergy had a mission.'

'Ah! but it would be no good,' said Lady Leven, sighing, 'if *she* were there!'

She threw out her small hand towards her hostess, and everybody laughed.

Up to the moment of the laugh, Lady Maxwell had been lying back in her chair listening, the beautiful mouth absently merry, and the eyes speaking—Tressady thought —of quite other things, of some hidden converse of her own, going on in the brain behind the eyes. A certain prophetess-air seemed natural to her. Nevertheless, that first impression of her he had carried away from the hospital scene was being somehow blurred and broken up.

She joined in the laugh against herself; then, with a little nod towards her assailant, she said to Edward Watton, who was sitting on her right hand—

'*You*'re not taken in, I know.'

'Oh, if you mean that I go in for "cases" and "causes" too,' cried Lady Leven, interrupting, 'of course I do—I can't be left alone. I must dance as my generation pipes.'

'Which means,' said her husband drily, 'that she went for two days filling soda-water bottles the week before last, and a day's shirt-making last week. From the first, I was told that she would probably return to me with an eye knocked out, she being totally inexperienced and absurdly rash. As to the second, to judge from the description she gave me of the den she had been sitting in when she came home, and the headache she had next day, I still expect typhoid. The fortnight isn't up till Wednesday.'

There was a shout of mingled laughter and inquiry.

'How did you do it?—and whom did you bribe?' said Bayle to Lady Leven.

'I didn't bribe anybody,' she said indignantly. 'You don't understand. My friends introduced me.'

Then, drawn out by him, she plunged into a lively account of her workshop experiences, interrupted every now and then by the sarcastic comments of her husband and the amusement of the two younger men who had brought their chairs close to her. Betty Leven ranked high among the lively chatterboxes of her day and set.

Lady Maxwell, however, had not laughed at Frank Leven's speech. Rather, as he spoke of his wife's experiences, her face had clouded, as though the blight of some too familiar image, some sad ever-present vision, had descended upon her.

Bennett also did not laugh. He watched the Levens indulgently for a few minutes, then insensibly he, Lady Maxwell, Edward Watton, and Tressady drew together into a circle of their own.

'Do you gather that Lord Fontenoy's speech on Friday has been much taken up in the country?' said Bennett, bending forward and addressing Lady Maxwell. Tressady, who was observing him, noticed that his dress was precisely the 'Sunday best' of the respectable workman, and was, moreover, reminded by the expression of the eyes and brow that Bennett was said to have been a well-known 'local preacher' in his north-country youth.

Lady Maxwell smiled, and pointed to Tressady.

'Here,' she said, 'is Lord Fontenoy's first-lieutenant.'

Bennett looked at George.

'I should be glad,' he said, 'to know what Sir George thinks?'

'Why, certainly—we think it has been very warmly taken up,' said George, promptly—'to judge from the newspapers, the letters that have been pouring in, and the petitions that seem to be preparing.'

Lady Maxwell's eyes gleamed. She looked at Bennett silently a moment, then she said;

'Isn't it amazing to you how strong an impossible case can be made to look?'

'It is inevitable,' said Bennett, with a little shrug, 'quite inevitable. These social experiments of ours are so young—there is always a strong case to be made out against any of them, and there will be for years to come.'·

'Well and good,' said George; 'then we cavillers are inevitable too. Don't attack us—praise us rather; by your own confession, we are as much a part of the game as you are.'

Bennett smiled slightly, but did not in reality quite follow. Lady Maxwell bent forward.

'Do you know whether Lord Fontenoy has any *personal* knowledge of the trades he was speaking about?' she said in her rich eager voice; 'that is what I want so much to find out.' ·

George was nettled by both the question and the manner.

'I regard Fontenoy as a very competent person,' he said drily. 'I imagine he did his best to inform himself. But there was not much need; the persons concerned—whom you think you are protecting—were so very eager to inform us!'

Lady Maxwell flushed.

'And you think that settles it—the eagerness of the cheap life to be allowed to maim and waste itself? But again and again English law has stepped in to prevent it—and again and again everybody has been thankful.'

'It is all a question of balance, of course,' said George. 'Must a few unwise people be allowed to kill themselves—or thousands lose their liberty?'

His blue eyes scanned her beautiful impetuous face with a certain cool hardness. Internally he was more and more in revolt against a 'monstrous regiment of

women ' and the influence upon the most complex economic problems of such a personality as that before him.

But his word 'liberty' pricked her. The look of feeling
passed away. Her eyes kindled as sharply and drily as
his own.

' Freedom ?—let me quote you Cromwell! " Every
sectary saith, ' O give me liberty ! ' But give it him, and
to the best of his power he will yield it to no one else." So
with your careless or brutal employer—give him liberty,
and no one else shall get it.'

' Only by metaphor—not legally,' said George, stubbornly. ' So long as men are not slaves by law there is
always a chance for freedom. Any way *we* stand for
freedom—as an end, not a means. It is not the business
of the State to make people happy—not at all !—at least
that is our view—but it *is* the business of the State to
keep them free.'

' Ah ! ' said Bennett, with a long breath, ' there you've
hit the nail—the whole difference between you and us.'

George nodded. Lady Maxwell did not speak immediately. But George was conscious that he was being
observed, closely considered. Their glances crossed an
instant, in antagonism, certainly, if not in dislike.

' How long is it since you came home from India ? '
she asked him suddenly.

' About six months.'

' And you were, I think, a long time abroad ? '

' Nearly four years. Does that make you think I have
not had much time to get up the things I am going to vote
about ? ' said the young man, laughing. ' I don't know !
On the broadest issues of politics, one makes up one's
mind as well in Asia as in Europe—better perhaps.'

' On the Empire, I suppose—and England's place in
the world ? That's a side which—I know—I remember
much too little. You think our life depends on a governing

class—and that *we* and democracy are weakening that class too much ? '

'That's about it. And for democracy it is all right. But *you*—you are the traitors ! '

His thrust, however, did not rouse her to any corresponding rhetoric. She smiled merely, and began to question him about his travels. She did it with great deftness, so that after an answer or two both his temper and manner insensibly softened, and he found himself talking with ease and success. His mixed personality revealed itself—his capacity for certain veiled enthusiasms, his respect for power, for knowledge, his pessimist beliefs as to the average lot of men.

Bennett, who listened easily, was glad to help her make her guest talk. Frank Leven left the group near the sofa and came to listen too. Tressady was more and more spurred, carried out of himself. Lady Maxwell's fine eyes and stately ways were humanised after all by a quick responsiveness, which for most people, however critical, made conversation with her draw like a magnet. Her intelligence, too, was competent, left the mere feminine behind in these connections that Tressady offered her, no less than in others. She had not lived in the world of high politics for nearly five years for nothing ; so that unconsciously, and indeed quite against his will, Tressady found himself talking to her, after a while, as though she had been a man and an equal, while at the same time taking more pains than he would ever have taken for a man.

'Well, you *have* seen a lot ! ' said Frank Leven at last, with a rather envious sigh.

Bennett's modest face suddenly reddened.

'If only Sir George will use his eyes to as good purpose at home——' he said involuntarily, then stopped. Few men were more unready and awkward in conversation; yet when roused he was one of the best platform speakers of his day.

George laughed.

'One sees best what appeals to one, I am afraid,' he said, only to be instantly conscious that he had made a rather stupid admission in face of the enemy.

Lady Maxwell's lip twitched; he saw the flash of some quick thought cross her face. But she said nothing.

Only when he got up to go, she bade him notice that she was always at home on Sundays, and would be glad that he should remember it. He made a rather cold and perfunctory reply. Inwardly he said to himself, 'Why does she say nothing of Letty, whom she knows— and of our marriage—if she wants to make friends?'

Nevertheless, he left the house with the feeling of one who has passed an hour not of the common sort. He had done himself justice, made his mark. And as for her—in spite of his flashes of dislike he carried away a strong impression of something passionate and vivid that clung to the memory. Or was it merely eyes and pose, that astonishingly beautiful colour, and touch of classic dignity which she got—so the world said—from some remote strain of Italian blood? Most probably! All the same, she had fewer of the ordinary womanly arts than he had imagined. How easy it would have been to send that message to Letty she had not sent! He thought simply that for a clever woman she might have been more adroit.

The door had no sooner closed behind Tressady than Betty Leven, with a quick look after him, bent across to her hostess, and said in a stage whisper:

'Who? Post me up, please.'

'One of Fontenoy's gang,' said her husband, before Lady Maxwell could answer. 'A new member, and as sharp as needles. He's been exactly to all the places where I want to go, Betty, and you won't let me.'

He glanced at his wife with a certain sharpness. For Tressady had spoken in passing of nilghai-shooting in the Himalayas, and the remark had brought the flush of an habitual discontent to the young man's cheek.

Betty merely held out a white child's wrist.

' Button my glove, please, and don't talk. I have got ever so many questions to ask Marcella.'

Leven applied himself rather sulkily to his task while Betty pursued her inquiries.

' Isn't he going to marry Letty Sewell?'

' Yes,' said Lady Maxwell, opening her eyes rather wide. ' Do you know her?'

' Why, my dear, she's Mr. Watton's cousin—isn't she?' said Betty, turning towards that young man. ' I saw her once at your mother's.'

' Certainly she is my cousin,' said that young man, smiling, ' and she is going to marry Tressady at Easter. So much I can vouch for, though I don't know her so well, perhaps, as the rest of my family do.'

' Oh!' said Betty drily, releasing her husband and crossing her small hands across her knee. ' That means— Miss Sewell isn't one of Mr. Watton's *favourite* cousins. You don't mind talking about your cousins, do you? You may blacken the character of all mine. Is she nice?'

' Who—Letty? Why, of course she is nice,' said Edward Watton, laughing. ' All young ladies are.'

' Oh goodness!' said Betty, shaking her halo of gold hair. ' Commend me to cousins for letting one down easy.'

' Too bad, Lady Leven!' said Watton, getting up to escape. ' Why not ask Bayle? He knows all things. Let me hand you over to him. He will sing you all my cousin's charms.'

'Delighted!' said Bayle as he, too, rose—'only unfortunately I ought at this moment to be at Wimbledon.'

He had the air of the typical official, well dressed, suave, and infinitely self-possessed, as he held out his hand—deprecatingly—to Lady Leven.

'Oh! you private secretaries!' said Betty, pouting and turning away from him.

'Don't abolish us,' he said, pleading. 'We must live.'

'*Je n'en vois pas la nécessité!*' said Betty over her shoulder.

'Betty, what a babe you are!' cried her husband, as Bayle, Watton, and Bennett all disappeared together.

'Not at all!' cried Betty. 'I wanted to get some truth out of somebody. For, of course, the real truth is that this Miss Sewell is——'

'Is what?' said Leven, lost in admiration all the time, as Lady Maxwell saw, of his wife's dainty grace and rose-leaf colour.

'Well—a—*minx!*' said Betty with innocent slowness, opening her blue eyes very wide; 'a mischievous—rather pretty—hard-hearted—flirting—little minx!'

'Really, Betty!' cried Lady Maxwell. 'Where have you seen her?'

'Oh, I saw her last year several times at the Wattons, and other places,' said Betty, composedly. 'And so did you too, please, madam. I remember very well one day Mrs. Watton brought her into the Winterbournes when you and I were there, and she chattered a great deal.'

'Oh yes!—I had forgotten.'

'Well, my dear, you'll soon have to remember her! so you needn't talk in that lofty tone. For they're going to be married at Easter, and if you want to make friends with the young man, you'll have to realise the wife!'

'Married at Easter? How do you know?'

I

'In the first place Mr. Watton said so, in the next there are such things as newspapers. But of course you didn't notice such trifles, you never do.'

'Betty, you're very cross with me to-day!' Lady Maxwell looked up at her friend with a little pleading air.

'Oh no! only for your good. I know you're thinking of nothing in the world but how to make that man take a reasonable view of Maxwell's Bill. And I want to impress upon you that *he*'s probably thinking a great deal more about getting married than about Factory Bills. You see, *your* getting married was a kind of accident. But other people are different. And oh, dear, you do know so little about them when they don't live in four pair backs! There, don't defend yourself—you sha'n't!'

And, stooping, Betty stifled her friend's possible protest by kissing her.

'Now then, come along, Frank—you've got your speech to write—and I've got to copy it out. Don't swear! you know you're going to have two whole days' golfing next week. Good-bye, Marcella! My love to Aldous—and tell him not to be so late next time I come to tea. Good-bye!'

And off she swept, pausing, however, on the landing to open the door again and put in an eager face.

'Oh! and, by the way, the young man has a mother— Frank reminded me. His womenkind don't seem to be his strong point—but as she doesn't earn *even* four-and-sixpence a week—very sadly the contrary—I won't tell you any more now, or you'll forget. Next time!'

When Marcella Maxwell was at last left alone, she began to pace slowly up and down the large bare room, as it was very much her wont to do.

She was thinking of George Tressady, and of the personality his talk had seemed to reveal.

'His heart is all in *power*—in what he takes for magnificence,' she said to herself. 'He talks as if he had no humanity, and did not care a rap for anybody. But it is a pose—I *think* it is a pose. He is interesting—he will develop. One would like—to show him things.'

After another pensive turn or two she stopped beside a photograph that stood upon her writing-table. It was a photograph of her husband—a tall, smooth-faced man, with pleasant eyes, features of no particular emphasis, and the free carriage of the country-bred Englishman. As she looked at it her face relaxed unconsciously, inevitably; under the stimulus of some habitual and secret joy. It was for his sake, for his sake only, that she was still thinking of George Tressady, still pondering the young man's character and remarks.

So much at least was true—no other member of Fontenoy's party had as yet given her even the chance of arguing with him. Once or twice in society she had tried to approach Fontenoy himself, to get somehow into touch with him. But she had made no way. Lord Fontenoy had simply turned his square-jawed face and red-rimmed eyes upon her with a stupid irresponsive air, which Marcella knew perfectly well to be a mask, while it protected him none the less effectively for that against both her eloquence and her charm. The other members of the party were young aristocrats, either of the ultra-exclusive or of the sporting type. She had made her attempts here and there among them, but with no more success. And once or twice, when she had pushed her attack to close quarters, she had been suddenly conscious of an underlying insolence in her opponent—a quick glance of bold or sensual eyes which seemed to relegate the mere woman to her place.

But this young Tressady, for all his narrowness and bitterness, was of a different stamp—or she thought so.

She began to pace up and down again, lost in reverie,
till after a few minutes she came slowly to a stop before
a long Louis Quinze mirror—her hands clasped in front
of her, her eyes half-consciously studying what she saw.

Her own beauty invariably gave her pleasure—though
very seldom for the reasons that would have affected
other women.   She felt instinctively that it made life
easier for her than it could otherwise have been ; that it
provided her with a natural and profitable 'opening' in
any game she might wish to play ; and that even among
the workmen, unionist leaders, and officials of the East
End it had helped her again and again to score the
points that she wanted to make.   She was accustomed to
be looked at, to be the centre, to feel things yielding
before her ; and without thinking it out, she knew perfectly well what it was she gained by this 'fair seeming
show' of eye and lip and form.   Somehow it made
nothing seem impossible to her ; it gave her a dazzling
self-confidence.

The handle of the door turned.   She looked round
with a smiling start and waited.

A tall man in a grey suit came in, crossed the room
quickly, and put his arms round her.   She leant back
against his shoulder, putting up one hand to touch his
cheek caressingly.

'Why, how late you are !   Betty left reproaches for
you.'

'I had a walk with Dowson.   Then two or three
people caught me on the way back—Rashdell among
others.'   (Lord Rashdell was Foreign Secretary.)   'There
are some interesting telegrams from Paris—I copied
them out for you.'

The country happened to be at the moment in the
midst of one of its periodical difficulties with France.
There had been a good deal of diplomatic friction, and a

certain amount of anxiety at the Foreign Office. Marcella
lit the silver kettle again and made her man some fresh
tea, while he told her the news, and they discussed the
various points of the telegrams he had copied for her,
with a comrade's freedom and vivacity. Then she said :

'Well, I have had an interesting time too ! That
young Tressady has been to tea.'

'Oh ! has he ? They say there is a lot of stuff in him,
and he may do us a great deal of mischief. How did you
find him ?'

'Oh, very clever, very limited—and a mass of prejudices,' she said, laughing. 'I never saw an odder mixture
of knowledge and ignorance.'

'What ? Knowledge of India and the East ?—that kind
of thing ?'

She nodded.

'Knowledge of everything except the subject he has
come home to fight about ! Do you know, Aldous——'

She paused. She was sitting on a stool beside him,
her arm upon his knee.

'What do I know ?' he said, his hand seeking hers.

'Well, I can't help feeling that that man might live
and learn. He isn't a mere obstructive block—like the
rest.'

Maxwell laughed.

'Then Fontenoy is not as shrewd as usual. They say
he regards him as their best recruit.'

'Never mind. I rather wish you'd try to make friends
with him.'

Maxwell, however, helped himself to cake and made no
response. On the two or three occasions on which he
had met George Tressady, he had been conscious, if the
truth were told, of a certain vague antipathy to the young
man.

Marcella pondered.

'No,' she said, 'no—I don't think after all he's your sort. Suppose *I* see what can be done !'

And she got up with her flashing smile—half love, half fun—and crossed the room to summon her little boy, Hallin, for his evening play. Maxwell looked after her, not heeding at all what she was saying, heeding only herself, her voice, the atmosphere of charm and life she carried with her.

CHAPTER VII

MARCELLA MAXWELL, however, had not been easily wooed
by the man who now filled all the horizon of her life. At
the time when Aldous Raeburn, as he then was—the
grandson and heir of old Lord Maxwell—came across
her first she was a handsome, undeveloped girl, of a type
not uncommon in our modern world, belonging by birth
to the country-squire class, and by the chances of a few
years of student life in London to the youth that takes
nothing on authority, and puts to fierce question whatever it finds already on its path—Governments, Churches,
the powers of family and wealth—that takes, moreover, its
social pity for the only standard, and spends that pity only
on one sort and type of existence. She accepted Raeburn,
then the best *parti* in the county, without understanding
or loving him, simply that she might use his power and
wealth for certain social ends to which the crude philan-
thropy of her youth had pledged itself. Naturally, they
were no sooner engaged than Raeburn found himself
launched upon a long wrestle with the girl who had thus
—in the selfishness of her passionate idealist youth—
opened her relation to him with a deliberate affront to the
heart offered her. The engagement had stormy passages,
and was for a time wholly broken off. Aldous was made
bitterly jealous, or miserably unhappy. Marcella left the
old house in the neighbourhood of the Maxwell property,
where her lover had first seen and courted her. She

plunged into London life, and into nursing, that common outlet for the woman at war with herself or society. She suffered and struggled, and once or twice she came very near to throwing away all her chances of happiness. But in the end, Maxwell tamed her; Maxwell recovered her. The rise of love in the unruly, impetuous creature, when the rise came, was like the sudden growth of some great forest flower. It spread with transforming beauty over the whole nature, till at last the girl who had once looked upon him as the mere tool of her own moral ambitions threw herself upon Maxwell's heart with a self-abandoning passion and penitence, which her developed powers and her adorable beauty made a veritable intoxication.

And Maxwell was worthy that she should do this thing. When he and Marcella first met, he was a man of thirty, very able, very reserved, and often painfully diffident as to his own powers and future. He was the only young representative of a famous stock, and had grown up from his childhood under the shadow of great sorrows and heavy responsibilities. The stuff of the poet and the thinker lay hidden behind his shy manners; and he loved Marcella Boyce with all the delicacy, all the idealising respect, that passion generates in natures so strong and so highly tempered. At the same time, he had little buoyancy or gaiety; he had a belief in his class, and a constitutional dislike of change, which were always fighting in his mind with the energies of moral debate; and he acquiesced very easily—perhaps indifferently—in many outward conventions and prejudices.

The crisis through which Marcella put him developed and matured the man. To the influences of love, moreover, were added the influences of friendship—of such a friendship as our modern time but seldom rears to perfection. In Raeburn's college days, a man of rare and delicate powers had possessed himself of Raeburn's

tenacious affection, and had thenceforward played the
leader to Raeburn's strength, physical and moral, availing
himself freely, wherever his own failed him, of the powers
and capacities of his friend.   For he himself bore in him
from his youth up the seeds of physical failure and early
death.   It was partly the marvellous struggle in him of
soul with body that subdued to him the homage of the
stronger man.   And it was clearly his influence that broke
up and fired Raeburn's slower and more distrustful temper, informing an inbred Toryism, a natural passion for
tradition, and the England of tradition with that 'repining
restlessness' which is the best spur of noble living.

Hallin was a lecturer and an economist; a man who
lived in the perception of the great paradox that in our
modern world political power has gone to the workman,
while yet socially and intellectually he remains little less
weak, or starved, or subject than before.   When he died
he left to Raeburn a legacy of feelings and ideas, all
largely concerned with this contrast between the huge
and growing 'tyranny' of the working class and the
individual helplessness or bareness of the working man.
And it was these feelings and ideas which from the
beginning made a link between Raeburn and the young
revolts and compassions of Marcella Boyce.   They were
at one in their love of Edward Hallin; and after Hallin's
death, in their sore and tender wish to make his thoughts
tell upon the English world.

The Maxwells had now been married some five years,
years of almost incredible happiness.   The equal comradeship of marriage at its best and finest, all the daily
disciplines, the profound and painless lessons of love, the
covetous bliss of parentage, the constant anxieties of power
nobly understood, had harmonised the stormy nature of
the woman, and had transformed the somewhat pessimist

and scrupulous character of the man. Not that life with
Marcella Maxwell was always easy. Now as ever she
remained on the moral side a creature of strain and effort,
tormented by ideals not to be realised, and eager to drive
herself and others in a breathless pursuit of them.

But if in some sort she seemed to be always dragging
those that loved her through the heart of a tempest,
the tempest had such golden moments! No wife had
ever more capacity for all the delicacies and depths of
passion towards the man of her choice. All the anxieties
she brought with her, all the perplexities and difficulties
she imposed, had never yet seemed to Maxwell anything
but divinely worth while. So far indeed he had never
even remotely allowed himself to put the question. Her
faults were her ; and she was his light of life.

For some time after their marriage, which took place
about a year after his accession to the title and estates,
they had lived at the stately house in Brookshire belonging
to the Maxwells, and Marcella had thrown herself into
the management of a large household and property with
characteristic energy and originality. She had tried new
ways of choosing and governing her servants ; new ways
of entertaining the poor, and of making Maxwell Court
the centre, not of one class, but of all. She ran up a fair
score of blunders, but not one of them was the blunder of
meanness or vulgarity. Her nature was inventive and
poetic, and the rich fulfilment that had overtaken her own
personal desires did but sting her eager passion to give
and to serve.

Meanwhile the family house in town was sold, and
what with the birth of her son, and the multiplicity
of the rural interests to which she had set her hand,
Marcella felt no need of London. But towards the end
of the second year she perceived—though he said little
about it—that there was in her husband's mind a strong

and persistent drawing towards his former political interests and associations. The late Lord Maxwell had sat
in several Conservative cabinets, and his grandson, after
a distinguished career in the House as a private member,
had accepted a subordinate place in the Government only
a few months before his grandfather's death transferred
him to the Lords. After that event, a scrupulous conscience had forced him to take landowning as a profession, and an arduous one. The Premier made him
flattering advances, and his friends remonstrated, but he
had none the less relinquished office, and buried himself
on his land.

Now, however, after some three years' hard and un-
remitting work, the estate was in excellent condition ; the
' new ways ' of the new owners had been well started;
and both Maxwell and Marcella had fitting lieutenants
who could be left in charge. Moreover, matters were
being agitated at the moment in politics which had
special significance for the man's idealist and reflective
mind. His country friends and neighbours hardly understood why.

For it was merely a question of certain further
measures of factory reform. A group of Labour leaders
were pressing upon the public and the Government a
proposal to pass a special Factory Act for certain districts
and trades of East London. In spite of Commissions, in
spite of recent laws, ' sweating,' so it was urged, was as
bad as ever—nay, in certain localities and industries was
more frightful and more oppressive than ever. The
waste of life and health involved in the great clothing
industries of East London, for instance, which had provoked law after law, inquiry after inquiry, still went—so
it was maintained—its hideous way.

' Have courage ! ' cried the reformers. ' Take, at last,
the only effectual step. Make it penal to practise certain

trades in the houses of the people—drive them, all into factories of a certain size, where alone these degraded industries can be humanised and controlled. Above all, make up your mind to a legal working day for East London men as well as East London women. Try the great experiment first of all in this omnivorous, inarticulate London, this dustbin for the rubbish of all nations. Here the problem is worst—here the victims are weakest and most manageable. London will bear what would stir a riot in Birmingham or Leeds. Make the experiment as partial and as tentative as you please—give the Home Office power to extend or revoke it at will—but *try it !* '

The change proposed was itself of vast importance, and was, moreover, but a prelude to things still more far-reaching. But, critical as it was, Maxwell was prepared for it. During the later years of his friend Hallin's life the two men had constantly discussed the industrial consequences of democracy with unflagging eagerness and intelligence. To both it seemed not only inevitable, but the object of the citizen's dearest hopes, that the rule of the people should bring with it, in ever-ascending degree, the ordering and moralising of the worker's toil. Yet neither had the smallest belief that any of the great civilised communities would ever see the State the sole landlord and the sole capitalist; or that Collectivism as a system has, or deserves to have, any serious prospects in the world. To both, possession—private and personal possession—from the child's first toy, or the tiny garden where it sows its passionately watched seeds, to the great business or the great estate, is one of the first and chiefest elements of human training, not to be escaped by human effort, or only at such a cost of impoverishment and disaster that mankind would but take the step—supposing it conceivable that it should take it—to retrace it instantly.

Maxwell's *heart*, however, was much less concerned with this belief, tenaciously as he held it, than with its relative—the limitation of private possession by the authority of the common conscience. That ' we are not our own ' has not, indeed, been left to Lassalle or Marx to discover. But if you could have moved this quiet Englishman to speak, he would have said—his strong, brooding face all kindled and alive—that the enormous industrial development of the past century has shown us the forces at work in the evolution of human societies on a gigantic scale, and by thus magnifying them has given us a new understanding of them. The vast extension of the individual will and power which science has brought to humanity during the last hundred years was always present to him as food for a natural exultation—a kind of pledge of the boundless prospects of the race. On the other hand, the struggle of society brought face to face with this huge increment of the individual power, forced to deal with it for its own higher and mysterious ends, to moralise and socialise it lest it should destroy itself and the State together ; the slow steps by which the modern community has succeeded in asserting itself against the individual, in protecting the weak from his weakness, the poor from his poverty, in defending the woman and child from the fierce claims of capital, in forcing upon trade after trade the axiom that no man may lawfully build his wealth upon the exhaustion and degradation of his fellow —these things stirred in him the far deeper enthusiasms of the moral nature. Nay more ! Together with all the other main facts which mark the long travail of man's ethical and social life, they were among the only ' evidences ' of religion a critical mind allowed itself—the most striking signs of something ' greater than we know ' working among the dust and ugliness of our common day. Attack wealth as wealth, possession as possession and civilisation is undone. But bring the force of the social conscience to bear as keenly and ardently as you may, upon the separate activities of factory and household, farm and office ; and from the results you will only get a richer individual freedom, one more illustration of the divinest law man serves—that he must 'die to live,' must surrender to obtain.

Such at least was Maxwell's persuasion; though as a practical man he admitted, of course, many limitations of time, occasion, and degree. And long companionship with him had impressed the same faith also on Marcella. With the natural conceit of the shrewd woman, she would probably have maintained that her social creed came entirely of mother-wit and her own exertions— her experiences in London, reading, and the rest. In reality it was in her the pure birth of a pure passion. She had learnt it while she was learning to love Aldous Raeburn; and it need astonish no one that the more dependent all her various philosophies of life had become on the mere personal influence and joy of marriage, the more agile had she grown in all that concerned the mere intellectual defence of them. She could argue better and think better; but at bottom, if the truth were told, they were Maxwell's arguments and Maxwell's thoughts.

So that when this particular agitation began, and he grew restless in his silent way, she grew restless too. They took down the old worn portfolios of Hallin's papers and letters, and looked through them, night after night, as they sat alone together in the great library of the Court. Both Marcella and Aldous could remember the writing of many of these innumerable drafts of Acts, these endless memoranda on special points, and must needs try, for love's sake, to forget the terrible strain and effort with which a dying man had put them to-

gether. She was led by them to think of the many
workmen friends she had made during the year of
her nursing life; while he had remembrances of much
personal work and investigation of his own, undertaken
during the time of his under-secretaryship, to add to hers.
Another Liberal government was slipping to its fall—if a
Conservative government came in, with a possible opening
in it for Aldous Maxwell, what then? Was the chance
to be seized?

One May twilight, just before dinner, as the two
were strolling up and down the great terrace just in front
of the Court, Aldous paused and looked at the majestic
house beside them.

‘ What’s the good of talking about these things while
we live *there* ? ’ he said, with a gesture towards the house,
half impatient, half humorous.

Marcella laughed. Then she sprang away from him,
considering, a sudden brightness in her eye. She had
an idea.

‘ The idea after all was a very simple one. But the
probability is that, had she not been there to carry him
through, Maxwell would have neither found it nor followed
it. However that may be, in a very few days she had
clothed it with fact, and made so real a thing of it that
she was amazed at her own success. She and Maxwell
had settled themselves in a small furnished house in the
Mile End Road, and Maxwell was once more studying
the problems of his measure that was to be in the midst
of the populations to whom it applied. The house had
been recently let in ‘ apartments ’ by a young tradesman
and his wife, well known to Marcella. In his artisan
days the man had been her friend, and for a time her
patient. She knew how to put her hand on him at
once.

They spent five months in the little house, while the

London that know them in St. James's Square looked on,
and made the comments—half amused, half inquisitive—
that the act seemed to invite. There was of course no
surprise. Nothing surprises the London of to-day. Or
if there were any, it was all Marcella's. In spite of her
passionate sympathy with the multitude who live in disagreeable homes on about a pound a week, she herself
was very sensitive to the neighbourhood of beautiful
things, to the charm of old homes, cool woods, green
lawns, and the rise and fall of Brookshire hills. Against
her wish, she had thought of sacrifice in thinking of the
Mile End Road in August.

But there was no sacrifice. Frankly, these five
months were among the happiest of her life. She and
Maxwell were constantly together, from morning till
night, doing the things that were congenial to them, and
seeing the things that interested them. They went in
and out of every factory and workshop in which certain
trades were practised, within a three-mile radius; they
became the intimate friends of every factory inspector
and every trade-union official in the place. Luckily,
Maxwell's shyness—at least in Mile End—was not of the
sort that can be readily mistaken for a haughty mind.
He was always ready to be informed; his diffident kindness asked to be set at ease; while in any real ardour of
debate his trained capacity and his stores of knowledge
would put even the expert on his mettle.

As for Marcella, it was her idiosyncrasy that these
tailors, furriers, machinists, shirtmakers, by whom she
was surrounded in East London, stirred her imagination far more readily than the dwellers in great houses
and the wearers of fine raiment had ever stirred it. And
Marcella, in the kindled sympathetic state, was always
delightful to herself and others. She revelled in the
little house and its ugly, druggetted rooms; in the

absence of all the usual paraphernalia of their life; in her undisturbed possession of the husband who was at once her lover and the best company she knew or could desire. On the few days when he left her for the day on some errand in which she could not share, to meet him at the train in the evening like any small clerk's wife, to help him carry the books and papers with which he was generally laden along the hot and dingy street, to make him tea from her little spirit kettle, and then to hear the news of the day in the shade of the little smutty back-garden, while the German charwoman who cooked for them had her way with the dinner—there was not an incident in the whole trivial procession that did not amuse and delight her. She renewed her youth; she escaped from the burdensome 'glories of our birth and state;' from that teasing 'duty to our equals' on which only the wisest preachers have ever laid sufficient stress; and her one trouble was that the little masquerade must end.

One other drawback indeed, one more blight upon a golden time there was. Not even Marcella could make up her mind to transplant little Hallin, her only child, from Maxwell Court to East London. It was springtime, and the woods about the Court were breaking into sheets of white and blue. Marcella must needs leave the boy to his flowers and his 'grandame earth,' sadly warned thereto by the cheeks of other little boys in and about the Mile End Road. But every Friday night she and Maxwell said good-bye to the two little workhouse girls, and the German charwoman, and the village boy from Mellor, who supplied them with all the service they wanted in Mile End, took with them the ancient maid who had been Marcella's mother's maid, and fled home to Brookshire. So on Saturday mornings it generally happened that little Hallin went out to inform his particular

K

friend among the garden boys, that 'Mummy had tum ome,' and that he was not therefore so much his own master as usual. He explained that he had to show mummy 'eaps of things '—the two new kittens, the ' edge-sparrer's nest,' and the ' ump they'd made in the church-yard over old Tom Collins from the parish ouses,' the sore place on the pony's shoulder, the ' ole that mummy's orse had kicked in the stable door,' and a host of other curiosities. By way of linking the child with the soil and its people, Marcella had taken care to give him nurse-maids from the village. And the village, being only some thirty miles from London, talked in the main the language of London, a language which it soon communicated to the tongue of Maxwell's heir. Marcella tried to school her boy in vain. Hallin chattered, laughed, broadened his a's and dropped all his h's into a bottomless limbo none the less.

What days of joy those Saturdays were for mother and child! All the morning and till about four o'clock, he and she would be inseparable, trailing about together over field and wood, she one of the handsomest of women, he one of the plainest of children—a little square-faced chubby fellow, with eyes monstrously black and big, fat cheeks that hung a little over the firm chin, a sallow complexion, and a large humorous mouth.

But in the late afternoon, alas! Hallin was apt to find the world grow tiresome. For against all his advice 'mummy' would allow herself to be clad by Annette, the maid, in a frock of state; carriages would drive up from the 5.10 train; and presently in the lengthening evening the great lawns of the Court would be dotted with strolling groups, or the red drawing-room, with its Romneys and Gainsboroughs, would be filled with talk and laughter circling round mummy at the tea-table; so that all that was left to Hallin was that seat on mummy's knee—his big, dark head pressed disconsolately against her breast, his thumb in his mouth for comfort—which no boy of any spirit would ever consent to occupy, so long as there was any chance of goading a slack companion into things better worth while.

Marcella herself was no less rebellious at heart, and would have asked nothing better than to be left free to spend her weekly holiday in roaming an April world with Hallin. But our country being what it is, the plans that are made in Mile End or Shoreditch have to be adopted by Mayfair or Mayfair's equivalent; otherwise they are apt to find an inglorious tomb in the portfolios that bred them. We have still, it seems, a 'ruling class'; and in spite of democracy it is still this 'ruling class' that matters. Maxwell was perfectly aware of it; and these Sundays to him were the mere complements of the Mile End weekdays. Marcella ruefully admitted that English life was so, and she did her best. But on Monday mornings she was generally left protesting in her inmost soul against half the women whom these peers and politicians, these administrators and journalists, brought with them, or wondering anxiously whether her particular share in the social effort just over might not have done Aldous more harm than good. She understood vaguely, without vanity, that she was a power in this English society, that she had many warm friends, especially among men of the finer and abler sort. But when a woman loved her, and insisted, as it were, on making her know it—and, after all, the experience was not a rare one—Marcella received the overture with a kind of grateful surprise She was accustomed, without knowing why, to feel herself ill at ease with certain types of women; even in her own house she was often aware of being furtively watched by hostile eyes; or she found herself suddenly the goal of some sharp little pleasantry that pricked like a stiletto.

K 2

She supposed that she was often forgetful and indiscreet. Perhaps the large court she held so easily on these occasions beneath the trees or in the great drawing-rooms of the old house had more to do with the matter. If so, she never guessed the riddle. In society she was conscious of one aim, and one aim only. Its very simplicity made other women incredulous, while it kept herself in the dark.

However, by dint of great pains, she had not yet done Aldous any harm that counted. During all the time of their East End sojourn, a Liberal Government, embarrassed by large schemes it had not force enough to carry, was sinking towards inevitable collapse. When the crash came, a weak Conservative Government, in which Aldous Maxwell occupied a prominent post, accepted office for a time without a dissolution. They came in on a cry of 'industrial reform,' and, by way of testing their own party and the country, adopted the Factory Bill for East London, which had now, by the common consent of all the workers upon it, passed into Maxwell's hands. The Bill rent the party in twain ; but the Ministry had the courage to go to the country with a programme in which the Maxwell Bill held a prominent place. Trade-unionism rallied to their support ; the forces both of reaction and of progress fought for them, in strangely mingled ways ; and they were returned with a sufficient, though not large, majority. Lord Ardagh, the veteran leader of the party, became Premier. Maxwell was made President of the Council, while his old friend and associate, Henry Dowson, became Home Secretary, and thereby responsible for the conduct of the long-expected Bill through the Commons.

When Maxwell came back to her on the afternoon of his decisive interview with Lord Ardagh, she was waiting for him in that same inner room where Tressady paid his first visit. At the sound of her husband's step outside, she sprang up, and they met halfway, her hands clasped in his, against his breast, her face looking up at him.

'Dear wife! at last we have our chance—our real chance,' he said to her.

She clung to him, and there was a moment of high emotion, in which thoughts of the past and of the dead mingled with the natural ambition of two people in the prime of life and power. Then Maxwell laughed and drew a long breath.

'The eggs have been all put into my basket in the most generous manner. We stand or fall by the Bill. But it will be a hard fight.'

And, in his acute, deliberate way, he began to sum up the forces against him—to speculate on the action of this group and that—Fontenoy's group first and foremost.

Marcella listened, her beautiful hand pensive against her cheek, her eyes on his. Half trembling, she realised what failure, if after all failure should come, would mean to him. Something infinitely tender and maternal spoke in her, pledging her to the utmost help that love and a woman could give.

Such for Maxwell and his wife had been the antecedents of a memorable session.

And now the session was here—was in full stream, indeed, rushing towards the main battle still to come. On the second night of Fontenoy's debate, George Tressady duly caught the Speaker's eye, and made a very fair maiden speech, which earned him a good deal more praise, both from his party and the press, than he—in a disgusted mood—thought at all reasonable. He had misplaced half his notes, and, in his own opinion, made a mess of his main argument. He remarked to Fontenoy afterwards that he had better hang himself, and stalked home after the division pleased with one thing only—that he had not allowed Letty to come.

In reality he had done nothing to mar the reputation that was beginning to attach to him. Fontenoy was content; and the scantiness of the majority by which the Resolution was defeated served at once to make the prospects of the Maxwell Bill, which was to be brought in after Easter, more doubtful, and to sharpen the temper of its foes.

CHAPTER VIII

' GOODNESS !—what an ugly place it is ! It wants five thousand spent on it at once to make it tolerable ! '

The remark was Letty Tressady's. She was standing disconsolate on the lawn · at Ferth, scanning the old-fashioned house to which George had brought her just five days before. They had been married a fortnight, and were still to spend another week in the country before going back to London and to Parliament. But already Letty had made up her mind that Ferth *must* be rebuilt and refurnished, or she could never endure it.

She threw herself down on a garden seat with a sigh, still studying the house. It was a straight barrack-like building, very high for its breadth, erected early in the last century by an architect who, finding that he was to be allowed but a very scanty sum for his performance, determined with considerable strength of mind to spend all that he had for decoration upon the inside rather than the outside of his mansion. Accordingly the inside had charm—though even so much Letty could not now be got to confess ; panellings, mantelpieces, and door-ways showed the work of a man of taste. But outside all that had been aimed at was the provision of a central block of building carried up to a considerable height so as to give the rooms demanded, while it economised in foundations and general space ; an outer wall pierced with the plainest openings possible at regular intervals ; a high-pitched roof to keep out the rain, whereof the original warm tiles had been long since replaced by the chilliest Welsh slates; and two low and disfiguring wings which held the servants and the kitchens. The stucco with which the house had been originally covered had blackened under the influence of time, weather, and the smoke from the Tressady coalpits. Altogether, what with its pitchy colour, its mean windows, its factory-like plainness and height, Ferth Place had no doubt a cheerless and repellent air; which was increased by its immediate surroundings. For it stood on the very summit of a high hill, whereon the trees were few and windbeaten; while the carriage drives and the paths that climbed the hill were all of them a coaly black. The flower garden behind the house was small and neglected; neither shrubberies nor kitchen garden, nor the small park had any character or stateliness; everything bore the stamp of bygone possessors who had been rich neither in money nor in fancy; who had been quite content to live small lives in a small way.

Ferth's new mistress thought bitterly of them, as she sat looking at their handiwork. What could be done with such a place? How could she have London people to stay there? Why, their very maids would strike! And, pray, what was a country house worth, without the usual country-house amenities and accessories?

Yet she already began to feel fretted and hampered about money. The inside of the house had been to some extent renovated. She had helped George to choose papers and curtains for the rooms that were to be her special domain, while they were in London together before Easter. But she knew that George had at one time meant to do much more than had actually been done; and he had been in a mood of lover-like apology on the first day of their arrival. 'Darling, I had hoped to buy you a hundred pretty things!—but times is bad—

dreadful bad!' he had said to her with a laugh. 'We will do it by degrees—you won't mind?'

Then she had tried to make him tell her why it was that he had abandoned some of the schemes of improvement that had certainly been in his mind during the first weeks of their engagement. But he had not been very communicative, and had put the blame mostly, as she understood him, on the 'beastly pits' and the very low dividends they had been earning during the past six months.

Letty, however, did not in the least believe that the comparatively pinched state of their finances, which, bride as she was, she was already brooding over, was wholly or even mainly due to the pits. She set her little white teeth in sudden anger as she said to herself that it was *not* the pits—it was Lady Tressady! George was crippled now because of the large sums his mother had not been ashamed to wring from him during the last six months. Letty—George's wife—was to go without comforts and conveniences, without the means of seeing her friends and taking her proper position in the world, because George's mother—a ridiculous painted old woman, who went in for flirtations and French gowns, when she ought to be subsiding quietly into caps and Bath chairs—would sponge upon his very moderate income, and take what did not belong to her.

'I am *certain* there is something in the background!' said Letty to herself, as she sat looking at the ugly house—'something that she is ashamed of, and that she doesn't tell George. She *couldn't* spend all that money on dress! I believe she is a wicked old woman—she has the most extraordinary creatures at her parties.'

. The girl's delicate face stiffened vindictively as she fell brooding for the hundredth time over Lady Tressady's enormities.

Then suddenly the garden door opened, and Letty, looking up, saw that George was on the threshold, waving his hand to her. He had left her that morning— almost for the first time since their marriage—to go and see his principal agent and discuss the position of affairs.

As he approached her, she noticed instantly that he was looking tired and ruffled. But the sight of her smoothed his brow. He threw himself down on the grass at her feet, and pressed his lips to the delicately tended hand that lay upon her lap.

'Have you missed me, madame?' he said, peremptorily.

Preoccupied as she was, Letty must needs flush and smile, so well she knew from his eager eye that she pleased him, that he noticed the pretty gown she had put on for luncheon, and that all the petting his absence had withdrawn from her for an hour or two had come back to her. Other women—more or less of her type—had found his ways beguiling before now. He took courtship as an art, and had his own rooted ideas as to how women should be treated. Neither too gingerly nor too sentimentally—but, above all, with variety!

He repeated his question insistently; whereupon Letty said, with her pert brightness, thinking all the time of the house, 'I'm *not* going to make you vain. Besides, I have been frightfully busy.'

'You're not going to make me vain? But I choose to be vain. I'll go away for the whole afternoon if I'm not made vain this instant. Ah! that's better. Do you know that you have the softest little curl on your soft little neck, and that your hair has caught the sun on it this morning?'

Letty instinctively put up a hand to tuck away the curl. But he seized the hand. 'Little vandal!—what have you been busy with?'

'Oh! I have been over the house with Mrs. Matthews,'

said Letty, in another tone. 'George, it's *dreadful*—the number of things that want doing. Do you know, *positively*, we could not put up more than two couples, if we tried ever so. And as for the state of the attics! Now do listen, George!'

And, holding his hand tight in her eagerness, she went through a vehement catalogue of all that was wanted— new furniture, new decoration, new grates, a new hot-water system, the raising of the wings, and so on to the alteration of the stables and the replanning of the garden. She had no sooner begun upon her list than George's look of worry returned. He got up from the grass, and sat on the bench beside her.

'Well, I'm sorry you dislike the place so much,' he said when her breath failed her, staring rather gloomily at his despised mansion. 'Of course it's quite true—it is an ugly hole. But the worst of it is, darling, I don't quite see how we're to do all this you talk about. I don't bring any good news from the pits, alas!'

He turned quickly towards her. The thought flashed through his mind—could he be justly charged with having married her on false pretences as to his affairs? No! There had been no misrepresentation of his income or his risks. Everything had been plainly and honestly stated to her father, and therefore to her. For Letty knew all that she wanted to know, and had managed her family since she was a baby.

Letty flushed at his last words.

'Do you mean to say,' she said with emphasis, 'that those men are really going to strike?'

'I am afraid so. We *must* enforce a reduction, to avoid working at sheer loss, and the men vow they'll come out.'

'They want you to make them a present of the mines, I suppose!' said Letty, bitterly. 'Why, the tales I hear of their extravagance and laziness! Mrs. Matthews says they'll have none but the best cuts of meat, that they all of them have an harmonium or a piano in the house, that their houses are *stuffed* with furniture—and the amount of money they spend in betting on their dogs and their football matches is perfectly sickening. And now I suppose they'll ruin themselves and us, rather than allow you to make a decent profit!'

'That's about it,' said George, flinging himself back on the bench. 'That's about it.'

There was a pause of silence. The eyes of both were turned to the colliery village far below, at the foot of the hill. From this high stretch of garden one looked across the valley and its straggling line of houses, to the pits on the further hillside, the straight black line of the 'bank,' the pulley wheels, and tall chimneys against the sky. To the left, along the ascending valley, similar chimneys and 'banks' were scattered at long intervals, while to the right the valley dipped in sharp wooded undulations to a blue plain bounded by far Welsh hills. The immediate neighbourhood of Ferth, for a coal country, had a woodland charm and wildness which often surprised a stranger. There were untouched copses, and little rivers and fern-covered hills, which still held their own against the ever-encroaching mounds of 'spoil' thrown out by the mines. Only the villages were invariably ugly. They were the modern creations of the coal, and had therefore no history and no originality. Their monotonous rows of red cottages were like fragments from some dingy town suburb, and the brick meeting-houses in which they abounded did nothing to abate the general unloveliness.

This view from the Ferth hill was one which had great familiarity for Tressady, and yet no charm. As a boy he had had no love for his home and very few acquaintances in the village. His mother hated the place and the people. She had been married very young—for the sake of money and position—to his dull old father, who nevertheless managed to keep his flighty wife in order by dint of a dumb, continuous stubbornness and tyranny, which would have overborne a stronger nature than Lady Tressady's. She was always struggling to get away from Ferth; he to keep her tied there. He was never at ease away from his estate and his pits; she felt herself ten years younger as soon as she had lost sight of the grim black house on its hilltop.

And this one opinion of hers she was able to impress upon her son—George, too, was always glad to turn his back on Ferth and its people. The colliers seemed to him a brutal crew, given over to coarse sports, coarse pleasures, and an odious religion. As to their supposed grievances and hardships, his intimate conviction as a boy had always been that the miner got the utmost both out of his employers and out of society that he was worth.

'Upon my word, I often think,' he said at last, his inward reverie finding speech, 'I often think it was a great pity my grandfather discovered the coal at all! In the long run I believe we should have done better without it. We should not at any rate have been bound up with these hordes, with whom you can no more reason than with so many blocks of their own coal!'

Letty made no answer. She had turned back towards the house. Suddenly she said, with an energy that startled him,

'George, what *are* we to do with that place? It gives me a nightmare. The extraordinary thing is the way that everything in it has gone to ruin. Did your mother really live here while you were away?'

George's expression darkened.

'I always used to suppose she was here,' he said. 'That was our bargain. But I begin to believe now that she was mostly in London. One can't wonder at it—she always hated the place.'

'Of course she was in London!' thought Letty to herself, 'spending piles of money, running shamefully into debt, and letting the house go to pieces. Why, the linen hasn't been darned for years!'

Aloud she said—

'Mrs. Matthews says a charwoman and a little girl from the village used to be left alone in the house for months, to play any sort of games, with nobody to look after them—*nobody*—while you were away!'

George looked at his wife—and then would only slip his arm round her for answer.

'Darling! you don't know how I've been worried all the morning—don't let's make worry at home. After all it *is* rather nice to be here together, isn't it?—and we shall do—we sha'n't starve! Perhaps we shall pull through with the pits after all—it is difficult to believe the men will make such fools of themselves—and—well! you know my angel mother can't always be swooping upon us as she has done lately. Let's just be patient a little—very likely I can sell a few bits of land before long that will give us some money in hand—and then this small person shall bedizen herself and the house as much as she pleases. And meanwhile, *madame ma femme*, let me point out to you that your George never professed to be anything but a very bad match for you!'

Letty remembered all his facts and figures perfectly. Only somehow she had regarded them with the optimism natural to a girl who is determined to be married. She had promptly forgotten the adverse chances he had insisted upon, and she had converted all his averages into minima. No, she could not say she had not been warned; but nevertheless the result promised to be quite different from what she had expected.

However, with her husband's arm round her, it was not easy to maintain her ill-humour, and she yielded. They wandered on into the wood which fringed the hill on its further side, she coquetting, he courting and flattering her in a hundred ways. Her soft new dress, her dainty lightness and freshness, made harmony in his senses with the April day, the building rooks, the breaths of sudden perfume from field and wood, the delicate green that was creeping over the copses, softening all the edges of the black scars left by the pits. The bridal illusion returned. George eagerly—hungrily—gave himself up to it. And Letty, though conscious all the while of a restless feeling at the back of her mind that they were losing time, must needs submit.

However, when the luncheon gong had sounded and they were strolling back to the house, he bethought himself, knit his brows again, and said to her—

'Do you know, darling, Dalling told me this morning'—Dalling was the Tressadys' principal agent— 'that he thought it would be a good thing if we could make friends with some of the people here? The Union are not—or *were* not—quite so strong in this valley as they are in some other parts. That's why that fellow Bewick—confound him!—has come to live here of late. It might be possible to make some of the more intelligent fellows hear reason. My uncles have always managed the thing with a very high hand—very natural!—the men *are* a set of rough, ungrateful brutes, who talk impossible stuff, and never remember anything that's done for them —but after all, if one has to make a living out of them, one may as well learn how to drive them, and what they want to be at. Suppose you come and show yourself in the village this afternoon?'

Letty looked extremely doubtful.

'I really don't get on very well with poor people,

George. It's very dreadful, I know, but there!—I'm not Lady Maxwell—and I can't help it. Of course, with the poor people at home in our own cottages it's different—they always curtsy and are very respectful—but Mrs. Matthews says the people here are so independent, and think nothing of being rude to you if they don't like you.'

George laughed.

'Go and call upon them in that dress and see! I'll eat my hat if anybody's rude. Beside, I shall be there to protect you. We won't go, of course, to any of the strong Union people. But there are two or three—an old nurse of mine I really used to be rather fond of—and a fireman that's a good sort—and one or two others. I believe it would amuse you.'

Letty was quite certain that it would not amuse her at all. However, she assented unwillingly, and they went in to lunch.

So in the afternoon the husband and wife sallied forth. Letty felt that she was being taken through an ordeal, and that George was rather foolish to wish it. However, she did her best to be cheerful, and to please George she still wore the pretty Paris frock of the morning, though it seemed to her absurd to be trailing it through a village street with only colliers and their wives to look at it.

'What ill luck,' said George suddenly, as they descended their own hill, 'that that fellow Bewick should have settled down here, in one's very pocket, like this!'

'Yes, you had enough of him at Malford, didn't you?' said Letty. 'I don't yet understand how he comes to be here.'

George explained that about the preceding Christmas there had been, temporarily, strong signs of decline in the Union strength of the Ferth district. A great many miners had quietly seceded; one of the periodical waves of suspicion as to funds and management to which all trade unions are liable had swept over the neighbourhood; and wholesale desertion from the Union standard seemed likely. In hot haste the Central Committee sent down Bewick as organising agent. The good fight he had made against Tressady at the Market Malford election had given him prestige; and he had both presence and speaking power. He had been four months at Ferth, speaking all over the district, and now, instead of leaving the Union, the men had been crowding into it, and were just as hot—so it was said—for a trial of strength with the masters as their comrades in other parts of the county.

'And before Bewick has done with us, I should say he'll have cost the masters in this district hundreds of thousands. I call him dear at the money!' said George finally, with a dismal cheerfulness.

He was really full of Bewick, and of the general news of the district which his agent had been that morning pouring into his ear. But he had done his best not to talk about either at luncheon. Letty had a curious way of making the bearer of unpleasant tidings feel that it was somehow all his own fault that things should be so; and George, even in this dawn of marriage, was beginning, half consciously, to recognise two or three such peculiarities of hers.

'What I cannot understand,' said Letty, vigorously, 'is why such people as Mr. Bewick are *allowed* to go about making the mischief he does.'

George laughed, but nevertheless repressed a sudden feeling of irritation. The inept remark of a pretty woman generally only amused him. But this Bewick matter was beginning to touch him home.

'You see we happen to be a free country,' he said drily, 'and Bewick and his like happen to be running us just now. Maxwell & Co. are in the shafts—Bewick sits up aloft and whips on the team. The extraordinary thing is that nothing personal makes any difference. The people here know perfectly well that Bewick drinks—that the woman he lives with is not his wife——'

'George!' cried Letty, 'how *can* you say such dreadful things!'

'Sorry, my darling! but the world is not a nice place. He picked her up somehow—they say she was a commercial traveller's wife—left on his hands at a country inn. Anyway she's not divorced, and the husband's alive. She looks like a walking skeleton, and is probably going to die. Nevertheless they say Bewick adores her. And as for my resentments—don't be shocked—I'm inclined to like Bewick all the better for *that* little affair. But then I'm not pious, like the people here. However, they don't mind—and they don't mind the drink—and they believe he spends their money on magnificent dinners at hotels— and they don't mind that. They don't mind anything— they shout themselves hoarse whenever Bewick speaks— they're as proud as Punch if he shakes hands with them —and then they tell the most gruesome tales of him behind his back, and like him all the better, apparently, for being a scoundrel. Queer, but true. Well, here we are—now, darling, you may expect to be stared at!'

For they had entered on the village street, and Ferth Magna, by some quick freemasonry, had become suddenly conscious of the bride and bridegroom. Here and there a begrimed man in his shirt-sleeves would open his front door cautiously and look at them; the children and womenkind stood boldly on the doorsteps and stared; while the people in the little shops ran back into the street, parcels and baskets in hand. The men working the morning shift had just come back from the pits, and their wives were preparing to wash their blackened lords, before the whole family sat down to tea. But both tea and ablutions were forgotten, so long as the owner of Ferth Place and the new Lady Tressady were in sight. The village eyes took note of everything; of the young man's immaculate serge suit and tan waistcoat, his thin, bronzed face and fair moustache; of the bride's grey gown, the knot of airy pink at her throat, the coils of bright brown hair on which her hat was set, and the buckles on her pretty shoes. Then the village retreated within doors again; and each house buzzed and gossiped its fill. There had been a certain amount of not very cordial response to George's salutations; but to Letty's thinking the women had eyed her with an unpleasant and rather hostile boldness.

'Mary Batchelor's house is down here,' said George, turning into a side lane, not without a feeling of relief. 'I hope we sha'n't find her out—no, there she is. You can't call these people affectionate, can you?'

They were close on a group of three brick cottages all close together. Their doors were all open. In one cottage a stout collier's wife was toiling through her wash. At the door of another the sewing-machine agent was waiting for his weekly payment; while on the threshold of the third stood an elderly tottering woman shading her eyes from the light as she tried to make out the features of the approaching couple.

'Why, Mary!' said George, 'you haven't forgotten me? I have brought my wife to see you.'

And he held out his hand with a boyish kindness.

The old woman looked at them both in a bewildered way. Her face, with its long chin and powerful nose, was blanched and drawn; her grey hair straggling from under her worn black-ribboned cap, and her black dress, had a neglected air, which drew George's attention. Mary Batchelor, so long as he remembered her, whether

as his old nurse, or in later days as the Bible-woman of
the village, had always been remarkable for a peculiar
dignity and neatness.

'Mary, is there anything wrong?' he asked her,
holding her hand.

'Coom yer ways in,' said the old woman, grasping his
arm, and taking no notice of Letty. 'He's gone—he'll
not freeten nobody—he wor here three days afore they
buried him. I could no let him go—but it's three weeks
now sen they put him away.'

'Why, Mary, what is it? Not *James !*—not your son !'
said George, letting her guide him into the cottage.

'Aye, it's James—it's my son,' she repeated drearily.
'Will yer be takkin a cheer—and perhaps'—she looked
round uncertainly, first at Letty, then at the wet floor where
she had been feebly scrubbing—'perhaps the leddy ull be
sittin down. I'm nobbut in a muddle. But I don't seem
to get forard wi my work a mornins—not sen they put
im away.'

And she dropped into a chair herself, with a long
sigh—forgetting her visitors apparently—her large and
bony hands, scarred with their life's work, lying along
her knees.

George stood beside her silent a moment.

'I hardly like to say I hadn't heard,' he said at last,
gently. 'You'll think I *ought* to have heard. But I
didn't know. I have been in town and very busy.'

'Aye,' said Mary, without looking up, 'aye, an yer've
been gettin married. I knew as yer didn't mean nothin
onkind.'

Then she stopped again—till suddenly, with a furtive
gesture, she raised her apron, and drew it across her
eyes, which had the look of perennial tears.

On the other side of the cottage meanwhile a boy of
about fourteen was sitting. He had just done his after-

hoon's wash, and was resting himself by the fire, enjoying
a thumbed football almanac. He had not risen when
the visitors entered, and while his grandmother was
speaking his lips still moved dumbly, as he went on
adding up the football scores. He was a sickly, rather
repulsive lad, with a callous expression.

'Let me wait outside, George,' said Letty, hurriedly.

Some instinct in her shrank from the poor mother
and her story. But George begged her to stay, and she
sat down nervously by the door, trying to protect her
pretty skirt from the wet boards.

'Will you tell me how it was?' said George, sitting
down himself in front of the bowed mother, and bending
towards her. 'Was it in the pit? Jamie wasn't one of
our men, I know. Wasn't it for Mr. Morrison he worked?'

Mrs. Batchelor made a sign of assent. Then she
raised her head quickly, and a flash of some passionate
convulsion passed through her face.

'It wor John Burgess as done it,' she said, staring at
George. 'It wor him as took the boy's life. But he's
gone himsel—so theer—I'll not say no more. It wor
Jamie's first week o hewin—he'd been a loader this
three year, an taken a turn at the hewin now an again—
an five weeks sen, John Burgess—he wor butty for Mr.
Morrison, yer know, in the Owd Pit—took him on, an the
lad wor arnin six an sixpence a day. An he wor that
pleased yo cud see it shinin out ov im. And it wor on
the Tuesday as he went on the afternoon shift. I saw
im go, an he wor down'earted. An I fell a cryin as he
went up the street, for I knew why he wor down'earted,
an I asked the Lord to elp him. And about six o'clock
they come runnin—an they towd me there'd bin an accident, an they wor bringin im—an he wor alive—an
I must bear up. They'd found him kneelin in his place
with his arm up, an the pick in it—just as the blast had

took him—An his poor back—oh! my God—scorched off him—*scorched off him.*'

A shudder ran through her. But she recovered herself and went on, still gazing intently at Tressady, her gaunt hand raised as though for attention.

'An they bräat him in, an they laid him on that settle' —she pointed to the bench by the fire—'an the doctors didn't interfere—there wor nowt to do—they left me alone wi un. But he come to, a minute after they laid im down—an I ses, "Jamie, ow did it appen?" an he ses, "Mother, it wor John Burgess—ee opened my lamp for to light hissen as had gone out—an I don't know no more." An then after a bit he ses, "Mother, don't you fret—I'm glad I'm goin—I'd got the drink in me," he ses. An then he give two three little breaths, as though he wor pantin—an I kiss him.'

She stopped, her face working, her trembling hands pressed hard against each other on her knee. Letty felt the tears leap to her eyes in a rush that startled herself.

'An he would a bin twenty-one year old, come next August—an allus a lad as yer couldn't help gettin fond on—not sen he were a little un. An when he wor layin there, I ses to myself, "He's the third as the coal-gettin ha took from me." An I minded my feyther an uncle—how they was bräat home both togither, when I wor nobbut thirteen years old—not a scar on em, nobbut a little blood on my feyther's forehead—but stone dead, both on em—from the afterdamp. Theer was thirty-six men killed in that explosion—an I recolleck how old Mr. Morrison—Mr. Walter's father—sent the coffins round— an how the men went on because they warn't good ones. Not a man would go down the pit till they was changed— if a man got the life choked out of im, they thowt the least the masters could do was to give un a dacent coffin to lie in. But theer—nobody helped me wi Jamie—I buried him mysel—an it wor all o the best.'

She dried her eyes again, sighing plaintively. George said what kind and consoling things he could think of. Mary Batchelor put up her hand and touched him on the arm as he leant over her.

'Aye, I knew yo'd be sorry—an yor wife——'

She turned feebly towards Letty, trying with her blurred and tear-dimmed sight to make out what Sir George's bride might be like. She looked for a moment at the small, elegant person in the corner—at the sheaf of nodding rosebuds on the hat—the bracelets—the pink cheeks under the dainty veil,—looked with a curious aloofness, as though from a great distance. Then, evidently, another thought struck her like a lash. She ceased to see or think of Letty. Her grip tightened on George's arm.

'An I'm allus thinkin,' she said, with a passionate sob, 'of that what he said about the drink. He'd allus bin a sober lad, till this last winter ɪt did seem as though he cudna keep hisself from it—it kep creepin on im—an several times lately he'd broke out very bad, pay-days—an he knew I'd been frettin. And who was ter blame—I ast yo, or onybody—who was it ter blame?'

Her voice rose to a kind of cry.

'His feyther died ov it, and his grandfeyther afore that. His grandfeyther wor found dead i the roadside, after they'd made him blind-drunk at owd Morse's public-house, where the butty wor reckonin with im an his mates. But he'd never ha gone near the drink if they'd hadn't druv him to't, for he wasn't inclined that way. But the butty as gave him work kep the public, an if yer didn't drink, yer didn't get no work. You must drink yoursel sick o Saturdays, or theer'd be no work for you o Mondays. "Noa, yer can sit at ome," they'd say to un, " ef yer so damned pertickler." I ast yor pardon, sir, for the bad word, but that's ow they'd say it. I've often heerd owd John say as he'd a been glad to ha given the butty·back a shillin ov is pay to be let off the drink. An Willum, that's my usband, he wor allus at it too—an the doctor towd me one day, as Willum lay a-dyin, as it ran in the blood—an Jamie heard im—I know he did—for I foun im on the stairs—listenin.'

She paused again, lost in a mist of incoherent memories, the tears falling slowly.

After a minute's silence, George said—not indeed knowing what to say—' We're *very* sorry for you, Mary— my wife and I—we wish we could do anything to help you. I am afraid it can't make any difference to you—I expect it makes it all the worse—to think that accidents are so much fewer—that so much has been done. And yet times are mended, aren't they?'

Mary made no answer.

George sat looking at her, conscious, as he seldom was, of raw youth and unreadiness—conscious, too, of Letty's presence in a strange, hindering way—as of something that both blunted emotion and made one rather ashamed to show it.

He could only pursue the lame topic of improvement, of changed times. The disappearance of old abuses, of ' butties ' and ' tommy-shops '; the greater care for life ; the accident laws; the inspectors. He found himself growing eloquent at last, yet all the time regarding himself, as it were, from a distance—ironically.

Mary Batchelor listened to him for a while, her head bent with something of the submission of the old servant, till something he said roused again the quick shudder, the look of anguished protest.

' Aye, I dessay it's aw reet, Mr. George !—I dessay it is—what yer say. The inspectors is very cliver—an the

wages is paid proper. But theer—say what yer will!
I've a son on the railway out Lichfield way—an he's
allus taakin about is long hours—they're killing im, he
says—an I allus ses to im, "Yer may jest thank the
Lord, Harry, as yer not in the pits." He never gets no
pity out o me. An soomtimes I wakes in the morning,
an I thinks o the men, cropin away in the dark—down
theer—under me and my bed—for they do say the pits now
runs right under Ferth village—an I think to mysel—
How long will it be before yo poor fellers is laying like my
Jim? Yer may be reet about the accidents, Mr. George—
but I *know*, ef yer wor to go fro house to house i this
village—it would be like tis in the Bible—I've often
thowt o them words—"*Theer was not a house*—no, nary
one!—*where there was not one dead.*" '

She hung her head again, muttering to herself.
George made out with difficulty that she was going
through one phantom scene after another—of burning,
wounds, and sudden death. One or two of the phrases—
of the fragmentary details that dropped out without name
or place—made his flesh creep. He was afraid lest
Letty should hear them, and was just putting out his
hand for his hat, when Mrs. Batchelor gripped his
arm again. Her face—so white and large-featured—
had the gleam of something like a miserable smile upon
it.

'Aye, an the men theirsels ud say jest as you do.
"Lor, Mrs. Batchelor," they'd say, "why, the pits is
as safe as a church"—an they'd *laff*—Jamie ud laff at
me times. But it's the *women*, Mr. George, as knows—
it's the women that ave to wash the bodies.'

A great trembling ran through her again. George
instinctively rose, and motioned to Letty to go. She too
rose, but she did not go. She stood by the door, her
wide grey eyes fixed with a kind of fascination on the

speaker; while behind her a ring of children could be seen in the street, staring at the pretty lady.

Mary Batchelor saw nothing but Tressady, whom she was still holding by the arm — looking up to him.

'Aye, but I didna disturb my Jamie, yer know. Noa!—I left im i the owd coat they'd thrown over im i the pit—I dursn't ha touched is back. Noa, I *dursn't*. But I made his shroud mysen, an I put it ower his poor workin clothes, an I washed his face, an is hands an feet —an then I kissed him, an I said, "Jamie, yo mun go an tell the Lord as yo ha done your best, an He ha dealt hardly by yer!—an that's the treuth—He ha dealt hardly by yer!"'

She gave a loud sob, and bowed her head on her hands a moment. Then, pushing back her grey locks from her face, she rose, struggling for composure.

'Aye, aye, Mr. George—aye, aye, I'll not keep yer no longer.'

But as she took his hand, she added passionately:

'An I towd the vicar I couldn't be Bible-woman no more. Theer's somethin broken in me sen Jamie died. I must keep things to mysen—I ain't got nuthin good to say to others—I'm allus *grievin* at the Lord. Good-bye to yer—good-bye to yer.'

Her voice had grown absent, indifferent. But when George asked her, just as they were leaving the cottage, who was the boy sitting by the fire, her face darkened. She came hurriedly to the door with them, and said in George's ear:

'He's my darter's child—my darter by my first usband. His feyther an mother are gone, an he come up from West Bromwich to live wi me. But he isn't no comfort to me. He don't take no notice of anybody. He set like that, with his football, when Jamie lay a-dyin.

I'd as lief be shut on him. But theer—I've got to put up wi im.'

Letty meanwhile had approached the boy and looked at him curiously.

'Do you work in the pits too?' she asked him.

The boy stared at her.

'Yes,' he said.

'Do you like it?'

He gave a rough laugh.

'I reckon yo've got to like it,' he said. And turning his back on his questioner, he went back to his almanac.

'Don't let us do any more visiting,' said George impatiently, as they emerged into the main street. 'I'm out of love with the village. We'll do our blandishments another day. Let's go a little further up the valley and get away from the houses.'

Letty assented, and they walked along the village, she looking curiously into the open doors of the houses, by way of return for the inquisitive attention once more lavished upon herself and George.

'The houses are *quite* comfortable,' she said, presently. 'And I looked into Mrs. Batchelor's back room while you were talking. It was just as Mrs. Matthews said—such good carpets and curtains, two chests of drawers, and an harmonium—and pictures—and flowers in the windows. George! what are "butties"?'

'"Butties" are sub-contractors,' he said absently— 'men who contract with the pit-owners to get the coal, either on a large or a small scale—now mostly on a small scale. They engage and pay the colliers in some pits, in others the owners deal direct.'

'And what is a "tommy-shop"?'

'"Tommy" is the local word for "truck"—paying in

kind instead of in money. You see, the butties and the
owners between them used to own the public-houses
and the provision-shops, and the amount of coin of the
realm the men got in wages in the bad old times was
infinitesimal. They were expected to drink the butty's
beer, and consume the butty's provisions—at the butty's
prices, of course—and the butty kept the accounts. Oh!
it was an abomination!—but of course it was done away
with long ago.'

'Of course it was!' said Letty, indignantly. 'They
never remember what's done for them. Did you see what
excellent teas there were laid out in some of the houses—
and those girls with their hats smothered in feathers?
Why, I should never dream of wearing so many!'

She was once more her quick, shrewd self. All trace
of the tears that had surprised her while Mary Batchelor
was describing her son's death had passed away. Her
half-malicious eyes glanced to right and left, peering into
the secrets of the village.

'And these are the people that talk of starving!' she
said to George, scornfully, as they emerged into the open
road. Why, anyone can see——'

George, suddenly returned from a reverie, understood
what she was saying, and remarked, with an odd look:

'You think their houses aren't so bad? One is
always a little surprised—don't you think?—when the
poor are comfortable. One takes it as something to
one's own credit—I detect it in myself scores of times.
Well!—one seems to say—they *could* have done without
it—one might have kept it for oneself—what a fine
generous fellow I am!'

He laughed.

'I didn't mean that at all,' said Letty, protesting.

'Didn't you? Well, after all, darling—you see, you
don't have to live in those houses, nice as they are—and

you don't have to do your own scrubbing.   Ferth may be a vile hole, but I suppose you could put a score of these houses inside it—and I'm a pauper, but I can provide you with two housemaids.   I say, why do you walk so far away from me ? '

And in spite of her resistance, he took her hand, put it through his arm and held it there.

' Look at me, darling,' he said imperiously.   'How *can* anyone spy upon us with these trees and high walls ?   I want to see how pretty and fresh you look—I want to forget that poor thing and her tale.   Do you know that somewhere—far down in me—there's a sort of black pool—and when anything stirs it up—for the moment I want to hang myself—the world seems such an awful place !   It got stirred up just now—not while she was talking—but just as I looked back at that miserable old soul, standing at her door.   She used to be such a jolly old thing—always happy in her Bible—and in Jamie, I suppose—quite sure that she was going to a nice heaven, and would only have to wait a little bit, till Jamie got there too.   She seemed to know all about the Almighty's plans for herself and everybody else.   Her drunken husband was dead ; my father left her a bit of money, so did an old uncle, I believe.   She'd gossip and pray and preach with anybody.   And now she'll weep and pine like that till she dies—and she isn't sure even about heaven any more—and instead of Jamie, she's got that oafish lad, that changeling, hung round her neck—to kick her and ill-treat her in another year or two.   Well ! and do you ever think that something like that has got to happen to all of us—something hideous—some torture—something that'll make us wish we'd never been born?   Darling, am I a mad sort of a fool ?   Stop here—in the shade— give me a kiss ! '

And he made her pause at a shady corner in the road,

between two oak copses on either hand—a river babbling
at the foot of one of them. He put his arm round her,
and stooping kissed her red lips with a kind of covetous
passion. Then, still holding her, he looked out from the
trees to the upper valley with its scattered villages, its
chimneys and engine-houses.

'It struck me—what she said of the men under our
feet. They're at it now, Letty, hewing and sweating.
Why are they there, and you and I here? I'm *precious*
glad, aren't you? But I'm not going to make believe
that there's no difference. Don't let's be hypocrites,
whatever we are.'

Letty was perplexed and a little troubled. He had
only shown her this excitability once before—on that odd
uncomfortable night when he made her sit with him on
the Embankment. Whenever it came it seemed to upset
her dominant impression of him. But yet it excited her
too—it appealed to something undeveloped—some yearning, protecting instinct which was new to her.

She suddenly put up her hand and touched his hair.

'You talk so oddly, George. I think sometimes '—she
laughed with a pretty gaiety—'you'll go bodily over to
Lady Maxwell and her " set " some day ! '

George made a contemptuous sound.

'May the Lord preserve us from quacks,' he · said
lightly. 'One had better be a hypocrite. Look, little
woman, there is a shower coming. Shall we turn home ? '

They walked home, chatting and laughing. At their
own front door the butler handed George a telegram.
He opened it and read—

'Must come down to consult you on important
business—shall arrive at Ferth about 9.30.—Amelia
Tressady.'

Letty, who was looking over George's shoulder, gave
a little cry of dismay.

Then, to avoid the butler's eyes and ears, they turned hurriedly into George's smoking-room which opened off the hall, and shut the door.

' George ! she has come to get more money out of you ! ' cried Letty, anger and annoyance written in every line of her little frowning face.

' Well, darling, she can't get blood out of a stone ! ' said George, crushing the telegram in his hand and throwing it away. ' It is a little too bad of my mother, I think, to spoil our honeymoon time like this. However, it can't be helped. Will you tell them to get her room ready ? '

CHAPTER IX

' Now, my dear George ! I do think I may claim at least
that you should remember I am your *mother !* '—the
speaker raised a fan from her knee, and used it with some
vehemence. ' Of course I can't help seeing that you don't
treat me as you ought to do. I don't want to complain
of Letty—I daresay she was taken by surprise—but all I
can say as to her reception of me last night is, that it
wasn't pretty—that's all ; it wasn't *pretty.* My room felt
like an ice-house—Justine tells me nobody has slept there
for months—and no fire until just the moment I arrived ;
and—and no flowers on the dressing-table—no little *attentions,* in fact. I can only say it was not what I am accustomed to. My feelings overcame me ; that poor dear
Justine will tell you what a state she found me in. She
cried herself, to see me so upset.'

Lady Tressady was sitting upright on the straight-
backed sofa of George's smoking-room. George, who
was walking up and down the room, thought, with discomfort, as he glanced at her from time to time, that she
looked curiously old and dishevelled. She had thrown a
piece of white lace round her head, in place of the more
elaborate preparation for the world's gaze that she was
wont to make. Her dress—a study in purples—had been
a marvel, but was now old, and even tattered ; the ruffles
at her wrist were tumbled ; and the pencilling under her
still fine eyes had been neglected. George, between his

wife's dumb anger and his mother's folly, had passed through disagreeable times already since Lady Tressady's arrival, and was now once more endeavouring to get to the bottom of her affairs.

'You forget, mother,' he said, in answer to Lady Tressady's complaint, 'that the house is not mounted for visitors, and that you gave us very short notice.'

Nevertheless he winced inwardly as he spoke at the thought of Letty's behaviour the night before.

Lady Tressady bridled.

'We will not discuss it, if you please,' she said, with an attempt at dignity. 'I should have thought that you and Letty might have known I should not have broken in on your honeymoon without most *pressing* reasons. George!'—her voice trembled, she put her lace handkerchief to her eyes—'I am an unfortunate and miserable woman, and if you—my own darling son—don't come to my rescue, I—I don't know what I may be driven to do!'

George took the remark calmly, having probably heard it before. He went on walking up and down.

'It's no good, mother, dealing in generalities, I am afraid. You promised me this morning to come to business. If you will kindly tell me at once what is the matter, and what is the *figure*, I shall be obliged to you.'

Lady Tressady hesitated, the lace on her breast fluttering. Then, in desperation, she confessed herself, first reluctantly, then in a torrent.

During the last two years, then, she said, she had been trying her luck for the first time in—well, in speculation!

'Speculation!' said George, looking at her in amazement. 'In what?'

Lady Tressady tried again to preserve her dignity. She had been investing, she said—trying to increase her income on the Stock Exchange. She had done it quite as much for George's sake as her own, that she might

M

improve her position a little, and be less of a burden upon him. Everybody did it! Several of her best women-friends were as clever at it as any man, and often doubled their allowances for the year. She, of course, had done it under the *best* advice. George knew that she had friends in the City who would do anything—positively *anything*—for her. But somehow——

Then her tone dropped. Her foot in its French shoe began to fidget on the stool before her.

Somehow, she had got into the hands of a reptile—there! No other word described the creature in the least—a sort of financial agent, who had treated her unspeakably, disgracefully. She had trusted him implicitly, and the result was that she now owed the reptile who, on the strength of her name, her son, and her aristocratic connections, had advanced her money for these adventures, a sum——

'Well, the truth is I am afraid to say what it is,' said Lady Tressady, allowing herself for once a cry of nature, and again raising a shaky hand to her eyes.

'How much?' said George, standing over her, cigarette in hand.

'Well—four thousand pounds!' said Lady Tressady, her eyes blinking involuntarily as she looked up at him.

'*Four thousand pounds!*' exclaimed George. 'Preposterous!'

And, raising his hand, he flung his cigarette violently into the fire and resumed his walk, hands thrust into his pockets.

Lady Tressady looked tearfully at his long, slim figure as he walked away, conscious, however, even at this agitated moment, of the quick thought that he had inherited some of her elegance.

'George!'

'Yes—wait a moment—Mother '—he faced round upon

her decidedly. 'Let me tell you at once, that at the present moment it is quite impossible for me to find that sum of money.'

Lady Tressady flushed passionately like a thwarted child.

'Very well, then,' she said—'very well. Then it will be bankruptcy—and I hope you and Letty will like the scandal!'

'So he threatens bankruptcy?'

'Do you think I should have come down here except for something like that?' she cried. 'Look at his letters!'

And she took a tumbled roll out of the bag on her arm and gave it to him. George threw himself into a chair, and tried to get some idea of the correspondence; while Lady Tressady kept up a stream of plaintive chatter he could only endeavour not to hear.

As far as he could judge on a first inspection, the papers concerned a long series of risky transactions—financial gambling of the most pronounced sort—whereof the few gains had been long since buried deep in scandalous losses. The outrageous folly of some of the ventures and the magnitude of the sums involved made him curse inwardly. It was the first escapade of the kind he could remember in his mother's history, and, given her character, he could only regard it as adding a new and real danger to his life and Letty's.

Then another consideration struck him.

'How on earth did you come to know so much about the ins and outs of Stock Exchange business,' he asked her suddenly, with surprise, in the midst of his reading. 'You never confided in me. I never supposed you took an interest in such things.'

In truth, he would have supposed her mentally incapable of the kind of gambling finance these papers bore witness of. She had never been known to do a sum or present an account correctly in her life; and he had often, in his own mind, accepted her density in these directions as a certain excuse for her debts. Yet this correspondence showed here and there a degree of financial legerdemain of which any City swindler might have been proud—so far, at least, as he could judge from his hasty survey.

Lady Tressady drew herself up sharply in answer to his remark, though not without a flutter of the eyelids which caught his attention.

'Of course, my dear George, I always knew you thought your mother a fool. As a matter of fact, all my friends tell me that I have a *very* clear head!'

George could not restrain himself from laughing aloud.

'In face of this?' he said, holding up the final batch of letters, which contained Mr. Shapetsky's last formidable account; various imperious missives from a 'sharp-practice' solicitor, whose name happened to be disreputably known to George Tressady; together with repeated and most explicit assurances on the part both of agent and lawyer, that if arrangements were not made at once by Lady Tressady for meeting at least half Mr. Shapetsky's bill—which had now been running some eighteen months—and securing the other half, legal steps would be taken immediately.

Lady Tressady at first met her son's sarcasm in angry silence, then broke into shrill denunciation of Shapetsky's 'villainies.' How could decent people, people in society, protect themselves against such creatures!

George walked to the window, and stood looking out into the April garden. Presently he turned, and interrupted his mother.

'I notice, mother, that these transactions have been going on for nearly two years. Do you remember, when

I gave you that large sum at Christmas, you said it would "all but" clear you; and when I gave you another large sum last month, you professed to be entirely cleared? Yet all the time you were receiving these letters, and you owed this fellow almost as much as you do now. Do you think it was worth while to mislead me in that way?'

He stood leaning against the window, his fingers drumming on the sill. The contrast between the youth of the figure and the absence of youth in face and voice was curious. Perhaps Lady Tressady felt vaguely that he looked like a boy and spoke like a master, for her pride rose.

'You have no right to speak to me like that, George! I did everything for the best. I always do everything for the best. It is my misfortune to be so—so confiding, so hopeful. I must always believe in some one—that's what makes my friends so *extremely* fond of me. You and your poor darling father were never the least like me——' And she went off into a tearful comparison between her own character and the characters of her husband and son—in which of course it was not she that suffered.

George did not heed her. He was once more staring out of window, thinking hard. So far as he could see, the money, or the greater part of it, would have to be found. The man of course was a scoundrel, but of the sort that keeps within the law; and Lady Tressady's monstrous folly had given him an easy prey. When he thought of the many sacrifices he had made for his mother, of her ample allowance, her incorrigible vanity and greed —and then of the natural desires of his young wife—his heart burned within him.

'Well, I can only tell you,' he said at last, turning round upon her, 'that I see no way out. How is that

man's claim to be met? I don't know. Even if I *could*
meet it—which I see no chance of doing—by crippling
myself for some time, how should I be at liberty to do it?
My wife and her needs have now the first claim upon
me.'

'Very well,' said Lady Tressady proudly, raising her
handkerchief, however, to hide her trembling lips.

'Let me remind you,' he continued, ceremoniously,
'that the whole of this place is in bad condition, except
the few rooms we have just done up, and that money
must be spent upon it—it is only fair to Letty that it
should be spent. Let me remind you also, that you are
a good deal responsible for this state of things.'

Lady Tressady moved uneasily. George was now
speaking in his usual half-nonchalant tone, and he had
provided himself with another cigarette. But his eye
held her.

'You will remember that you promised me while I was
abroad to live here and look after the house. I arranged
money affairs with you, and other affairs, upon that basis.
But it appears that during the four years I was away you
were here altogether, at different times, about three
months. Yet you made me believe you were here; if I
remember right, you dated your letters from here. And
of course, in four years, an old house that is totally
neglected goes to the bad.'

'Who has been telling you such falsehoods?' cried
Lady Tressady. 'I was here a great deal more than
that—a great deal more!'

But the scarlet colour, do what she would, was dyeing
her still delicate skin, and her eyes, alternately obstinate
and shuffling, tried to take themselves out of the range
of George's.

As for George, as he stood there coolly smoking, he
was struck—or, rather, the critical mind in him was

struck—by a sudden perception of the meanness of aspect
which sordid cares of the kind his mother was now
plunged in can give to the human face. He felt the rise
of a familiar disgust. How many scenes of ugly battle
over money matters could he not remember in his boyhood between his father and mother! And later—in
India—what things he had known women do for money
or dress! He thought scornfully of a certain intriguing
lady of his acquaintance at Madras—who had borrowed
money of him—to whom he had given ball-dresses; and
of another, whose selfish extravagance had ruined one of
the best of men. Did all women tend to be of this make,
however poetic might be their outward seeming?

Aloud, he said quietly, in answer to his mother's
protest:

'I think you will find that is about accurate. I
mention it merely to show you how it is that I find
myself now plunged in so many expenses. And, now,
doesn't it strike you as a *little* hard that I should be
called upon to strip and cripple myself still further—
not to give my wife the comforts and conveniences I
long to give her, but to pay such debts as those?'

Involuntarily he struck his hand on the papers lying
in the chair where he had been sitting.

Lady Tressady, too, rose from her seat.

'George, if you are going to be *violent* towards your
mother, I had better go,' she said with an attempt at
dignity. 'I suppose Letty has been gossiping with her
servants about me. Oh! I knew what to expect!' cried
Lady Tressady, gathering up fan and handkerchief from
the sofa behind her with a hand that shook. 'I always
said from the beginning that she would set you against
me! She has never treated me as—as a daughter—
never! And that is my weakness—I must be cared for
—I must be treated with—with tenderness.'

'I wouldn't give way, mother, if I were you,' said George, quite unmoved by the show of tears. 'I think, if you will reflect upon it, that it is Letty and I who have the most cause to give way. If you will allow me, I will go and have a talk with her. I believe she is sitting in the garden.'

His mother turned sullenly away from him, and he left the room.

As he passed through the long oak-panelled hall that led to the garden, he was seized with an odd sense of pity for himself. This odious scene behind him, and now this wrestle with Letty that must be gone through— were these the joys of the honeymoon?

Letty was not in the garden. But as he passed into the wood on the farther side of the hill he saw her sitting under a tree halfway down the slope, with some embroidery in her hand. The April sun was shining into the wood. A larch beyond Letty was already green, and the twigs of the oak beneath which she sat made a reddish glow in the bright air. Patches of primroses and anemones starred the ground about her, and trails of periwinkle touched her dress. She was stooping, and her little hand went rapidly—impatiently—to and fro.

The contrast between this fresh youth amid the spring and that unlovely, reluctant age he had just left behind him in the smoking-room struck him sharply. His brow cleared.

As she heard his step she looked round eagerly. 'Well?' she said, pushing aside her work.

He threw himself down beside her.

'Darling, I have had my talk. It is pretty bad— worse than we had even imagined!'

Then he told her his mother's story. She could

hardly contain herself, as she listened, as he mentioned the total figure of the debts. It was evidently with difficulty that she prevented herself from interrupting him at every word. And when he had barely finished she broke out:

'And what did you say?'

George hesitated.

'I told her, of course, that it was monstrous and absurd to expect that we could pay such a sum.'

Letty's breath came fast. His voice and manner did not satisfy her at all.

'Monstrous? I should think it was! Do you know how she has run up this debt?'

George looked at her in surprise. Her little face was quivering under the suppressed energy of what she was going to say.

'No!—do you?'

'Yes!—I know all about it. I said to my maid last night—I hope, George, you won't mind, but you know Grier has been an age with me, and knows all my secrets—I told her she must make friends with your mother's maid, and see what she could find out. I felt we *must*, in self-defence. And of course Grier got it all out of Justine. I knew she would! Justine is a little fool; and she doesn't mean to stay much longer with Lady Tressady, so she didn't mind speaking. It is exactly as I supposed! Lady Tressady didn't begin speculating for herself at all—but for—somebody—else! Do you remember that absurd-looking singer who gave a "musical sketch" one day that your mother gave a party in Eccleston Square—in February?'

She looked at him with eagerness, an ugly half shrinking innuendo in her expression.

George had suddenly moved away, and was sitting now some little distance from his wife, his eyes bent on the ground. However, at her question he made a sign of assent.

'You do remember? Well,' said Letty, triumphantly, 'it is he who is at the bottom of it all. I *knew* there must be somebody. It appears that he has been getting money out of her for years—that he used to come and spend hours, when she had that little house in Bruton Street, when you were away—I don't believe you ever heard of it—flattering her, and toadying her, paying her compliments on her dress and her appearance, fetching and carrying for her—and of course living upon her! He used to arrange all her parties. Justine says that he used even to make her order all his favourite wines —*such* bills as there used to be for wine! He has a wife and children somewhere, and of course the whole family lived upon your mother. It was he made her begin speculating. Justine says he has lost all he ever had himself that way, and your mother couldn't, in fact, " *lend* " him '—Letty laughed scornfully—'money fast enough. It was he brought her across that odious creature Shapetsky—isn't that his name? And that's the whole story. If there have been any gains, he has made off with them—leaving her, of course, to get out of the rest. Justine says that for months there was nothing but business, as she calls it, talked in the house—and she knew, for she used to help wait at dinner. And such a crew of people as used to be about the place!'

She looked at him, struck at last by his silence and his attitude, or pausing for some comment, some appreciation of her cleverness in ferreting it all out.

But he did not speak, and she was puzzled. The angry triumph in her eyes faltered. She put out her hand and touched him on the arm.

'What is it, George? I thought—it would be more satisfactory to us both to know the truth.'

He looked up quickly.

'And all this your maid got out of Justine? You asked her?'

She was struck, offended, by his expression. It was so cool and strange—even, she could have imagined, contemptuous.

'Yes, I did,' she said passionately. 'I thought I was quite justified. We must protect ourselves.'

He was silent again.

'I think,' he said at last, drily, she watching him— 'I think we will keep Justine and Grier out of it, if you please.'

She took her work, and laid it down again, her mouth trembling.

'So you had rather be deceived?'

'I had rather be deceived than listen behind doors,' he said, beginning in a light tone, which, however, passed immediately into one of bitterness. 'Besides, there is nothing new. For people like my mother there is always some adventurer or adventuress in the background—there always used to be in old days. She never meant any serious harm; she was first plundered, then we. My father used to be for ever turning some impostor or other out of doors. Now I suppose it is my turn.'

This time it was Letty who kept silence. Her needle passed rapidly to and fro. George glanced at her queerly. Then he rose and came to stand near her, leaning against the tree.

'You know, Letty, we shall have to pay that money,' he said suddenly, pulling at his moustache.

Letty made an exclamation under her breath, but went on working faster than before.

He slipped down to the moss beside her, and caught her hand.

'Are you angry with me?'

'If you insult me by accusing me of listening behind doors you can't wonder,' said Letty, snatching her hand away, her breast heaving.

He felt a bitter inclination to laugh, but he restrained it, and did his best to make peace. In the midst of his propitiations Letty turned upon him.

'Of course, I know you think I did it all for selfishness,' she said, half crying, 'because I want new furniture and new dresses. I don't; I want to protect you from being—being—plundered like this. How can you do what you ought as a member of Parliament? how can we ever keep ourselves out of debt if—if—— ? How *can* you pay this money?' she wound up, her eyes flaming.

'Well, you know,' he said, hesitating—'you know I suggested yesterday we should sell some land to do up the house. I am afraid we must sell the land, and pay this scoundrel—a proportion, at all events. Of course, what I should *like* to do would be to put him—and the other—to instant death, with appropriate tortures! Short of that, I can only take the matter out of my mother's hands, get a sharp solicitor on my side to match *his* rascal, and make the best bargain I can.'

Letty rolled up her work with energy, two tears of anger on her cheeks. 'She *ought* to suffer!' she cried, her voice trembling—'she *ought* to suffer!'

'You mean that we ought to let her be made a bankrupt?' he said coolly. 'Well, no doubt it would be salutary. Only, I am afraid it would be rather more disagreeable to us than to her. Suppose we consider the situation. Two young married people—charming house —charming wife—husband just beginning in politics— people inclined to be friends. Then you go to dine with them in Brook Street—excellent little French dinner— bride bewitching. Next morning you see the bankruptcy of the host's mamma in the "Times." "And he's the only son, isn't he?—he must be well off. They say she's been dreadfully extravagant. But, hang it! you know, a man's mother!—and a widow—no, I can't stand that. Sha'n't dine with them again!" There! do you see, darling? Do you really want to rub all the bloom off the peach?'

He had hardly finished his little speech before the odiousness of it struck himself.

'Am I come to talking to her like *this?*' he asked himself in a kind of astonishment.

But Letty, apparently, was not astonished.

'Everybody would understand if you refused to ruin yourself by going on paying these frightful debts. I am sure *something* could be done,' she said, half-choked.

George shook his head.

'But everybody wouldn't want to understand. The dear world loves a scandal—doesn't really *like* being amiable to new-comers at all. You would make a bad start, dear—and all the world would pity mamma.'

'Oh! if you are only thinking what people would say,' cried Letty.

'No,' said George, reflectively, but with a mild change of tone. 'Damn people! I can pull myself to pieces so much better than they can. You see, darling, you're such an optimist. Now, if you'd only just believe, as I do, that the world is a radically bad place, you wouldn't be so surprised when things of this sort happen. Eh, little person, has it been a radically bad place this last fortnight?'

He laid his cheek against her shoulder, rubbing it gently up and down. But something hard and scornful lay behind his caress—something he did not mean to inquire into.

'Then you told your mother,' said Letty after a pause, still looking straight before her, 'that you would clear her?'

'Not at all. I said we could do nothing. I laid it on about the house. And all the time I knew perfectly well in my protesting soul, that if this man's claim is sustainable we should *have* to pay up. And I imagine that mamma knew it too. You can get out of anybody's debts but your mother's—that's apparently what it comes to. Queer thing, civilisation! Well now'—he sprang to his feet—'let's go and get it over.'

Letty also rose.

'I can't see her again!' she said quickly. 'I sha'n't come down to lunch. Will she go by the three-o'clock train?'

'I will arrange it,' said George.

They walked through the wood together silently. As they came in sight of the house Letty's face quivered again with restrained passion—or tears. George, whose *sangfroid* was never disturbed outwardly for long, had by now resigned himself, and had, moreover, recovered that tolerance of woman's various weaknesses which was in him the fruit of a wide, and at bottom hostile, induction. He set himself to cheer her up. Perhaps, after all, if he could sell a particular piece of land which he owned near a neighbouring large town, and sell it well—he had had offers for it before—he might be able to clear his mother, and still let Letty work her will on the house. She mustn't take a gloomy view of things—he would do his best. So that by the time they got into the drawing-room she had let her hand slip doubtfully into his again for a moment.

But nothing would induce her to appear at lunch. Lady Tressady, having handed over all Shapetsky's papers and all her responsibilities to George, graciously told him

that she could understand Letty's annoyance, and didn't
wish for a moment to intrude upon her. She then called
on Justine to curl her hair, put on a blue shot silk with
marvellous pink fronts just arrived from Paris, and
came down to lunch with her son in her most smiling
mood. She took no notice of his monosyllables, and in
the hall, while the butler discreetly retired, she kissed
him with tears, saying that she had always known his
generosity would come to the rescue of his poor darling
mamma.

'You will oblige me, mother, by not trying it again
too soon,' was George's ironical reply as he put her into
the carriage.

In the afternoon Letty was languid and depressed.
She would not talk on general topics, and George shrank
in nervous disgust from reopening the subjects of the
morning. Finally, she chose to be tucked up on the sofa
with a novel, and gave George free leave to go out.

It surprised him to find as he walked quickly down
the hill, delighting in the April sun, that he was glad to
be alone. But he did not in the least try to fling the
thought away from him, as many a lover would have
done. The events, the feelings of the day had been alike
jarring and hateful; he meant to escape from them.

But he could not escape from them all at once. A
fresh and unexpected debt of somewhere about four
thousand pounds does not sit lightly on a comparatively
poor man. In spite of his philosophy for Letty's benefit,
he must needs harass himself anew about his money
affairs, planning and reckoning. How many more such
surprises would his mother spring upon him—and how
was he to control her? He realised now something of
the life-long burden his dull old father had borne—a burden which the absences of school, college, and travel had

hitherto spared himself. What was he to appeal to in her? There seemed to be nothing—neither will nor conscience. She was like the women without backs in the fairy-tale.

Then, with one breath he said to himself that he must kick out that singer-fellow, and with the next, that he would not touch any of his mother's crew with a barge-pole. Though he never pleaded ideals in public, he had been all his life something of a moral epicure, taking 'moral' as relating rather to manners than to deeper things. He had done his best not to soil himself by contact with certain types—among men especially. Of women he was less critical and less observant.

As to this ugly feud opening between his mother and his wife, it had quite ceased to amuse him. Now that his marriage was a reality, the daily corrosion of such a thing was becoming plain. And who was there in the world to bear the brunt of it but he? He saw himself between the two—eternally trying to make peace—and his face lengthened.

And if Letty would only leave the thing to him!—would only keep her little white self out of it! He wished he could get her to send away that woman Grier—a forward second-rate creature, much too ready to meddle in what did not concern her.

Then, with a shake of his thin shoulders, he passionately drove it all out of his thoughts.

Let him go to the village, sound the feeling there if he could, and do his employer's business. His troubles as a pit-owner seemed likely to be bad enough, but they did not canker one like domestic miseries. They were a man's natural affairs; to think of them came as a relief to him.

He had but a disappointing round, however.

In the first place he went to look up some of the older 'hewers,' men who had been for years in the employ of the Tressadys. Two or three of them had just come back from the early shift, and their wives, at any rate, were pleased and flattered by George's call. But the men sat like stocks and stones while he talked. Scarcely a word could be got out of them, and George felt himself in an atmosphere of storm, guessing at dangers, everywhere present, though not yet let loose —like the foul gases in the pits under his feet.

He behaved with a good deal of dignity, stifling his pride here and there sufficiently to talk simply and well of the general state of trade, the conditions of the coal industry in the West Mercian district, the position of the masters, the published accounts of one or two large companies in the district, and so on. But in the end he only felt his own anger rising in answer to the sullenness of the men. Their sallow faces and eyes weakened by long years of the pit expressed little—but what there was spelt war.

Nor did his visits to what might be called his own side give him much more satisfaction.

One man, a brawny 'fireman,' whom George had been long taught to regard as one of the props of law and order in the district, was effusively and honestly glad to see his employer. His wife hurried the tea, and George drank and ate as heartily as his own luncheon would let him in company with Macgregor and his very neat and smiling family. Nothing could be more satisfactory than Macgregor's general denunciations of the Union and its agent. Bewick, in his opinion, was a 'drunken, low-livin scoundrel,' who got his bread by making mischief; the Union was entering upon a great mistake in resisting the masters' proposals; and if it weren't for the public-house and idleness there wasn't a

N

man in Ferth that couldn't live *well*, ten per cent. reduction and all considered. Nevertheless, he did not conceal his belief that battle was approaching, and would break out, if not now, at any rate in the late summer or autumn. Times, too, were going to be specially bad for the non-society men. The membership of the Union had been running up fast; there had been a row that very morning at the pit where he worked, the Union men refusing to go down in the same cage with the blacklegs. He and his mates would have to put their backs into it. Never fear but they would! Bullying might be trusted only to make them the more 'orkard.'

Nothing could have been more soothing than such talk to the average employer in search of congenial opinions. But George was not the average employer, and the fastidious element in him began soon to make him uncomfortable. Sobriety is, no doubt, admirable, but he had no sooner detected a teetotal cant in his companion than that particular axiom ceased to matter to him. And to think poorly of Bewick might be a salutary feature in a man's character, but it should be for some respectable reason. George fidgeted on his chair while Macgregor told the usual cock-and-bull stories of monstrous hotel-bills seen sticking out of Bewick's tail-pockets, and there deciphered by a gaping populace; and his mental discomfort reached its climax when Macgregor wound up with the remark :

'And *that*, Sir George, is where the money goes to!—not to the poor starving women and children, I can tell yer, whose husbands are keepin him in luxury. I've always said it. *Where's the accounts ?* I've never seen no balance-sheet—*never !*' he repeated solemnly. 'They do say as there's one to be seen at the "lodge "——'

'Why, of course there is, Macgregor,' said George

with a nervous laugh, as he got up to depart; 'all the big Unions publish their accounts.'

The fireman's obstinate mouth and stubbly hair only expressed a more pronounced scepticism.

'Well, I shouldn't believe in em,' he said, 'if they did. I've never seen a balance-sheet, and I don't suppose I ever shall. Well, good-bye to you, Sir George, and thank you kindly. Yo take my word, sir, if it weren't for the public-house the men could afford to lose a trifle now and again to let the masters make their fair profit!'

And he looked behind him complacently at his neat cottage and well-clothed children.

But George walked away, impatient.

'*His* wages won't go down, anyway,' he said to himself —for the wages of the 'firemen,' whose work is of the nature of superintendence, hardly vary with the state of trade. 'And what suspicious idiocy about the accounts!'

His last visit was the least fortunate of any. The fireman in question, Mark Dowse, Macgregor's chief rival in the village, was a keen Radical, and George found him chuckling over his newspaper, and the defeat of the Tory candidate in a recently decided County Council election. He received his visitor with a surprise which George thought not untinged with insolence. Some political talk followed, in which Dowse's Yorkshire wit scored more than once at his employer's expense. Dowse, indeed, let himself go. He was on the point of taking the examination for an under-manager's certificate and leaving the valley. Hence there were no strong reasons for servility, and he might talk as he pleased to a young 'swell' who had sold himself to reaction. George lost his temper somewhat, was furiously ashamed of himself, and could only think of getting out of the man's company with dignity.

He was by no means clear, however, as he walked
away from the cottage, that he had succeeded in doing
so. What was the good of trying to make friends with
these fellows? Neither in agreement nor in opposition
had he any common ground with them. Other people
might have the gifts for managing them; it seemed to
him that it would be better for him to take up the line
at once that he had none. Fontenoy was right. Nothing
but a state of enmity was possible—veiled enmity at some
times, open at others.

What were those voices on the slope above him?

He was walking along a road which skirted his own
group of pits. To his left rose a long slope of refuse,
partly grown over, ending in the 'bank' whereon stood
the engine-house and winding-apparatus. A pathway
climbed the slope and made the natural ascent to the pit
for people dwelling in the scattered cottages on the
farther side of it.

Two men, he saw, were standing high up on the
pathway, violently disputing. One was Madan, his own
manager, an excellent man of business and a bitter Tory.
The other was Valentine Bewick.

As Tressady neared the road-entrance to the pathway
the two men parted. Madan climbed on towards the
pit. Bewick ran down the path.

As he approached the gate, and saw Tressady passing
on the road, the agent called:

'Sir George Tressady!'

George stopped.

Bewick came quickly up to him, his face crimson.

'Is it by your orders, Sir George, that Mr. Madan
insults and browbeats me when he meets me on a
perfectly harmless errand to one of the men in your
engine-house?'

'Perhaps Mr. Madan was not so sure as you were,

Mr. Bewick, that the errand *was* a harmless one,' said George, with a cool smile.

By this time, however, Bewick was biting his lip, and very conscious that he had made an impulsive mistake.

'Don't imagine for a moment,' he said hotly, ' that Madan's opinion of anything I may be doing matters one brass farthing to me! Only I give you and him fair warning that if he blackguards me again in the way he has done several times lately, I shall have him bound over.'

'He might survive it,' said George. 'But how will you manage it? You have had ill-luck, rather, with the magistrates—haven't you?'

He stood drawn up to his full height, thin, venomous, alert, rather enjoying the encounter, which 'let off the steam' of his previous irritations.

Bewick threw him a furious look.

'You think that a damaging thing to say, do you, Sir George? Perhaps the day will come—not so far off, neither—when the magistrates will be no longer your creatures, but ours. Then we shall see!'

'Well, prophecy is cheap,' said George. 'Console yourself with it, by all means.'

The two men measured each other eye to eye.

Then, unexpectedly, after the relief of his outburst, the philosopher's instincts which were so oddly inter-woven with the rest of Tressady's nature reasserted themselves.

'Look here,' he said in another manner, advancing a step. 'I think this is all great nonsense. If Madan has exceeded his duty, I will see to it. And, meanwhile, don't you think it would be more worthy of us, as a couple of rational beings, if, now we have met, we had a few serious words on the state of things in this valley? You and I

fought a square fight at Malford—you at least said as
much. Why can't we fight a square fight here?'

Bewick eyed him doubtfully. He was leaning on his
stick, recovering breath and composure. George noticed
that since the Malford election, even he had lost youth
and looks. He had the drunkard's skin and the
drunkard's eyes. Yet there were still the make and
proportions of the handsome athlete. He was now a
man of about thirty-two; but in his first youth he had
carried the miner's pick for some four or five years, and
during the same period had been one of the most famous
football-players of the county. As George knew, he was
still the idol of the local clubs, and capable in his sober
spells of amazing feats both of strength and endurance.

'Well, I have no objection to some conversation with
you,' said Bewick at last, slowly.

'Let's walk on, then,' said George.

And they walked past the gate of Ferth, towards
the railway-station, which was some two miles off.

About an hour later the two men returned along the
same road. Both had an air of tension; both were
rather pale.

'Well, it comes to this,' said George, as he stopped
beside his own gate, 'you believe our case—the badness
of trade, the disappearance of profits, pressure of
contracts, and all the rest of it—and you still refuse on
your part to bear the smallest fraction of the burden?
You will claim all you can get in good times—you will
give back nothing in bad?'

'That is so,' said Bewick, deliberately; 'that is so,
precisely. We will take no risks; we give our labour,
and in return the workman must live. Make the consumer
pay, or pay yourselves out of your good years'—he turned
imperceptibly towards the barrack-like house on the hill.
'We don't care a ha'porth which it is!—only don't you

come on the man who risks his life, and works like a
galley-slave five days a week for a pittance of five-and-
twenty shillings, or thereabouts, to pay—for he *won't*.
He's tired of it. Not till you starve him into it, at any
rate!'

George laughed.

'One of the best men in the village has been giving
me his opinion this afternoon that there isn't a man in
that place '—he pointed to it—'that couldn't live, and
live well—ay, and take the masters' terms to-morrow—
but for the drink!'

His keen look ran over Bewick from head to foot.

'And I know who *that* is,' said Bewick, with a
sneer. 'Well, I can tell you what the rest of the men in
that place think, and it's this: that the man in that
village who *doesn't* drink is a mean skunk, who's betraying his own flesh and blood to the capitalists! Oh! you
may preach at us till you're black in the face, but drink
we *shall* till we get the control of our own labour. For,
look here! Directly we cease to drink—directly we become good boys on your precious terms—the standard of
life falls, down come wages, and *you* sweep off our beer-
money to spend on your champagne. Thank you, Sir
George! but we're not such fools as we look—and that
don't suit us! Good-day to you.'

And he haughtily touched his hat in response to
George's movement, and walked quickly away.

George slowly mounted his own hill. The chequered
April day was declining, and the dipping sun was flooding the western plain with quiet light. Rooks were
circling round the hill, filling the air with long-drawn
sound. A cuckoo was calling on a tree near at hand,
and the evening was charged with spring scents —
scents of leaf and grass, of earth and rain. Below, in

an oak-copse across the road, a stream rushed; and
from a distance came the familiar rattle and thud of
the pits.

George stood still a moment under a ragged group of
Scotch firs—one of the few things at Ferth that he
loved—and gazed across the Cheshire border to the distant
lines of Welsh hills. The excitement of his talk with
Bewick was subsiding, leaving behind it the obstinate
resolve of the natural man. He should tell his uncles
there was nothing for it but to fight it out. Some blood
must be let; somebody must be master.

What poor limited fools, after all, were the best of
the working men—how incapable of working out any
serious problem, of looking beyond their own noses and
the next meal! Was he to spend his life in chronic battle
with them—a set of semi-civilised barbarians—his country-
men in nothing but the name? And for what cause—to
what cry? That he might defend against the toilers of
this wide valley a certain elegant house in Brook Street,
and find the means to go on paying his mother's debts?—
such debts as he carried the evidence of, at that moment,
in his pocket.

Suddenly there swept over his mind with pricking
force the thought of Mary Batchelor at her door, blind
with weeping and pain—of the poor boy, dead in his
prime. Did those two figures stand for the *realities*
at the base of things—the common labours, affections,
agonies, which uphold the world?

His own life looked somehow poor and mean to him
as he turned back to it. The Socialist of course—Bewick
—would say that he and Letty and his mother were
merely living, and dressing, and enjoying themselves,
paying butlers, and starting carriages out of the labour
and pain of others—that Jamie Batchelor and his like
risked and brutalised their strong young lives that

Lady Tressady and her like might 'jig and amble' through theirs.

Pure ignorant fanaticism, no doubt! But he was not so ready as usual to shelter himself under the big words of controversy. Fontenoy's favourite arguments had momentarily no savour for a kind of moral nausea.

'I begin to see it was a "cursed spite" that drove me into the business at all,' he said to himself as he stood under the trees.

What he was really suffering from was an impatience of new conditions—perhaps surprise that he was not more equal to them. Till his return home—till now, almost—he had been an employer and a coalowner by proxy. Other people had worked for him, had solved his problems for him. Then a transient impulse had driven him home—made him accept Fontenoy's offer— worse luck!—at least, Letty apart! The hopefulness and elation about himself, his new activities, and his Parliamentary prospects, that had been his predominant mood in London seemed to him at this moment of depression mere folly. What he really felt, he declared to himself, was a sort of cowardly shrinking from life and its tests—the recognition that at bottom he was a weakling, without faiths, without true identity.

Then the quick thought-process, as it flowed on, told him that there are two things that protect men of his stamp from their own lack of moral stamina : perpetual change of scene, that turns the world into a spectacle— and love. He thought with hunger of his travel-years; holding away from him, as it were, for a moment the thought of his marriage.

But only for a moment. It was but a few weeks since a woman's life had given itself wholly into his hands. He was still thrilling under the emotion and astonishment of it. Tender, melting thoughts flowed upon him. His little Letty! Had he ever thought her perfect, free from natural covetousness and weaknesses? What folly! *He* to ask for the grand style in character!

He looked at his watch. How long he had left her! Let him hurry, and make his peace.

However, just as he was turning, his attention was caught by something that was passing on the opposite hillside. The light from the west was shining full on a white cottage with a sloping garden. The cottage belonged to the Wesleyan minister of the place, and had been rented by Bewick for the last six months. And just as George was turning away he saw Bewick come out of the door with a burden—a child, or a woman little larger than a child—in his arms. He carried her to an armchair, which had been placed on the little grass-plat. The figure was almost lost in the chair, and sat motionless while Bewick brought cushions and a stool. Then a baby came to play on the grass, and Bewick hung over the back of the chair, bending so as to talk to the person in it.

'Dying?' said George to himself. 'Poor devil! he must hate something.'

He sped up the hill, and found Letty still on the sofa and in the last pages of her novel. She did not resent his absence apparently,—a freedom, so far, from small exaction for which he inwardly thanked her. Still, from the moment that she raised her eyes as he came in, he saw that if she was not angry with him for leaving her alone, her mind was still as sore as ever against him and fortune on other accounts—and his revived ardour drooped. He gave her an account of his adventures, but she was neither inquiring nor sympathetic; and her manner all the evening had a nervous dryness that took away the pleasure of their *tête-à-tête*. Any old friend of Letty's, indeed, could hardly have failed to ask what had become of that small tinkling charm of manner, that girlish flippancy and repartee, that had counted for so much in George's first impressions of her? They were no sooner engaged than it had begun to wane. Was it like the bird or the flower, that adorns itself only for the wooing time, and sinks into relative dinginess when the mating effort is over?

On this particular evening, indeed, she was really absorbed half the time in gloomy thoughts of Lady Tressady's behaviour and the poorness of her own prospects. She lay on the sofa again after dinner—her white slimness and bright hair showing delicately against the cushions—playing still with her novel, while George read the newspapers. Sometimes she glanced at him unsteadily, with a pinching of the lips. But it was not her way to invite a scene.

Late at night he went up to his dressing-room.

As he entered it Letty was talking to her maid. He stopped involuntarily in the darkness of his own room, and listened. What a contrast between this Letty and the Letty of the drawing-room! They were chattering fast, discussing Lady Tressady, and Lady Tressady's gowns, and Lady Tressady's affairs. What eagerness, what malice, what feminine subtlety and acuteness! After listening for a few seconds, it seemed to him as though a score of new and ugly lights had been thrown alike upon his mother and on human nature. He stole away again without revealing himself.

When he returned the room was nearly dark, and Letty was lying high against her pillows, waiting for him. Suddenly, after she had sent her maid away, she had felt depressed and miserable, and had begun to cry. And for some reason hardly clear to herself she had lain pining for George's footstep. When he came in she looked at him with eyes still wet, reproaching him gently for being late.

In the dim light, surrounded with lace and whiteness, she was a pretty vision; and George stood beside her, responding and caressing.

But that black depth in his nature, of which he had spoken to her—which he had married to forget—was, none the less, all ruffled and vocal. For the first time since Letty had consented to marry him he did not think or say to himself, as he looked at her, that he was a lucky man, and had done everything for the best.

CHAPTER X

THUS, with the end of the honeymoon, whatever hopes or illusions George Tressady had allowed himself in marrying were already much bedimmed. His love-dream had been meagre and ordinary enough. But even so, it had not maintained itself.

Nevertheless, such impressions and emotions pass. The iron fact of marriage outstays them, tends always to modify, and, at first, to conquer them.

Upon the Tressadys' return to London, Letty, at any rate, endeavoured to forget her great defeat of the honeymoon in the excitement of furnishing the house in Brook Street. Certainly there could be no question, in spite of all her high speech to Miss Tulloch and others, that in her first encounter with Lady Tressady, Lady Tressady had won easily. Letty had forgotten to reckon on the hard realities of the filial relation, and could only think of them now, partly with exasperation, partly with despair.

Lady Tressady, however, was for the moment somewhat subdued, and on the return of the young people to town she did her best to propitiate Letty. In Letty's eyes, indeed, her offence was beyond reparation. But, for the moment, there was outward amity at least between them; which for Letty meant chiefly that she was conscious of making all her purchases for the house and planning all her housekeeping arrangements under a constant critical inspection; and, moreover, that she was liable to find all her afternoon-teas with particular friends, or those persons of whom she wished to make particular friends, broken up by the advent of the over-dressed and berouged lady, who first put the guests to flight, and was then out of temper because they fled.

Meanwhile George found the Shapetsky matter extremely harassing. He put on a clever lawyer; but the Shapetsky would have scorned to be overmatched by anybody else's abilities, and very little abatement could be obtained. Moreover, the creditor's temper had been roughened by a somewhat unfortunate letter George had written in a hurry from Ferth, and he showed every sign of carrying matters with as high a hand as possible.

Meanwhile George was discovering, like any other landowner, how easy it is to talk of selling land, how difficult to sell it. The buyer who would once have bought was not now forthcoming; the few people who nibbled were, naturally, thinking more of their own purses than Tressady's; and George grew red with indignation over some of the offers submitted to him by his country solicitor. With the payment of a first large instalment to Shapetsky out of his ordinary account, he began to be really pressed for money, just as the expenses of the Brook Street settling-in were at their height. This pecuniary strain had a marked effect upon him. It brought out certain features of character which he no doubt inherited from his father. Old Sir William had always shown a scrupulous and petty temper in money matters. He could not increase his possessions: for that he had apparently neither brains nor judgment; nor could he even protect himself from the more serious losses of business, for George found heavy debts in existence— mortgages on the pits and so forth—when he succeeded. But as the head of a household Sir William showed extraordinary tenacity and spirit in the defence of his petty cash; and the exasperating extravagance of the wife whom, in a moment of infatuation, he had been cajoled into marrying, intensified and embittered a natural characteristic.

George so far resembled him that both at school and college he had been a rather careful and abstemious boy. Probably the spectacle of his mother's adventures had revealed to him very early the humiliations of the debtor. At any rate, during his four years abroad he had never exceeded the modest yearly sum he had reserved for himself on leaving England; and the frugality of his personal expenditure had counted for something in the estimates formed of him during his travels by competent persons.

Nevertheless, at this beginning of household life he was still young and callow in all that concerned the management of money; and it had never occurred to him that his somewhat uncertain income of about four thousand a year would not be amply sufficient for anything that he and Letty might need; for housekeeping, for children—if children came—for political expenses, and even for those supplementary presents to his mother which he had all along recognised as inevitable. Now, however, what with the difficulty he found in settling the Shapetsky affair, what with Letty's demands for the house, and his revived dread of what his mother might be doing, together with his overdrawn account and the position of his colliery property, a secret fear of embarrassment and disaster began to torment him, the offspring of a temperament which had never perhaps possessed any real buoyancy.

Occasionally, under the stimulus of this fear, he would leave the House of Commons on a Wednesday or Saturday afternoon, walk to Warwick Square, and appear precipitately in his mother's drawing-room, for the purpose of examining the guests—or possible harpies—who might be gathered there. He did his best once or twice to dislodge the 'singer-fellow'—an elderly gentleman with a flabby face and long hair, who seemed to George to be equally boneless, physically and morally. Nevertheless, he was not to be dislodged. The singer, indeed, treated the young legislator with a mixture of deference and artistic condescension, which was amusing or enraging as you chose to take it. And once, when George attempted very plain language with his mother, Lady Tressady went into hysterics, and vowed that she would not be parted from her friends, not even by the brutality of young married people who had everything they wanted, while she was a poor lone widow, whose life was not worth living. The whole affair was, so to speak, sordidly innocent. Mr. Fullerton—such was the gentleman's name—wanted creature-comforts and occasional loans ; Lady Tressady wanted company, compliments, and 'musical sketches' for her little tea-parties. Mrs. Fullerton was as ready as her husband to supply the two former ; and even the children, a fair-haired, lethargic crew, painfully like their boneless father in Tressady's opinion, took their share in the general exploitation of Tressady's mamma. Lady Tressady meanwhile posed as the benefactor of genius in distress ; and vowed, moreover, that 'poor dear Fullerton' was in no way responsible for her recent misfortunes. The 'reptile,' and the 'reptile' only, was to blame.

After one of these skirmishes with his mother, George, ruffled and disgusted, took his way home, to find Letty eagerly engaged in choosing silk curtains for the drawing-room.

'Oh! how lucky!' she cried when she saw him. 'Now you can help me decide—*such* a business !'

And she led him into the drawing-room, where lengths of pink and green brocade were pinned against the wall in conspicuous places.

George admired, and gave his verdict in favour of a particular green. Then he stooped to read the ticket on the corner of the pattern, and his face fell.

'How much will you want of this stuff, Letty?' he asked her.

'Oh! for the two rooms, nearly fifty yards,' said Letty, carelessly, opening another bundle of patterns as she spoke.

'It is twenty-six shillings a yard!' said George, rather gloomily, as he fell, tired, into an armchair.

'Well, yes, it *is* dear. But then, it is so good that it will last an age. I think I must have some of it for the sofa, too,' said Letty, pondering.

George made no reply.

Presently Letty looked up.

'Why, George?—George, what *is* the matter? Don't you want anything pretty for this room? You never take any interest in it at all.'

'I'm only thinking, darling, what fortunes the upholsterers must make,' said George, his hands penthouse over his eyes.

Letty pouted and flushed. The next minute she came to sit on the edge of his chair. She was dressed—rather overdressed, perhaps—in a pale blue dress whereof the inventive ruffles and laces pleased her own critical mind extremely. George, well-accustomed by now to the items in his mother's bills, felt uncomfortably, as he looked at the elegance beside him, that it was a question of guineas —many guineas. Then he hated himself for not simply admiring her—his pretty little bride—in her new finery. What was wrong with him? This beastly money had put everything awry!

Letty guessed shrewdly at what was the matter. She bit her lip, and looked ready to cry.

'Well, it *is* hard,' she said, in a low, emphatic voice,

_O

'that we can't please ourselves in a few trifles of this sort—when one thinks *why!*'

George took her hand, and kissed it affectionately.

'Darling, only just for a little—till I get out of this brute's clutches. There are such pretty, cheap things nowadays—aren't there?'

'Oh! if you want to have a South Kensington drawing-...e..y, indignantly, 'with fo.. _
..........s and art pots, you can do *that* for nothing. ...u. I'd rather go back to horsehair and a mahogany table in the middle at once!'

'You needn't wear "greenery-yallery" gowns, you know,' said George, laughing; 'that's the one unpardonable thing. Though, if you did wear them, you'd become them.'·

And he held her at arm's length that he might properly admire her new dress.

Letty, however, was not to be flattered out of her lawful dues in the matter of curtains—that Lady Tressady's debts might be paid the sooner. She threw herself into a long wrestle with George, half-angry, half-plaintive, and in the end she wrung out of him much more considerable matters than the brocades originally in dispute. Then George went down to his study, pricked in his conscience, and vaguely sore with Letty. Why? Women in his eyes were made for silken gauds and trinkets: it was the price that men were bound to pay them for their society. He had watched the same sort of process that had now been applied to himself many times already in one or more of the Anglo-Indian households with which he had grown familiar, and had been philosophically amused by it.· But the little comedy, transferred to his own hearth, seemed somehow to have lost humour and point.

Still, with two young people, under thirty, just entering upon that fateful second act of the play of life which makes or mars us all, moments of dissatisfaction and depression—even with Shapetskys and Lady Tressadys in the background—were but rare specks in the general sum of pleasure. George had fallen once more under the Parliamentary illusion, as soon as he was again within reach of the House of Commons and in frequent contact with Fontenoy. The link between him and his strange leader grew daily stronger as they sat side by side, through some hard-fought weeks of Supply, throwing the force of their little group now on the side of the Government, now on that of the Opposition, always vigilant, and often successful. George' became necessary to Fontenoy in a hundred ways; for the younger man had a mass of *connaissances*—to use the irreplaceable French word—the result of his more normal training and his four years of intelligent travel, which Fontenoy was almost wholly without. Many a blunder did George save his chief; and no one could have offered his brains for the picking with a heartier goodwill. On the other hand, the instinctive strength and acuteness of Fontenoy's judgment were unmatched, according to Tressady's belief, in the House of Commons. He was hardly ever deceived in a man, or in the significant points of a situation. His followers never dreamt of questioning his verdict on a point of tactics. They followed him blindly; and if the gods sent defeat, no one blamed Fontenoy. But in success his grunt of approval or congratulation rewarded the curled young aristocrats who made the nucleus of his party as nothing else did; while none of his band ever affronted or over-rode him with impunity. He wielded a natural kingship, and, the more battered and gnarled became his physical presence, the more remarkable was his moral ascendency.

One discouragement, however, he and his group suf-fered during the weeks between Easter and Whitsuntide

They were hungry for battle, and the best of the battle was for the moment denied them; for, owing to a number of controverted votes in Supply and the slipping-in of two or three inevitable debates on pressing matters of current interest, the Second Reading of the Maxwell Bill was postponed till after Whitsuntide, when it was certainly to take precedence. There was a good deal of grumbling in the House, led by Fontenoy; but the Government could only vow that they had no choice, and that their adversaries could not possibly be more eager to fight than they were to be fought.

Life, then, on this public side, though not so keen as it would be presently, was still rich and stirring. And meanwhile society showed itself gracious to the bride and bridegroom. Letty's marriage had made her unusually popular for the time with her own acquaintance. For it might be called success; yet it was not of too dazzling a degree. What, therefore, with George's public and Parliamentary relations, the calls of officials, the attentions of personal friends, and the good offices of Mrs. Watton, who was loftily determined to 'launch' her niece, Letty was always well-pleased with the look of her hall-table and the cards upon it when she returned home in her new brougham from her afternoon round. She left them there for George to see, and it delighted her particularly if Lady Tressady came in during the interval.

Meanwhile they dined with many folk, and made preliminary acquaintance with the great ones of the land. Letty's vanity swelled within her as she read over the list of her engagements. Nevertheless, she often came home from her dinner-parties flat and disappointed. She did not feel that she made way; and she found herself constantly watching the triumphs of other women with annoyance or perplexity. What was wrong with her? Her dress was irreproachable, and, stirred by this great roaring world, she recalled for it the little airs and graces she had almost ceased to spend on George. But she con·stantly found herself, as she thought, neglected ; while the slightest word or look of some happy person in a simple gown, near by, had power to bring about her that flatter-ing crowd of talkers and of courtiers for which Letty pined.

The Maxwells called very early on the newly-wedded pair, and left an invitation to dinner with their cards. But, to Letty's chagrin, she and George were already en-gaged for the evening named, and when they duly pre-sented themselves at St. James's Square on a Sunday afternoon, it was to find that the Maxwells were in the country. Once or twice in some crowded room Letty or George had a few hurried words with Lady Maxwell, and Marcella would try to plan a meeting. But what with her engagements and theirs, nothing that she suggested could be done.

'Ah! well, after Whitsuntide,' she said, smiling, to Letty one evening that they had interchanged a few words of polite regret on the stairs at some official party. 'I will write to you in the country, if I may. Ferth Place, is it not?'

'No,' said Letty, with easy dignity; 'we shall not be at home,—not at first, at any rate. We are going for two or three days to Mrs. Allison, at Castle Luton.'

'Are you? You will have a pleasant time. Such a glorious old house!'

And Lady Maxwell swept on ; not so fast, however, but that she found time to have a few words of Parliamentary chat with Tressady on the landing.

Letty made her little speech about Castle Luton with a delightful sense of playing the rare and favoured part. Nothing in her London career, so far, had pleased her so much as Mrs. Allison's call and Mrs. Allison's invitation.

For, although on the few occasions when she had seen this gentle, white-haired lady, Letty had never felt for one moment at ease with her, still, there could be no question that Mrs. Allison was, socially, distinction itself. She had a following among all parties. For, although she was Fontenoy's friend and inspirer, a strong Churchwoman, and a great aristocrat, she had that delicate, long-descended charm which shuts the lions' mouths, and makes it possible for certain women to rule in any company. Even those who were most convinced that the Mrs. Allisons of this world are the chief obstacles in the path of progress, deliberated when they were asked to Castle Luton, and fell—protesting. And for a certain world, high-born, cultivated, and virtuous, she was almost a figure of legend, so widespread was the feeling she inspired, and so many were the associations and recollections that clustered about her.

So that when her cards, those of her son Lord Ancoats, and a little accompanying note in thin French handwriting—Mrs. Allison had been brought up in Paris —arrived, Letty had a start of pleasure. 'To meet a few friends of mine'—that meant, of course, one of *the* parties. She supposed it was Lord Fontenoy's doing. He was said to ask whom he would to Castle Luton. Under the influence of this idea, at any rate, she bore herself towards her husband's chief at their next meeting with an effusion which made Fontenoy supremely uncomfortable.

The week before Whitsuntide happened to be one of special annoyance for Tressady. His reports from Ferth were steadily more discouraging; his attempts to sell his land made no way; and he saw plainly that, if he was to keep their London life going, to provide for Shapetsky's claims, and to give Letty what she wanted for renovations at Ferth, he would have to sell some of the very small list of good securities left him by his father. Most young men in his place, perhaps, would have taken such a thing with indifference; he brooded over it. 'I am beginning to spend my capital as income,' he said to himself. 'The strike will be on in July; next half-year I shall get almost nothing from the pits; rents won't come to much; Letty wants all kinds of things. How long will it be before I, too, am in debt, like my mother, borrowing from this person and that?'

Then he would make stern resolutions of economy, only to be baffled by Letty's determination to have everything that other people had; above all, not to allow her own life to be stinted because he had so foolishly adopted his mother's debts. She said little; or said it with smiles and a bridal standing on her rights not to be answered. But her persistence in a particular kind of claim, and her new refusal to be taken into his confidence and made the partner of his anxieties, raised a miserable feeling in his mind as the weeks went on.

'No!' she said to herself, all the time resenting bitterly what had happened at Ferth; 'if I let him talk to me about it, I shall be giving in, and letting *her* trample on me! If George will be so weak, he must find the money somehow. Of course he can! I am not in the *least* extravagant. I am only doing what everybody expects me to do.'

Meanwhile this state of things did not make Lady Tressady any more welcome in Brook Street, and there were symptoms of grievances and quarrels of another sort. Lady Tressady heard that the young couple had already given one or two tiny dinner-parties, and to none of them had she been invited. One day that George had been obliged to go to Warwick Square to consult her on business, he was suddenly overwhelmed with reproaches on this point.

'I suppose Letty thinks I should spoil her parties!

She is ashamed of me, perhaps '—Lady Tressady gave an angry laugh. 'Oh! very well; but I should like you and her to understand, George, that I have been a good deal more admired in my time than ever Letty need expect to be!'

And George's mother, in a surprising yellow teagown, threw herself back on her chair, bridling with wrath and emotion. George declared, with good temper, that he and Letty were well aware of his mother's triumphs; whereupon Lady Tressady, becoming tearful, said she knew it wasn't a pretty thing to say—of course it wasn't—but if one was treated unkindly by one's only son and his wife, what could one do but assert oneself?

George soothed her as best he could, and on his return home said tentatively to Letty, that he believed it would please his mother if they were to ask her to a small impromptu dinner of Parliamentary friends which they were planning for the following Friday.

'George!' exclaimed Letty, her eyes gleaming, 'we can't ask her! I don't want to say anything disagreeable, but you must see that people don't like her—her dress is so *extraordinary*, and her manners—it sets people against the house. I do think it's too bad that——'

She turned aside with a sudden sob. George kissed her, and sympathised with her; for he himself was never at ease now for an instant while his mother was in the room. But the widening of the breach which Letty's refusal brought about only made his own position between the two women the more disagreeable to a man whose ideal of a home was that it should be a place of perpetual soothing and amusement.

On the very morning of their departure for Castle Luton matters reached a small crisis. Letty, tired with some festivity of the night before, took her breakfast in bed; and George, going upstairs toward the middle of the morning to make some arrangement with her for the journey, found her just come down, and walking up and down the drawing-room, her pale pink dress sweeping the floor, her hands clasped behind her. She was very pale, and her small lips were tightly drawn.

He looked at her with astonishment.

'What is the matter, darling?'

'Oh! nothing,' said Letty, trying to speak with sarcasm. 'Nothing at all. I have only just been listening to an account of the way in which your mother speaks of me to her friends. I ought to be flattered, of course, that she notices me at all! But I think I shall have to ask you to *request* her to put off her visit to Ferth a little. It could hardly give either of us much enjoyment.'

George first pulled his moustaches, then tried, as usual, to banter or kiss her into composure. Above all, he desired not to know what Lady Tressady had said. But Letty was determined he should know. 'She was heard'—she began passionately, holding him at arm's-length—'she was heard saying to a *whole roomful* of people yesterday, that I was "pretty, of course—rather pretty—but *so* second rate—and so provincial! It was such a pity dear George had not waited till he had been a few months in London. Still, of course one could only make the best of it!"'

Letty mimicked her mother-in-law's drawling voice, two red spots burning on either cheek the while, and her little fingers gripping George's arm.

'I don't believe she ever said such things. Who told you so?' said George, stiffening, his arm dropping from her waist.

Letty tossed her head.

'Never mind! I *ought* to know, and it doesn't really matter how I know. She *did* say them.'

'Yes, it does matter,' said George quickly, walking away to the other side of the room. 'Letty! if you would only send away that woman Grier, you can't think how much happier we should both be.'

Letty stood still, opening her blue eyes wide.

'You want me—to get rid—of Grier,' she said, 'my own particular pet maid? And why—please?'

George had the courage to stick to his point, and the result was a heated and angry scene—their first real quarrel—which ended in Letty's rushing upstairs in tears, and declaring she would go *nowhere*. *He* might go to Castle Luton, if he pleased; she was far too agitated and exhausted to face a houseful of strangers.

The inevitable reconciliation, with its usual accompaniments of headache and eau de cologne, took time, and they only just completed their preparations and caught their appointed train.

Meanwhile the storm of the day had taken all savour from Letty's expectations, and made George feel the whole business an effort and a weariness. Letty sat pale and silent in her corner, devoured with regrets that she had not put on a thicker veil to hide the ravages of the morning; while George turned over the pages of a political biography, and could not prevent his mind from falling back again and again into dark places of dread and depression.

'You are my earliest guests,' said Mrs. Allison, as she placed a chair for Letty beside herself, on the lawn at Castle Luton. 'Except, indeed, that Lady Maxwell and her little boy are here somewhere, roaming about. But none of our other friends could get down till later. I am glad we shall have a little quiet time before they come.'

'Lady Maxwell!' said Letty. 'I had no idea they were coming. Oh, what a lovely day! and how beautiful

it all is!' she cried, as she sat down and looked round
her. The colour came back into her cheeks. She forgot
her determination to keep her veil down, and raised it
eagerly.

Mrs. Allison smiled.

'We never look so well as in May—the river is so
full, and the swans are so white. Ah! I see Edgar has
already taken Sir George to make friends with them.'

And Letty, looking across the broad green lawn, saw
the flash of a brimming river and a cluster of white swans,
beside which stood her husband and a young man in a
serge suit, who was feeding the swans with bread—Lord
Ancoats, no doubt, the happy owner of all this splendour.
To the left of their figures rose a stone bridge with a high,
carved parapet, and beyond the river she saw green hills
and woods against a radiant sky. Then, to her right was
this wonderful yellowish pile of the old house.. She began
to admire and exclaim about it with a great energy and
effusion, trying hard to say the correct and cultivated
thing, and, in fact, repeating with a good deal of exact-
ness what she had heard said of it by others.

Her hostess listened to her praises with a gentle smile.
Gentleness, indeed, a rather sad gentleness, was the characteristic of Mrs. Allison. It seemed to make an atmosphere about her—her delicate blanched head and soft
face, her small figure, her plain black dress, her hands in
their white ruffles. Her friends called it saintliness. At
any rate, it set her apart, giving her a peculiar ethereal
dignity which made her formidable in society to many
persons who were not liable to shyness. Letty from the
beginning had felt her formidable.

Yet nothing could be kinder or simpler than her
manner. In response to Letty's enthusiasms she let herself be drawn at once into speaking of her own love for
the house, and on to pointing out its features.

'I am always telling these things to new-comers,' she said, smiling. 'And I am not clever enough to make variations. But I don't mind, somehow, how often I go through it. You see, this front is Tudor, and the south front is a hundred years later, and both of them, they say, are the finest of their kind. Isn't it wonderful that two men, a hundred years apart, should each have left such a noble thing behind him! One inspired the other. And then we—we poor moderns come after, and must cherish what they left us as we best can. It's a great responsibility, don't you think? to live in a beautiful house.'

'I am afraid I don't know much about it,' said Letty, laughing; 'we live in such a very ugly one.'

Mrs. Allison looked sympathetic.

'Oh! but then, ugly ones have character; or they are pretty inside, or the people one loves have lived in them. That would make any place a House Beautiful. Aren't you near Ferth?'

'Yes; and I am afraid you'll think me *dreadfully* dis-contented,' said Letty, with one of her little laughing airs; 'but there really isn't anything to make up in our barrack of a place. It's like a blackened brick set up on end at the top of a hill. And then the villages are so hideous.'

'Ah! I know that coal-country,' said Mrs. Allison, gravely—'and I know the people. Have you made friends with them yet?'

'We were only there for our honeymoon. George says that next month the whole place will be out on strike. So just now they hate us—they will hardly look at us in the street. But, of course, we shall give away things at Christmas.'

Mrs. Allison's lip twitched, and she shot a glance at the bride which betrayed, for all her gentleness, the woman of a large world and much converse with mankind. What a curious, hard little face was Lady Tressady's under the outer softness of line and hue, and what an amazing costume ! Mrs. Allison had no quarrel with beautiful gowns, but the elaboration, or, as one might say, the research of Letty's dress struck her unpleasantly. The time that it must have taken to think out !

Aloud she said :

' Ah ! the strike. Yes, I fear it is inevitable. Ancoats has some property not very far from you, and we get reports. Poor fellows ! if it weren't for the wretched agitators who mislead them—but there, we mustn't talk of these things. I see Lady Maxwell coming.'

And Mrs. Allison waved her hand to a tall figure in white with a child beside it that had just emerged on the far distance of the lawn.

' Is Lord Maxwell here, too ? ' asked Letty.

' He is coming later. It seems strange, perhaps, that you should find them here this Sunday, for Lord Fontenoy comes to morrow, and the great fight will be on so soon. But when I found that they were free, and that Maxwell would like to come, I was only too glad. After all, rival politicians in England can still meet each other, even at a crisis. Besides, Maxwell is a relation of ours, and he was my boy's guardian—the kindest possible guardian. Politics apart, I have the greatest respect for him. And her too. Why is it always the best people in the world that do the most mischief ? '

At the mention of Lord Fontenoy it had been Letty's turn to throw a quick side look at Mrs. Allison. But the name was spoken in the quietest and most natural way ; and yet, if one analysed the tone, in a way that did imply something exceptional, which, however, all the world knew, or might know.

' Is Lady Maxwell an old friend of yours, too ? ' asked

Letty, longing to pursue the subject, and vexed to see how fast the mother and child were approaching.

'Only since her marriage. To see her and Maxwell together is really a poem. If only she wouldn't identify herself so hotly, dear woman! with everything he does and wishes in politics. There is no getting her to hear a word of reason. She is another Maxwell in petticoats. And it always seems to me so unfair. Maxwell without beauty and without petticoats is quite enough to fight! Look at that little fellow with his flowers!—such an oddity of a child!'

Then she raised her voice.

'My dear, what a ramble you must have made. Come and have a shady chair and some tea.'

For answer Marcella, laughing, held up a glorious bunch of cuckoo-pint and marsh marigold, while little Hallin at her skirts waved another trophy of almost equal size. The mother's dark face was flushed with exercise and pleasure. As she moved over the grass, the long folds of a white dress falling about her, the flowers in her hand, the child beside her, she made a vision of beauty lovely in itself and lovely in all that it suggested. Frank joy and strength, happiness, purity of heart—these entered with her. One could almost see their dim heavenly shapes in the air about her.

Neither Letty nor Mrs. Allison could take their eyes from her. Perhaps she knew it. But if she did, it made no difference to her perfect ease of bearing. She greeted Letty kindly.

'You didn't expect to see me here, did you, Lady Tressady? But it is the unexpected that happens.',

Then she put her hand on Mrs. Allison's shoulder, bending her height to her small hostess.

'What a day, and what a place! Hallin and I have been over hill and dale. But he is getting such a botanist,

the little monkey! He will hardly forgive me because I
forgot one of the flowers we found out yesterday in his
botany book.'

'She said it was " Robin-run-in-the-'edge," and it
isn't—it's 'edge mustard,' said Hallin, severely, holding
up a little feathery stalk.

Mrs. Allison shook her head, endeavouring to suit her
: , ` the gravity of the offence.

'Mother must learn her lessons better, mustn't she?
Go and shake hands, little man, with Lady Tressady.'

Hallin went gravely to do as he was told. Then he
stood on one foot, and looked Letty over with a considering eye.

'Are you going to a party?' he said suddenly, putting
out a small and grimy finger, and pointing to her dress.

'Hallin! come here and have your tea,' said his mother,
hastily. Then she turned to Letty with the smile that
had so often won Maxwell a friend.

'I am sorry to say that he has a rooted objection to
anything that isn't rags in the way of clothes. He
entirely declined to take me across the river till I had
rolled up my lace cloak and put it in a bush. And he
won't really be friends with me again till we have both
got back to the scarecrow garments we wear at home.'

'Oh! children are so much happier when they are
dirty,' said Letty, graciously, pleased to feel herself on
these easy terms with her two companions. 'What
beautiful flowers he has! and what an astonishing little
botanist he seems to be!'

And she seated herself beside Hallin, using all her
blandishments to make friends with him, which, however,
did not prove to be an easy matter. For when she praised
his flowers, Hallin only said, with his mouth full: 'Oh! but
mammy's bunch is *never* so much bigger;' and when she
offered him cake, the child would sturdily put the cake

away, and hold it and her at arm's length till his mute
look across the table had won his mother's nod of per-
mission.

Letty at last thought him an odd, ill-mannered child,
and gave up courting him, greatly to Hallin's satisfaction.
He edged closer and closer to his mother, established
himself finally in her pocket, and browsed on all the
good things with which Mrs. Allison provided him, undisturbed.

'How late they are!' said Marcella, looking at her
watch. 'Tell me the names again, dear lady'—she bent
forward, and laid her hand affectionately on Mrs. Allison's
knee. 'Your parties are always a work of art.'

Mrs. Allison flushed a little, as though she liked the
compliment, and ran laughingly through the names.

'Lord and Lady Maxwell.'

'Ah!' said Marcella, 'the least said about them the
soonest mended. Go on.'

'Lord and Lady Cathedine.'

Marcella made a face.

'Poor little thing! I always think of the remark about
the Queen in " Alice in Wonderland." " A little kindness,
and putting her hair in curl-papers, would do wonders
for her." She is so limp and thin and melancholy. As
for him—isn't there a race or a prize-fight we can send
him to?'

Mrs. Allison tapped her lightly on the lips.

'I won't go on unless my guests are taken prettily.'

Marcella kissed the delicate wrinkled hand.

'I'll be good. What do you keep such an air here for?
It gets into one's head?'

Letty Tressady, indeed, was looking on with a feeling
of astonishment. These merry, childlike airs had absolutely no place in her conception of Lady Maxwell. Nor
could she know that Mrs. Allison was one of the very few

people in the world to whom Marcella was ever drawn to show them.

'Sir Philip Wentworth,' pursued Mrs. Allison, smiling. 'Say anything malicious about him, if you can!'

'Don't provoke me. What a mercy I brought a volume of "Indian Studies" in my bag! I will go up early, before dinner, and finish them.'

'Then there is Madeleine Penley, and Elizabeth Kent.'

A quick involuntary expression crossed Marcella's face. Then she drew herself up with dignity, and crossed her hands primly on her lap.

'Let me understand. Are you going to protect me from Lady Kent this time? Because, last time you threw me to the wolves in the most dastardly way.'

Mrs. Allison laughed out.

'On the contrary, we all enjoyed your skirmish with her in November so much, we shall do our best to provoke another in May.'

Marcella shook her head.

'I haven't the energy to quarrel with a fly. And as for Aldous—please warn his lady at dinner that he may go to sleep upon her shoulder!'

'You poor thing!'—Mrs. Allison put out a sympathetic hand. 'Are you so tired? Why will you turn the world upside down?'

Marcella took the hand lightly in both hers.

'Why will you fight reform?'

And the eyes of the two women met, not without a sudden grave passion. Then Marcella dropped the hand, and said, smiling:

'Castle Luton isn't full yet. Who else?'

'Oh! some young folk—Charlie Naseby.'

'A nice boy—a very nice boy—not half such a cox-comb as he looks. Then the Levens—I know the Levens

P

are coming, for Betty told me that she got out of two other engagements as soon as you asked her.'

'Oh! and, by the way, Mr. Watton—Harding Watton,' said Mrs. Allison, turning slightly towards Lady Tressady.

The exclamation on Lady Maxwell's lips was checked by something she saw on her hostess's face, and Letty eagerly struck in:

'Harding coming?—my cousin? I am so glad. I suppose I oughtn't to say it, but he is such a *clever*, such an *agreeable* creature. But you know the Wattons, don't you, Lady Maxwell?'

Marcella was busying herself with Hallin's tea.

'I know Edward Watton,' she said, turning her beautiful clear look on Letty. 'He is a real friend of mine.'

'Oh! but Harding is *much* the cleverer,' said Letty. And pleased both to find the ball of talk in her hands, and to have the chance of glorifying a relation in this world of people so much bigger than herself, she plunged into an extravagant account—all adjectives and superlatives—of Harding Watton's charms and abilities, to which Lady Maxwell listened in silence.

'Tactless!' thought Mrs. Allison, with vexation, but she did not know how to stop the stream. In truth, since she had given Lord Fontenoy leave to invite Harding Watton she had had time to forget the invitation, and she was sorry now to think of his housing with the Maxwells. For Watton had been recently Lord Fontenoy's henchman and agent in a newspaper attack upon the Bill, and upon Maxwell personally, that even Mrs. Allison had thought violent and unfair. Well, it was not her fault. But Lady Tressady ought to have better information and better sense than to be chattering like this. She was just about to interpose, when Marcella held up her hand.

'I hear the carriages!'

The hostess hastened towards the house, and Marcella followed her, with Hallin at her skirts. Letty looked after Lady Maxwell with the same mixture of admiration and jealous envy she had felt several times before. 'I don't feel that I shall get on with her,' she said to herself. impatiently. 'But I don't think I want to. George took her measure at once.'

Part of this reflection, however, was not true. Letty's ambition would have been very glad to 'get on' with Marcella Maxwell.

Just as his wife was ready for dinner, and Grier had disappeared, George entered Letty's room. She was standing before a tall glass, putting the last touches to her dress—smoothing here, pinning there, turning to this side and to that. George, unseen himself, stood and watched her—her alternate looks of anxiety and satisfaction, her grace, the shimmering folds of the magnificent wedding-dress in which she had adorned herself.

He, however, was neither happy nor gay. But he had come in feeling that he must make an effort—many efforts, if their young married life was to be brought back to that level of ease and pleasure which he had once taken for granted, and which now seemed so hard to maintain. If that ease and pleasure were ultimately to fail him, what should he do? He shrank impatiently from the idea. Then he would scoff at himself. How often had he read and heard that the first year of marriage is the most difficult! Of course it must be so. Two individualities cannot fuse without turmoil, without heat. Let him only make his effort.

So he walked up to her and caught her in his arms.

'Oh, George!—my hair!—and my flowers!'

'Never mind,' he said, almost with roughness. 'Put your head there. Say you hate the thought of our day, as I do! Say there shall never be one like it again! Promise me!'

She felt the beating of his heart beneath her cheek. But she stood silent. His appeal, his unwonted agitation, revived in her all the anger and irritation that had begun to prey upon her thoughts. It was all very well, but why were they so pinched and uncomfortable? Why must everybody—Mrs. Allison, Lady Maxwell, a hundred others—have more wealth, more scope, more consideration than she? It was partly his fault.

So she gradually drew herself away, pushing him softly with her small gloved hand.

'I am sure I hate quarrelling,' she said. 'But there! Oh, George! don't let's talk of it any more! And look what you have done to my poor hair. You dear, naughty boy!'

But though she called him 'Dear,' she frowned as she took off her gloves that she might mend what he had done.

George thrust his hands into his pockets; walked to the window, and waited. As he descended the great stairs in her wake he wished Castle Luton and its guests at the deuce. What pleasure was to be got out of grimacing and posing at these country-house parties? And now, according to Letty, the Maxwells were here. A great *gêne* for everybody!

CHAPTER XI

THAT lady sitting by Sir George? What! Lady Maxwell? No—the other side? Oh! that's Lady Leven. Don't you know her? She's tremendous fun!'

And the dark-eyed, rosy-cheeked young man who was sitting beside Letty nodded and smiled across the table to Betty Leven, merely by way of reminding her of his existence. They had greeted before dinner—a greeting of comrades.

Then he turned back, with sudden decorum, to this Lady Tressady, whom he had been commissioned to take in to dinner. 'Quite pretty, but rather—well, ordinary!' he said to himself, with a critical coolness bred of much familiarity with the best things of Vanity Fair. He had been Ancoats's friend at Cambridge, and was now disporting himself in the Guards, but still more—as Letty of course assumed—in the heart of the English well-born world. She knew that he was Lord Naseby, and that some day he would be a marquis. A halo, therefore, shone about him. At the same time, she had a long experience of young men, and, if she flattered him, it was only indirectly, by a sort of teasing aggression that did not allow him to take his attention from her.

'I declare you are better than any peerage!' she said to him presently, when he had given her a short biography, first of Lord Cathedine, who was sitting opposite, then of various other members of the company.

'I should like to tie you to my fan when I go out to dinner.'

'Would you?' said the young man, drily. 'Oh! you will soon know all you want to know.'

'How are poor little people from Yorkshire to find their way about in this big world? You are all so dreadfully absorbed in each other. In the first place, you all marry each other.'

'Do we?—though I don't quite understand who "we" means. Well, one must marry somebody, I suppose, and cousins are less trouble than other people.'

Involuntarily, the young man's eyes travelled along the table to a fair girl on the opposite side, dazzlingly dressed in black. She was wielding a large fan of black feathers, which threw both hair and complexion into amazing relief; and she seemed to be amusing herself in a nervous, spasmodic way with Sir Frank Leven. Letty noticed his glance.

'Oh! you have not earned your testimonial yet, not by any manner of means,' she said. 'That is Lady Madeleine Penley, isn't it? Is she a relation of Mrs. Allison's?'

'She is a cousin. That is her mother, Lady Kent, sitting beside poor Ancoats. Such an old character! By the end of dinner she will have got to the bottom of Ancoats, or know the reason why.'

'.Is Lord Ancoats such a mystery?' said Letty, running an inquisitive eye over the black front, sharp nose, and gorgeously bejewelled neck of a somewhat noisy and forbidding old lady sitting on the right hand of the host.

Young Naseby's expression in answer rather piqued her. There was a quick flash of something that was instantly suppressed, and the youth said, composedly,

'Oh! we are all mysteries for Lady Kent.'

But Letty noticed that his eyes strayed back to Lord Ancoats, and then again to Lady Madeleine. He seemed to be observing them, and Letty's sharpness at once took the hint. No doubt the handsome, large-featured girl was here to be 'looked at.' Probably a good many maidens would be passed in review before this young Sultan made his choice ! By the way, he must be a good deal older than George had imagined. Clearly he left college some time ago. What a curious face he had—a small, crumpled face, with very prominent blue eyes ; curly hair of a reddish colour, piled high, as though for effect, above his white brow ; together with a sharp chin and pointed moustache, which gave him the air of an old French portrait. He was short in stature, but at the same time agile and strongly built. He wore one or two fine old rings, which drew attention to the delicacy of his hands ; and his manner struck her as at once morose and excitable. Letty regarded him with involuntary respect as the son of Mrs. Allison—much more as the master of Castle Luton and fifty thousand a year. But if he had not been the master of Castle Luton she would have probably thought, and said, that he had a disagreeable Bohemian air.

'Haven't you really made acquaintance with Lady Kent ? ' said Lord Naseby, returning to the charge—his laziness was somewhat at a loss for conversation. ' I should have thought she was the person one could least escape knowing in the three kingdoms.'

' I have seen her, of course,' said Letty, lightly, though, alas ! untruly. ' But I am afraid you can hardly realise that I have only been three short seasons in London— two with an old aunt, who never goes out, in Cavendish Square, poor dull old dear ! and another with Mrs. Watton, of Malford.'

Oh ! with Mrs. Watton, of Malford,' said Lord Naseby, vaguely. Then he became suddenly aware that Lady Leven, on the other side of the table, was beckoning to him.

He leant across, and they exchanged a merry war of words about something of which Letty knew nothing.

Letty, rather incensed, thought him a puppy, drew herself up, and looked round at the ex-Governor beside her. She saw a fine head, the worn yellow face and whitened hair of a man who has suffered under a hot climate, and an agreeable, though somewhat courtly, smile. Sir Philip Wentworth was not troubled with the boyish fastidious-ness of Lord Naseby. He perceived merely that a pretty young woman wished to make friends with him, and met her wish at once. Moreover, he identified her as the wife of that ' promising and well-informed fellow, Tressady,' with whom he had first made friends in India, and had now— just before dinner—renewed acquaintance in the most cordial fashion.

He talked graciously to the wife, then, of Tressady's abilities and Tressady's career. Letty at first liked it. Then she was seized with a curious sense of discom-fort.

Her eyes wandered towards the head of the table, where George was talking—why! actually talking earn-estly, and as though he were enjoying himself, to Lady Maxwell, whose noble head and neck, rising from a silver-white dress, challenged a great Genoese Vandyck of a Marchesa Balbi which was hanging just behind her, and challenged it victoriously.

So other people thought and said these things of George? Letty was for a moment sharply conscious that they had not occupied much place in her mind since her marriage, or, for the matter of that, since her engage-ment. She had taken it for granted that he was ' distin-guished '—that was part of the bargain. Only, she never seemed as yet to have had either time or thought to give to those parts and elements in his life which led people to talk of him as this old Indian was doing.

Curtains, carpets, gowns, cabinets ; additions to Ferth ; her own effect in society ; how to keep Lady Tressady in her place—of all these things she had thought, and thought much. But George's honourable ambitions, the esteem in which he was held, the place he was to make for himself in the world of men—in thinking of *these* her mind was all stiff and unpractised. She was conscious first of a moral prick, then of a certain irritation with other people.

Yet she could not help watching George wistfully. He looked tired and pale, in spite of the animation of his talk. Well ! no doubt she looked pale too. Some of the words and phrases of their quarrel flashed across her. In this beautiful room, with its famous pictures and its historical associations, amid this accumulated art and wealth, the whole thing was peculiarly odious to remember. Under the eyes of Vandyck's Marchesa one would have liked to think of oneself as always dignified and refined, always elegant and calm.

Then Letty had a revulsion, and laughed at herself.

'As if these people didn't have tempers, and quarrel about money ! Of course they do ! And if they don't— well, we all know how easy it is to be amiable on fifty thousand a year.'

After dinner Mrs. Allison led the way to the 'Green Drawing-room.' This room, hung with Gainsborough portraits, was one of the sights of the house, and to-night Marcella Maxwell especially looked round her on entering it, with enchantment.

'You happy people !' she said to Mrs. Allison. 'I never come into this room without anxiously asking myself whether I am fit to make one of the company. I look at my dress, or I am doubtful about my manners, or I wish some one had taught me to dance the minuet !'

'Yes,' said Betty Leven, running up to a vast picture,

a life-size family group, which covered the greater part of
the farther wall of the room. 'What a vulgar, insignificant chit one feels oneself without cap or powder!—
without those ruffles, or those tippets, or those quilted
petticoats! Mrs. Allison, *may* my maid come down to-
morrow while we are at dinner and take the pattern of
those ruffles? No—no! she sha'n't! Sacrilege! You
pretty thing!' she said, addressing a figure—the figure of
a girl in white with thin virginal arms and bust, who
seemed to be coming out of the picture, almost to be
already out of it and in the room. 'Come and talk to me.
Don't think any more of your father and mother there.
You have been curtseying to them for a hundred years;
and they are rather dull, stupid people, after all. Come
and tell us secrets. Tell us what you have seen in
this room—all the foolish people making love, and the
sad people saying good-bye.'

Betty was kneeling on a carved chair, her pretty arms
leaning on the back of it, her eyes fixed half in laughter,
half in sentiment, on the figure in the picture.

Lady Maxwell suddenly moved closer to her, and
Letty heard her say in a low voice, as she put her hand
on Lady Leven's arm:

'Don't, Betty! *don't!* It was in this room he proposed
to her, and it was in this room he said good-bye. Maxwell has often told me. I believe, she never comes in here
alone—only for ceremony and when there is a crowd.'

A look of consternation crossed Lady Leven's lively
little face. She glanced shyly towards Mrs. Allison.
That lady had moved hastily away from the group in
front of the picture. She was sitting by herself, looking
straight before her, with a certain stiffness, her thin hands
crossed on her knee. Betty impetuously went towards
her, and was soon sitting on a stool beside her, chattering
to her and amusing her.

Meanwhile Marcella invited Lady Tressady to come and sit with her on a sofa beneath the great picture.

Letty followed her, settled her satin skirts in their most graceful folds, put one little foot on a Louis Quinze footstool which seemed to invite it, and then began to inform herself about the house and the family.

At the beginning of their talk it was clear that Lady Maxwell wished to ingratiate herself. A friendly observer would have thought that she was trying to make a stranger feel more at ease in this house and circle, where she herself was a familiar guest. Betty Leven, catching sight of the pair from the other side of the room, said to herself, with inward amusement, that Marcella was 'realising the wife.'

At any rate, for some time Lady Maxwell talked with sympathy, with effusion even, to her companion. In the first place she told her the story of their hostess.

Thirty years before, Mrs. Allison, the daughter and heiress of a Leicestershire squire, had married Henry Allison, old Lord Ancoats's second son, a young captain in the Guards. They enjoyed three years of life together; then the chances of a soldier's career, as interpreted by two high-minded people, took Henry Allison out to an obscure African coast, to fight one of the innumerable 'little wars' of his country. He fell, struck by a spear, in a single-file march through some nameless swamp; and a few days afterwards the words of a Foreign Office telegram broke a pining woman's heart.

Old Lord Ancoats's death, which followed within a month or two, was hastened by the shock of his son's loss; and before the year was out the eldest son, who was sickly and unmarried, also died, and Mrs. Allison's boy, a child of two, became the owner of Castle Luton. The mother saw herself called upon to fight down her grief, to relinquish the quasi-religious life she had entered upon,

and instead to take her boy to the kingdom he was to
rule, and bring him up there.

'And for twenty-two years she has lived a wonderful
life here,' said Marcella; 'she has been practically the
queen of a whole countryside, doing whatever she pleased,
the mother and friend and saint of everybody. It has
been all very paternal and beautiful, and—abominably
Tory and tyrannous! Many people, I suppose, think it
perfect. Perhaps I don't. But then, I know very well
I can't possibly disagree with her a tenth part as strongly
as she disagrees with me.'

'Oh! but she admires you so much,' cried Letty with
effusion; 'she thinks you mean so nobly!'

Marcella opened her eyes, involuntarily wondering
a little what Lady Tressady might know about it.

'Oh! we don't hate each other,' she said, rather drily,
'in spite of politics. And my husband was Ancoats's
guardian.'

'Dear me!' said Letty. 'I should think it wasn't
easy to be guardian to fifty thousand a year.'

Marcella did not answer—did not, indeed, hear. Her
look had stolen across to Mrs. Allison—a sad, affectionate
look, in no way meant for Lady Tressady. But Letty
noticed it.

'I suppose she adores him,' she said.

Marcella sighed.

'There was never anything like it. It frightens one
to see.'

'And that, of course, is why she won't marry Lord
Fontenoy?'

Marcella started, and drew away from her companion.

'I don't know,' she said stiffly; 'and I am sure that
no one ever dared to ask her.'

'Oh! but of course it's what everyone says,' said
Letty, gay and unabashed. 'That's what makes it so

exciting to come here, when one knows Lord Fontenoy so very well.'

Marcella met this remark with a discouraging silence.

Letty, however, was determined this time to make her impression. She plunged into a lively and often audacious gossip about every person in the room in turn, asking a number of intimate or impertinent questions, and yet very seldom waiting for Marcella's reply, so anxious was she to show off her own information and make her own comments. She let Marcella understand that she suspected a great deal, in the matter of that handsome Lady Madeleine. It was *immensely* interesting, of course ; but wasn't Lord Ancoats a trifle wild?—she bent over and whispered in Marcella's ear ; was it likely that he would settle himself so soon ?—didn't one hear sad tales of his theatrical friends and the rest ? And what could one expect ! As if a young man in such a position was not certain to have his fling ! And his mother would have to put up with it. After all, men quieted down at last. Look at Lord Cathedine !

And with an air of boundless knowledge she touched upon the incidents of Lord Cathedine's career, hashing up, with skilful deductions of her own, all that Lord Naseby had said or hinted to her at dinner. Poor Lady Cathedine ! didn't she look a walking skeleton, with her strange, melancholy face, and every bone showing? Well, who could wonder ! And when one thought of their money difficulties, too ! '

Lady Tressady lifted her white shoulders in compassion.

By this time Marcella's black eyes were wandering insistently round the room, searching for means of escape. Betty, far away, noticed her air, and concluded that the · ' realisation ' was making rapid, too rapid progress. Presently, with a smiling shake of her little head, she left her own seat and went to her friend's assistance.

At the same moment Mrs. Allison, driven by her conscience as a hostess, got up for the purpose of introducing Lady Tressady to a lady in grey who had been sitting quiet, and, as Mrs. Allison feared, lonely, in a corner, looking over some photographs. Marcella, who had also risen, put out a hand to Betty, and the two moved away together.

They stopped on the threshold of a large window at the side of the room, which stood wide-open to the night. Outside, beyond a broad flight of steps, stretched a formal Dutch garden. Its numberless small beds, forming stiff scrolls and circles on a ground of white gravel, lay in bright moonlight. Even the colours of the hyacinths and tulips with which they were planted could be seen, and the strong scent from them filled the still air. At the far end of this flat-patterned place a group of tall cypress and ilex, black against the sky, struck a note of Italy and the South ; while, through the yew hedges which closed in the little garden, broad archways pierced at intervals revealed far breadths of silvery English lawn and the distant gleam of the river.

'Well, my dear,' said Betty, laughing, and slipping her arm through Marcella's as they stood in the opening of the window, 'I see you have been doing your duty for once. Let me pat you on the back. All the more that I gather you are not exactly enchanted with Lady Tressady. You really should keep your face in order. From the other end of the room I know exactly what you think of the person you are talking to.'

'Do you ? ' said Marcella, penitently. 'I wish you didn't.'

'Well you may wish it, for it doesn't help the political lady to get what she wants. However, I don't think that Lady Tressady has found out yet that

you don't like her. She isn't thin-skinned. If you had
looked like that when you were talking to me, I would
have paid you out somehow. What is the matter with
her?'

'Oh! I don't know,' said Marcella, impatiently,
raising her shoulders. 'But she jarred. I pined to
get away—I don't think I ever want to talk to her
again.'

'No,' said Betty, ruminating; 'I'll tell you what it is
—she isn't a gentleman! Don't interrupt me! I mean
exactly what I say—*she isn't a gentleman.* She would
do and say all the things that a nice man squirms at. I
always have the oddest fancy about that kind of person.
I see them as they must be at night—all the fine clothes
gone—just a little black soul scrawled between the bed-
clothes!'

'*You* to call me censorious!' said Marcella, laughing,
and pinching her friend's arm.

'My dear, as I have often before remarked to you, *I* am
not a great lady, with a political campaign to fight. If
you knew your business, you would make friends with the
mammon of unrighteousness in the shape of Lady
Tressadys. *I* may do what I please—I have only a
husband to manage!' and Betty's light voice dropped into
a sigh.

'Poor Betty!' said Marcella, patting her hand. 'Is
Frank as discontented as ever?'

'He told me yesterday he hated his existence, and
thought he would try whether the Serpentine would
drown him. I said I was agreeable, only he would never
achieve it without me. I should have to 'tice away the
police while he looked for the right spot. So he has
promised to take me into partnership, and it's all right
so far.'

Then Betty fell to sighing in earnest.

'It's all very well "chaffing," but I am a miserable woman. Frank says I have ruined his life; that it's all my ambition; that he might have made a decent country gentleman if I hadn't sown the seed of every vice in him by driving him into politics. Pleasant, isn't it, for a model wife like me?'

'You'll have to let him give it up,' said Marcella, smiling; 'I don't believe he'll ever reconcile himself to the grind and the town life.'

Betty clenched her small hands.

'My dear! I never promised to marry a sporting boor, and I can't yet make up my mind to sink to it. Don't let's talk of it! I only hope he'll vote straight in the next few months. But the thought of being kept through August drives him desperate already. Ah! here they are—plagues of the human race!'—and she waved an accusing hand towards the incoming stream of gentlemen. 'Now, I'll prophesy, and you watch. Lady Tressady will make two friends here—Harding Watton—oh! I forgot, he's her cousin!—and Lord Cathedine. Mark my words. By the way—' Betty caught Marcella's arm and spoke eagerly into her friend's ear. Her eyes meanwhile glanced over her shoulder towards Lady Madeleine and her mother, who were seated on the farther side of the room.

Marcella's look followed Betty's, but she showed no readiness to answer Betty's questions. When Letty had made her astonishing remarks on the subject of Madeleine Penley, Lady Maxwell had tried to stop her with a hauteur which would have abashed most women, though it had but small effect on the bride. And now, even to Betty, who was Madeleine Penley's friend, Marcella was not communicative; although when Betty was carried off by Lord Naseby, who came in search of her as soon as he entered the drawing-room, the elder woman stood for a moment by the window, watching the girl they had been talking of with a soft serious look.

But the softness passed. A slight incident disturbed it. For the spectator saw Lady Kent, who was sitting beside her daughter, raise a gigantic fan and beckon to Lord Ancoats. He came unwillingly, and she made some bantering remark. Lady Madeleine meanwhile was bending over a book of photographs, with a flushed cheek and a look of constraint. Ancoats stood near her for a moment uneasily, frowning and pulling at his moustache. Then with an abrupt word to Lady Kent, he turned away and threw himself on a sofa beside Lord Cathedine. Lady Madeleine bent lower over her book, her beautiful hair making a spot of fire in the room. Marcella caught the expression of her profile, and her own face took a look of pain. She would have liked to go instantly to the girl's side, with some tenderness, some caress. But that gorgon Lady Kent, now looking extremely fierce, was in the way, and moreover other young men had arrived to take the place Ancoats had apparently refused.

Meanwhile Letty saw the arrival of the gentlemen with delight. She had found but small entertainment in the lady to whom Mrs. Allison had introduced her. Miss Paston, the sister of Lord Ancoats's agent, was a pleasant-looking spinster of thirty-five in a Quakerish dress of grey silk. Her face bore witness that she was capable and refined. But Letty felt no desire whatever to explore capability and refinement. She had not come to Castle Luton to make herself agreeable to Miss Paston.

So the conversation languished. Letty yawned a little, and flourished her fan a great deal, till the appearance of the men brought back the flush to her cheek and

Q

animation to her eye. She drew herself up at once, hungry for notice and success. Mrs. Hawkins, the vicar's wife at Malford, would have been avenged could she have watched her old tyrant under these chastening circumstances.

Harding Watton crossed the room when he saw his cousin, and took the corner of the sofa beside her. Letty received him graciously, though she was perhaps disappointed that it was not Lord Ancoats or Lord Cathedine. Looking round before she gave herself to conversation with him, she saw that George was standing near the open window with Lord Maxwell and Sir Philip Wentworth, the ex-Governor. They were talking of India, and Sir Philip had his hand on George's arm.

'Yes, I saw Dalhousie go,' he said eagerly. 'I was only a lad of twenty, but I can't think of it now without a lump in my throat. When he limped on to the Hooghly landing-stage on his crutches we couldn't cheer him—I shall never forget that sudden silence! In eight years he had made a new India, and there we saw him—our little hero—dying of his work at forty-six before our eyes! . . . Well, I couldn't have imagined that a young man like you would have known or cared so much about that time. What a talk we have had! Thank you!'

And the veteran tightened his grip cordially for a moment on Tressady's arm, then dropped it and walked away.

Tressady threw his wife a bright glance, as though to ask her how she fared. Letty smiled graciously in reply, feeling a sudden softening pleasure in being so thought of. As her eyes met her husband's she saw Marcella Maxwell, who was still standing by the window, turn towards George and call to him. George moved forward with alacrity. Then he and Lady Maxwell slowly walked down the steps to the garden, and disappeared through one of the archways to the left.

'That great lady and George seem at last to have made friends,' said Harding Watton to Letty, in a laughing under-tone. 'I have no doubt she is trying to win him over. Well she may! Before the next few weeks are over the Government will be in a fix with this Bill; and not even their "beautiful lady" will help them out. Maxwell looks as glum as an owl to-night.'

Letty laughed. The situation pleased her vanity a good deal. The thought of Lady Maxwell humiliated and defeated—partly by George's means—was decidedly agreeable to her. Which would seem to show that she was, after all, more sensitive or more quick-eyed than Betty Leven had been ready to allow.

Meanwhile Marcella and George Tressady were strolling slowly towards the river, along a path that crossed the great lawns. In front of them the stretches of grass, bathed in silvery light and air, ran into far distances of shade under majestic trees just thickening to a June wealth of foliage. Below, these distant tree-masses made sharp capes and promontories on the white grass; above, their rounded tops rose dark against a blue, light-breathing sky. At one point the river pierced the blackness of the wood, and in the space thus made the spire of a noble church shot heavenward. Swans floated dimly along the stream and under the bridge. The air was fresh, but the rawness of spring was gone. It was the last week of May; the 'high midsummer pomps' were near—a heavenly prophecy in wood and field.

And not even Tressady's prejudice—which, indeed, was already vanishing—could fail to see in the beautiful woman beside him the fitting voice and spirit of such a scene.

Q 2

To-night he said to himself that one must needs believe her simple, in spite of report. During their companionship this evening she had shown him more and more plainly that she liked his society; her manner towards him, indeed, had by now a soft surrender and friendliness that no man could possibly have met with roughness, least of all a man young and ambitious. But at the same time he noticed again, as he had once noticed with anger, that she was curiously free from the usual feminine arts and wiles. After their long talk at dinner, indeed, he began, in spite of himself, to feel her not merely an intellectual comrade—that he had been conscious of from the first—but rather a most winning and attaching companion. It was a sentiment of friendly ease, that seemed to bring with it a great relief from tension. The sordid cares and frictions of the last few weeks, and the degrading memories of the day itself, alike ceased to wear him.

Yet all the time he said to himself, with inward amusement, that he must take care! They had not talked directly of the Bill at dinner, but they had talked round and about it incessantly. It was clear that the Maxwells were personally very anxious; and George knew well that the public position of the Ministry was daily becoming more difficult. There had been a marked cooling on the subject of the Bill among their own supporters; one or two London members originally pledged to it were even believed to be wavering; and this campaign lately started by Fontenoy and Watton against two of the leading clauses of the measure, in a London 'daily,' bought for the purpose, had been so far extremely damaging. The situation was threatening indeed, and Maxwell might well look harassed.

Yet Tressady had detected no bitterness in Lady Maxwell's mood. Her temper rather seemed to him very strenuous, very eager, and a little sad. Altogether, he had been touched, he knew not exactly why, by his conversation with her. 'We are going to win,' he said to himself, 'and she knows it.' Yet to think thus gave him, for the first time, no particular pleasure.

As they strolled along they talked a little of some of the topics that had been started at dinner, topics semi-political and semi-social, till suddenly Lady Maxwell said, with a change of voice:

'I heard some of your conversation with Sir Philip just now. How differently you talk when you talk of India!'.

'I wonder what that means,' said George, smiling. 'It means, at any rate, that when I am not talking of India, but of English labour, or the poor, you think I talk like a brute.' .

'I shouldn't put it like that,' she said quietly. 'But when you talk of India, and people like the Lawrences or Lord Dalhousie, then it is that one sees what you really admire—what stirs you—what makes you feel.'

'Well, ought I not to feel? Is there to be no gratitude towards the people that have made one's country?'

He looked down upon her gaily, perfectly conscious of his own tickled vanity. To be observed and analysed by such a critic was in itself flattery.

'That have made one's country?' she repeated, not without a touch of irony. Then suddenly she became silent.

George thrust his hands into his pockets and waited a little.

'Well?' he said presently. 'Well? I am waiting to hear you prove that the Dalhousies and the Lawrences have done nothing for the country, compared to—what shall we say?—some trade-union secretary whom you particularly admire.'

She laughed, but he did not immediately draw his answer. They had reached the river-bank and the steps of the little bridge. Marcella mounted the bridge and paused midway across it, hanging over the parapet. He followed her, and both stood gazing at the house. It rose from the grass like some fabric of yellowish ivory cut and scrolled and fretted by its Tudor architect, who had been also a goldsmith. There were lights like jewels in its latticed windows; the dark fulness of the trees, disposed by an artist-hand, enwrapped or fell away from it as the eye required; and on the dazzling lawns, crossed by soft bands of shadow, scattered forms moved up and down—women in trailing dresses, and black-coated men. There were occasional sallies of talk and laughter, and from the open window of the drawing-room came the notes of a violin.

'Brahms!' said Marcella with delight. 'Nothing but music and he could express this night—or the river—or the rising glow and bloom of everything.'

As she spoke George felt a quick gust of pleasure and romance sweep across him. It was as though senses that had been for long on the defensive, tired, or teased merely, by the world, gave way in a moment to joy and poetry. He looked from the face beside him to the pictured scene in which they stood—the soft air filled his lungs—what ailed him?—he only knew that after many weeks he was, somehow, happy and buoyant again!

Lady Maxwell, however, soon forgot the music and the moonlight.

'That have made one's country?' she repeated, pausing on the words. 'And of course that house appeals to you in the same way? Famous people have lived in it—people who belong to history. But for *me*, the real making of one's country is done out of sight, in garrets and workshops and coalpits, by people who die every minute—forgotten—swept into heaps like autumn leaves, their lives mere soil and foothold for the generation that comes after them. All yesterday morning, for instance, I spent trying to feed a woman I know. She is a shirtmaker; she has four children, and her husband is a docker out of work. She had sewed herself sick and blind. She couldn't eat, and she couldn't sleep. But she had kept the children alive—and the man. Her life will flicker out in a month or two; but the children's lives will have taken root, and the man will be eating and earning again. What use would your Dalhousies and Lawrences be to England without her and the hundreds of thousands like her?'

'And yet it is you,' cried George, unable to forbear the chance she gave him, 'who would take away from this very woman the power of feeding her children and saving her husband—who would spoil all the lives in the clumsy attempt to mend one of them. How can you quote me such an instance! It amazes me.'

'Not at all. I have only to use my instance for another purpose, in another way. You are thinking of the Bill, of course? But all we do is to say to some of these victims, " Your sacrifice, as it stands, is *too* costly ; the State in its own interest cannot go on exacting or allowing it. We will help you to serve the community in ways that shall exhaust and wound it less." '

' And as a first step, drive you all comfortably into the workhouse ! ' said George. ' Don't omit that.'

'Many individuals must suffer,' she said steadily. ' But there will be friends to help—friends that will strain every nerve to help.'

All her heart showed itself in voice and emphasis. Almost for the first time in their evening's talk her natural passionateness came to sight—the Southern, impulsive temper, that so often made people laugh at or dislike her.

Under the lace shawl she had thrown round her on coming
out he saw the quick rise and fall of the breast, the
nervous clasp of the hands lying on the stonework of the
bridge.   These were her prophetess airs again.   To night
they still amused him, but in a gentler and more friendly
way.

'And so, according to your own account, you will protect your tailoress and unmake your country.   I am sorry
for your dilemma,' he said, laughing.

'Ah! well'—she shrugged her shoulders with a sigh—
'don't let's talk of it.   It's all too pressing—and sore—
and hot.   And to think of the weeks that are just coming
on!'

George, hanging over the parapet beside her, felt reply
a little awkward, and said nothing.   For a minute or two
the night made itself heard, the gentle slipping of the
river, the fitful breathings from the trees.   A swan passed
and repassed below them, and an owl called from the
distant woods.

Presently Marcella lifted a white finger and pointed
to the house.

'One wouldn't want a better parable,' she said.
'It's like the State as you see it—magnificent, inspiring, a
thing of pomp and dignity.   But we women, who have
to drive and keep going a house like that—*we* know what
it all rests upon.   It rests upon a few tired kitchenmaids
and boot-boys and scullery-girls, hurrying, panting
creatures, whom a guest never sees, who really run it all.
I know, for I have tried to unearth them, to organise
them, to make sure that no one was fainting while we
were feasting.   But it is incredibly hard; half the human
race believes itself born to make things easy for the other
half.   It comes natural to them to ache and toil while
we sit in easy chairs.   What they resent is that we should
try to change it.'

'Goodness!' said George, pulling at his moustaches. 'I don't recognise my own experience of the ordinary domestic polity in that summary.'

'I daresay. You have to do with the upper servant, who is always a greater tyrant than his master,' she retorted, her voice expressing a curious medley of laughter and feeling. 'I am speaking of the people that are not seen, like the tailoress and shirtmaker, in your drum-and-trumpet State.'

'Well, you may be right,' said George, drily. 'But I confess—if I may be quite frank—that I don't altogether trust you to judge. I want at least, before I strike the balance between my Dalhousie and your tailoress, to hear what those people have to say who have not crippled their minds—by pity!'

'Pity!' she said, her lip trembling in spite of herself. 'Pity!—you count pity a disease?'

'As you—and others—practise it,' he replied coolly, turning round upon her. 'It is no good; the world can't be run by pity. At least, living always seems to me a great brutal, rushing, rough-and-tumble business, which has to be carried on whether we like it or no. To be too careful, too gingerly over the separate life, brings it all to a standstill. Meddle too much, and the Demiurge who set the machine going turns sulky and stops working. Then the nation goes to pieces—till some strong ruffian without a scruple puts it together again.'

'What do you mean by the Demiurge?'

He laughed.

'Why do you make me explain my flights? Well, I suppose, the natural daimonic power in things, which keeps them going and set them off; which is not us, or like us, and cares nothing for us.'

His light voice developed a sudden energy during his little speech.

'Ah!' said Marcella, wistfully. 'Yes, if one thought that, I could understand. But, even so, if the power behind things cares nothing for us, I should only regard it as challenging us to care more for each other. Do you mind my asking you a few plain questions? Do you know anything personally of the London poor? I mean, have you any real friends among them, whose lives you know?'

'Well, I sit with Fontenoy while he receives deputations from all those tailoresses and shirtmakers and fur-sewers that *you* want to put in order. The harassed widow streams through his room perpetually—wailing to be let alone!'

Marcella made a sound of amused scorn.

'Oh! you think that nothing,' said George, indignant. 'I vow I could draw every type of widow that London contains—I know them intimately.'

She shook her head.

'I give up London. Then, in the North, aren't you a coalowner? Do you know your miners?'

'Yes, and I detest them!' said George, shortly; 'pigheaded brutes! They will be on strike next month, and I shall be defrauded of my lawful income till their lordships choose to go back. Pity *me*, if you please—not them!'

'So I do,' she said with spirit—'if you hate the men by whom you live!'

There was silence. Then suddenly George said, in another tone:

'But sometimes, I don't deny, the beggars wring it out of one—your pity. I saw a mother last week—— Suppose we stroll on a little. I want to see how the river gets out of the wood.'

They descended the bridge, and turned again into the river-path. George told the story of Mary Batchelor in his half-ironic way, yet so that here and there Marcella shivered. Then gradually, as though it were a relief to him to talk, he slipped into a half-humorous, half-serious discussion of his mine-owner's position and its difficulties. Incidentally and unconsciously a good deal of his history betrayed itself in his talk : his bringing-up, his mother ; the various problems started in his mind since his return from India ; even his relations to his wife. Once or twice it flashed across him that he was confessing himself with an extraordinary frankness to a woman he had made up his mind to dislike. But the reflection did not stop him. The balmy night, the solitude, this loveliness that walked beside him so willingly and kindly—with every step they struck his defences from him ; they drew ; they penetrated.

With her, too, everything was simple and natural. She had felt his attraction at their first meeting ; she had determined to make a friend of him ; and she was succeeding. As he disclosed himself she felt a strange compassion for him. It was plain to her woman's instinct that he was at heart lonely and uncompanioned. Well, what wonder with that hard, mean little being for a wife ! Had she captured him, or had he thrown himself away upon her in mere wantonness, out of that defiance of sentiment which appeared to be his favourite *parti-pris* ? In any case, it seemed to this happy wife that he had done the one fatal and irreparable thing; and she was genuinely sorry for him. She felt him very young, too. As far as she could gather, he was about two years her junior ; but her feeling made the gap much greater.

Yet, of course, the situation—Maxwell, Fontenoy—all that those names implied to him and her, made a thrilling under-note in both their minds. She never forgot her husband and his straits ; and in George's mind Fontenoy's rugged figure stood sentinel. Given the circumstances, both her temperament and her affections drove her inevitably into trying, first to attract, then to move and influence her companion. And given the circumstances, he could but yield himself bit by bit to her woman's charm; while full all the time of a confident scorn for her politics.

Insensibly, the stress upon them drew them back to London and to current affairs, and at last she said to him, with vehemence:

'You *must* see these people in the flesh—and not in your house, but in theirs. Or, first come and meet them in mine?'

'Why, please, should you think St. James's Square a palace of truth compared to Carlton House Terrace?' he asked her, with amusement. Fontenoy lived in Carlton House Terrace.

'I am not inviting you to St. James's Square,' she said quietly. 'That house is only my home for one set of purposes. Just now my true home is not there at all. It is in the Mile End Road.'

George asked to be informed, and opened his eyes at her account of the way in which she still divided her time between the West End and the East, spending always one or two nights a week among the trades and the work-people she had come to know so intimately, whose cause she was fighting with such persistence.

'Maxwell doesn't come now,' she said. 'He is too busy, and his work there is done. But I go because I love the people, and to talk with them and live with them part of every week keeps one's mind clear as to what one wants, and why. Well'—her voice showed that she smiled—'will you come? My old maid shall give you coffee, and you shall meet a roomful of tailors and shirt-makers. You shall see what people look like in the flesh—not on paper—after working fourteen hours at a stretch, in a room where you and I could not breathe!'

'Charming!'—he bowed ironically. 'Of course I will come.'

They had paused under the shadow of a grove of beech-trees, and were looking back towards the moonlit garden and the house. Suddenly George said, in an odd voice :

'Do you mind my saying it? You know, nobody is ever converted—politically—nowadays.'

In the darkness her flush could not be seen. But he felt the mingled pride and soreness in her voice, under its forced brightness.

'I know. How long is it since a speech turned a vote in the House of Commons! One wonders why people take the trouble to speak. Shall we go back? Ah! there is some one pursuing us—my husband and Ancoats!'

And two figures, dark for an instant against the brightness of the lawns, plunged into the shadow of the wood.

'You wanderers!' said Maxwell, as he distinguished his wife's white dress. 'Is this path quite safe in this darkness? Suppose we get out of it.'

The river, indeed, beneath a steep bank, ran close beside them, and the trees meeting overhead all but shut out the moon. Maxwell, in some anxiety, caught his wife's arm, and made her pause till his eye should be once more certain of the path. Meanwhile Ancoats and Tressady walked quickly back to the lawn, Ancoats talking and laughing with unusual vigour.

The Maxwells did not hurry themselves. As they emerged from the wood Marcella slipped her hand into her husband's. It was her characteristic caress. The slim, strong hand loved to feel itself in the shelter of his ; while to him that seeking touch was the symbol of all

that she brought him—the inventive, inexhaustible arts
of a passion which was a kind of genius.

'Don't go in!' she pleaded. 'Why should we?'

'No!—why should we?' he repeated, sighing. 'Why
are we here at all?—that is what I have been asking
myself all the evening. And now more than ever since
my walk with that boy Ancoats.'

'Tell me about it,' she said eagerly. 'Could you get
nothing out of him?'

Maxwell shrugged his shoulders.

'Nothing. He vows that everything is all right; that
he knows a pack of slanderers have been "yelping at
him," and he wishes both they and his mother would let
him alone.'

'His mother!' cried Marcella, outraged.

'Well, I suppose I said to him the kind of thing you
would evidently like to say. But with no result. He
merely laughed, and chattered about everything under the
sun—his racehorses, new plays, politics—Heaven knows
what! He is in an excited state—feverish, restless, and,
I should think, unhappy. But he would tell nothing—to
me.'

'How much do you think she knows?'

'His mother? Nothing, I should say. Every now
and then I detect a note of extra anxiety when she talks to
him ; and there is evidently something in her mind, some
impression from his manner, perhaps, which is driving
her more keenly than ever towards this marriage. But I
don't believe a single one of the stories that have reached
us has reached her. And now—here is this poor girl—
and even my dull eyes have noticed that to-night he has
purposely, markedly, avoided her.'

Marcella felt her cheek flame.

'And when one thinks of his behaviour in the winter!'
she cried.

They wandered on along a path that skirted the wood, talking anxiously about the matter which had in truth brought them to Castle Luton. In spite of the comparative gentleness of English political relations, neither Maxwell nor Marcella, perhaps, would willingly have become Charlotte Allison's guests at a moment when her house was actually the headquarters of a violent and effective opposition to Maxwell's policy, when moreover the leader of that opposition was likely to be of the party. But about a fortnight before Whitsuntide some tales of young Ancoats had suddenly reached Maxwell's ears, with such effect that on his next meeting with Ancoats's mother he practically invited himself and Marcella—greatly to Mrs. Allison's surprise—to Castle Luton for Whitsuntide.

For the boy had been Maxwell's ward, and Henry Allison had been the intimate friend and comrade of Maxwell's father. And Maxwell's feeling for his father, and for his father's friends, was of such a kind that his guardian's duties had gone deep with him. He had done his best for the boy, and since Ancoats had reached his majority his ex-guardian had still kept him anxiously in mind.

Of late indeed Ancoats had troubled himself very little about his guardian, or his guardian's anxieties. He seemed to have been devoting a large share of his mind to the avoidance of his mother's old friends; and the Maxwells, for months, in spite of many efforts on their part, had seen little or nothing of him. Maxwell for various reasons had begun to suspect a number of uncomfortable things with regard to the young fellow's friends and pleasures. Yet nothing could be taken hold of till this sudden emergence of a particular group of stories, coupling Ancoats's name with that of a notorious little actress whose adventures had already provided a certain class of newspaper with abundant copy.

Then Maxwell, who cared personally very little for the red-haired youth himself, took alarm for the mother's sake. For in the case of Mrs. Allison a scandal of the kind suggested meant a tragedy. Her passion for her son was almost a tragedy already, so closely mingled in it were the feelings of the mother and those of the Christian, to whom 'vice' is not an amusement, but an agony.

Yet, as Marcella said and felt, it was a hard fate that had forced Maxwell to concern himself with Ancoats's love-affairs at this particular moment.

'Don't think of it,' she said at last, urgently, as they walked along. 'It is too bad; as if there were not enough!'

Maxwell stood still, with a little smile, and put his arm round her shoulders.

'Dear, I shall soon have time enough, probably, to think about Ancoats's affairs or anything else. Do you know that I was planning this morning what we would do when we go out? Shall we slip over to the Australian colonies in the autumn? I would give a good deal to see them for myself.'

She gave a low cry of pain.

'Why are you so depressed to-night? Is there any fresh news?'

'Yes. And, altogether, things look increasingly bad for us, and increasingly well for them. It will be extraordinarily close any way—probably a matter of a vote or two.'

And he gave her a summary of his after-dinner conversation with Lord Cathedine, a keen ally of Fontenoy's in the Lords, and none the less a shrewd fellow because he happened to be also a detestable person.

Marcella heard the news of one or two fresh defections from the Government with amazement and indignation. She stood there in the darkness, leaning against the man she loved, her heart beating fast and stormily. How could the world thus misconceive and thwart him? And what could she do? Her mind ran passionately through a hundred schemes, refusing to submit—to see him baffled and defeated.

CHAPTER XII

To Lord Ancoats himself this party of his mother's was an oppression and a nuisance. He had only been induced to preside over it with difficulty; and his mother had been both hurt and puzzled by his reluctance to play the host.

If you had asked Maxwell's opinion on the point, he would have told you that Ancoats's bringing up had a good deal to do with the present anxieties of Ancoats's mother. He—Maxwell—had done his best, but he had been overmatched.

First and foremost, Ancoats had been to no public school. It was not the custom of the family; and Mrs. Allison could not be induced to break the tradition. There was accordingly a succession of tutors, whose Church-principles at least were sound. And Ancoats showed himself for a time an impressionable, mystical boy, entirely in sympathy with his mother. His confirmation was a great family emotion, and when he was seventeen Mrs. Allison had difficulty in making him take food enough in Lent to keep him in health. Maxwell was beginning to wonder where it would end, when the lad was sent to Cambridge, and the transformation scene, that might always perhaps have been expected, began.

He had been two years at Trinity when he went to pay the Maxwells a visit at the Court. Maxwell could hardly believe his eyes or ears. The boy who at nineteen was an authority on church music and ancient 'uses,' by twenty-one talked and thought of nothing in heaven or earth but the stage and French *bric-à-brac*. His conversation swarmed with the names of actors, singers, and dancers; but they were names that meant nothing except to the initiated. They were the small people of the small theatres; and Ancoats was a Triton among them, not at all, so he carefully informed his kindred, because of his wealth and title, but because he too was an artist, and could sing, revel, write, and dance with the best of them.

For some time Maxwell was able to console Mrs. Allison with the historical reflection that more than one son of the Oxford Movement had found in a passion for the stage a ready means of annoying the English Puritan. When it came, however, to the young man's producing risky plays of his own composing at extremely costly *matinées*, there was nothing for it but to interfere. Maxwell at last persuaded him to give up the farce of Cambridge and go abroad. But Ancoats would only go with a man of his own sort; and their time was mostly spent in Paris, where Ancoats divided his hard-spent existence between the furious pursuit of Louis Quinze *bibelots* and the patronage of two or three minor theatres. To be the king of a first night raining applause and bouquets from his stage-box seemed to give him infinite content; but his vanity was hardly less flattered by the compliments say of M. Tournonville, the well-known dealer on the Quai Voltaire, who would bow himself before the young Englishman with the admiring cry, 'Mon Dieu! milord, que vous êtes fin connaisseur!' while the dealer's assistant grinned among the shadows of the back-shop.

At last, at twenty-four, he must needs return to England for his coming of age under his grandfather's

R 2

will and the taking over of his estate. Under the sober-
ing influence of these events his class and his mother
seemed for a time to recover him. He re-furnished a
certain number of rooms at Castle Luton, and made
a special marvel of his own room, which was hung thick
with Boucher, Greuze, and Watteau engravings, littered
with miniatures and trinkets, and encumbered here and
there with portfolios of drawings which he was not
anxious to unlock in his mother's presence.

Moreover, he. was again affectionate to his mother,
and occasionally even went to church with her. The
instincts of the English aristocrat reappeared amid the
accomplishments of the *petit-maitre*, and poor Mrs.
Allison's spirits revived. Then the golden-haired Lady
Madeleine was asked to stay at Castle Luton. When
she came Ancoats devoted himself with extraordinary
docility. He drew her, made songs for her, and devised
French charades to act with her; he even went so far
as to compare her with enthusiasm to the latest and
most wonderful 'Salome' just exhibited in the Salon by
the latest and most wonderful of the impressionists. But
Lady Madeleine fortunately had not seen the picture.

Then suddenly, one morning, Ancoats went up to town
without notice and remained there. After a while his mother
pursued him thither; but Ancoats was restless at sight
of her, and she was not long in London, though long
enough to show the Maxwells and others, that her heart
was anxiously set upon Lady Madeleine as a daughter-
in-law.

This then—taken together with the stories now be-
sprinkling the newspapers—was the situation. Naturally, Ancoats's affairs, as he himself was irritably aware,
were now, in one way or another, occupying the secret
thoughts or the private conversations of most of his
mother's guests.

For instance—

'Are you nice?' said Betty Leven, suddenly, to young Lord Naseby, in the middle of Sunday morning. 'Are you in a charitable, charming, humble, and trusting frame of mind? Because, if not, I shall go away—I have had too much of Lady Kent!'

Charlie Naseby laughed. He was sitting reading in the shade at the edge of one of the Castle Luton lawns. For some time past he had been watching Betty Leven and Lady Kent, as they talked under a cedar-tree some little distance from him. Lady Kent conversed with her whole bellicose person—her cap, her chin, her nose, her spreading and impressive shoulders. And from her gestures young Naseby guessed that she had been talking to Betty Leven rather more in character than usual.

He felt a certain curiosity about the *tête-à-tête*. So that when Betty left her companion and came tripping over the lawn to the house, the young man lifted his face and gave her a smiling nod, as though to invite her to come and visit him on the way. Betty came, and then as she stood in front of him delivered the home question already reported.

'Am I nice?' repeated young Naseby. 'Far from it. I have not been to church, and I have been reading a French novel of which I do not even propose to tell you the name.'

And he promptly slipped his volume into his pocket.

'Which is worst?' said Betty, pensively: 'to break the fourth Commandment or the ninth? Lady Kent, of course, has been trampling on them both. But the ninth is her particular victim. She calls it "getting to the roots of things."'

'Whose roots has she been delving at this morning?' said Naseby.

Betty looked behind her, saw that Lady Kent had gone into the house, and let herself drop into the corner of Naseby's bench with a sigh of fatigue.

'One feels as though one were a sort of house-dog tussling with a burglar. I have been keeping her off all my friends' secrets by main force; so she had to fall back on George Tressady, and tell me ugly tales of his mamma.'

'George Tressady! Why on earth should she do him an ill turn? I don't believe she ever saw him before.'

Betty pressed her lips. She and Charlie Naseby had been friends since they wore round pinafores and sat on high nursery chairs side by side.

'One needn't go to the roots of things,' she said severely, 'but one should have eyes in one's head. Has it ever occurred to you that Ancoats has taken a special fancy to Sir George—that he sat talking to him last night till all hours, and that he has been walking about with him the whole of this morning, instead of walking about —well! with somebody else—as he was meant to do? Why do men behave in this ridiculous manner? Women, of course. But *men!* It's like a trout that won't let itself be landed. And what's the good? It's only prolonging the agony.'

'Not at all,' said Naseby, laughing. 'There's always the chance of slipping the hook.' Then his lively face became suddenly serious. 'But it's time, I think,' he added, almost with vehemence, 'that Lady Kent stopped trying to land Ancoats. In the first place, it's no good. He won't be landed against his will. In the next—well, I only know,' he broke off, 'that if I had a sister in love with Ancoats at the present moment, I'd carry her off to the North Pole rather than let her be talked about with him!'

Betty opened her eyes.

'Then there *is* something in the stories!' she cried.
'Of course, Frank told me there was nothing. And the
Maxwells have not said a word. And *now* I understand
why Lady Kent has been dinning it into my ears—I could
only be thankful Mrs. Allison was safe at church—that
Ancoats should marry early. "Oh! my dear, it's always
been the only hope for them!"' Betty mimicked Lady
Kent's deep voice and important manner : '"Why, there
was the grandfather—*his* wife had a time!—I could tell
you things about *him!*—oh! and her too.—And even
Henry Allison!——" There, of course, I stopped her.'

'Old ghoul!' said Naseby, in disgust. 'So she knows.
And yet—Good Heavens! where does that charming girl
come from?'

He knocked the end off his cigarette, and returned it
to his mouth with a rather unsteady hand.

'Knows?—knows what?' said Betty. There was a
pink flush, perhaps of alarm, on her pretty cheek, but her
eyes said plainly that if there were risks she must run
them.

Naseby hesitated The natural reticence of one young
man about another held him back—and he was Ancoats's
friend. But he liked Lady Madeleine, and her mother's
ugly manœuvres in the sight of gods and men filled him
with a restless ill-temper.

'You say the Maxwells have told you nothing?' he
said at last. 'But all the same I am pretty certain that
Maxwell is here for nothing else. What on earth should
he be doing in this *galère* just now! Look at him and
Fontenoy! They've been pacing that lime-walk for a
good hour. No one ever saw such a spectacle before.
Of course something's up!'

Betty followed his eyes, and caught the figures of the
two men between the trunks as they moved through the
light and shadow of the lime-walk—Fontenoy's massive

head sunk in his shoulders, his hands clasped behind his
back; Maxwell's taller and alerter form beside him.
Fontenoy had, in fact, arrived that morning from town,
just too late to accompany Mrs. Allison and her flock to
church; and Maxwell and he had been together since
the moment when Ancoats, having brought his guest into
the garden, had gone off himself on a walk with Tressady.

'Ancoats and Tressady came back past here,' Naseby
went on. 'Ancoats stood still, with his hands on his
sides, and looked at those two. His expression was not
amiable. "Something hatching," he said to Tressady.
I suppose Ancoats got his sneer from his actor-friends—
none of us could do it without practice. "Shall we go and
pull the chief out of that?" But they didn't go. Ancoats
turned sulky, and went into the house by himself.'

'I'm glad I don't have to keep that youth straight,'
said Betty, devoutly. 'Perhaps I don't care enough
about him to try. But his mother's a darling saint!—
and if he breaks her heart he ought to be hung.'

'She knows nothing—I believe—' said Naseby,
quickly.

'Strange!' cried Betty. 'I wonder if it pays to be a
saint. I shall know everything about *my* boy when he's
that age.'

'Oh! will you?' said Naseby, looking at her with a
mocking eye.

'Yes, sir, I shall. Your secrets are not so difficult to
know, if one *wants* to know them. Heaven forbid, however, that I should want to know anything about any of
you till Bertie is grown up! Now, please tell me everything. Who is the lady?'

'Heaven forbid I should tell you!' said Naseby, drily.

'Don't trifle any more,' said Betty, laying a remon-
strating hand on his arm; 'they will be home from church
directly.'

'Well, I won't tell you any names,' said Naseby, reluctantly. 'Of course, it's an actress—a very small one. And, of course, she's a bad lot—and pretty.'

'Why, there's no of course about it—about either of them!' said Betty, with more indignation than grammar. She also had dramatic friends, and was sensitive on the point.

Naseby protested that if he must argue the ethics of the stage before he told his tale, the tale would remain untold. Then Betty, subdued, fell into an attitude of meek listening, hands on lap. The tale when told indeed proved to be a very ordinary affair, marked out perhaps a trifle from the ruck by the facts that there was another pretender in the field with whom Ancoats had already had one scene in public, and would probably have more; that Ancoats being Ancoats, something mad and conspicuous was to be expected, which would bring the matter inevitably to his mother's ears; and that Mrs. Allison was Mrs. Allison.

'Can he marry her?' said Betty, quickly.

'Thank Heaven! no. There is a husband somewhere in Chili. So that it doesn't seem to be a question of driving Mrs. Allison out of Castle Luton. But—well, between ourselves, it would be a pity to give Ancoats so fine a chance of going to the bad, as he'll get, if this young woman lays hold of him. He mightn't recover it.'

Betty sat silent a moment. All her gaiety had passed away. There was a fierceness in her blue eyes.

'And that's what we bring them up for!' she exclaimed at last—'that they may do all these ugly, stale, stupid things over again. Oh! I'm not thinking so much of the morals!'—she turned to Naseby with a defiant look. 'I am thinking of the hateful cruelty and unkindness!'

'To his mother?' said Naseby. He shrugged his shoulders.

Betty allowed herself an outburst. Her little hand trembled on her knee. Naseby did not reply. Not that he disagreed; far from it. Under his young and careless manner he was already a person of settled character, cherishing a number of strong convictions. But since it had become the fashion to talk as frankly of a matter of this kind to your married-women friends as to anybody else, he thought that the women should take it with more equanimity.

Betty, indeed, regained her composure very quickly, like a stream when the gust has passed. They fell into a keen, practical discussion of the affair. Who had influence with Ancoats? What man? Naseby shook his head. The difference in age between Ancoats and Maxwell was too great, and the men too unlike in temperament. He himself had done what he could, in vain, and Ancoats now told him nothing; for the rest, he thought Ancoats had very few friends amid his innumerable acquaintance, and such as he had, of a third-rate dramatic sort, not likely to be of much use at this moment.

'I haven't seen him take to any fellow of his own kind as much as he has taken to George Tressady these two days, since he left Cambridge. But that's no good, of course—it's too new.'

The two sat side by side, pondering. Suddenly Naseby said, smiling, with a change of expression:

'This party is really quite interesting. Look there!'

Betty looked, and saw George Tressady, with his hands in his pockets, lounging along a distant path beside Marcella Maxwell.

'Well!' said Betty, 'what then?'

Naseby gave his mouth a twist.

'Nothing; only it's odd. I ran across them just now

—I was playing ball with that jolly little imp, Hallin. You never saw two people more absorbed. Of course he's *sous le charme*—we all are. Our English politics are rather rum, aren't they? They don't indulge in this amiable country-house business in a South American republic, you know. They prefer shooting.'

'And you evidently think it a healthier state of things. Wait till we come to something nearer to *our* hearths and bosoms than Factory Acts,' said Betty, with the wisdom of her kind. 'All the same, Lord Fontenoy is in earnest.'

'Oh yes, Fontenoy is in earnest. So, I suppose, is Tressady. So—good Heavens!—is Maxwell. I say, here comes the church party.'

And from a side-door in a venerable wall, beyond which could be seen the tower of a little church, there emerged a small group of people—Mrs. Allison, Lady Cathedine, and Madeleine Penley in front, escorted by the white-haired Sir Philip; and behind, Lady Tressady, between Harding Watton and Lord Cathedine.

'Cathedine!' cried Naseby, staring at the group. 'Cathedine been to church?'

'For the purpose, I suppose, of disappointing poor Laura, who might have hoped to get rid of him,' said Betty, sharply. 'No!—if I were Mrs. Allison I should draw the line at Lord Cathedine.'

'Nobody need see any more of Cathedine than they want,' said Naseby, calmly; 'and, of course, he behaves himself here. Moreover, there is no doubt at all about his brains. They say Fontenoy expects to make great use of him in the Lords.'

'By the way,' said Betty, turning round upon him 'where are you?'

'Well, thank God! I'm not in Parliament,' was Naseby's smiling reply. 'So don't trouble me for opinions.

I have none. Except that, speaking generally, I should like Lady Maxwell to get what she wants.'

Betty threw him a sly glance, wondering if she might tease him about the news she heard of him from Marcella.

She had no time, however, to attack him, for Mrs. Allison approached.

'What is the matter with her?—with Madeleine?— with all of them?' thought Betty, suddenly.

For Mrs. Allison, pale and discomposed, did not return, did not apparently notice Lady Leven's greeting. She walked hastily past them, and would have gone at once into the house but that, turning her head, she perceived Lord Fontenoy hurrying towards her from the lime-walk. With an obvious effort she controlled herself, and went to meet him, leaning heavily on her silver-topped stick.

The others paused, no one having, as it seemed, anything to say. Letty poked the gravel with her parasol; Sir Philip made a telescope of his hands, and fixed it upon Maxwell, who was coming slowly across the lawn; while Lady Madeleine turned a handsome, bewildered face on Betty.

Betty took her aside to look at a flower on the house.

'What's the matter?' said Lady Leven under her breath.

'I don't know,' said the other. 'Something dreadful happened on the way home. There was a girl——'

But she broke off suddenly. Ancoats had just opened and shut the garden-door, and was coming to join his guests.

'Poor dear!' thought Betty to herself, with a leap of pity. It was so evident the girl's whole nature thrilled to the approaching step. She turned her head towards

Ancoats, as though against her will, her tall form drawn erect, in unconscious tension.

Ancoats's quick eyes ran over the group.

'He thinks we have been talking about him,' was Betty's quick reflection, which was probably not far from the truth. For the young man's face at once assumed a lowering expression, and, walking up to Lady Tressady, whom as yet he had noticed no more than civility required, he asked whether she would like to see the 'houses' and the rose-garden.

Letty, delighted by the attention, said Yes in her gayest way, and Ancoats at once led her off. He walked quickly, and their figures soon disappeared among the trees.

Madeleine Penley gazed after them. Betty, who had a miserable feeling that the girl was betraying herself to men like Harding Watton or Lord Cathedine—a feeling which was, however, the creation of her own nervous excitement—tried to draw her away. But Lady Madeleine did not seem to understand. She stood mechanically buttoning and unbuttoning her long gloves. 'Yes, I'm coming,' she said, but she did not move.

Then Betty saw that Lord Naseby had approached her; and it seemed to the observer that all the young man's vivid face was suffused with something at once soft and fierce.

'The thorn-blossom on the hill is a perfect show just now, Lady Madeleine,' he said. 'Come and look at it. There will be just time before lunch.'

The girl looked at him. The colour rushed to her cheeks, and she walked submissively away beside him.

Meanwhile Letty and Ancoats pursued their way towards the greenhouses and walled gardens. Letty tripped along, hardly able to keep up with her com-

panion's stride, but chattering fast all the time. At every
turn of the view she overflowed with praise and wonder;
nor could anything have been at once more enthusiastic
or more impertinent than the questions with which she
plied him as to his gardeners, his estate, and his affairs,
in the intervals of panegyric.

. Ancoats at first hardly listened to her. A perfunctory
'Yes' or 'No' seemed to be all that the situation demanded. Then, when he did sufficiently emerge from the
tempest of his own thoughts to catch some of the things
she was saying, his irritable temper rebelled at once.
What had Tressady been about?—ill-bred, tiresome
woman!

His manner stiffened; he stalked along in front of
her, doing his bare host's duty, and warding off her conversation as much as possible; while Letty, on her side,
soon felt the familiar chill and mortification creeping over
her. Why, she wondered angrily, should he have asked
her to walk with him if he could not be a more agreeable companion?

Towards the end of the lime-walk they came across
Mrs. Allison and Lord Fontenoy. As they passed the
older pair the pale mother lifted her eyes to her son with
a tremulous smile.

But Ancoats made no response, nor had he any
greeting for Fontenoy. He carried his companion
quickly on, till they found themselves in a wilderness
of walled gardens opening one into another, each, as it
seemed, more miraculously ordered and more abundantly
stocked than its neighbour.

'I wonder you know your way,' laughed Letty. 'And
who can possibly consume all this?'

'I haven't an idea,' said Ancoats, abruptly, as he
opened the door of the tenth vinery. 'I wish you'd tell
me.'

Letty raised her eyebrows with a little cry of protest.

'Oh! but it makes the whole place so magnificent, so complete.'

'What is there magnificent in having too much?' said Ancoats, shortly. 'I believe the day of these huge country places, with all their dull greenhouses and things, is done.'

Much he cared, indeed, about his gardeners and his grapes! He was in the mood to feel his whole inheritance a burden round his neck. But at the same time to revile his own wealth gave him a pungent sense of playing the artist.

'Have you argued that with Lord Fontenoy?' she inquired archly.

'I should not take the trouble,' he said, with careless hauteur. 'Ah!'—Letty's vanity winced under his involuntary accent of relief—'I see your husband and Lady Maxwell.'

Marcella and George came towards them. They were strolling along a broad flowery border, which was at the moment a blaze of pæonies of all shades, interspersed with tall pyramidal growths of honeysuckle. Marcella was loitering here and there, burying her face in the fragrance of the honeysuckle, or drawing her companion's attention in delight to the glowing clumps of pæonies. Hallin hovered round them, now putting his hand confidingly into· Tressady's, now tugging at his mother's dress, and now gravely wooing the friendship of a fine St. Bernard that made one of the party. George, with his hands in his pockets, walked or paused as the others chose; and it struck Letty at once that he was talking with unusual freedom and zest.

Yes, it was true, indeed, as Harding said—they had made friends. As she looked at them the first movement of a jealous temper stirred in Letty. She was angry with Lady Maxwell's beauty, and angry with George's enjoyment. It was like the great lady all over to slight the wife and annex the husband. George certainly might have taken the trouble to come and look for her on their return from church!

So, while Ancoats talked stiffly with Marcella, the bride, a few paces off, let George understand through her bantering manner that she was out of humour.

'But, dear, I had no notion you would be let out so soon,' pleaded George. 'That good man really can't earn his pay.'

'Oh! but of course you knew it was High Church—all split up into little bits,' said Letty, unappeased. 'But naturally——'

She was about to add some jealous sarcasm when it was arrested by the arrival of Sir Philip Wentworth and Watton, whose figures appeared in a side-archway close to her.

'Ah! well guessed,' said Sir Philip. 'I thought we should find you among the pæonies. Lady Tressady, did you ever see such a show? Ancoats, is your head gardener visible on a Sunday? I ask with trembling, for there is no more magnificent member of creation. But if I *could* get at him, to ask him about an orchid I saw in one of your houses yesterday, I should be grateful.'

'Come into the next garden, then,' said Ancoats, 'where the orchid-houses are. If he isn't there, we'll send for him.'

'Then, Lady Tressady, you must come and see me through,' said Sir Philip, gallantly. 'I want to quarrel with him about a label—and you remember Dizzy's saying —"a head gardener is always opinionated"? Are you coming, Lady Maxwell?'

Marcella shook her head, smiling.

'I am afraid I hate hothouses,' she said.

'My dear lady, don't pine for the life according to nature at Castle Luton!' said Sir Philip, raising a finger. 'The best of hothouses, like the best of anything, demands a thrill.'

Marcella shrugged her shoulders.

'I get more thrill out of the pæonies.'

Sir Philip laughed, and he and Watton carried off Letty, whose vanity was once more happy in their society; while Ancoats, glad of the pretext, hurried along in front to find the great Mr. Newmarch.

'I believe there are some wonderful irises out in the Friar's Garden,' said Marcella. 'Mrs. Allison told me there was a show of them somewhere. Let me see if I can find the way. And Hallin would like the goldfish in the fountain.'

Her two companions followed her gladly, and she led them through devious paths till there was a shout from Hallin, and the most poetic corner of a famous garden revealed itself. Amid the ruins of a cloister that had once formed part of the dissolved Cistercian priory on whose confiscated lands Castle Luton had arisen, a rich medley of flowers was in full and perfect bloom. Irises in every ravishing shade of purple, lilac, and gold, carpets of daffodils and narcissus, covered the ground, and ran into each corner and cranny of the old wall. Yellow banksia and white clematis climbed the crumbling shafts, or made new tracery for the empty windows, and where the ruin ended, yew hedges, adorned at top with a whole procession of birds and beasts, began. The flowery space thus enclosed was broken in the centre by an old fountain; and as one sat on a stone seat beside it, one looked through an archway, cut through

s

the darkness of the yews, to the blue river and the hills.

The little place breathed perfume and delight. But Marcella did not, somehow, give it the attention it deserved. She sat down absently on the bench by the fountain, and presently, as George and Hallin were poking among the goldfish, she turned to her companion with the abrupt question:

'You didn't know Ancoats, I think, before this visit, did you?'

'Only as one knows the merest acquaintance. Fontenoy introduced me to him at the club.'

Marcella sighed. She seemed to be arguing something with herself. At last, with a quick look towards the approaches of the garden, she said in a low voice:

'I think you must know that his friends are not happy about him?'

It so happened that Watton had found opportunity to show Tressady that morning a paragraph from one of the numerous papers that batten on the British peer, his dress, his morals, and his sport. The paragraph, without names, without even initials, contained an outline of Lord Ancoats's affairs which Harding, who knew everything of a scandalous nature, declared to be well informed. It had made George whistle; and afterwards he had watched Mrs. Allison go to church with a new interest in her proceedings.

So that when Marcella threw out her hesitating question, he said at once:

'I know what the papers are beginning to say—that is, I have seen a paragraph——'

'Oh! those newspapers!' she said in distress. 'We are all afraid of some madness, and any increase of talk may hasten it. There is no one who can control him, and of late he has not even tried to conceal things.'

'It is a determined face,' said George. 'I am afraid he will take his way. How is it that he comes to be so unlike his mother?'

'How is it that adoration and sacrifice count for so little? said Marcella, sadly. 'She has given him all the best of her life.'

And she drew a rapid sketch of the youth's career and the mother's devotion.

George listened in silence. What she said showed him that in his conversations with Ancoats that young man had been talking round and about his own case a good deal! and when she paused he said, drily:

'Poor Mrs. Allison! But, you know, there must be some crumples in the rose-leaves of the great.'

She looked at him with a momentary astonishment.

'Why should one think of her as "great"? Would not any mother suffer? First of all, he is so changed; it is so difficult to get at him—his friends are so unlike hers—he is so wrapped up in London, so apathetic about his estate. All the religious sympathy that meant so much to her is gone. And now he threatens her with this—what shall I call it?'—her lip curled—'this entanglement. If it goes on, how shall we keep her from breaking her heart over it? Poor thing! poor mothers!'

She raised her white hand, and let it fall upon her knee with one of the free, instinctive gestures that made her beauty so expressive.

But George would not yield himself to her feeling.

'Ancoats will get through it—somehow—as other men do,' he said stubbornly, 'and she must get through it too—and *not* break her heart.'

Marcella was silent. He turned towards her after a moment.

'You think that a brutal doctrine? But if you'll let me say it, life and ease and good temper are really not the

brittle things women make them ! Why do they put all
their treasure into that one bag they call their affections ?
There is plenty else in life—there is indeed ! It shows
poverty of mind ! '

He laughed, and taking up a pebble dropped it sharply
among the goldfish.

' Alack ! ' said Marcella, caressing her child's head as
he stood playing beside her. ' Hallin, I can't have you
kiss my hand like that. Sir George says it's poverty of
mind.'

' It ain't,' said Hallin, promptly. But his remark had
a deplorable lack of unction, for the goldfish, startled by
George's pebble, were at that moment performing evolu-
tions of the greatest interest, and his black eyes were
greedily bent upon them.

Both laughed, and George let her remark alone. But
his few words left on Marcella a painful impression,
which renewed her compassion of the night before. This
young fellow, just married, protesting against an over-
exaltation of the affections !—it struck her as half tragic,
half grotesque. And, of course, it was explained by the
idiosyncrasies of that little person in a Paris gown now
walking about somewhere with Sir Philip !

Yet, just as she had again allowed herself to think of
him as some one far younger and less mature than herself, he quietly renewed the conversation, so far as it
concerned Ancoats, talking with a caustic good sense, a
shrewd perception, and at bottom with a good feeling,
that first astonished her, and then mastered her friendship
more and more. She found herself yielding him a fuller
and fuller confidence, appealing to him, taking pleasure
in anything that woke the humour of the sharp, long face,
or that rare blink of the blue eyes that meant a leap of
some responsive sympathy he could not quite conceal.

And for him it was all pleasure, though he never

stopped to think of it. The lines of her slender form, as she sat with such careless dignity beside him, her lovely eyes, the turns of her head, the softening tones of her voice, the sense of an emerging bond that had in it nothing ignoble, nothing to be ashamed of, together with the child's simple liking for him, and the mere physical delight of this morning of late May—the rush and splendour of its white, thunderous clouds, its penetrating, scented air : each and all played their part in the rise of a new emotion he would not have analysed if he could.

He was particularly glad that in this fresh day of growing intimacy she had as yet talked politics or ' questions ' of any sort so little ! It made it all the more possible to escape from, to wholly overthrow in his mind that first hostile image of her, impressed—strange unreason on his part !—by that first meeting with her in the crowd round the injured child, and in the hospital ward. Had she started any subject of mere controversy he would have held his own as stoutly as ever. But so long as she let them lie, *herself*, the woman, insensibly argued for her, and wore down his earlier mood.

So long, indeed, as he forgot Maxwell's part in it all ! But it was not possible to forget it long. For the wife's passion, in spite of a noble reticence, shone through her whole personality in a way that alternately touched and challenged her new friend. No; let him remember that Maxwell's ways of looking at things were none the less pestilent because *she* put them into words.

After luncheon Betty Leven found herself in a corner of the Green Drawing-room. On the other side of it Mrs. Allison and Lord Fontenoy were seated together, with Sir Philip Wentworth not far off. Lord Fontenoy was describing his week in Parliament. Betty, who knew and generally shunned him, raised her eyebrows occasionally, as she caught the animated voice, the queer laughs, and fluent expositions, which the presence of his muse was drawing from this most ungainly of worshippers. His talk, indeed, was one long invocation; and the little white-haired lady in the arm-chair was doing her best to play Melpomene. Her speech was very soft. But it made for battle; and Fontenoy was never so formidable as when he was fresh from Castle Luton.

Betty's thoughts, however, had once more slipped away from her immediate neighbours, and were pursuing more exciting matters—the state of Madeleine Penley's heart and the wiles of that witch-woman in London, who must be somehow plucked like a burr from Ancoats's skirts—when Marcella entered the room, hat in hand.

'Whither away, fair lady?' cried Betty; 'come and talk to me.'

'Hallin will be in the river,' said Marcella, irresolute.

'If he is, Sir George will fish him out. Besides, I believe Sir George and Ancoats have gone for a walk, and Hallin with them. I heard Maxwell tell Hallin he might go.'

Marcella turned an uncertain look upon Lord Fontenoy and Mrs. Allison. But directly Maxwell's wife entered the room, Maxwell's enemy had dropped his talk of political affairs, and he was now showing Sir Philip a portfolio of Mrs. Allison's sketches, with a subdued ardour that brought a kindly smile to Marcella's lip. In general, Fontenoy had neither eye nor ear for anything artistic; moreover, he spoke barbarous French, and no other European tongue; while of letters he had scarcely a tincture. But when it became a question of Mrs. Allison's accomplishments, her drawing, her embroidery still more her admirable French and excellent Italian, the books she had read, and the poetry she knew by heart, he was all appreciation—one might almost say, all feeling. It was Cymon and Iphigenia in a modern and middle-aged key.

His mien he fashioned and his tongue he filed.

And did a blunder come, Iphigenia gently and deftly put it to rights.

'Where is Madeleine?' asked Betty, as Marcella approached her sofa.

'Walking with Lord Naseby, I think.'

'What was the matter on the way from church?' asked Betty in a low voice, raising her face to her friend.

Marcella looked gravely down upon her.

'If you come into the garden I will tell you. Madeleine told me.'

Betty, all curiosity, followed her friend through the open window to a seat in the Dutch garden outside.

'It was a terrible thing that happened,' said Marcella, sitting erect, and speaking with a manner of suppressed energy that Betty knew well; 'one of the things that make my blood boil when I come here. You know how she rules the village?'—she turned imperceptibly towards the distant drawing-room, where Mrs. Allison's white head was still visible. 'Not only must all the cottages be beautiful, but all the people must reach a certain standard of virtue. If a man drinks, he must go; if a girl loses her character, she and her child must go. It was such a girl that threw herself in the way of the party this morning. Her mother would not part with her; so the decree went forth—the whole family must go. They say the girl has never been right in her head since the baby's birth; she raved and wept this morning, said her parents could find no work elsewhere—they must die, she and her child must die. Mrs. Allison tried to stop her, but couldn't; then she hurriedly sent the others on, and stayed behind herself—only for a minute or two; she overtook Madeleine almost immediately. Madeleine is sure she was inexorable; so am I; she always is. I once argued with her about a case of the kind—a *cruel* case! "Those are the sins that make me *shudder!*" she said, and one could make no impression on her whatever. You see how exhausted she looks this afternoon. She will wear herself out, probably, praying and weeping over the girl.'

Betty threw up her hands.

'My dear!—when she knows ——'

'It may perfectly well kill her,' said Marcella, steadily. Then, after a pause, Betty saw her face flush from brow to chin, and she added, in a low and passionate voice: 'Nevertheless, from all tyrannies and cruelties in the name of Christ, good Lord, deliver us!'

The two lingered together for some time without speaking. Both were thinking of much the same things, but both were tired with the endless talking of a country-house Sunday, and the rest was welcome.

And presently Marcella rambled away from her friend, and spent an hour pacing by herself in a glade beside the river.

And there her mind instantly shook itself from every care but one—the yearning over her husband and his work.

Two years of labour—she caught her breath with a little sob—labour which had aged and marked the labourer; and now, was it really to be believed, that after all the toil, after so much hope and promise of success, everything was to be wrecked at last?

She gave herself once more to eager forecasts and combinations. As to individuals—she recalled Tressady's blunt warning with a smile and a wince. But it did not prevent her from falling into a reverie of which he, or some one like him, was the centre. Types, incidents, scenes, rose before her—if they could only be pressed upon, *burnt into* such a mind, as they had been burnt into her mind and Maxwell's! That was the whole difficulty—lack of vision, lack of realisation. Men were to have the deciding voice in this thing, who had no clear conception of how poverty and misery live, no true knowledge of this vast tragedy of labour perpetually acted in our midst, no rebellion of heart against conditions of life for other men they themselves would die a thousand times rather than accept. She saw herself, in a kind of despair, driving such persons through streets, and into houses she knew, forcing them to look, and *feel.* Even now, at the last moment——

How much better she had come to know this interesting, limited being, George Tressady, during these twenty-four hours! She liked his youth, his sincerity—even the stubbornness with which he disclaimed inconvenient enthusiasms; and she was inevitably flattered by the way in which his evident prejudice against herself had broken down.

His marriage was a misfortune, a calamity! She thought of it with the instinctive repulsion of one who has never known any temptation to the small vulgarities of life. One could have nothing to say to a little being like that. But all the more reason for befriending the man!

An hour or two later Tressady found himself strolling home along the flowery bank of the river. It was not long since he had parted from Lady Maxwell and Hallin, and on leaving them he had turned back for a while towards the woods on the hill, on the pretext that he wanted more of a walk. Now, however, he was hurrying towards the house, that there might be time for a chat with Letty before dressing. She would think he had been away too long. But he had proposed to take her on the river after tea, and she had preferred a walk with Lord Cathedine.

Since then—— He looked round him at the river
and the hills. There was a flush of sunset through the
air, and the blue of the river was interlaced with rosy or
golden reflections from a sky piled with stormy cloud and
aglow with every 'visionary majesty' of light and colour.
The great cloud-masses were driving in a tragic splendour
through the west; and hue and form alike, throughout
the wide heaven, seemed to him to breathe a marvellous
harmony and poetry, to make one vibrating 'word' of
beauty. Had some god suddenly gifted him with new
senses and new eyes? Never had he felt so much joy
in Nature, such a lifting up to things awful and divine.
Why? Because a beautiful woman had been walking
beside him?—because he had been talking with her of
things that he, at least, rarely talked of—realities of
feeling, or thought, or memory, that no woman had ever
shared with him before?

How had she drawn him to such openness, such
indiscretions? He was half-ashamed, and then forgot
his discomfort in the sudden, eager glancing of the
mind to the future, to the opportunities of the day
just coming—for Mrs. Allison's party was to last till
Whit Tuesday—to the hours and places in London
where he was to meet her on those social errands of
hers. What a warm, true heart! What a woman,
through all her dreams and mistakes, and therefore
how adorable!

He quickened his pace as the light failed. Presently
he saw a figure coming towards him, emerging from the
trees that skirted the main lawn. It was Fontenoy,
and Fontenoy's supporter must needs recollect himself as
quickly as possible. He had not seen much of his leader
during the day. But he knew well that Fontenoy never
forgot his *rôle*, and there were several points, newly arisen

within the last forty-eight hours, on which he might have
expected before this to be called to counsel.

But Fontenoy, when he came up with the wanderer,
seemed to have no great mind for talk. He had evidently
been pacing and thinking by himself, and when he was
fullest of thought he was as a rule most silent and inarticulate.

'You are late; so am I,' he said, as he turned back
with Tressady.

George assented.

'I have been thinking out one or two points of tactics.'

But instead of discussing them he sank into silence
again. George let him alone, knowing his ways.

Presently he said, raising his powerful head with a
jerk, 'But tactics are not of such importance as they were.
I think the thing is done—*done!*' he repeated with
emphasis.

George shrugged his shoulders.

'I don't know. We may be too sanguine. It is not
possible that Maxwell should be easily beaten.'

Fontenoy laughed—a strange, high laugh, like a jay's,
that seemed to have no relation to his massive frame, and
died suddenly away.

'But we shall beat him,' he said quietly; 'and her, too.
A well-meaning woman—but what a foolish one!'

George made no reply.

'Though I am bound to say,' Fontenoy went on
quickly, 'that in private matters no man could be
kinder and show a sounder judgment than Maxwell.
And I believe Mrs. Allison feels the same with regard to
her.'

His look first softened, then frowned; and as he
turned his eyes towards the house, George guessed
what subject it was that he and Maxwell had discussed
under the limes in the morning.

He found Letty in very good spirits, owing, as far as he could judge, to the civilities and attentions of Lord Cathedine. Moreover, she was more at ease in her surroundings, and less daunted by Mrs. Allison.

'And of course, to-morrow,' she said, as she put on her diamonds, 'it will be nicer still. We shall all know each other so much better.'

In her good-humour she had forgotten her twinge of jealousy, and did not even inquire with whom he had been wandering so long.

But Letty was disappointed of her last day at Castle Luton. For the party broke up suddenly, and by ten o'clock on Monday morning all Mrs. Allison's guests but Lord Fontenoy and the Maxwells had left Castle Luton.

It was on this wise.

After dinner on Sunday night Ancoats, who had been particularly silent and irritable at table, suddenly proposed to show his guests the house. Accordingly, he led them through its famous rooms and corridors, turned on the electric light to show the pictures, and acted cicerone to the china and the books.

Then, suddenly it was noticed that he had somehow slipped away, and that Madeleine Penley, too, was missing. The party straggled back to the drawing-room without their host.

Ancoats, however, reappeared alone in about half an hour. He was extremely pale, and those who knew him well, and were perforce observing him at the moment, like Maxwell and Marcella, drew the conclusion that he was in a state of violent though suppressed excitement. His mother, however, strange to say, noticed nothing. But she was clearly exhausted and depressed, and she gave an early signal for the ladies' withdrawal.

The great house sank into quietness. But about an hour after Marcella and Betty had parted at Betty's door, Betty heard a quick knock, and opened it in haste.

'Mrs. Allison is ill!' said Marcella in a low, rapid voice. 'I think everyone ought to go quite early to-morrow. Will you tell Frank? I am going to Lady Tressady. The gentlemen haven't come up.'

Betty caught her arm. 'Tell me——'

'Oh! my dear,' cried Marcella under her breath, 'Ancoats and Madeleine had an explanation in his room. He told her everything—that child! She went to Mrs. Allison—he asked her to! Then the maid came for me in terror. It has been a heart-attack—she has often had them. She is rather better. But *do* let everybody go!' and she wrung her hands. 'Maxwell and I must stay and see what can be done.'

Betty flew to ring for her maid and look up trains. Lady Maxwell went on to Letty Tressady's room.

But on the way, in the half-dark passage, she came across George Tressady coming up from the smoking-room. So she gave her news of Mrs. Allison's sudden illness to him, begging him to tell his wife, and to convey their hostess's regrets and apologies for this untoward break-up of the party. It was the reappearance of an old ailment, she said, and with quiet would disappear.

George heard her with concern, and though his mind was active with conjectures, asked not a single question. Only, when she said good-night to him, he held her hand a friendly instant.

'We shall be off as early as possible, so it is good-bye. But we shall meet in town—as you suggested?'

'Please!' she said, and hurried off.

But just as he reached his own door, he turned with a long breath towards the passage where he had just seen her. It seemed that he saw her still—her white face and dress, the trouble and pity under her quiet manner, her pure sweetness and dignity. He said to himself, with a sort of pride, that he had made a friend, a friend whose sympathy, whose heart and mind, he was now to explore.

Who was to make difficulties? Letty? But already as he stood there, with his hand upon the handle of her door, his mind, in a kind of flashing dream, was already making division of his life between the woman he had married with such careless haste, and this other, who at highest thought of him with a passing kindness, and at lowest regarded him as a mere pawn in the political game.

What could he win by this friendship, that would injure Letty? Nothing! absolutely nothing!

PART II

CHAPTER XIII

On a hot morning at the end of June, some four weeks after the Castle Luton visit, George Tressady walked from Brook Street to Warwick Square, that he might obtain his mother's signature to a document connected with the Shapetsky negotiations, and go on from there to the House of Commons.

She was not in the drawing-room, and George amused himself during his minutes of waiting by inspecting the various new photographs of the Fullerton family that were generally to be found on her table. What a characteristic table it was, littered with notes and bills, with patterns from every London draper, with fashion-books and ladies' journals innumerable ! And what a characteristic room, with its tortured decorations and crowded furniture, and the flattered portraits of Lady Tressady, in every caprice of costume, which covered the walls ! George looked round it all with an habitual distaste ; yet not without the secret admission that his own drawing-room was very like it.

His mother might, he feared, have a scene in preparation for him.

For Letty, under cover of some lame excuse or other, had persisted in putting off the visit which Lady Tressady had intended to pay them at Ferth during the Whitsun-

tide recess, and since their return to town there had been
no meeting whatever between the two ladies. George,
indeed, had seen his mother two or three times. But
even he had just let ten days pass without visiting her.
He supposed he should find her in a mood of angry complaint; nor could he deny that there would be some
grounds for it.

'Good morning, George,' said a sharp voice, which
startled him as he was replacing a photograph of the
latest Fullerton baby. 'I thought you had forgotten your
way here by now.'

'Why, mother, I am very sorry,' he said, as he kissed
her. 'But I have really been terribly busy, what with
two Committees and this important debate.'

'Oh! don't make excuses, pray. And of course—for
Letty—you won't even attempt it. I wouldn't if I were
you.'

Lady Tressady settled herself on a chair with her back
to the light, and straightened the ribbons on her dress
with hasty fingers. Something in her voice struck
George. He looked at her closely.

'Is there anything wrong, mother? You don't look
very well.'

Lady Tressady got up hurriedly, and began to move
about the room, picking up a letter here, straightening a
picture there. George felt a sudden prick of alarm. Were
there some new revelations in store for him? But before
he could speak she interrupted him.

'I should be very well if it weren't for this heat,' she
said pettishly. 'Do put that photograph down, George!
—you do fidget so! Haven't you got any news for me—
anything to amuse me? Oh! those horrid papers!—I see.
Well! they'll wait a little. By the way, the "Morning
Post" says that young scamp, Lord Ancoats, has gone
abroad. I suppose that girl was bought off.'

She sat down again in a shady corner, fanning herself vigorously.

'I am afraid I can't tell you any secrets,' said George, smiling, 'for I don't know any. But it looks as though Mrs. Allison and Maxwell between them had somehow found a way out.'

'How's the mother?'

'You see, she has gone abroad, too—to Bad Wildheim. In fact, Lord Ancoats has taken her.'

'That's the place for heart, isn't it?' said his mother, abruptly. 'There's a man there that cures everybody.'

'I believe so,' said George. 'May we come to business, mother? I have brought these papers for you to sign, and I must get to the House in good time.'

Lady Tressady seemed to take no notice. She got up again, restlessly, and walked to the window.

'How do you like my dress, George? Now, don't imagine anything absurd! Justine made it, and it was quite cheap.'

George could not help smiling—all the more that he was conscious of relief. She would not be asking him to admire her dress if there were fresh debts to confess to him.

'It makes you look wonderfully young,' he said, turning a critical eye, first upon the elegant gown of some soft pinky stuff in which his mother had arrayed herself, then upon the subtly rouged and powdered face above it. 'You are a marvellous person, mother! All the same, I think the heat must have been getting hold of you, for your eyes are tired. Don't racket too much!'

He spoke with his usual careless kindness, laying a hand upon her arm.

Lady Tressady drew herself away, and, turning her back upon him, looked out of the window.

T

'Have you seen any more of the Maxwells?' she said over her shoulders.

George gave a slight involuntary start. Then it occurred to him that his mother was making conversation in an odd way,

'Once or twice,' he said, reluctantly, in reply. 'They were at the Ardaghs' the other night, of course.'

'Oh! you were there?'—Lady Tressady's voice was sharp again. 'Well, of course. Letty went as your wife, and you're a member of Parliament. Lady Ardagh knows *me* quite well—but I don't count now; she used to be glad enough to ask me.'

'It was a great crush, and very hot,' said George, not knowing what to say.

Lady Tressady frowned as she looked out of the window.

'Well!—and Lady Maxwell—is she as absurd as ever?'

'That depends upon one's point of view,' said George, smiling. 'She seemed as convinced as ever.'

'Who sent Mrs. Allison to that place? Barham, I suppose. He always sends his patients there. They say he's in league with the hotel-keepers.'

George stared. What was the matter with her? What made her throw out these jerky sentences with this short, hurried breath.

Suddenly Lady Tressady turned.

'George!'

'Yes, mother.' He stepped nearer to her. She caught his sleeve.

'George'—there was something like a sob in her voice—'you were quite right. I am ill. There, don't talk about it. The doctors are all fools. And if you tell Letty anything about it, I'll never forgive you.'

George put his arm round her, but was not, in truth, much disturbed. Lady Tressady's repertory, alas! had

many *rôles*. He had known her play that of the invalid
at least as effectively as any other.

'You are just overdone with London and the heat,'
he said. 'I saw it at once. You ought to go away.'

She looked up in his face.

'You don't believe it?' she said.

Then she seemed to stagger. He saw a terrible drawn
look in her face, and, putting out all his strength, he
held her, and helped her to a sofa.

'Mother!' he exclaimed, kneeling beside her, 'what
is the matter?'

Voice and tone were those of another man, and Lady
Tressady quailed under the change. She pointed to a
small bag on a table near her. He opened it, and she
took out a box, from which she swallowed something.
Gradually breath and colour returned, and she began
to move restlessly.

'That was nothing,' she said, as though to herself—
'nothing—and it yielded at once. Well, George, I knew
you thought me a humbug!'

Her eyes glanced at him with a kind of miserable
triumph. He looked down upon her, still kneeling,
horror-struck against his will. After a life of acting, was
this the truth—this terror, which spoke in every movement, and in some strange way had seized upon and
infected himself?

He urgently asked her to be frank with him. And
with a sob she poured herself out. It was the tragic,
familiar story that every household knows. Grave
symptoms, suddenly observed—the hurried visit to a
specialist—his verdict and his warnings.

'Of course, he said at first I ought to give up everything and go abroad—to this very same place—Bad-what-
do-you-call it? But I told him straight out I couldn't and
wouldn't do anything of the sort. I am just eaten up

with engagements. And as to staying at home and lying-
up, that's nonsense—I should die of that in a fortnight.
So I told him to give me something to take, and that
was all I could do. And in the end he quite came round
—they always do if you take your own line—and said I
had much better do what suited me, and take care.
Besides, what do any of them know? They all confess
they're just fumbling about. Now, surgery, of course—
that's different. Battye '—Battye was Lady Tressady's
ordinary medical adviser—' doesn't believe all the other
man said. I knew he wouldn't. And as for making an
invalid of me, he sees, of course, that it would kill me at
once. There, my dear George, don't make too much of
it. I think I was a fool to tell you.'

‎ And Lady Tressady struggled to a sitting position,
looking at her son with a certain hostility. The frown
on her white face showed that she was already angry
with him for his emotion—this rare emotion, that she had
never yet been able to rouse in him.

He could only implore her to be guided by her doctor—
to rest, to give up at least some of the mill-round of her
London life, if she would not go abroad. Lady Tressady
listened to him with increasing obstinacy and excitability.

'I tell you I know best!' she said passionately, at
last. 'Don't go on like this—it worries me. Now, look
here——'

She turned upon him with emphasis.

'Promise me not to tell Letty a word of this. Nobody
shall know—she least of all. I shall do just as usual.
In fact, I expect a very gay season. Three "drums" this
afternoon and a dinner-party—it doesn't look as though
I were quite forgotten yet, though Letty does think me
an old fogey!'

She smiled at him with a ghastly mixture of defiance

and conceit. The old age in her pinched face, fighting with the rouged cheeks and the gaiety of her fanciful dress, was pitiful.

'Promise,' she said. 'Not a word—to her!'

George promised, in much distress. While he was speaking she had a slight return of pain, and was obliged to submit to lie down again.

'At least,' he urged, 'don't go out to-day. Give yourself a rest. Shall I go back, and ask Letty to come round to tea?'

Lady Tressady made a face like a spoilt child.

'I don't think she'll come,' she said. 'Of course, I know from the first she took an ungodly dislike to me. Though, if it hadn't been for me—— Well, never mind! Yes, you can ask her, George—do! I'll wait and see if she comes. If she comes, perhaps I'll stay in. It would amuse me to hear what she has been doing. I'll behave quite nicely—there!'

And, taking up her fan, Lady Tressady lightly tapped her son's hand with it in her most characteristic manner.

He rose, seeing from the clock that he should only just have time to drive quickly back to Letty if he was to be at the House in- time for an appointment with a constituent, which had been arranged for one o'clock.

'I will send Justine to you as I go out,' he said, taking up his hat, 'and I shall hear of you from Letty this evening.'

Lady Tressady said nothing. Her eyes, bright with some inner excitement, watched him as he looked for his stick. Suddenly she said, 'George! kiss me!'

Her tone was unsteady. Infinitely touched and bewildered, the young man approached her, and, kneeling down again beside her, took her in his arms. He felt a quick sobbing breath pass through her; then she pushed him lightly away, and, putting up the slim, pink-nailed hand of which she was so proud, she patted him on the cheek.

'There—go along! I don't like that coat of yours, you know. I told you so the other day. If your figure weren't so good, you'd positively look badly dressed in it. You should try another man.'

Tressady hailed a hansom outside, and drove back to Brook Street. On the way his eyes saw little of the crowded streets. So far, he had had no personal experience of death. His father had died suddenly while he was at Oxford, and he had lost no other near relation or friend. Strange! this grave, sudden sense that all was changed, that his careless, half-contemptuous affection for his mother could never again be what it had been. Supposing, indeed, her story was all true! But in the case of a character like Lady Tressady's, there are for long, recurrent, involuntary scepticisms on the part of the bystander. It seems impossible, unfitting, to grant to such persons *le beau rôle* they claim. It outrages a certain ideal instinct, even, to be asked to believe that they too can yield, in their measure, precisely the same tragic stuff as the hero or the saint.

Letty was at home, just about to share her lunch with Harding Watton, who had dropped in. Hearing her husband's voice, she came out to the stairhead to speak to him.

But after a minute or two George dashed down again to his study, that he might write a hurried note to a middle-aged cousin of his mother's, asking her to go round to Warwick Square early in the afternoon, and making excuses for Letty, who was ' very much engaged.'

For Letty had met his request with a smiling disdain. Why, she was simply ' crowded up ' with engagements of all sorts and kinds!

'Mother is really unwell,' said George, standing with his hands on his sides, looking down upon her. He was fuming with irritation and hurry, and had to put a force on himself to speak persuasively.

'My dear old boy!'—she rose on tiptoe and twisted his moustache for him—'don't we know all about your mother's ailments by this time? I suppose she wants to give me a scolding, or to hear about the Ardaghs, or to tell me all about the smart parties *she* has been to—or something of the sort. No, really, it's quite impossible—this afternoon. I know I must go and see her some time—of course I will.'

She said this with the air of some one making a great concession. It was, indeed, her first formal condonement of the offence offered her just before the Castle Luton visit.

George attempted a little more argument and entreaty, but in vain. Letty was rather puzzled by his urgency, but quite obdurate. And as he ran down the stairs, he heard her laugh in the drawing-room mingled with Harding Watton's. No doubt they were making merry over the ' discipline ' which Letty found it necessary to apply to her mother-in-law.

In the House of Commons the afternoon was once more given up to the adjourned debate on the second reading of the Maxwell Bill. The House was full, and showing itself to advantage. On the whole, the animation and competence of the speeches reflected the general rise in combative energy and the wide kindling of social passions which the Bill had so far brought about, both in and out of Parliament. Those who figured as the defenders of industries harassed beyond bearing by the Socialist meddlers spoke with more fire, with more semblance, at any rate, of putting their hearts into it, than any men of their kind had been able to attain since the ' giant' days of the first Factory debates. Those, on the other hand, who were urging the House to a yet sterner vigilance in protecting the worker—even the grown man —from his own helplessness and need, who believed that law spells freedom, and that the experience of half a century was · wholly on their side—these friends of a strong cause were also at their best, on their mettle. Owing to the widespread flow of a great reaction, the fight had become a representative contest between two liberties—a true battle of ideas.

Yet George, sitting below the Gangway beside his leader, his eyes staring at the ceiling, and his hands in his pocket, listened to it all in much languor and revolt. He himself had made his speech on the third day of the debate. It had cost him endless labour, only to seem to him in the end—by contrast with the vast majority of speeches made in the course of the debate, even those by men clearly inferior to himself in mind and training—to be a hollow and hypocritical performance. What did he really think and believe? What did he really desire? He vowed to himself once more, as he had vowed at Ferth, that his mind was a chaos, without convictions, either intellectual or moral ; that he had begun what he was not able to finish ; and that he was doomed to make a failure of his parliamentary career, as he was already making a failure of coal-owning and a failure——

He curbed something bitter and springing that haunted his most inmost mind. But his effort could not prevent his dwelling angrily for a minute on the thought of Letty laughing with Harding Watton—laughing because he had asked her a small kindness, and she had most unkindly refused it.

Yet she *must* help him with his poor mother. How softened were all his thoughts about that difficult and troublesome lady! As it happened, he had a good deal of desultory medical knowledge, for the problems and perils of the body had always attracted his pessimist sense. Yet it did not help him much at this juncture. At one moment he said to himself, 'Eighteen months— she will live eighteen months,' and at another, 'Battye was probably right; Barham took an unnecessarily gloomy view—she may quite well last as long as the rest of us.'

Suddenly he was startled by a movement beside him.

'The honourable member has totally misunderstood me,' cried Fontenoy, springing to his feet and looking eagerly towards the Speaker.

The member who was speaking on the Government side smiled, put on his hat, and sat down. Fontenoy flung out a few stinging sentences, was hotly cheered both by his own supporters and from a certain area of the Liberal benches, and sat down again triumphant, having scored an excellent point.

George turned round to his companion.

'Good!' he said, with emphasis. 'That rubbed it in!'

But when the man opposite was once more on his legs, labouring to undo the impression which had been made, George found himself wondering whether, after all, the point had been so good, and why he had been so quick to praise. *She* would have said, of course, that it was a point scored against common-sense, against humanity. He began to fancy the play of her scornful eyes, the eloquence of her white hand moving and quivering as she spoke.

How long was it—one hurried month only—since he had walked with her along the river at Castle Luton? While the crowded House about him was again listening

with attention to the speech which had just brought
the protesting Fontenoy to his legs; while his leader
was fidgeting and muttering beside him; while to his
left the crowd of members round the door was constantly
melting, constantly reassembling, Tressady's mind withdrew itself from its surroundings, saw nothing, heard
nothing but the scenes of a far-off London and a figure
that moved among them.

How often had he been with her since Castle Luton?
Once or twice a week, certainly, either at St. James's
Square or in the East End, in spite of Parliament, and
Fontenoy, and his many engagements as Letty's husband.
Strange phenomenon—that little *salon* of hers in the far
East! For it was practically a *salon*, though it existed for
purposes the Hôtel Rambouillet knew nothing of. He
found himself one of many there. And, like all *salons*, it
had an inner circle. Charles Naseby, Edward Watton,
Lady Madeleine Penley, the Levens—some or all of these
were generally to be found in Lady Maxwell's neighbourhood, rendering homage or help in one way or another.
It was touching to see that girl, Lady Madeleine, looking
at the docker or the shirt-maker, with her restless greenish
eyes, as though she realised for the first time what a
hideous bond it is—the one true commonalty—that crushes
the human family together!

Well!—and what had he seen? Nothing, certainly, of
which he had not had ample information before. Under
the fresh spur of the talk that occupied the Maxwell
circle he had made one or two rounds through some
dismal regions in Whitechapel, Mile End, and Hackney,
where some of the worst of the home industries to which,
at last, after long hesitation on the part of successive
Governments, Maxwell's Bill was intended to put an end,
crowded every house and yard. He saw some of it in the
company of a lady rent-collector, an old friend of the

Maxwells, who had charge of several tenement blocks where the trouser and vest trade was largely carried on; and he welcomed the chance of one or two walks in quest of law-breaking workshops with a young inspector, who could not say enough in praise of the Bill. But if it had been only a question of fact, George would have felt when the rounds were done merely an added respect for Fontenoy, perhaps even for his own party as a whole. Not a point raised by his guides but had been abundantly discussed and realised—on paper, at any rate—by Fontenoy and his friends. The young inspector, himself a hot partisan, and knowing with whom he had to deal, would have liked to convict his companion of sheer and simple ignorance; but, on the contrary, Tressady was not to be caught napping. As far as the trade details and statistics of this gruesome slopwork of East London went, he knew all that could be shown him.

Nevertheless, cool and impassive as his manner was throughout, the experience in the main did mean the exchange of a personal for a paper and hearsay knowledge. When, indeed, had he, or Fontenoy, or anyone else ever denied that the life of the poor was an odious and miserable struggle, a scandal to gods and men? What then? Did they make the world and its iron conditions? And yet this long succession of hot and smelling dens, this series of pale, stooping figures, toiling hour after hour, at fever pace, in these stifling backyards, while the June sun shone outside, reminding one of English meadows and the ripple of English grass; these panting, dishevelled women, slaving beside their husbands and brothers, amid the rattle of the machines and the steam of the pressers' irons, with the sick or the dying, perhaps, in the bed beside them, and their blanched children at their feet—sights of this sort, thus translated from the commonplace of reports and newspapers into a poignant, unsavoury truth, had at least

this effect—they vastly quickened the personal melancholy
of the spectator, they raised and drove home a number of
piercing questions which, probably, George Tressady would
never have raised, and would have lived happily without
raising, if it had not been for a woman, and a woman's
charm.

For that woman's *solutions* remained as doubtful to
him as ever. He would go back to that strange little house
where she kept her strange court, meet her eager eyes,
and be roused at once to battle. How they had argued!
He knew that she had less hope than ever of persuading
him even to modify his view of the points at issue between
the Government and his own group. She could not hope
for a moment that any act of his would be likely to stand
between Maxwell and defeat. He had not talked of his
adventures to Fontenoy—would rather, indeed, that Fontenoy knew nothing of them. But he and she knew that
Fontenoy, so far, had little to fear from them.

And yet she had not turned from him. To her
personal mood, to her wifely affection even, he must
appear more plainly than ever as the callous and selfish
citizen, ready and glad to take his own ease while his
brethren perished. He had been sceptical and sarcastic ;
he had declined to accept her evidence ; he had shown
a persistent preference for the drier and more brutal
estimate of things. Yet she had never parted from him
without gentleness, without a look in her beautiful eyes
that had often tormented his curiosity. What did it
mean ? Pity ? Or some unspoken comment of a personal kind she could not persuade her womanly reticence
to put into words ?

Or, rather : had she some distant inkling of the real
truth—that he was beginning to hate his own convictions — to feel that to be right with Fontenoy was
nothing, but to be wrong with her would be delight ?

What absurdity! With a strong effort, he pulled himself together—steadied his rushing pulse. It was like some one waking at night in a nervous terror, and feeling the pressure of some iron dilemma, from which he cannot free himself—cold vacancy and want on the one side, calamity on the other.

For that cool power of judgment in his own case which he had always possessed did not fail him now. He saw everything nakedly and coldly. His marriage was not three months old, but no spectator could have discussed its results more frankly than he was now prepared to discuss them with himself. It was monstrous, no doubt. He felt his whole position to be as ugly as it was abnormal. Who could feel any sympathy with it or him? He himself had been throughout the architect of his own misfortune. Had he not rushed upon his marriage with less care—relatively to the weight of the human interest in such a matter—than an animal shows when it mates?

Letty's personal idiosyncrasies even — her way of entering a room, her mean little devices for attracting social notice, the stubborn extravagance of her dress and personal habits, her manner to her servants, her sharp voice as she retailed some scrap of slanderous gossip— her husband had by now ceased to be blind or deaf to any of them. Indeed, his senses in relation to many things she said and did were far more irritable at this moment—possibly far less just—than a stranger's would have been. Often and often he would try to recall to himself the old sense of charm, of piquancy. In vain. It was all gone—he could only miserably wonder at the past. Was it that he knew now what charm might mean, and what divinity may breathe around a woman?

'I say, where are you off to?'

Tressady looked up with a start as Fontenoy rose beside him.

'Good opportunity for dinner, I think,' said Fontenoy, with a motion of the head towards the man who had just caught the Speaker's eye. 'Are you coming? I should like a word with you.'

George followed him into the Lobby. As the swing-door closed behind him, they plunged into a whirlpool of talk and movement. All the approaches to the House were full of folk; everybody was either giving news or getting it. For the excitement of a coming crisis was in the air. This was Friday, and the division on the second reading was expected on the following Monday.

'What a crowd, and what a temperature!' said Fontenoy. 'Come on to the Terrace a moment.'

They made their way into the air, and as they walked up and down Fontenoy talked in his hoarse, hurried voice of the latest aspect of affairs. The Government would get their second reading, of course—that had never been really doubtful; though Fontenoy was certain that the normal majority would be a good deal reduced. But all the hopes of the heterogeneous coalition which had been slowly forming throughout the spring hung upon the Committee stage, and Fontenoy's mind was now full of the closest calculations as to the voting on particular amendments.

For him the Bill fell into three parts. The first part, which was mainly confined to small amendments and extensions of former Acts, would be sharply criticised, but would probably pass without much change. The second part contained the famous clause by which it became penal to practise certain trades, such as tailoring, boot-finishing, and shirt-making, in a man's or woman's own home—in the same place, that is to say, as the worker uses for eating and sleeping. This clause, which represented the climax of a long series of restrictions upon the right of a man to stitch even his own life away, still more upon his right to force his children or bribe his neighbour to a like waste of the nation's force, was by now stirring the industrial mind of England far and wide.

And not the mind of England only. Ireland and Scotland, town and country, talked of it, seethed with it. The new law, if it passed, was to be tried, indeed, at first, in London only. But every provincial town and every country district knew that, if it succeeded, there was not a corner of the land that would not ultimately feel the yoke, or the deliverance, of it. Every workman's club, every trade-union meeting, every mechanics' institute was ringing with it. Organised labour, dragged down at every point—in London, at any rate—by the competition of the starving and struggling crew of home-workers, clamoured for the Bill. The starving and struggling crew themselves were partly voiceless, partly bewildered ; now drawn by the eloquence of their trade-union fellows to shout for the revolution that threatened them, now surging tumultuously against it.

On this vital clause, in Fontenoy's belief, the Government would go down. But if, by amazing good-fortune and good generalship, they should get through with it, then the fight would but rage the more fiercely round the last two sections of the Bill.

The third section dealt with the hours of labour in the new workshops that were to be. For the first time it became directly penal for a man, as well as a woman, to work more than the accepted factory-day of ten and a half hours, with a few exceptions and exemptions in the matter of overtime. On this clause, if it were ever reached, the Socialist vote, were it given solidly for the Government, might, no doubt, pull them through. 'But if we have any luck—damn it ! they won't get the chance!' Fontenoy would say, with that grim, sudden reddening which revealed from moment to moment the feverish tension of the man.

In the last section of the Bill the Government, having made its revolution, looked round for a class on which to lay the burden of carrying it into action, and found it in the landlords. The landlords were to be the policemen of the new Act. To every owner of every tenement or other house in London the Bill said : *You* are responsible. If, after a certain date, you allow certain trades to be carried on within your walls at all, even by the single man or the single woman working in their own room, penalty and punishment shall follow.

Of this clause in the Bill Fontenoy could never speak with calmness. One might see his heart thumping in his breast as he denounced it. At bottom it was to him the last and vilest step in a long and slanderous campaign against the class to which he belonged—against property—against the existing social order.

He fell upon the subject to-night *à propos* of a Socialist letter in the morning papers ; and George, who was mostly conscious at the moment of a sick fatigue with Fontenoy and Fontenoy's arguments, had to bear it as best he might. Presently he interrupted :

'One assumption you make I should like to contest. You imagine, I think, that if they carry the prohibition and the hours clauses we shall be able to whip up a still fiercer attack on the "landlords" clause. Now, that isn't my view.'

Fontenoy turned upon him, startled.

'Why isn't it your view?' he said abruptly.

'Because there are always waverers who will accept a *fait accompli;* and you know how opposition has a trick of cooling towards the end of a Bill. Maxwell has carried his main point, they will say ; this is a

question of machinery. Besides, many of those Liberals
who will be with us on the main point don't love the
landlords. No! don't flatter yourself that, if we lose
the main engagement, there will be any Prussians to
bring up. The thing will be done.'

'Well, thank God!' grumbled Fontenoy, 'we don't
mean to lose the main engagement. But if one of *our* men
were to argue in that way, I should know what to say to
him.'

George made no reply.

They walked on in silence, the summer twilight falling
softly over the river and the Hospital, over the Terrace
with its groups, and the towering pile of buildings beside
them.

Presently Fontenoy said, in another voice:

'I have really never had the courage to talk to you of
the matter, Tressady, but didn't you see something of
that lad Ancoats before he went off abroad?'

'Yes, I saw him several times: first at the club;
then he came and dined with me here one night.'

'And did he confide in you?'

'More or less,' said George, smiling rather queerly at
the recollection.

Fontenoy made a sound between a growl and a sigh.

'Really, it's rather too much to have to think out that
young man's affairs as well as one's own. And the
situation is so extraordinary!—Maxwell and I have to be
in constant consultation. I went to see him in his room
in the House of Lords the other night, and met a man
coming out, who stopped, and stared as though he were
shot. Luckily I knew him, and could say a word to him,
or there would have been all sorts of cock-and-bull stories
abroad.'

'Well, and what are you and Maxwell doing?'

'Trying to get at the young woman. One can't buy

U

290 SIR GEORGE TRESSADY

her off, of course. Ancoats is his own master, and could
outbid us. But Maxwell has found a brother—a decent
sort of fellow—a country solicitor. And there is a
Ritualist curate, a Father somebody'—Fontenoy raised
his shoulders—'who seems to have an intermittent hold
on the girl. When she has fits of virtue she goes to
confess to him. Maxwell has got hold of *him.*'

'And meanwhile Ancoats is at Bad Wildheim?'

'Ancoats is at Bad Wildheim, and behaving himself,
as I hear from his poor mother.' Fontenoy sighed. 'But
the boy was frightened, of course, when they went abroad.
Now she is getting better, and one can't tell——'

'No, one can't tell,' said George.

'I wish I knew what the thing really *meant,*' said
Fontenoy presently, in a tone of perplexed reverie.
'What do you think? Is it a passion——?'

'Or a pose?'

George pondered.

'H'm,' he said at last—'more of a pose, I think, than
a passion. Ancoats always seems to me the *jeune premier*
in his own play. He sees his life in scenes, and plays
them according to all the rules.'

'Intolerable!' said Fontenoy, in exasperation. 'And
at least he might refrain from dragging a girl into it! We
weren't saints in my day, but we weren't in the habit of
choosing well-brought-up maidens of twenty in our own
set for our confidantes. You know, I suppose, what
broke up the party at Castle Luton?'

'Ancoats told me nothing. I have heard some gossip
from Harding Watton,' said George, unwillingly. It was
one of his strongest characteristics, this fastidious and
even haughty dislike of chatter about other people's
private affairs, a dislike which, in the present case, had
been strengthened by his growing antipathy to Harding.

'How should he know?' said Fontenoy, angrily. He

was glad enough to use Watton as a political tool, but had never yet admitted him to the smallest social intimacy.

Yet with Tressady he felt no difficulty in talking over these private affairs; and he did, in fact, report the whole story—that same story with which Marcella had startled Betty Leven on the night in question: how Ancoats on this Sunday evening had decoyed this handsome, impressionable girl, to whom throughout the winter he had been paying decided and even ostentatious court, into a *tête-à-tête*—had poured out to her frantic confessions of his attachment to the theatrical lady—a woman he could never marry, whom his mother could never meet, but with whom, nevertheless, come what might, he was determined to live and die. She—Madeleine—was his friend, his good angel. Would she go to his mother and break it to her? Would she understand, and forgive him? There must be no opposition, or he would shoot himself. And so on, till the poor girl, worn out with excitement and grief, tottered into Mrs. Allison's room more dead than alive.

But at that point Fontenoy stopped abruptly.

George agreed that the story was almost incredible, and added the inward and natural comment of the public-school man—that if people will keep their boys at home, and defraud them of the kickings that are their due, they may look out for something unwholesome in the finished product. Then, aloud, he said:

'I should imagine that Ancoats was acting through the greater part of that. He had said to himself that such a scene would be effective—and would be new.'

'Good Heavens!—why, that makes it ten thousand times more abominable than before!'

'I daresay,' said George, coolly. 'But it also makes the future, perhaps, a little more hopeful—throws some light on the passion or pose alternative. My impression

is, that if we can only find an effective exit for Ancoats—
a last act that he would consider worthy of him—he will
bow himself out of the business willingly enough.'

Fontenoy smiled rather gloomily, and the two walked
on in silence.

Once or twice, as they paced the Terrace, George
glanced sidelong at his leader. A corner of Fontenoy's
nightly letter to Mrs. Allison was, he saw, sticking out
of the great man's coat-pocket. Every night he wrote a
crowded sheet upon his knee, under the shelter of a Blue
Book, and on one or two nights George's quick eyes had
not been able to escape from the pencilled address on the
envelope to which it was ultimately consigned. The
sheet was written with the regularity and devotion of a
Prime Minister reporting to the Sovereign.

Well! it was all very touching and very remarkable.
But George had some sympathy with Ancoats. To be
virtually saddled with a stepfather, with whom your
minutest affairs are confidentially discussed, and yet to
have it said by all the world that your poor mother is too
unselfish and too devoted to her son to marry again—the
situation is not without its pricks. And that Ancoats
was acutely conscious of them George had good reason
to know.

'I say, Tressady, will you pair till eleven?' cried a
man swinging bareheaded along the Terrace with his
hat in his hand. 'I want an hour or two off badly, and
there will be no big guns on till eleven or so.'

George exchanged a word or two with Fontenoy, then
stood still, and thought a moment. A sudden animation
flushed into his face. Why not?

'All right!' he said; 'till eleven.'

Then he and Fontenoy went back to dine. As they
mounted the dark staircase leading from the Terrace
another man caught Tressady by the arm.

'The strike notices are out,' he said. 'I have just had a wire. Everyone leaves work to-night.'

George shrugged his shoulders. He had been expecting the news at any moment, and was glad that the long shilly-shallying on both sides was at last over.

'Good luck to them!' he said. 'I'm glad. The fight had to come.'

'Oh! we shall be in the middle of arbitration before a fortnight's up. The men won't stand.'

George shook his head. He himself believed that the struggle would last on through the autumn.

'Well, to be sure, there's Bewick,' said his informant, himself a large coalowner in the Ferth district; 'if Bewick keeps sober, and if somebody doesn't buy him, Bewick will do his worst.'

'That we always knew,' said George, laughing, and passed on. He had but just time to catch his train.

He walked across to the Underground station, and by the time he reached it he had clean forgotten his pits and the strike, though as he passed the post-office in the House a sheaf of letters and telegrams had been put into his hands. Rather, he was full of a boy's eagerness and exultation. He had never supposed he could be let off to-night, till the offer of Dudley's pair tempted him. And now, in half an hour he would be in that queer Mile End room, watching her—quarrelling with her.

A little later, however, as he was sitting quietly in the train, quick composite thoughts of Letty, of his miners, and his money difficulties began to clutch at him again. Perhaps, now that the strike was a reality, it might even be a help to him and a bridle to his wife. Preposterous, what she was doing and planning at Ferth! His face flushed and hardened as he thought of their many wrangles during the past fortnight, her constant drag upon his

purse, his own weakness, the annoyance and contempt
that made him yield rather than argue.

· What was that fellow, Harding Watton, doing in the
house at all hours, and beguiling Letty, by his collector's
airs, into a hundred foolish wants and whims? ˙ And that
brute Cathedine! Was it decent, was it bearable, that
a bride of three months should take no more notice of
her husband's wishes and dislikes in such a matter than
Letty had shown with regard to her growing friendship
with that disreputable person? It seemed to George
that he called most afternoons. Letty laughed, excused
herself, or abused her visitor as soon as he had departed;
but the rebuff which George's pride would not let him
ask of her directly, while yet his whole manner demanded
it, was never given.

He sat solitary in his brilliantly lit carriage, staring at
the advertisements opposite, his long chin thrust forward,
his head, with its fair curls, thrown moodily back. And
all the time his mind was working with an appalling
clearness. This cold light, in which he was beginning to
see his wife and all she did—it was already a tragedy.

What was he flying to, what was he in search of—
there in the East End? His whole being flung the
answer. A little sympathy, a little heart, a little tenderness and delicacy of soul!—nothing else. He had once
taken it for granted that every woman possessed them in
some degree. Or, was it only since he had found them
in this unexampled fulness and wealth that he had begun
to thirst for them in this way? He made himself face
the question. 'One needn't lie to oneself!'

· At Aldgate, as he was making his way out of the
station, he stumbled upon Edward Watton.

'Hullo! You bound for No. 20, too?'

'No; there is no function to-night. Lady Maxwell is
at a meeting. It has grown rather suddenly from small

beginnings, and two days ago they made her promise to speak. I came down because I am afraid of a row. Things are beginning to look ugly down here, and I don't think she has much idea of it. Will you come?'

'Of course.'

Watton looked at him with an amused and friendly eye.

It was another instance of her power—that she had been able to bind even this young enemy to her chariot-wheels. He hoped Letty had the sense to approve! As a matter of fact, Watton had never, by his own choice, become well acquainted with his cousin Letty, and had always secretly marvelled at Tressady's sudden marriage.

CHAPTER XIV

Tʜᴇ two men were soon on the top of the Mile End Road tramcar, on their way eastward. It was a hot, dull evening. The setting sun behind them was already swallowed up in mist, and the heavy air held down and made palpable all the unsavoury odours of street and shop. Before them stretched the wide, interminable road which was once the highway from the great city to Colchester and East Anglia. A broad and comely thoroughfare on the whole, save that from end to end it has now the dyed and patched look that an old village street inevitably puts on when it has been swallowed up by the bricks and mortar of an overtaking town.

Tressady looked round him in a reverie, interested in the place and the streets because *she* cared for them, and had struck one of her roots here. Strange medley everywhere—in this main street, at all events—of old and new! Here were the Trinity almshouses, with their Jacobean gables and their low, spreading quadrangle behind the fine ironwork that shelters them from the street—a poetic fragment from the days of Wren and Dryden, sore threatened now by an ever-advancing London, hungry for ground and space. Here was a vast mission-hall, there a still vaster brewery ; on the right, the quiet entrance to the old-world quiet of Stepney Green ; and to the left a huge flame-ringed gin-palace, with shops on either side, hung to the roof with carpets, or brooms, or umbrellas, plastered with advertisements, and blazing with gas. While in the street between streamed the ever-moving crowd of East London folk, jostling, chattering, loafing, doing their business or their pleasure, and made perpetually interesting, partly by their frank preoccupation with the simplest realities of life : with eating, drinking, earning, marrying, child-rearing ; still more, perhaps, by the constant presence among them of that 'leisured class' which, alike at the bottom and the top of things, has time to be gay, curious, and witty.

As he rolled along, watching the scene, Tressady thought to himself, as he had often thought before, that the East End, in many of its aspects, is a very decentish sort of place, about which many people talk much nonsense. He made the remark, carelessly, to Watton.

Watton shrugged his shoulders, and pointed silently to the entrances, right and left, of two side-streets, the typical streets of the East End : long lines of low houses —two storeys always, or two storeys and a basement— all of the same yellowish brick, all begrimed by the same smoke, every door-knocker of the same pattern, every window-blind hung in the same way, and the same corner 'public' on either side, flaming in the hazy distance.

Watton hardly put his comment into words ; but Tressady, who knew him well, understood, and nodded over his cigarette. Watton meant, of course, to suggest the old commonplace of the mean and dull monotony that weighs like a nightmare upon this vast East London and its human hive, which hums and toils, drones and feeds, by night and day, in these numberless featureless boxes of wood and stone, on this flat, interminable earth that stretches eastward to Essex marshes and southward to the river, and bears yellow brick and cemeteries for corn.

Well! Tressady knew that the thought of this monotony, and of the thousands under its yoke, was to

Watton a constant sting and oppression ; he knew, too, or guessed, the religious effects it produced in him. For Watton was a religious man, and the action of the dream within showed itself in him and all he did. But why should everyone make a grief of East London ? He was in the mood again to-night to feel it a kind of impertinence, this endless, peering anxiety about a world you never planned and cannot mend. Whose duty is it to cry for the moon ?

'Better get down here, I think,' said Watton, signalling to the tram-conductor, 'and find out whether they have really gone, or not.'

They stopped, half way down the Mile End Road, before a piece of wall with a door in it. A trim maiden of fifteen in a spotless cotton frock and white apron opened to them.

Inside was a small flagged courtyard and the old-fashioned house that Marcella Maxwell, a year before —some time after their first lodging had been given up— had rescued from demolition and the builder, to make an East End home out of it. Somewhere about 1750 some City tradesman had built it among fields, and taken his rest there ; while somewhat later, in a time of Evangelical revival, a pious widow had thrown out a low room to one side for class-meetings. In this room Marcella now held her gatherings, and both Tressady and Watton knew it well.

The little handmaid bubbled over with willing talk. Oh, yes, there was a meeting up Manx Road, and her Ladyship had gone with Lord Naseby, and Lady Madeleine, and Mr. Everard, the inspector, and, she thought, one or two besides. She expected the ladies back about ten, and they were to stay the night.

'An they do say, sir,' she said eagerly, looking up

at Watton, whom she knew, 'as there'll be a lot o rough people at the meetin.'

'Oh! I daresay,' said Watton. 'Well, we're going up, too, to look after her.'

As they walked on they talked over the general situation in the district, and Watton explained what he knew of this particular meeting. In the first place, he repeated, he could not see that Lady Maxwell understood as yet the sort of opposition that the Bill was rousing, especially in these East End districts. The middle-class and parliamentary resistance she had always appreciated; but the sort of rage that might be awakened among a degraded class of workers by proposals that seemed to threaten their immediate means of living, he believed she had not yet realised, in anything like its full measure and degree. And he feared that this meeting might be a disagreeable experience.

· For it was the direct fruit of an agitation that, as Tressady knew, was in particular Fontenoy's agitation. The Free Workers' League, which had called upon the trade-unionists of Mile End to summon the meeting, and to hear therein what both sides had to say, was, in fact, Fontenoy's creation. It had succeeded especially in organising the women home-workers of Mile End and Poplar. Two or three lady-speakers employed by the League had been active to the point of frenzy in denouncing the Bill and shrieking 'Liberty!' in the frightened ear of Mile End. Watton could not find a good word for any of them—was sure that what mostly attracted them was the notoriety of the position, involving, as it did, a sort of personal antagonism to Lady Maxwell, who had, so to speak, made Mile End her own. And to be Lady Maxwell's enemy was, Watton opined, the next best thing, from the point of view of advertisement, to being her friend.

'Excellent women, I daresay,' said Tressady, laughing—'talking excellent sense. But, tell me, what is this about Naseby—why Naseby?—on all these occasions?'

'Why not, indeed?' said Watton. 'Ah! you don't know? It seems to be Naseby that's going to get the egg out of the hat for us.'

And he plunged eagerly into the description of certain schemes wherewith Naseby had lately astonished the Maxwell circle. Tressady listened, languidly at first, then with a kind of jealous annoyance that scandalised himself. How well he could understand the attraction of such things for her quick mind! Life was made too easy for these 'golden lads.' People attributed too much importance to their fancies.

Naseby, in fact—but so much George already knew—had been for some months now the comrade and helper of both the Maxwells. His friends still supposed him to be merely the agreeable and fashionable idler. In reality, Naseby for some years past had been spending all the varied leisure that his commission in the Life Guards allowed him upon the work of a social and economic student. He had joined the staff of a well-known sociologist, who was at the time engaged in an inquiry into certain typical East London trades. The inquiry had made a noise, and the evidence collected under it had already been largely used in the debates on the Maxwell Bill. Tressady, for instance, had much of it by heart, although he never knew, until he became a haunter of Lady Maxwell's circle, that Naseby had played any part in the gathering of it.

At the same time, as George had soon observed, Naseby was no blind follower of the Maxwells. In truth, under his young gaiety and coolness he had the temper of the student, who is more in love with his problem itself than with any suggested solution of it. As he had told Lady Betty, he had 'no opinions'—would himself rather leave the sweated trades alone, and trust to much slower and less violent things than law-making. All this the Maxwells knew perfectly, and liked and trusted him none the less.

Now, however, it seemed there was a new development. If the Bill passed, Naseby had a plan. He was already a rich man, independently of the marquisate to come. His grandmother had left him a large preliminary fortune, and through his friends and connections besides he seemed to command as much money as he desired. And of this money, supposing the Bill passed, he proposed to make original and startling use. He had worked out the idea of a syndicate furnished with, say, a quarter of a million of money, which should come down upon a given district of the East End, map it out, buy up all the existing businesses in its typical trade, and start a system of new workshops proportioned to the population, supplying it with work just as the Board schools supply it with education. The new scheme was to have a profit-sharing element: the workers were to be represented on the syndicate, and every nerve was to be strained to secure the best business-management. The existing middlemen would be either liberally bought out, or absorbed into the new machine. It was by no means certain that they would show it any strong resistance.

Tressady made a number of unfriendly comments on the scheme as Watton detailed it. A bit of amateur economics, which would only help the Bill to ruin a few more people than would otherwise have gone down !

'Ah ! well,' said Watton, 'if this thing passes there are bound to be experiments, and Naseby means to be in 'em. So do I, only I haven't got a quarter of a million. Here's our road ! We're late, of course—the meeting's begun. I say, just look at this ! '

For Manx Road, as they turned into it, was already held by another big meeting of its own. The room in the Board school which crossed the end of the street must be full, and this crowd represented, apparently, those who had been turned away.

As the two friends pushed their way through, Tressady's quick eye recognised in the throng a number of familiar types. Well-to-do 'pressers' and machinists, factory-girls of different sorts, hundreds of sallow women, representing the home-workers of Mile End, Bow, and Stepney—poor souls bowed by toil and maternity, whose marred fingers labour day and night to clothe the Colonies and the army; their husbands and brothers, too, English slop-tailors for the most part, of the humbler sort—the short side-street was packed with them. It was an anxious, sensitive crowd, Tressady thought, as he elbowed his passage through it. A small thing might inflame it; and he saw a number of rough lads on the skirts of it.

Jews, too, there were in plenty. For the stress of this Bill had brought Jew and Gentile together in a new comradeship that amazed the East End. Here were groups representing the thrifty, hard-working London Jew of the second generation—small masters for the most part, pale with the confinement and 'drive' of the workshop—men who are expelling and conquering the Gentile East-ender, because their inherited passion for business is not neutralised by any of the common English passions for spending—above all by the passion for drink. Here, too, were men of a far lower type and grade—the waste and refuse of the vast industrial mill. Tressady knew a good many of them by sight—sullen, quick-eyed folk, who buy their 'greeners' at the docks, and work them day and night at any time of pressure; whose workshops are still flaring at two o'clock in the morning, and alive again by the winter dawn; who fight and flout the law by a hundred arts, and yet, brutal and shifty as many of them are, have a curious way of winning the Gentile inspector's sympathy, even while he fines and harasses them, so clearly are they and their 'hands' alike the victims of a huge world-struggle that does but toss them on its surge.

These gentry, however, were hard hit by more than one clause of the Maxwell Bill, and they were here to-night to protest, as they had been already protesting at many meetings, large and small, all over the East End. And they had their slaves with them—ragged, hollow-eyed creatures, newly arrived from Russian Poland, Austria, or Roumania, and ready to shout or howl in Yiddish as they were told—men whose strange faces and eyes under their matted shocks of black or reddish hair suggested every here and there the typical history and tragic destiny of the race which, in other parts of the crowd, was seen under its softer and more cosmopolitan aspects.

As the two men neared the door of the school, where the press was densest, they were recognised as probably belonging to the Maxwell party, and found themselves a good deal jeered and hustled, and could hardly make any way at all. However, a friendly policeman came to their aid. They were passed into a lobby, and at last, with much elbowing and pushing, found themselves inside the schoolroom.

So crowded was the place and so steaming the atmosphere, that it was some minutes before Tressady could make out what was going on. Then he saw that Naseby was speaking—Naseby, looking remarkably handsome and well-curled, and much at his ease, besides, in the production of a string of Laodicean comments on the Bill, his own workshop scheme, and the general prospects of East-End labour. He described the scheme, but in such a way as rather to damn it than praise it; and as for the Bill itself, which he had undertaken to compare with former Factory Bills, when he sat down he left it, indeed, in a parlous case—a poor, limping, doubtful thing, quite as likely to ruin the East End as to do it a hand's turn of good.

Just as the speaker was coming to his peroration, Tressady suddenly caught sight of a delicate upraised profile on the platform, behind Naseby. The repressed smile on it set him smiling, too.

'What on earth do they make Naseby speak for!' said Watton, indignantly. 'Idiocy! He spoils everything he touches. Let him give the money, and other people do the talking. You can see the people here don't know what to make of him in the least. Look at their faces.—Who's he talking to?'

'Lady Madeleine, I think,' said Tressady. 'What amazing red hair that girl has! and what queer, scared eyes! It is like an animal—one wants to stroke her.'

'Well, Naseby strokes her,' said Watton, laughing. 'Look at her; she brightens up directly he comes near.'

Tressady thought of the tale Fontenoy had just told him, and wondered. Consolation seemed to come easy to maidens of quality.

Meanwhile various trade unionists—sturdy, capable men, in black coats—were moving and seconding resolutions; flinging resentful comments, too, at Naseby whenever occasion offered. Tressady heard very little of what they had to say. His eyes and thoughts were busy with the beautiful figure to the left of the chair. Its dignity and charm worked upon him like a spell—infused a kind of restless happiness.

When he woke from his trance of watching, it was to turn upon Watton with impatience. How long was this thing going on? The British workman spoke with

deplorable fluency. Couldn't they push their way through
to the platform?

Watton looked at the crowd, and shrugged his shoulders.

'Not yet—I say! who's this they've put up. Come,
my dear fellow, that looks like the real thing!'

Tressady turned, and saw an old man, a Jew, with
a long greyish beard, coming slowly to the front of the
platform. His eyes were black and deep, sunk under
white brows; he was decently but poorly dressed; and
he began to speak with a slight German accent, in an
even, melancholy voice, rather under-pitched, which soon
provoked the meeting. He was vociferously invited to
speak up or sit down; and at the first interruption he
stopped timorously, and looked towards the Chair.

An elderly, grey-haired woman was presiding—no
doubt to mark the immense importance of the Bill for the
women of the East End. She came forward at the man's
appeal.

'My friends,' she said quietly, 'you let this man
speak, and don't you be hard on him. He's got a sad story
to tell you, and he won't be long about it. You give him
his chance. Some of you shall have yours soon.'

The speaker was the paid secretary of one of the
women's unions; but she had been a tailoress for years,
and had known a tragic life. Once, at a meeting where
some flippant speaker had compared the reality and frequency of 'starvation' in London to the reality and
frequency of the sea serpent, Tressady had seen her get
up and, with a sudden passion, describe the death of her
own daughter from hardship and want, with the tears
running down her cheeks.

Her appeal to the justice of the meeting succeeded,
and the old man was allowed to go on. It soon appeared
that he had been put up by one of the tailoring unions to

                                                      x

denounce the long hours worked in some of the Whitechapel and Spitalfields workshops. His facts were
appalling. But he put them badly, with a dull, stumbling
voice, and he got no hold on the meeting at all till suddenly he stepped forward, paused—his miserable face
working, his head turning from side to side—and finally
said, with a sharp change of note :

'And now, if you please, I will tell you how it was
about Isaac—my brother Isaac. It was Mr. Jacobs'—he
looked round, and pointed to the trade union secretary who
had been speaking before him—'Mr. Jacobs it was that
put it in my mind to come here and tell you about Isaac.
For the way Isaac died was like this. He and I were born
in Spitalfields; he wasn't one of your greeners—he was
a reg'lar good worker, first-rate general coat-hand, same
as me. But he got with a hard master. And last winter
season but one there came a rush. And Isaac must be
working six days a week—and he must be working fourteen hours a day—and, more'n that, he must be doing
his bastes overtime, two hours one time, and an hour or
so, perhaps, another; anyway, they made it up to half a
day—eight hours and more in the week. *You* know how
they reckon it.'

He stopped, grinning feebly. The trade unionists
about the platform shouted or groaned in response. The
masters round the door, with their 'greeners,' stood silent.

'And about Wednesday in the third week,' he went
on, 'he come to the master, and he says—Isaac was older
than me, and his chest it would be beginning to trouble
him pretty bad, so he says : " I'm done," he says ; " I must
go home. You can get another chap to do my bastes to-
night—will you ? " And the master says to Isaac : "If
you don't do your bastes overtime, if you're too high and
mighty," he says, " why, there's plenty as will, and you
don't need to come to-morrow neither." And Isaac had

his wife Judith at home, and four little uns; and he stopped and done his bastes, of *course*. And next night he couldn't well see, and he'd been dreadful sick all day, and he says to the master again, he says as he must go home. And the master, he says the same to him—and Isaac stops. And on Friday afternoon he come home. And the shop had been steamin hot, but outside it was a wind to cut yer through. And his wife Judith says to him, " Isaac, you look starved !" and she set him by the fire. And he sat by the fire, and he didn't say nothing. Then his hands fell down sudden like that——'

The old man let his hands drop heavily by his side with a simple dramatic gesture. By this time there was not a sound in the crowded room. Even the wildest and most wolfish of the greeners were staring silently, craning brown necks forward.

'And his wife ran to him, and he falls against her ; and he says, " Lay me down, Judith, and don't you let em wake me—not the young uns," he says—"not for nothing and nobody. For if it was the trump of the Most High," he says—and Isaac was a religious man, and careful in his speech—"I must have my sleep." And she laid him down, and the children and she watched—and by midnight Isaac turned himself over. He just opened his eyes once, and groaned. And he never spoke no more —he was gone before mornin.—And his master gave Judith five shillings towards the coffin, and the men in the shop, they raised the rest.'

The old man paused. He stood considering a moment, his face and ragged beard thrown out—a spot of greyish white — against the figures behind, his eyes blinking painfully under the gas.

'Well, we've tried many things,' he said at last. ' We've tried strikes and unions, and it isn't no good. There's always one treading on another, and if you don't

do it, some one else will. It's the *law* as'll have to do it.
You may take that and smoke it!—you won't get nothing
else. Why!'—his hoarse voice trembled—'why, they
use us up cruel in the sort of shop I work for. Ten or
twelve years, and a man's all to pieces. It's the irons,
and the heat, and the sitting—*you* know what it is. I've
lasted fifteen year, but I'm breaking up now. If my
master give me the sack for speaking here I'll have
nothing but the Jewish Board of Guardians to look to.
All the same, I made up my mind as I'd come and say
how they served Isaac.'

He stopped abruptly, and stood quite still a moment,
fronting the meeting, as though appealing to them,
through the mere squalid physical weakness he could
find no more words to express. Then, with a sort of
shambling bow, he turned away, and the main body of
the meeting clapped excitedly, while at the back some of
the 'sweaters' grinned, and chatted sarcastic things in
Yiddish with their neighbours. Tressady saw Lady Maxwell rise eagerly as the old man passed her, take his hand,
and find him a seat.

'That, I suppose, was an emotion,' said Tressady,
looking down upon his companion.

'Or an argument,' said Watton—'as you like!'

One other 'emotion' of the same kind—the human
reality at its simplest and cruellest—Tressady afterwards
remembered.

A 'working-woman' was put up to second an amend-
ment condemning the workshops clause, which had been
moved in an angry speech by one of 'Fontenoy's ladies,'
a shrill-voiced, fashionable person, the secretary to the
local branch of the Free Workers' League. Tressady
had yawned impatiently through the speech, which had
seemed to him a violent and impertinent performance.

But as the speaker sat down he was roused by an exclamation from a man beside him.

'*That* woman!' cried a tall curate, straining on tiptoe to see. 'No! They ought to be ashamed of themselves!'

Tressady wondered who and why; but all that he saw was that a thin, tall woman was being handed along the bench in front of him, while her neighbours and friends clapped her on the back as she passed, laughing and urging her on. Then, presently, there she stood on the platform, a thin, wand-like creature, with her battered bonnet sideways on her head, a woollen crossover on her shoulders, in spite of July, her hands clasped across her chest, her queer light eyes wandering and smiling hither and thither. In her emaciation, her weird cheerfulness, she was like a figure from a Dance of Death. But what was amazing was her self-possession.

'Now yer laffin at me,' she began in a conversational tone, nodding towards the group of women she had just left. 'You go long! I told the lidy I'd speak, an I will. Well, they comes to me, an they ses, Mrs. Dickson, yer not to work at ome no longer—they'll put yer in prison if yer do't, they ses; yer to go out ter work, same as the shop ands, they ses; and what's more, if they cotch Mr. Butterford—that's my landlord; p'raps yer dunno im——'

She looked down at the meeting with a whimsical grin, her eyes screwed up and her crooked brows lifted, so that the room roared merely to look at her. The trim lady-secretary, however, bent forward with an air of annoyance. She had not, perhaps, realised that Mrs. Dickson was so much of a character.

'If they cotch Mr. Butterford, they'll make im pay up smart for lettin yer do such a thing as make knickers in is ouse. So I asks the lidy, Wot's ter become o me an the little uns? An she says she done know, but yer mus

come and speak Tuesday night, she says—Manx Road
Schools, she says—if yer want to perwent em making a
law ov it.   Which I'm a doin of—ain't I?'

Fresh laughter and response from the room.   She went
on satisfied.

'An, yer know, if I can't make the knickers at ome, I
can't make em away from ome.   For ther ain't no shops
as want kids squallin round, as fer as I can make out.
An Jimmy's a limb, as boys mos'ly are in my egsperience.
Larst week ee give the biby a alfpenny and two o my
biggest buttons to swaller, an I ony jest smacked em
out of er in time.   Ther'd be murder done if I was to
leave em.   An ow ud I be able to pay anyone fer
lookin after em?   I can't git much, yer know, shop or
no shop.   I ain't wot I was.'

She stopped, and pointed significantly to her chest.
Tressady shuddered as the curate whispered to him.

'I've been in orspital—cut about fearful.   I can't go
at the pace them shops works at.   They'd give me the
sack, double-quick, if I was to go tryin em.   No, it's
settin as does it—settin an settin.   I'm at it by seven,
an my usband—yer can see im there—ee'll tell yer.'

She stopped, and pointed to a burly ruffian standing
amid a group of 'pals' round the door.   This gentleman had his arms folded, and was alternately frowning
and grinning at this novel spectacle of his wife as a public
performer.   Bribes had probably been necessary to bring
him to consent to the spectacle at all.   But he was not
happy, and when his wife pointed at him, and the meeting
turned to look, he suddenly took a dive head-foremost
into the crowd about him; so that when the laughter
and horse-play that followed had subsided, it was seen
that Mr. Tom Dickson's place knew him no more.

Meanwhile Mrs. Dickson stood grinning—grinning wide
and visibly.   It was the strangest mirth, as though hollow

pain and laughter strove with each other for the one poor
indomitable face.

'Well, ee *could* a told yer, if ee'd ad the mind,' she
said, nodding, 'for ee knows. Ee's been out o work this
twelve an a arf year—well, come, I'll bet yer, anyway, as
ee asn't done a and's turn this three year—an I don't
blime im. Fust, there isn't the work to be got, and then
yer git out o the way o wantin it. An beside, I'm used
to im. When Janey—no, it were Sue!—were seven
month old, ee come in one night from the public, an
after ee'd broke up most o the things, ee says to me,
"Clear out, will yer!" An I cleared out, and Sue and
me set on the doorstep till mornin. And when mornin
come, Tom opened the door, an ee says, "What are you
doin there, mother? Why ain't yer got my breakfast?"
An I went in an got it. But, bless yer, nowadays—the
women won't do it!——'

Another roar went up from the meeting. Mrs. Dickson still grinned.

'An so there's nothink but *settin*, as I said before—
settin till yer can't set no more. If I begin o seven, I
gets Mr. Dickson to put the teathings an the loaf andy,
so as I don't ave to get up more'n jes to fetch the
kettle; and the chillen gets the same as me—tea an bread,
and a red erring Sundays; an Mr. Dickson, ee gets is
meals' out. I gives im the needful, and ee don't make no
trouble; an the chillen is dreadful frackshus sometimes,
and gets in my way fearful. But there, if I can *set*—set
till I ear Stepney Church goin twelve—I can earn my
ten shillin a week, an keep the lot of em. Wot does any
lidy or genelman want, a comin meddlin down ere?
Now, that's the middle an both ends on it. Done? Well,
I dessay I is done. Lor, I ses to em in the orspital
it do seem rummy to me to be layin abed like that. If
Tom was ere, why, ee'd——'

She made a queer, significant grimace. But the audience laughed no longer. They stared silently at the gaunt
creature, and with their silence her own mood changed.

Suddenly she whipped up her apron. She drew it
across her eyes, and flung it away again passionately.

'I dessay we shall be lyin abed in Kingdom Come,'
she said defiantly, yet piteously. 'But we've got to git
there fust. An I don't want no shops, thank yer!'

She rambled on a little longer, then, at a sign from the
lady-secretary, made a grinning curtsy to the audience
and departed.

'What do they get out of that?' said Watton in
Tressady's ear—'Poor galley-slave in praise of servitude!'

'Her slavery keeps her alive, please.'

'Yes—and drags down the standard of a whole class!'

'You'll admit she seemed content?'

'It's that content we want to kill.—Ah! *at last!*' and
Watton clapped loudly, followed by about half the meeting, while the rest sat silent. Then Tressady perceived
that the chairwoman had called upon Lady Maxwell to
move the next resolution, and that the tall figure had risen.

She came forward slowly, glancing from side to side,
as though doubtful where to look for her friends. She
was in black, and her head was covered with a little
black lace bonnet, in the strings of which, at her throat,
shone a small diamond brooch. The delicate whiteness
of her face and hands, and this sparkle of light on her
breast, that moved as she moved, struck a thrill of
pleasure through Tressady's senses. The squalid
monotony and physical defect of the crowd about him
passed from his mind. Her beauty redressed the balance.
' " Loveliness, magic, and grace—they are here; they are
set in the world! "—and ugliness and pain have not
conquered while this face still looks and breathes.' This,
and nothing less, was the cry of the young man's heart

and imagination as he strained forward, waiting for her voice.

Then he settled himself to listen—only to pass gradually from expectation to nervousness, from nervousness to dismay.

What was happening? She had once told him that she was not a speaker, and he had not believed her. She had begun well, he thought, though with a hesitation he had not expected. But now—had she lost her thread—or what? Incredible! when one remembered her in private life, in conversation. Yet those stumbling sentences, this evident distress!

Tressady found himself fidgeting in sympathetic misery. He and Watton looked at each other.

A little more, and she would have lost her audience. She *had* lost it. At first there had been eager listening, for she had plunged straightway into a set explanation and defence of the Bill point by point, and half the room knew that she was Lord Maxwell's wife. But by the end of ten minutes their attention was gone. They were only staring at her because she was handsome and a great lady. Otherwise, they seemed not to know what to make of her. She grew white; she wavered. Tressady saw that she was making great efforts, and all in vain. The division between her and her audience widened with every sentence, and Fontenoy's lady-organiser, in the background, sat smilingly erect. Tressady, who had been at first inclined to hate the thought of her success in this Inferno, grew hot with wrath and irritation. His own vanity suffered in her lack of triumph.

Amazing! How *could* her personal magic—so famous on so many fields—have deserted her like this in an East-End schoolroom, before people whose lives she knew, whose griefs she carried in her heart?

Then an idea struck him. The thought was an

illumination—he understood. He shut his eyes and listened. Maxwell's sentences, Maxwell's manner—even, at times, Maxwell's voice! He had been rehearsing to her his coming speech in the House of Lords, and she was painfully repeating it! To his disgust, Tressady saw the reporters scribbling away—no doubt they knew their business! Aye, there was the secret. The wife's adoration showed through her very failure—through this strange conversion of all that was manly, solid, and effective in Maxwell, into a confused mass of facts and figures, pedantic, colourless, and cold!

Edward Watton began to look desperately unhappy. 'Too long,' he said, whispering in Tressady's ear, 'and too technical. They can't follow.'

And he looked at a group of rough factory-girls beginning to scuffle with the young men near them, at the restless crowd of 'greeners,' at the women in the centre of the hall lifting puzzled faces to the speaker, as though in a pain of listening.

Tressady nodded. In the struggle of devotion with a half-laughing annoyance he could only crave that the thing should be over.

But the next instant his face altered. He pushed forward instinctively, turning his back on Watton, hating the noisy room, that would hardly let him hear.

Ah!—those few last sentences, that voice, that quiver of passion—they were her own—herself, not Maxwell. The words were very simple, and a little tremulous— words of personal reminiscence and experience. But for one listener there they changed everything. The room, the crowd, the speaker—he saw them for a moment under another aspect: that poetic, eternal aspect, which is always there, behind the veil of common things, ready to flash out on mortal eyes. He *felt* the woman's heart, oppressed with a pity too great for it; the delicate, trembling consciousness, like a point in space, weighed on by the burden of the world; he stood, as it were, beside her, hearing with her ears, seeing the earth-spectacle as she saw it, with that terrible second sight of hers : the all-environing woe and tragedy of human things—the creeping hunger and pain—the struggle that leads no whither—the life that hates to live and yet dreads to die—the death that cuts all short, and does but add one more hideous question to the great pile that hems the path of man.

A hard, reluctant tear rose in his eyes. Is it starved tailoresses and shirtmakers alone who suffer? Is there no hunger of the heart, that matches and overweighs the physical? Is it not as easy for the rich as the poor to miss the one thing needful, the one thing that matters and saves? Angrily, and in a kind of protest, he put out his hand, as it were, to claim his own share of the common pain.

'Make way there ! make way ! ' cried a police-sergeant, holding back the crowd, 'and let the lady pass.'

Tressady did his best to push through with Lady Maxwell on his arm. But there was an angry hum of voices in front of him, an angry pressure round the doors.

' We shall soon get a cab,' he said, bending over her. ' You are very tired, I fear. Please lean upon me.'

Yet he could but feel grateful to the crowd. It gave him this joy of protecting and supporting her. Nevertheless, as he looked ahead, he wished that they were safely off, and that there were more police !

For this meeting, which had been only mildly disorderly and inattentive while Marcella was speaking, had suddenly flamed, after she sat down, into a fierce confusion and tumult—why, Tressady hardly now understood. A man had sprung up to speak as she sat down who was apparently in bad repute with most of the unions of the

district. At any rate, there had been immediate uproar and
protest. The trade unionists would not hear him—hurled
names at him—'thief,' 'blackleg'—as he attempted to
speak. Then the Free Workers, for whom this dubious
person had been lately acting, rose in a mass and booed at
the unionists; and finally some of the dark-eyed, black-
bearded 'greeners' near the door, urged on, probably, by
the masters, whose slaves they were, had leaped the
benches near them, shouting strange tongues, and making
for the hostile throng around the platform.

Then it had been time for Naseby and the police to
clear the platform and open a passage for the Maxwell
party. Unfortunately, there was no outlet to the back,
no chance of escaping the shouting crowd in Manx Road.
Tressady, joining his friends at last by dint of his height
and a free play of elbows, found himself suddenly alone
with Lady Maxwell, Naseby and Lady Madeleine borne
along far behind, and no chance but to follow the current,
with such occasional help as the police stationed along
the banks of it might be able to give.

Outside, Tressady strained his eyes for a cab.

'Here, sir!' cried the sergeant in front, carving a
passage by dint of using his own stalwart frame as a ram.

They hurried on, for some rough lads on the edges of
the crowd had already begun stone-throwing. The faces
about them seemed to be partly indifferent, partly hostile.
'Look at the bloomin bloats!' cried a wild factory-girl
with a touzled head as Lady Maxwell passed. 'Let em
stop at ome and mind their own usbands—yah!'

'Garn! who paid for your bonnet?' shouted another,
until a third girl pulled her back, panting, 'If you say
that any more I'll scrag yer!' For this third girl had
spent a fortnight in the Mile End Road house, getting fed
and strengthened before an operation.

But here was the cab! Lady Maxwell's foot was

already on the step, when Tressady felt something fly past him.

There was a slight cry. The form in front of him seemed to waver a moment. Then Tressady himself mounted, caught her, and in another moment, after a few plunges from the excited horse, they were off down Manx Road, followed by a shouting crowd that gradually thinned.

'You are hurt!' he said.

'Yes,' she said faintly, 'but not much. Will you tell him to drive first to Mile End Road?'

'I have told him. Can I do anything to stop the bleeding?'

He looked at her in despair. The handkerchief, and the delicate hand itself that she was holding to her brow, were dabbled in blood.

'Have you a silk handkerchief to spare?' she asked him, smiling slightly and suddenly through her pallor, as though at their common predicament.

By good-fortune he had one. She took off her hat, and gave him a few business-like directions. His fingers trembled as he tried to obey her; but he had the practical sense that the small vicissitudes and hardships of travel often develop in a man, and between them they adjusted a rough but tolerable bandage.

Then she leant against the side of the cab, and he thought she would have swooned. There was a pause, during which he watched the quivering lines of the lips and nostrils and the pallor of the cheeks with a feeling of dismay.

But she did not mean to faint, and little by little her will answered to her call upon it. Presently she said, with eyes shut and brow contracted:

'I *trust* the others are safe. Oh! what a failure—what a failure! I am afraid I have done Aldous harm!'

The tone of the last words touched Tressady deeply. Evidently she could hardly restrain her tears.

'They were not worthy you should go and speak to them,' he said quickly. 'Besides, it was only a noisy minority.'

She did not speak again till they drew up before the house in the Mile End Road. Then she turned to him.

'I was to have stayed here for the night, but I think I must go home. Aldous might hear that there had been a disturbance. I will leave a message here, and drive home.'

'I trust you will let me go with you. We should none of us be happy to think of you as alone just yet. And I am due at the House by eleven.'

She smiled, assenting, then descended, leaning heavily upon him in her weakness.

When she reappeared, attended by her two little servants, all frightened and round-eyed at their mistress's mishap, she had thrown a thick lace scarf round her head, which hid the bandage and gave to her pale beauty a singularly touching, appealing air.

'I wish I could see Madeleine,' she said anxiously, standing beside the cab and looking up the road. 'Ah!'

For she had suddenly caught sight of a cab in the distance driving smartly up. As it approached, Naseby and Lady Madeleine were plainly to be seen inside it. The latter jumped out almost at Marcella's feet, looking more scared than ever as she saw the bandage and the black scarf twisted round the white face. But in a few moments Marcella had soothed her, and given her over, apparently, to the care of another lady staying in the house. Then she waved her hand to Naseby, who, with his usual coolness, asked no questions and made no remarks, and she and Tressady drove off.

'Madeleine will stay the night,' Marcella explained as

they sped towards Aldgate. 'That was our plan. My
secretary will look after her. She has been often here
with me lately, and has things of her own to do. But I
ought not to have taken her to-night. Lady Kent would
never have forgiven me if she had been hurt. Oh! it
was all a mistake—all a great mistake! I suppose I
imagined—that is one's folly—that I could really do
some good—make an effect.'

She bit her lip, and the furrow reappeared in the.
white brow.

Tressady felt by sympathy that her heart was all
sore, her moral being shaken and vibrating. After these
long months of labour and sympathy and emotion, the
sudden touch of personal brutality had unnerved her.

Mere longing to comfort, to 'make-up,' overcame him.

'You wouldn't talk of mistake—of failing—if you
knew how to be near you, to listen to you, to see you,
touches and illuminates some of us!'

His cheek burnt, but he turned a manly, eager look
upon her.

Her cheek, too, flushed, and he thought he saw her
bosom heave.

'Oh no!—no!' she cried. 'How *impossible!*—when
one feels oneself so helpless, so clumsy, so useless.
Why couldn't I do better? But perhaps it is as well. It
all prepares one—braces one—against——'

She paused and leaned forward, looking out at the
maze of figures and carriages on the Mansion House
crossing, her tight-pressed lips trembling against her will.

'Against the last inevitable disappointment.' That,
no doubt, was what she meant.

'If you only understood how loth some of us are to
differ from you,' he cried—'how hard it seems to have
to press another view—to be already pledged.'

'Oh yes!—*please*—I know that you are pledged,' she

said, in hasty distress, her delicacy shrinking as before
from the direct personal argument.

They were silent a little. Tressady looked out at the
houses in Queen Victoria Street, at the lamplit summer
night, grudging the progress of the cab, the approach of
the river, of the Embankment, where there would be less
traffic to bar their way—clinging to the minutes as they
passed.

' Oh ! how could they put up that woman ? ' she said
presently, her eyes still shut, her hand shaking as it
rested on the door. ' How *could* they ? It is the thought
of women like that—the hundreds and thousands of them
—that goads one on. A clergyman who knows the East
End well said to me the other day, " The difference between
now and twenty years ago is that the women work much
more, the men less." I can never get away from the
thought of the women ! Their lives come to seem to me
the mere refuse, the rags and shreds, that are thrown
every day into the mill and ground to nothing—without a
thought—without a word of pity, an hour of happiness !
Cancer—three children left out of nine—and barely forty,
though she looked sixty ! They tell me she may live eighteen months. Then, when the parish has buried her, the
man has only to hold up his finger to find some one else to
use up in the same way. And she is just one of thousands.'

' I can only reply by the old, stale question,' said Tressady, sturdily. ' Did we make the mill ? Can we stop its
grinding ? And if not, is it fair even, to the race that
has something to gain from courage and gaiety—is it
reasonable to take all our own poor little joy and drench
it in this horrible pain of sympathy, as you do ? But we
have said all these things before.'

He bent over to her, smiling. But she did not look up.
And he saw a tear which her weakness, born of shock

and fatigue, could not restrain, steal from the lashes on the cheek.   Then he added, still leaning towards her :

'Only, what I never have said—I think—is what is true to-night.   At last you have made one person feel— if that matters anything !—the things you feel.   I don't know that I am particularly grateful to you !   And, practically, we may be as far apart as ever.   But I was without a sense when I went into this game of politics ; and now——'

His heart beat.   What would he not have said, mad youth !—within the limits imposed by her nature and his own dread—to make her look at him, to soften this preposterous sadness !

But it needed no more.   She opened her eyes, and looked at him with a wild sweetness and gratitude which dazzled him, and struck his memory with the thought of the Southern, romantic strain in her.

'You are very kind and comforting !' she said ; 'but then, from the first—somehow—I knew you were a friend to us.   One felt it—through all difference.'

The little sentences were steeped in emotion— emotion springing from many sources, fed by a score of collateral thoughts and memories—with which Tressady had, in truth, nothing to do.   Yet the young man gulped inwardly.   She had been a, tremulous woman till the words were said.   Now—strange !—through her very gentleness and gratefulness, a barrier had risen between them.   Something stern and quick told him this was the very utmost of what she could ever say to him—the farthest limit of it all.

They passed under Charing Cross railway bridge. Beside them, as they emerged, the moon shone out above the darks and silvers of the river, and in front, the towers of Westminster rose purplish grey against a west still golden,

Y

'How were things going in the House this afternoon?' she asked, looking at the towers. 'Oh! I forgot. You see, the clock says close on eleven. Please let me drop you here. I can manage by myself quite well.'

He protested, and she yielded, with a patient kindness that made him sore. Then he gave his account, and they talked a little of Monday's division and of the next critical votes in Committee—each of them; so he felt in his exaltation, a blow dealt to her—that he must help to deal. Yet there was a fascination in the topic. Neither could get away from it.

Presently, Pall Mall being very full of traffic, they had to wait a moment at the corner of the street that turns into St. James's Square. In the pause Tressady caught sight of a man on the pavement. The man smiled, looked astonished, and took off his hat. Lady Maxwell bowed coldly, and immediately looked away. Tressady recognised Harding Watton. But neither he nor she mentioned his name.

In another minute he had seen her vanish within the doors of her own house. Her hand had rested gently, willingly, in his.

'I am so grateful!' she had said; 'so will Maxwell be. We shall meet soon, and laugh over our troubles!'

And then she was gone, and he was left standing a moment, bewildered.

Eleven? What had he to do?

Then he remembered his pair, and that he had promised to call for Letty at a certain house, and take her on to a late ball. The evening, in fact, instead of ending, was just beginning. He could have laughed, as he got back into his cab.

Meanwhile Marcella had sped through the outer hall into the inner, where one solitary light, still burning, made a rather desolate dark-in-light through the broad, pillared space. A door opened at the farther side.

'Aldous!'

'You!'

He came out, and she flew to him. He felt her trembling as she touched him. In ten words she told him something of what had happened. Then he saw the bandage round her temple. His countenance fell. She knew that he turned white, and loved him for it. How few things had power to move him so!

He wanted to lead her back into his library, where he was at work. But she resisted.

'Let me go up to Annette,' she said. 'The little wound —oh! it is not much, I *know* it is not much—ought to be properly seen to. We will do it between us in a moment. Then come—I will send her down for you. I want to tell you.'

But in her heart of hearts she was just a little afraid of telling him. What if an exaggerated version should get into the papers—if it should really do him harm— at this critical moment! She was always tormented by this dread, a dread born of long-past indiscretions and mistakes.

He acquiesced, but first he insisted on half-leading, half-carrying her upstairs; and she permitted it, delighting in his strong arm.

Half an hour later she sent for him. The maid found him pacing up and down the hall, waiting.

When he entered her room she was lying on her sofa in a white wrapper of some silky stuff. The black lace had been drawn again round her head, and he saw nothing but a very pale face and her eager, timid eyes—timid for no one in the world but him. As he caught sight of her, she produced in him that exquisite mingled impression of grace, passion, self-yielding, which in all its infinite variations and repetitions made up for him the constant poem of her beauty. But though she knew it, she glanced at him anxiously as he approached her. It had been to her a kind of luxury of feeling, in the few moments that she had been waiting for him, to cherish a little fear of him—of his displeasure.

'Now describe exactly what you have been doing,' he said, sitting down by her with a troubled face and taking her hand, as soon as he had assured himself that the cut was slight and would leave no scar.

She told her tale, and was thrilled to see that he frowned. She laid her hand on his shoulder.

'It is the first public thing I have done without consulting you. I meant to have asked you yesterday, but we were both so busy. The meeting was got up rather hurriedly, and they pressed me to speak, after all the arrangements were made.'

'We are both of us too busy,' he said, rather sadly ; ' we glance, and nod, and bustle by——'

He did not finish the quotation, but she could. Her eyes scanned his face. 'Do you think I ought to have avoided such a thing at such a time ? Will it do harm ?'

His brow cleared. He considered the matter.

'I think you may expect some of the newspapers to make a good deal of it,' he said, smiling.

And, in fact, his own inherited tastes and instincts were all chafed by her story. His wife—the wife of a Cabinet Minister—pleading for her husband's Bill, or, as the enemy might say, for his political existence, with an East-End meeting, and incidentally with the whole public—exposing herself, in a time of agitation, to the rowdyism and the stone-throwing that wait on such things ! The notion set the fastidious old-world temper of the man all on edge. But he would never have dreamed of arguing the matter so with her. A sort of high chivalry forbade it. In marrying her he had not made a single condition—would have suffered tortures rather than lay the smallest fetter upon her. In consequence, he had been often thought a weak, uxorious person. Maxwell knew that he was merely consistent. No sane man lays his heart at the feet of a Marcella without counting the cost.

She did not answer his last remark. But he saw that she was wistful and uneasy, and presently she laid her fingers lightly on his.

'Tell me if I am too much away from you—too much occupied with other people.'

He sighed—the slightest sigh—but she winced.

'I had just an hour before dinner,' he said; 'you were not here, and the house seemed very empty. I would have come down to fetch you, but there were some important papers to read before to-morrow.' A Cabinet meeting was fixed, as she knew, for the following day. 'Then, I have been making Saunders draw up a statement for the newspapers in answer to Watton's last attack, and it would have been a help to talk to you before we sent it off. Above all, if I had known of the meeting I should have begged you not to go. I ought to have warned you yesterday, for I knew that there was some ugly agitation developing down there. But I never thought of you as likely to face a mob. . Will you please reflect'—he pressed her hand almost roughly against his lips—'that if that stone had been a little heavier, and flung a little straighter——'

He paused. A dew came to her eyes, a happy glow to her cheek. As for her, she was grateful to the stone that had raised such heart-beats.

Perhaps some instinct told him not to please her in this way too much, for he rose and walked away a moment.

'There! don't let's think of it, or I shall turn tyrant after all, and plunge into "shalls" and "sha'n'ts"! You *know* you carry two lives, and all the plans that either of us care about, in your hand. You say that Tressady brought you home?'

He turned and looked at her.

'Yes. Edward Watton brought him to the meeting.'

'But he has been down to see you there several times before, as well as coming here?'

'Oh yes! almost every week since we met at Castle Luton.'

'It is curious,' said Maxwell, thoughtfully; 'for he will certainly vote steadily with Fontenoy all through. His election speeches pledged him head over ears.'

'Oh! of course he will vote,' said Marcella, moving a little uneasily; 'but one cannot help trying to modify his way of looking at things. And his tone *is* changed.'

Maxwell stood at the foot of her sofa, considering, a host of perplexed and unwelcome notions flitting across his mind. In spite of his idealist absorption in his work, his political aims, and the one love of his life, he had the training of a man of the world, and could summon the shrewdness of one when he pleased. He had liked this young Tressady, for the first time, at Castle Luton, and had seen him fall under Marcella's charm with some amusement. But this haunting of their camp in the East End, at such a marked and critical moment, was strange, to say the least of it. It must point, one would think, to some sudden and remarkable strength of personal influence.

Had she any real consciousness of the power she wielded? Once or twice, in the years since they had been married, Maxwell had watched this spell of his wife's at work, and had known a moment of trouble. 'If

I were the fellow she had talked and walked with so,'
he had once said to himself, ' I must have fallen in love
with her had she been twenty times another man's wife ! '
Yet no harm had happened; he had only reproached
himself for a gross mind without daring to breathe a word
to her.

And he dared not now. Besides, how absurd ! The
young man was just married, and, to Maxwell's absent,
incurious eyes, the bride had seemed a lively, pretty little
person enough. No doubt it was the nervous strain of
his political life that made such fancies possible to him.
Let him not cumber her ears with them !

Then gradually, as he stood at her feet, the sight of
her, breathing weakness, submission, loveliness, her eyes
raised to his, banished every other thought from his
happy heart, and drew him like a magnet.

Meanwhile she began to smile. He knelt down beside
her, and she put both hands on his shoulders.

'Dear !' she said, half-laughing and half-crying, 'I
did speak so badly ; you would have been ashamed of me.
I couldn't hold the meeting. I didn't persuade a soul.
Lord Fontenoy's ladies had it all their own way. And
first I was dreadfully sorry I couldn't do such a thing
decently—sorry because of one's vanity, and sorry
because I couldn't help you. And now I think I'm rather
glad.'

'Are you?' said Maxwell, drily; 'as for me, I'm
enchanted ! There !—so much penalty you *shall* have.'

She pressed his lips with her hand.

'Don't spoil my pretty speech. I am only glad
because—because public life and public success make
one stand separate—alone. I have gone far enough to
know how it might be. A new passion would come in,
and creep through one like a poison. I should win you

votes—and our hearts would burn dry! There! take me —scold me—despise me. I am a poor thing—but yours!'

With such a humbleness might Diana have wooed her shepherd, stooping her goddess head to him on the Latmian steep.

CHAPTER XV

GEORGE went back to the House, and stayed for half an hour or so, listening to a fine speech from a member of a former Liberal Cabinet. The speech was one more sign of the new cleavage of parties that was being everywhere brought about by the pressure of the new Collectivism.

'We always knew,' said the speaker, referring to a Ministry in which he had served seven years before, ' that we should be fighting Socialism in good earnest before many years were over ; and we knew, too, that we should be fighting it as put forward by a Conservative Government. The hands are the hands of the English Tory, the voice is the voice of Karl Marx.'

The Socialists sent forth mocking cheers, while the Government benches sat silent. The rank-and-file of the Conservative party already hated the Bill. The second reading must go through. But if only some rearrangement were possible without rushing the country into the arms of revolutionists—if it were only conceivable that Fontenoy, or even the old Liberal gang, should form a Government, and win the country, the Committee stage would probably not trouble the House long.

Meanwhile in the smoking-rooms and lobbies the uncertainties of the coming division kept up an endless hum of gossip and conjecture. Tressady wandered about it all like a ghost, indifferent and preoccupied, careful above all to avoid any more talk with Fontenoy. While he was in the House itself he stood at the door or sat in the cross-benches, so as to keep a space between him and his leader.

A little before twelve he drove home, dressed hastily, and went off to a house in Berkeley Square, where he was to meet Letty. He found her waiting for him, a little inclined to be reproachful, and eager for her ball. As they drove towards Queen's Gate she chattered to him of her evening, and of the people and dresses she had seen.

' And, you foolish boy ! ' she broke out, laughing, and tapping him on the hand with her fan—' you looked so glum this morning when I couldn't go and see Lady Tressady—and—what do you think? Why, she has been at a party to-night—at a party, my dear !—and *dressed !* Mrs. Willy Smith told me she had seen her at the Webers'.'

' I daresay,' said George, rather shortly ; ' all the same, this morning she was very unwell.'

Letty shrugged her shoulders, but she did not want to be disagreeable and argue the point. She was much pleased with her dress—with the last glance of herself that she had caught in the cloak-room looking-glass before leaving Berkeley Square—and, finally, with this well-set-up, well-dressed husband beside her. She glanced at him every now and then as she put on a fresh pair of gloves. He had been very much absorbed in this tiresome Parliament lately, and she thought herself a very good and forbearing wife not to make more fuss. Nor had she made any fuss about his going down to see Lady Maxwell at the East End. It did not seem to have made the smallest difference to his opinions.

The thought of Lady Maxwell brought a laugh to her lips.

' Oh ! do you know, Harding was so amusing about the Maxwells to-day ! ' she said, turning to Tressady in her most good-humoured and confiding mood. ' He says people are getting so tired of her—of her meddling, and her preaching, and all the rest of it—and that everybody thinks him so absurd not to put a stop to it. And Harding says that it doesn't succeed even—that Englishmen will never stand petticoat government. It's all very well—they have to stand it in some forms ! '

And, stretching her slim neck, she turned and gave her husband a tiny flying kiss on the cheek. Mechanically grateful, George took her hand in his, but he did not make her the pretty speech she expected. Just before she spoke he was about to tell her of his evening—of the meeting, and of his drive home with Lady Maxwell. He had been far too proud hitherto, and far too confident in himself, to make any secret to Letty of what he did. And, luckily, she had raised no difficulties. In truth, she had been too well provided with amusements and flatteries of her own since their return from the country to leave her time or opportunities for jealousy. Perhaps, secretly, the young husband would have been more flattered if she had been more exacting.

But as she quoted Harding something stiffened in him. Later, after the ball, when they were alone, he would tell her—he would try and make her understand what sort of a woman Marcella Maxwell was. In his trouble of mind a confused plan crossed his thoughts of trying to induce Lady Maxwell to make friends with Letty. But a touch of that charm, that poetry !—he asked no more.

He glanced at his wife. She looked pretty and young as she sat beside him, lost in a pleasant pondering of social successes. But he wondered, uncomfortably, why she must use such a thickness of powder on her still un- spoilt complexion ; and her dress seemed to him fantastic, and not over-modest. He had begun to have the strangest feeling about their relation, as though he possessed a double personality, and were looking on at himself and her, wondering how it would end. It was characteristic, perhaps, of his half-developed moral life that his sense of ordinary husbandly responsibility towards her was not strong. He always thought of her as he thought of himself—as a perfectly free agent, dealing with him and their common life on equal terms.

The house to which they were going belonged to very wealthy people, and Letty was looking forward feverishly to the cotillon.

'They say, at the last dance they gave, the cotillon gifts cost eight hundred pounds,' she said, gleefully, to George. 'They always do things extraordinarily well.'

No doubt it was the prospect of the cotillon that had brought such a throng together. The night was stifling; the stairs and the supper-room were filled with a struggling mob; and George spent an hour of purgatory wondering at the gaieties of his class.

He had barely more than two glimpses of Letty after they had fought their way into the room. On the first occasion, by stretching himself to his full height so as to look over the intervening crowd, he saw her seated in a chair of state, a mirror in one hand and a lace handkerchief in the other. Young men were being brought up behind her to look into the glass over her shoulder, and she was merrily brushing their images away. Presently a tall, dark fellow advanced, with jet-black moustache and red cheeks. Letty kept her handkerchief suspended a moment over the reflection in the glass. George could see the corners of her lips twitching with amusement. Then she quietly handed the mirror to the leader of the cotillon, rose, gathered up her white skirt a little, the music struck up joyously, and she and Lord Cathedine spun round the room together, followed by the rest of the dancers.

George meanwhile found few people to talk to. He danced a few dances, mostly with young girls in the white frocks of their first season—a species of partner for which, as a rule, he had no affinity at all. But on the whole he passed the time leaning against the wall in a corner, lost in a reverie which was a vague compound of this and that, there and here; of the Manx Road schoolroom, its odours and heats, its pale, uncleanly crowd absorbed in the things of daily bread, with these gay, scented rooms, and this extravagance of decoration, that made even flowers a vulgarity, with these costly cotillon gifts—pins, bracelets, rings—that were being handed round and wondered over by people who had already more of such things than they could wear; of these rustling women, in their silks and diamonds, with that gaunt stooping image of the loafer's wife, smiling her queer defiance at pain and fate, and letting meddling 'lidies' know that without sixteen hours' 'settin' she could not keep her husband and children alive. Stale commonplace, that all the world knows by heart!—the squalor of the *pauperum tabernæ* dimming the glory of the *regum turres*. Yet there are only a few men and women in each generation who really pass into the eclipsing shadow of it. Others talk—*they* feel and struggle. There were many elements in Tressady's nature that might seem destined to force him into their company. Yet hitherto he had resolutely escaped his destiny—and enjoyed his life.

About supper-time he found himself near Lady Cathedine, a thin-faced, silent creature, whose eyes suddenly attracted him. He took her down to supper, and spent an exceedingly dull time. She had the air of one pining to talk, to confide herself. Yet in practice it was apparently impossible for her to do it. She fell back into monosyllables or gentle banalities; and George

noticed that she was always restlessly conscious of the
movements in the room—who came in, who went out
—and throwing little frightened glances towards the
door.

He was glad indeed when his task was over. On
their way to the drawing-rooms they passed a broad
landing, which on one side led out to a balcony, and had
been made into a decorated bower for sitting-out. At the
farther end he saw Letty sitting beside Harding Watton.
Letty was looking straight before her, with a flushed and
rather frowning face. Harding was talking to her, and,
to judge from his laughing manner, was amusing himself, if not her.

George duly found Lady Cathedine a seat, and
returned himself to ask Letty whether it was not time to
go. He found, however, that she had been carried off by
another partner, and could only resign himself to a fresh
twenty minutes of boredom. He leant, yawning, against
the wall, feeling the evening interminable.

Then a Harrow and Oxford acquaintance came up to
him, and they chatted for a time behind a stand of flowers
that stood between them and one of the doorways to the
ballroom. At the end of the dance George saw Lady
Cathedine hurrying up to this door with the quick,
furtive step that was characteristic of her. She passed
on the other side of the flowers, and George heard her
say to some one just inside the room :

'Robert, the carriage has come!'

A pause; then a thick voice said, in an emphatic
undertone :

'Damn the carriage!—go away!'

'But, Robert, you know we *promised* to look in at
Lady Tuam's on the way home.'

The thick voice dropped a note lower.

'Damn Lady Tuam! I shall come when it suits me.'

Lady Cathedine fell back, and George saw her cross the landing, and drop into a chair beside an old general, who was snoozing in a peaceful corner till his daughters should see fit to take him home. The old general took no notice of her, and she sat there, playing with her fan, her rather prominent grey eyes staring out of her white face.

Both George and his friend, as it happened, had heard the conversation. The friend raised his eyebrows in disgust.

'What a brute that fellow is! They have been married four months. However, she was amply warned.'

'Who was she?'

'The daughter of old Wickens, the banker. He married her for her money, and lives upon it religiously. By now, I should think, he has dragged her through every torture that marriage admits of.'

'So soon?' said George, drily.

'Well,' said the friend, laughing, 'no doubt it admits of a great many.'

'I am ready to go home,' said a voice at Tressady's elbow.

Something in the intonation surprised him, and he turned quickly.

'By all means,' he said, throwing an astonished look at his wife, who had come up to him on Lord Cathedine's arm. 'I will go and look for the carriage.'

What was the matter, he asked himself as he ran downstairs—what was the meaning of Letty's manner and expression?

But by the time he had sent for the carriage the answer had suggested itself. No doubt Harding Watton had given Letty news of that hansom in Pall Mall, and no doubt, also—— He shrugged his shoulders in annoyance. The notion of having to explain and excuse himself was particularly unpalatable. What a fool he had been not to tell Letty of his East-End adventure on their way to Queen's Gate.

He was standing in a little crowd at the foot of the stairs when Letty swept past him in search of her wraps. He smiled at her, but she held her head erect as though she did not see him.

So there was to be a scene. George felt the rise of a certain inner excitement. Perhaps it was as well. There were a good many things he wanted to say.

At the same time, the Cathedine episode had filled him with a new disgust for the violences and brutalities to which the very intimacy of the marriage relation may lead. If a scene there was to be, he meant to be more or less frank, and at the same time to keep both himself and her within bounds.

'You can't deny that you made a secret of it from me,' cried Letty, angrily. 'I asked you what had been doing in the House, and you never let me suspect that you had been anywhere else the whole evening.'

'I daresay,' said George, quietly. 'But I never meant to make any mystery. Something you said about Lady Maxwell put me off telling you—then. I thought I would wait till we got home.'

They were in George's study—the usual back-room on the ground-floor, which George could not find time to make comfortable, while Letty had never turned her attention to it. Tressady was leaning against the mantel-piece. He had turned up a solitary electric light, and in the cold glare of it Letty was sitting opposite to him, angrily upright. The ugly light had effaced the half-tones of the face and deepened the lines of it, while it had taken all the grace from her extravagant dress and tumbled flowers. She seemed to have lost her prettiness.

'Something I said about Lady Maxwell?' she repeated

scornfully. 'Why shouldn't I say what I like about
Lady Maxwell? What does she matter either to you or to
me that I should not laugh at her if I please? Everybody
laughs at her.'

'I don't think so,' said Tressady, quietly. 'I have
seen her to-night in a curious and touching scene—in a
meeting of very poor people. She tried to make a speech,
by the way, and spoke badly. She did not carry the
meeting with her, and towards the end it got noisy. As
we came out she was struck with a stone, and I got a
hansom for her, and drove her home to St. James's Square.
We were just turning into the Square when Harding saw
us. I happened to be with her in the crowd when the
stone hit her. What do you suppose I could do but bring
her home?'

'Why did you go? and why didn't you tell me at
once?'

'Why did I go?' Tressady hesitated, then looked
down upon his wife. 'Well!—I suppose I went because
Lady Maxwell is very interesting to watch—because she
is sympathetic and generous, and it stirs one's mind to
talk to her.'

'Not at all!' cried Letty, passionately. 'You went
because she is handsome—because she is just a superior
kind of flirt. She is always making women anxious
about their husbands under this pretence of politics.
Heaps of women hate her, and are afraid of her.'

She was very white, and could hardly save herself
from the tears of excitement. Yet what was working in
her was not so much Harding Watton's story as this new
and strange manner of her husband's. She had sat
haughtily silent in the carriage on their way home, fully
expecting him to question her—to explain, entreat, excuse
himself, as he had generally been ready to do whenever
she chose to make a quarrel. But he, too, said nothing,

z

and she could not make up her mind how to begin. Then,
as soon as they were shut into his room her anger had
broken out, and he had not yet begun to caress and appease
her.   Her surprise had brought with it a kind of shock.
What was the matter?   Why was she not mistress as
usual?

As she made her remark about Marcella, Tressady
smiled a little, and played with a cigarette he had taken up.

'Whom do you mean?' he asked her.   'One often
hears these things said of her in the vague, and never
with any details.   I myself don't believe it.   Harding, of
course, believes anything to her disadvantage.'

Letty hesitated; then, remembering all she could of
Harding's ill-natured gossip, she flung out some names,
exaggerating and inventing freely.   The emphasis with
which she spoke reddened all the small face again—made
it hot and common.

Tressady raised his shoulders as she came to the end
of her tirade.

'Well, you know I don't believe all that—and I don't
think Harding believes it.   Lady Maxwell, as you once
said yourself, is not, I suppose, a woman's woman.   She
gets on better, no doubt, with men than with women.
These men you speak of are all personal and party friends.
They support Maxwell, and they like her.   But if anybody
is jealous, I should think they might remember that there
is safety in numbers.'

'Oh, that's all very well!   But she wants *power*, and
she doesn't care a rap how she gets it.   She is a dangerous, intriguing woman—and she just trades upon her
beauty!'

Tressady, who had been leaning with his face averted
from her, turned round with sparkling eyes.

'You foolish child!' he said slowly—'you foolish
child!'

Her lips twitched. She put out a shaking hand to her cloak, that had fallen from her arms.

'Oh! very well. I sha'n't stay here to be talked to like that, so good-night.'

He took no notice. He walked up to her and put his hands on her shoulders.

'Don't you know what it is '—he spoke with a curious imperiousness—'that protects any woman—or any man either for the matter of that—from Marcella Maxwell's beauty? Don't you know that she adores her husband?'

'That's a pose, of course, like everything else,' cried Letty, trying to move herself away ; 'you once said it was.'

'Before I knew her. It's not a pose—it's the secret of her whole life.'

He walked back to the mantelpiece, conscious of a sudden rise of inward bitterness.

'Well, I shall go to bed,' said Letty, again half-rising. 'You might, I think, have had the kindness and the good taste to say you were sorry I should have the humiliation of finding out where my husband spends his evenings, from Harding Watton!'

Tressady was stung.

'When have I ever concealed what I did from you?' he asked her hotly.

Letty, who was standing stiff and scornful, tossed her head without speaking.

'That means,' said Tressady after a pause, 'that you don't take my word for it—that you suspect me of deceiving you before to-night?'

Letty still said nothing. His eyes flashed. Then a pang of conscience smote him. He took up his cigarette again with a laugh.

'I think we are both a pair of babies,' he said, as he pretended to look for matches. 'You know very well that you don't really think I tell you mean lies. And let

z 2

me assure you, my dear child, that fate did not mean Lady
Maxwell to have lovers—and that she never will have
them.   But when that's said there's something else to say.'

He went up to her again, and touched her arm.

'You and I couldn't have this kind of scene, Letty,
could we, if everything was all right?'

Her breast rose and fell hurriedly.

'Oh! I supposed you would want to retaliate—to complain on your side!'

'Yes,' he said, deliberately, 'I think I do want to
complain. Why is it that—— I began to like going down
to see Lady Maxwell—why did I like talking to her at
Castle Luton?   Well! of course it's pleasant to be with a
beautiful person—I don't deny that in the least.   But she
might have been as beautiful as an angel, and I mightn't
have cared twopence about her.   She has something
much less common than beauty.   It's very simple, too—
I suppose it's only *sympathy*—just that.   Everybody feels
the same.   When you talk to her she seems to care
about it; she throws her mind into yours.   And there's
a charm about it—there's no doubt of that.'

He had begun his little speech meaning to be perfectly
frank and honest—to appeal to her better nature and his
own.   But something stopped him abruptly, perhaps the
sudden perception that he was after playing the hypocrite
—perhaps the consciousness that he was only making
matters worse.

'It's a pity you didn't say all these things before,'
she said, with a hard laugh, 'instead of denouncing the
political woman, as you used to do.'

He sat down on the arm of the chair beside her,
balancing lightly, with his hands in his pockets.

'Did I denounce the political woman? Well, the Lord
knows I'm not in love with her now! It isn't politics, my
dear, that are attaching—it's the kind of human being.

Ah ! well, don't let's talk of it. Let's go back to that point of sympathy. There's more in it than I used to think. Suppose, for instance, you were to try and take a little more interest in my political work than you do ? Suppose you were to try and see money matters from my point of view, instead of driving us '—he paused a moment, then went on coolly, lifting his thin, long-chinned face to her as she stood quivering beside him—' driving us into expenses that will, sooner or later, be the ruin of us—that rob us, too, of self-respect. Suppose you were to take a little more account, also, of my taste in people ? I am afraid I don't like Harding, though he is your cousin, and I don't certainly see why he should furnish our drawing-rooms and empty our purse for us as he has been doing. Then, as to Lord Cathedine, I'm really not over-particular, but when I hear that fellow's in the house, my impulse is to catch the nearest hansom and drive away from it. I heard him speak to his wife to-night in a way for which he ought to be kicked down Oxford Street—and, in general, I should say that it takes the shine off a person to be much seen with Cathedine.'

The calm attitude—the voice, just a shade interrogative, exasperated Letty still more. She, too, sat down, her cheeks flaming.

'I am *extremely* obliged to you ! You really couldn't have been more frank. I am sorry that *nothing* I do pleases you. You must be quite sorry by now you married me—but really I didn't force you ! Why should I give up my friends ? You know very well you won't give up Lady Maxwell.'

She looked at him keenly, her little foot beating the ground. George started.

'But what is there to give up?' he cried. 'Come and see her yourself—come with me, and make friends with her. You would be quite welcome.'

But as he spoke he knew that he was talking absurdly, and that Letty had reason for her laugh.

'Thank you! Lady Maxwell made it *quite* plain to me at Castle Luton that she didn't want *my* acquaintance. I certainly sha'n't force myself upon her any more. But if you'll give up going to see her—well, perhaps I'll see what can be done to meet your wishes ; though, of course, I think all you say about Harding and Lord Cathedine is just unreasonable prejudice ! '

George was silent. His mind was torn between the pricks of a conscience that told him Letty had in truth, as far as he was concerned, a far more real grievance than she imagined, and a passionate intellectual contempt for the person who could even distantly imagine that Marcella Maxwell belonged to the same category as other women, and was to be won by the same arts as they. At last he broke out impatiently :

'I cannot possibly show discourtesy to one who has been nothing but kindness to me, as she is to scores of others—to old friends like Edward Watton, or new ones like——'

'She wants your vote, of course ! ' threw in Letty, with an excited laugh. ' *Either* she is a flirt—*or* she wants your vote. Why should she take so much notice of you ? She isn't your side—she wants to get hold of you—and it makes you ridiculous. People just laugh at you and her ! ' She turned upon him passionately. A little more, and the wish to say the wounding, venomous thing would have grown like a madness upon her. But George kept his self-possession.

'Well, they may laugh,' he said, with a strong effort to speak good-humouredly. ' But politics aren't managed like that, as you and they will find out. Votes are not so simple as they sound.'

He got up and walked away from her as he spoke.

As usual, his mood was beginning to cool. He saw no way out. They must both accept the *status quo*. No radical change was possible. It is character that makes circumstance, and character is inexorable.

'Well, of course I didn't altogether believe that you would really be such a fool, and wreck all your prospects!' said Letty violently, her feverish eyes intent the while on her husband and on the thin fingers once more busied with the cigarette. 'There now! I think we have had enough of this! It doesn't seem to have led to much, does it?'

'No,' said George, coolly; 'but perhaps we shall come to see more alike in time. I don't want to tyrannise—only to show you what I think. Shall I carry up your cloak for you?'

He approached her punctiliously. Letty gathered her wraps upon her arm in a disdainful silence, warding him off with a gesture. As he opened the door for her she turned upon him:

'You talk of my extravagance, but you never seem to consider what you might do to make up to me for the burden of being your mother's relation! You expect me to put up with the annoyance and ridicule of belonging to her—and to let her spend all your money besides. I give you fair warning that I sha'n't do it! I shall try and spend it on my side, that she sha'n't get it.'

She was perfectly conscious that she was behaving like a vixenish child, but she could not restrain herself. This strange new sense that she could neither bend nor conquer him was becoming more than she could bear.

George looked at her, half-inclined to shake her first, and then insist on making friends. He was conscious that he could probably assert himself with success if he tried. But the impulse failed him. He merely said, without any apparent temper, 'Then I shall have to see if I can invent some way of protecting both myself and you.'

She flung through the door, and almost ran through the long passage to the stairs, in a sobbing excitement. A sudden thought struck George as he stood looking after her. He pursued her, caught her at the foot of the stairs, and held her arm strongly.

'Letty! I wasn't to tell you, but I choose to break my promise. Don't be too cruel, my dear, or too angry. My mother is dying!'

She scanned him deliberately, the flushed face—the signs of strongly felt yet strongly suppressed emotion. The momentary consciousness flew through her that he was at bottom a very human, impressionable creature— that if she could but have broken down and thrown herself on his neck, this miserable evening might open for both of them a new way. But her white-heat of passion was too strong. She pushed him away.

'She made you believe that this morning? Then I'd better hurry up at Ferth; for of course it only means that there will be a fresh list of debts directly!'

He let her go, and she heard him walk quickly back to his study and shut the door. She stared after him triumphantly for a moment, then rushed upstairs.

In her room her maid was waiting for her. Grier's sallow face and gloomy eyes showed considerable annoyance at being kept up so late. But she said nothing, and Letty, who in general was only too ready to admit the woman to a vulgar familiarity, for once held her tongue. Her state of excitement and exhaustion, however, was evident, and Grier bestowed many furtive, examining glances upon her mistress in the course of the undressing. She thought she had heard 'them' quarrelling on the stairs. What a pity she had been too tired and cross to listen!

Of course they must come to quarrelling! Grier's sympathies were tolerably impartial. She had no affection

for her mistress, and she cordially disliked Sir George,
knowing perfectly well that he thought ill of her.   But
she had a good place, and meant to keep it if she could.
To which end she had done her best to strengthen a mean
hold on Letty.   Now, as she was brushing out Letty's
brown hair, and silently putting two and two together
the while, an idea occurred to her which pleased her.

After Grier had left her, Letty could not make up her
mind to go to bed.   She was still pacing up and down
the room in her dressing-gown, when she heard a knock
—Grier's knock.

'Come in !'

'Please, my lady,' said Grier, appearing with something in her hand, ' doesn't this belong to your photograph-
box ?   I found it on the floor in Sir George's dressing-
room this morning.'

Letty hastily took it from her, and, in spite of an
instant effort to control herself, the red flushed again
into a cheek that had been very pale when Grier came in.

'Where did you find it ?'

'It had tumbled off Sir George's table, I think,' said
Grier, with elaborate innocence ; 'some one must have
took it out of your photo-box.'

'Thank you,' said Letty, shortly.   'You may go,
Grier.'

The maid went, and Letty was left standing with the
photograph in her hands.

Two days before Tressady had been in Edward
Watton's room in St. James's Street, and had seen this
amateur photograph of Marcella Maxwell and her boy on
Watton's table.   The poetic charm of it had struck him
so forcibly that he had calmly put it in his pocket, telling
the protesting owner that he in his *rôle* of great friend
could easily procure another, and must beware of a
grudging spirit.   Watton had laughed and submitted, and

Tressady had carried off the picture, honestly meaning to present it to Letty for a collection of contemporary 'beauties' she had just begun to make.

Later in the day, as he was taking off his coat in the evening to dress for dinner, Tressady drew out the photograph. A sudden instinct, which he himself could hardly have explained, made him delay handing it over to Letty. He thrust it into the top tray of his collar-and-shirt wardrobe. Two days later the butler, coming in a hurry before breakfast to put out his master's clothes, shook the photograph out of the folds of the shirt, where it had hidden itself, without noticing what he had done. The picture slipped between the wardrobe and the wall of the recess in which it stood, was discovered later in the day by the housemaid, and given to Lady Tressady's maid.

Letty laid the photograph down on the dressing-table, and stood leaning upon her hands, looking at it. Marcella was sitting under one of the cedars of Maxwell Court with her boy beside her. A fine corner of the old house made a background, and the photographer had so dealt with his picture as to make it a whole, full of significance, and culminating in the two faces—the sensitive, speaking beauty of the mother, the sturdy strength of the child. Marcella had never looked more wistful, more attaching. It was the expression of a woman at rest, in the golden moment of her life, yet conscious—as all happiness is conscious—of the common human doom that nothing escapes. Meanwhile the fine, lightly furrowed brow above the eyes spoke action and power; so did the strong waves of black hair blown back by the breeze. A noble, strenuous creature, yet quivering through and through with the simplest, most human instincts. So one must needs read her, as one looked from the eyes to the eager clasp of the arm about the boy.

Letty studied it, as though she would pierce and stab it with looking. Then, with a sudden wild movement, she took up the picture, and tore it into twenty pieces. The pieces she left strewn on the floor, so that they must necessarily strike the eye of anyone coming into the room. And in a few more minutes she was in bed, lying still and wakeful, with her face turned away from the door.

About an hour afterwards there was a gentle knock at her door. She made no answer, and Tressady came in. He stepped softly, thinking she was asleep, and presently she heard him stop, with a stifled exclamation. She made no sound, but from his movement she guessed that he was picking up the litter on the floor. Then she heard it thrown into the basket under her writing-table, and she waited, holding her breath.

Tressady walked to a far window, drew a curtain back softly, and stood looking out at the starlight over the deserted street. Once, finding him so still, she ventured a hasty glance at him over the edge of the sheet. But she could see nothing. And after a time he turned and came to his accustomed place beside her. In twenty minutes at latest, she knew, much to her chagrin, that he was asleep.

She herself had no sleep. She was stung to wakefulness by that recurrent sense of the irrevocable which makes us say to ourselves in wonder, 'How can it have happened? Two hours ago—such a little while—it had not happened!' And the mind clutches at the bygone hour, so near, so eternally distant—clutches at its ghost, in vain.

Yet it seemed to her now that she had been jealous from the first moment when she and George had come into contact with Marcella Maxwell. During the long hours of this night her jealousy burnt through her like a hot pain—jealousy, mixed with reluctant memory. Half

consciously she had always assumed that it had been a
piece of kindness on her part to marry George Tressady
at all. She had almost condescended to him. After all,
she had played with ambitions so much higher ! At any
rate, she had taken for granted that he would always
admire and be grateful to her—that in return for her
pretty self she might at least dispose of him and his as
she pleased.

And now, what galled her intolerably was this discern-
ment of the way in which—at least since their honeymoon
—he must have been criticising and judging her—judging
her by comparison with another woman. She seemed to
see at a glance the whole process of his mind, and her
vanity writhed under it.

How much else than vanity ? As she turned restlessly
from side to side, possessed by plans for punishing George,
for humiliating Lady Maxwell, and avenging herself, she
said to herself that she did not care—that it was not worth
caring about—that she would either bring George to his
senses, or manage to amuse herself without him.

But in reality she was held tortured and struggling all
the time in the first grip of that masterful hold wherewith
the potter lifts his clay when he lays it on the eternal
whirring of the wheel.

CHAPTER XVI

THE newspapers of the morning following these events—
that is to say, of Saturday, July 5—gave very lively
accounts of the East-End meeting, at which, as some put
it, Lady Maxwell ' had got her answer ' from the East-End
mob. The stone-throwing, the blow, the woman, and the
cause were widely discussed that same day throughout
the clubs and drawing-rooms of Mayfair and Belgravia,
no less than among the clubs and ' publics ' of the East
End ; and the guests at country-house parties as they
hurried out of town for the Sunday, carried the gossip
of the matter far and wide. The Maxwells went down
alone to Brookshire, and the curious visitors who called
in St. James's Square ' to inquire ' came away with
nothing to report.

' A put-up thing, the whole business,' said Mrs.
Watton, indignantly, to her son Harding, as she handed
him the ' Observer,' on the Sunday morning, in the dining-
room of the family house in Tilney Street. ' Of course, a
little martyrdom just now suits her book excellently. How
that man *can* let her make him a laughing-stock in this
way——'

' A laughing-stock ? ' said Harding, smiling. ' Not at
all. Don't spoil your first remark, mother. For, of course,
it is all practical politics. The handsomest woman in
England doesn't give her temple to be gashed for nothing.

You will see what her friends will make out of it !—and out of the brutal violence of our mob.'

' Disgusting ! ' said Mrs. Watton, playing severely with the lid of the mustard-pot that stood beside her.

She and Harding were enjoying a late breakfast *tête-à-tête*. The old Squire had finished long before, and was already doing his duty with a volume of sermons in the library upstairs, preparatory to going to church. Mrs. Watton and Harding, however, would accompany him thither presently ; for Harding was a great supporter of the Establishment.

The son raised his shoulders at his mother's adjective.

' What I want to know,' he said, ' is whether Lady Maxwell is going to bag George Tressady, or not. He brought her home from the meeting on Friday.'

' Brought her home from the meeting ?—*George Tressady* ? '

Mrs. Watton raised her masculine head and frowned at her son, as though he were, in some sense, personally responsible for this unseemly fact.

' He has been haunting her in the East End for weeks. I got that out of Edward. But, of course, one knew that was going to happen as soon as one saw them together at Castle Luton. She throws her flies cleverly, that woman ! '

' All I can say is,' observed Mrs. Watton, ponderously, ' that in any decent state of society such a woman would be banned ! '

Harding rose, and stood by the open window caressing his moustache. It was a perception of long standing with him, that life would have been better worth living had his mother possessed a sense of humour.

' It seems to me,' his mother resumed after a pause, ' that some one at least should give Letty a hint.'

' Oh ! Letty can take care of herself,' said Watton,

laughing. He might have said, if he had thought it worth
while, that somebody had already given Letty a hint.
Tressady, it appeared, disliked him. Well, people that
disliked you were fair game. However, in spite of
Tressady's dislike, he had been able to amuse himself a
good deal with Letty and Letty's furnishing during the last
few months. Harding, who prided himself on the finest of
tastes, liked to be consulted ; he liked anything, also, that
gave him importance, if it were only with the master of
a curiosity shop, and, under cover of Letty's large dealings, he had carried off various spoils of his own for his
rooms in the Temple—spoils which were not to be despised—at a very moderate price indeed.

'Who could have thought George Tressady would turn
out such a weak creature,' said his mother, rising, 'when
one remembers how Lord Fontenoy believed in him ? '

'And does still believe in him, more or less,' said
Harding ; 'but Fontenoy will have to be warned.'

He looked at the clock, to see if there was time for a
cigarette before church, lit it, and, leaning against the
window, gazed towards the hazy park with a meditative
air.

'Do you mean there is any question of his ratting ? '
said his mother.

Harding raised his eyebrows.

'Well, no—hardly anything so gross as that. But you
can see all the spirit has gone out of him. He does no
work for us. The party gets nothing out of him.'

Harding spoke as if he had the party in his pocket.
His mother looked at him with a severely concealed
admiration. There were few limits to her belief in
Harding. But it was not her habit to flatter her sons.

'What makes one so mad,' she said, as she sailed
towards the door in a stiff rustle of Sunday brocade, ' is
the way in which the people who admire her talk of her.

When one thinks that all this " slumming," and all this stuff about the poor, only means keeping her husband in office and surrounding herself with a court of young men, it turns one sick ! '

' My dear mother, we all keep our little hypocrisies,' said Harding, indulgently. ' Don't forget that Lady Maxwell provides me with a deal of good copy.'

And after his mother had left him he smoked on, thinking with pleasure of an article of his on ' The Woman of the Slums,' packed with allusions to Marcella Maxwell, which was to appear in the next number of the ' Haymarket Reporter,' the paper that he and Fontenoy were now running. Harding was not the editor. He disliked drudgery and office-hours ; and his father was good for enough to live upon. But he was a powerful adviser in the conduct of the new journal, and wrote, perhaps, the smartest articles.

The paper, indeed, was written by the smartest people conceivable, and had achieved the smartest combinations. ' Liberty' was its catchword ; but the employer must be absolute. To care or think about religion was absurd ; but whoso threw a stone at the Established Church, let him die the death. Christianity must be steadily, even ferociously supported ; in the policing of an unruly world it was indispensable. But the perennial butt of the paper was the fool who ' went about doing good.' The young men who lived in ' settlements,' for instance, and gave University Extension Lectures—the paper pursued all such with a hungry malice, only less biting than that wherewith day by day it attacked Lord Maxwell, the arch offender of all the philanthropic tribe. To help a man who had toiled his ten or twelve hours in the workshop or the mine to read Homer or Dante in the evening—well ! in the language of Hedda Gabler, ' people don't do these things,'—not people with any sense of the humorous or the seemly. Harding and his crew had required a good deal of help in their time towards the reading of those authors; that, however, was only their due, and in the order of the universe. The same universe had sent the miner below to dig coals for his betters, while Harding Watton went to college.

But the last and worst demerit in the eyes of Harding and his set was that old primitive offence that Cain already found so hard to bear. Half the violence which the new paper had been lavishing on Maxwell—apart from passionate conviction of the Fontenoy type, which also spoke through it—sprang from this source. Maxwell, in spite of his obvious drawbacks, threatened to succeed, to be accepted, to take a large place in English political life. And his wife, too, reigned, and had her way without the help of clever young men who write. There was the sting. Harding at any rate found it intolerable.

Meanwhile, in spite of newspapers to right of it and newspapers to left of it, the political coach clattered on.

The following day—Monday—was a day of early arrivals, packed benches, and much excitement in the House of Commons; for the division on the second reading was to be taken after the Home Secretary's reply on the debate. Dowson was expected to get up about ten o'clock, and it was thought that the division would be over by eleven.

On this afternoon and evening Fontenoy was ubiquitous. At least so it seemed to Tressady. Whenever one put one's head into the Smoking-room or the Library, whenever one passed through the Lobby, or rushed on to the Terrace for ten minutes' fresh air, Fontenoy's great brow and rugged face were always to be seen, and always in fresh company.

The heterogeneous character of the Opposition with which the Government was confronted, the conflicting groups and interests into which it was split up, offered large scope for the intriguing, contriving genius of the man. And he was spending it lavishly. The small eyes were more invisible, the circles round them more saucer-like than ever.

Meanwhile George Tressady had never been so keenly conscious as on this critical afternoon that his party had begun to drop him out of its reckonings. Consultations that would once have included him as a matter of course were going on without him. During the whole of this busy day Fontenoy even had hardly spoken to him; the battle was leaving him on one side.

Well, what room for bitterness?—though, with the unreason that no man escapes, he was not without bitterness. He had disappointed them as a debater—and, in other ways, what had he done for them since Whitsun-tide? No doubt also the mention of his name in the reports of the Mile End meeting had not been without its effect. He believed that Fontenoy's personal regard for him still held. Otherwise, he was beginning to feel himself placed in a tacit isolation.

What wonder, good Lord! During the dinner-hour he found himself in a corner of the Library, dreaming over a biography of Lord Melbourne. Poor Melbourne! in those last tragic years of waiting and pining, every day expecting the proffer of office that never came and the familiar recognition that would be his no more. But Melbourne was old, and had had his day.

'I wanted to speak to you,' said a hoarse voice over his shoulder.

'Say on, and sit down,' said George, smiling, and pushing forward a chair beside him. 'I should think you'll want a week's sleep after this.'

'Have you got some time to spare this week,' said Fontenoy, abruptly, as he sat down.

George hesitated.

'Well, no. I ought to go down to the country immediately, and see after my own affairs and the strike, before Committee begins. There is a meeting of coalowners on Wednesday.'

'What I want wouldn't take long,' said Fontenoy, persistently, after a pause. 'I hear you have been going round workshops lately?'

His keen, peremptory eyes fixed his companion.

'I had a round or two with Everard,' said George. 'We saw a fairly representative lot.'

The thought that flashed through Fontenoy's mind was, 'Why the deuce didn't you speak of it to me?' Aloud, he said with impatience :

'Representing what Everard chose to show, I should think. However, what I want is this. You know the series of extracts from reports that has been going on lately in the "Chronicle."'

George nodded.

'We want something done to correct the impression that has been made. You and I know perfectly well that the vast majority of workshops work factory-hours and an average of four and a half days a week. You have just had personal experience, and you can write. Will you do three or four signed articles for the "Reporter" this week or next? Of course the office will give you every help.'

George considered.

'I think not,' he said presently, looking up. 'I shouldn't do it well. Perhaps I have become too conscious of the exceptions—the worst cases. Frankly, the whole thing has become more of a problem to me than it was.'

Fontenoy moved, and grunted uneasily.

'Does that mean,' he said at last, in his harshest manner, ' that you will feel any difficulty in——? '

- 'In voting? No. I shall vote right enough. I am all for delay. This particular Bill doesn't convince me any more than it did. But I don't want to take a strong public part just at present.'

The two men eyed each other in silence.

'I thought there was something brewing,' said Fontenoy at last.

' Well, I'm not sorry to have had these few words,' was George's reply, after a pause. 'I wanted to tell you that, though I shall vote, I don't think I shall speak much more. I don't believe I'm the stuff people in Parliament ought to be made of. I shall be remorseful presently for having led you into a mistake ! ' He forced a smile.

' I made no mistake,' said Fontenoy, grimly, and departed. Then, as he walked down the corridor, he completed his sentence—' except in not seeing that you were the kind of man to be made a fool of by women ! '

First of all, a hasty marriage with a silly girl who could be no help to him or to the cause ; now, according to Watton—who had called upon Fontenoy that morning, at his private house, to discuss various matters of business —the Lady-Maxwell fever in a pronounced form. Most likely. It was the best explanation.

The leader's own sense of annoyance and disappointment was considerable. There was no man for whom he had felt so much personal liking as for Tressady since the fight began.

Somewhere before midnight the division on the second reading was taken, amid all those accompaniments of crowd, expectation, and commotion, that are usually evoked by the critical points of a contested measure. The majority for Government was forty-four—less by twenty-four votes than its normal figure.

As the cheers and ·counter-cheers subsided, George found himself borne into the Lobby with the crowd pouring out of the House. As he approached the door leading to the outer lobby, a lady in front of him turned. George received a lightning impression of beauty, of a kind of anxious joy, and recognised Marcella Maxwell.

She held out her hand.

'Well, the first stage is over!' she said.

'Yes, and well over,' he said, smiling. 'But you have shed a great many men already.'

'Oh! I know—I know. The next few weeks will be intolerable; one will feel sure of nobody.' Then her voice changed—took a certain shyness. 'A good many people from here are coming down to us at Mile End during the next few weeks—will you come some time, and bring Lady Tressady?'

'Thank you,' said George, rather formally. 'It is very kind of you.' Then, in another voice : 'And you are really none the worse?'

His eyes sought the injured temple, and she instinctively put up her hand to the black wave of hair that had been drawn forward so as to conceal the mark.

'Oh no! That boy was not an expert, luckily. How absurd the papers have been!'

George shook his head.

'I don't know what else one could expect,' he said, laughing.

'Not at all!'—the flush mounted in the delicate hollow of the cheek. 'Why should there be any more fuss about a woman's being struck than a man? We don't want any of this extra pity and talk.'

'Human nature, I am afraid,' said George, raising

his shoulders. Did she really suppose that women could mix in the political fight on the same terms as men— could excite no more emotion there than men? Folly!

Then Maxwell, who was standing behind her, came forward, greeted Tressady kindly, and they talked for a few minutes about the evening's debate. The keen look of the elder scanned the younger's face and manner the while with some minuteness. As for George, his dialogue with the Minister, at which more than one passer-by threw looks of interest and amusement, gave him no particular pleasure. Maxwell's qualities were not of the kind that specially appealed to him; nor was he likely to attract Maxwell. Nevertheless, he could have wished their ten minutes' talk to last interminably, merely because of the excuse it gave him to be near her!—played upon by her movements and her tones. He talked to Maxwell of speeches, and votes, and little incidents of the day. And all the time he knew how she was surrounded; how the crowd that was always gathering about her came and went; with whom she talked; above all, how that eager, sensitive charm which she had shown in its fulness to him—perhaps to him only, beside her husband, of all this throng—played through her look, her voice, her congratulations and her dismays. For had he not seen her in distress and confusion—seen her in tears, wrestling with herself? His heart caressed the thought like a sacred thing, all the time that he was conscious of her as the centre of this political throng—the adored, detested, famous woman, typical in so many ways of changing custom and of an expanding world.

Then, in a flash, as it were, the crowd had thinned, the Maxwells had gone, and George was running down the steps of the members' entrance, into the rain outside. He seemed to carry with him the scent of a rose—the rose she had worn on her breast—and his mind was tormented with the question he had already asked himself: 'How is it going to end?'

He pushed on through the wet streets, lost in a hundred miseries and exaltations. The sensation was that of a man struggling with a rising tide, carried helplessly in the rush and swirl of it. Yet conscience had very little to say, and, when it did speak, got little but contempt for its pains. What had any clumsy code, social or moral, to do with it? When would Marcella Maxwell, by word or look or thought, betray the man she loved? Not till

> A' the seas gang dry, my dear,
> An the rocks melt wi' the sun!

How he found his way home he hardly knew; for it was a moment of blind crisis with him. All that crowded, dramatic scene of the House—its lights, its faces, its combinations—had vanished from his mind. What remained was a group of three people, contemplated in a kind of terror—terror of what this thing might grow to! Once, in St. James's Street, the late hour, the soft, gusty night, suddenly reminded him of that other gusty night in February when he had walked home after his parting with Letty, so well content with himself and the future, and had spoken to Marcella Maxwell for the first time amid that little crowd in the Mall. Nothing had been irreparable then. He had his life in his hands.

As for this passion, that was creeping into all his veins, poisoning and crippling all his vitalities, he was still independent enough of it to be able to handle it with the irony it deserved. For it was almost as ludicrous as it was pitiable. He did not want any man of the world, any Harding Watton, to tell him that.

What amazed him was the revelation of his own nature that was coming out of it. He had always been rather proud to think of himself as an easy-going fellow with no particular depths. Other men were proud of a 'storm period,'—of feasting and drinking deep—made a pose of it. Tressady's pose had been the very opposite. Out of a kind of good taste, he had wished to take life lightly, with no great emotion. And marriage with Letty had seemed to satisfy this particular canon.

Now, for the first time, certain veils were drawn aside, and he knew what this hunger for love, and love's response, can do with a man—could do with *him*, were it allowed its scope!

Had Marcella Maxwell been another woman, less innocent, less secure!

As it was, Tressady no sooner dared to give a sensuous thought to her beauty than his own passion smote him back—bade him beware lest he should be no longer fit to speak and talk with her, actually or spiritually. For in this hopeless dearth of all the ordinary rewards and encouragements of love he had begun to cultivate a sort of second, or spiritual, life, in which she reigned. Whenever he was alone he walked with her, consulted her, watched her dear eyes, and the soul playing through them. And so long as he could maintain this dream he was conscious of a sort of dignity, of reconciliation with himself; for the passions and tragedies of the soul always carry with them this dignity, as Dante, of all mortals, knew first and best.

But with the turn into Upper Brook Street, the dream suddenly and painfully gave way. He saw his own house, and could forget Letty and the problem of his married life no more. What was he going to do with her and it? What relation was he going to establish with his wife, through all these years that stretched so interminably before them? Remorse mingled with the question. But perhaps impatience, still more—impatience of his own misery, of this maze of emotion in which he felt himself entangled, as it were against his will.

During the three days which had passed since his quarrel with Letty, their common life had been such a mere confusion of jars and discomforts that George's hedonist temper was almost at the end of its patience; yet so far, he thought, he had not done badly in the way of forbearance. After the first moment of angry disgust, he had said to himself that the tearing up of the photograph was a jealous freak, which Letty had a right to if it pleased her. At any rate, he had made no comment whatever upon it, and had done his best to resume his normal manner with her the next day. She had been, apparently, only the more enraged; and, although there had been no open quarrelling since, her cutting, contemptuous little airs had been very hard to bear. Nor was it possible for George to ignore her exasperated determination to have her own way in the matter both of friends and expenses.

As he took his latchkey out of the lock, and turned up the electric light, he saw two handsome marqueterie chairs standing in the hall. He went to look at them in some perplexity. Ah! no doubt they had been sent as specimens. Letty had grown dissatisfied with the chairs originally bought for the dining-room. He remembered to have heard her say something about a costly set at a certain Asher's, that Harding had found.

He studied them for a few moments, his mouth tightening. Then, instead of going upstairs, he went into his study, and sat down to his table to write a letter.

Yes—he had better go off to Staffordshire by the early train; and this letter, which he would put upon her writing-desk in the drawing-room, should explain him to Letty.

The letter was long and candid, yet by no means without tenderness. 'I have written to Asher,' it said, 'to direct him to send in the morning for the chairs I found in the hall. They are too expensive for us, and I have told him that I will not buy them. I need not say that in writing to him I have avoided every word that could be annoying to you. If you would only trust me, and consult me a little about such things—trifles as they be—life just now would be easier than it is.'

Then he passed to a very frank statement of their financial position, and of his own steady resolve not to allow himself to drift into hopeless debt. The words were clear and sharp, but not more so than the course of the preceding six weeks made absolutely necessary. And their very sharpness led him to much repentant kindness at the end. No doubt she was disappointed both in him and in his circumstances; and, certainly, differences had developed between them that they had never foreseen at the time of their engagement. But to 'make a good thing' of living together was never easy. He asked her not to despair, not to judge him hardly. He would do his best—let her only give him back her confidence and affection.

He closed the letter, and then paced restlessly about the little room for a time. It seemed to him that he was caught in a vice—that neither happiness, nor decent daily comfort, nor even the satisfactions of ambition, were ever to be his.

Next day he was off to Euston before Letty was properly awake. She found his letter waiting for her when she descended, and spent the day in a pale excitement. Yet by the end of it she had pretty well made up her mind. She would have to give in on the money question. George's figures and her natural shrewdness convinced her that the ultimate results of fighting him in this matter could only be more uncomfortable for herself than for him. But as to her freedom in choosing her own friends, or as to her jealousy of Lady Maxwell, she would never give in. If George had ceased to court his wife, then he could have nothing to say if she looked for the amusement and admiration that were her due from other people. There was no harm in that. Everybody else did it ; and she was not going to be pretty and young for nothing. Whereupon she sat down and wrote a line to Lord Cathedine to tell him that she and 'Tully' would be at the Opera on the following night, and to beg him to make sure that she got her 'cards for Clarence House.' Moreover, she meant to make use of him to procure her a card for a very smart ball, the last of the season, which was coming off in a fortnight. That could be arranged, no doubt, at the Opera.

George returned from the North in a few days looking, if possible, thinner and more careworn than when he went. He had found the strike a very stubborn business. Bewick was riding the storm triumphantly ; and while upon his own side Tressady looked in vain for a 'man,' there was a dogged determination to win among the masters. George's pugnacity shared it fully. But he was beginning to ask himself a number of questions about these labour disputes which, apparently, his co-employers did not ask themselves. Was it that here, no less than in matters that concerned the Bill before Parliament, *her* influence, helped by the power of an expanding mind, had developed in him that fatal capacity for sympathy, for the double-seeing of compromise, which takes from a man all the joy of battle ?

Letty, at any rate, was not troubled by anything of the sort. When he came back he found that she was ready to be on fairly amicable terms with him. Moreover, she had postponed the more expensive improvements and changes she had begun to make at Ferth against his

will ; nor was there any sign of the various new purchases
for the London house with which she had threatened him.
On the other hand, she ceased to consult him about her
own engagements ; and she let him know, though without
any words on the subject, that she had entirely broken
with his mother—would neither see her nor receive her.
As her attitude on this point involved—or, apparently,
must involve—a refusal to accept her husband's statement
made solemnly under strong emotion, George's pride took
it in absolute silence.   No doubt it was her revenge upon
him for their crippled income—and for Lady Maxwell.

The effect of her behaviour on this point was to increase his own pity for his mother.   He told her frankly
that Letty could not get over the inroads upon their
income and the shortening of their resources produced by
the Shapetsky debt, just at a time when they should have
been able to spend, and were already hampered by the
state of the coal trade.   It would be better that she and
Letty should not meet for a time.   He would do his best
to make it up.

Lady Tressady took his news with a curious equanimity.

'Well, she always hated me ! ' she said—'I don't
exactly know why—and was a little jealous of my gowns,
too, I think.   Don't mind, George.   I must say it out.
You know, she doesn't really dress very well—Letty
doesn't.   Though, my goodness, the bills !   Wait till you
see them before you call *me* extravagant.   You should
make her go to that new woman—what do they call her ?
She's a *darling*, and such a style !   Never mind about
Letty ; you needn't bother.   I daresay she isn't very nice
to *you* about it.   But if you don't come and see me, I shall
cut my throat, and leave a note on the dressing-table.   It
would spoil your career dreadfully, so you'd better take
care.'

But, indeed, George came, without any pressing, almost every day. He saw her in her bursts of gaiety and affectation, when the habits of a lifetime asserted themselves as strongly as ever; and he saw her in her moments of pain and collapse, when she could hide the omens of inexorable physical ill neither from herself nor him. By the doctor's advice, he ceased to press her to give in, to resign herself to bed and invalidism. It was best, even physically, to let her struggle on. And he was both astonished and touched by her pluck. She had never been so repellent to him as on those many occasions in the past when she had feigned illness to get her way. Now that Death was really knocking, the half-gay, half-frightened defiance with which she walked the palace of life, one moment listening to the sounds at the gate, the next throwing herself passionately into the revelry within, revealed to the son a new fact about her—a fact of poetry unutterably welcome.

Even her fawning dependents, the Fullertons, ceased to annoy him. They were poor parasites, but she thought for them, and they professed to love her in return. She had emptied her life of finer things, but this relation of patron and flatterer, such as it was, did something to fill the vacancy; and George made no further effort to disturb it.

It was surprising, indeed, how easily, as the weeks went on, he came to bear many of those ways of hers which had once set him most on edge—even her absurd outbursts of affection towards him, and preposterous praise of him in public. In time he submitted even to being flown at and kissed before the Fullertons. Amazing into what new relations that simple perspective of *the end* will throw all the stuff of life!

In Parliament the weeks rushed by. The first and

comparatively non-contentious sections of the Bill passed with a good deal of talk and delay. George spoke once or twice, without expecting to speak, instinctively pleasing Fontenoy where he could. They had now but little direct intercourse. But George did not feel that his leader had become his enemy, and was not slow to recognise a magnanimity he had not foreseen. Yet, after all, he had not offered the worst affront to party discipline. Fontenoy could still count on his vote. As to the rest of his party, he saw that he was to be finally reckoned as a 'crank,' and let alone. It was not, he found, altogether to be regretted. The position gave him a new freedom of speech.

Meanwhile he and Marcella Maxwell rarely met. Week after week passed, and still Tressady avoided those gatherings at the Mile End house, of which he heard full accounts from Edward Watton. He once formally asked Letty if she would go with him to one of Lady Maxwell's East-End 'evenings,' and she, with equal formality, refused. But he did not take advantage of her refusal to go himself. Was it fear of his own weakness, or compunction towards Letty, or the mere dread of being betrayed into something at once ridiculous and irreparable ?

At the same time, it was surprising how often during these weeks he had occasion to pass through St. James's Square. Once or twice he saw her go out or come in, and sometimes was near enough to catch the sudden smile and look which surely must be the smile and look she gave her friends, and not to every passing stranger! Once or twice, also, he met her for a few minutes in the Lobby, or on the Terrace, but always in a crowd. She never repeated her invitation. He divined that she was, perhaps, vexed with herself for having seemed to press the point on the night of the second reading.

July drew to an end. The famous 'workshop clause' had been debated for nearly ten days, the whole country, as it were, joining in. One evening in the last week of the month Naseby and Lady Madeleine were sitting together in a corner of a vast drawing-room in Carlton House Terrace. The drawing-room was Mrs. Allison's. She had returned about a fortnight before from Bad Wildheim, and was now making an effort, for the boy's sake, to see some society. As she moved about the room in her black silk and lace she was more gentle, but in a sense more inaccessible, than ever. She talked with everyone, but her eyes followed her son's auburn head, with its strange upstanding tufts of hair above the fair, freckled face; or they watched the door, even when she was most animated. She looked ill and thin, and the many friends who loved her would have gladly clung about her and cherished her. But it was not easy to cherish Mrs. Allison.

'Do you see how our hostess keeps a watch for Fontenoy,' said Naseby, in a low voice, to Lady Madeleine.

Madeleine turned her startled face to him. Nature had given her this hunted look—the slightly open mouth, the wide eyes of one who perpetually hears or expects bad news. Naseby did not like it, and had tried to laugh her out of her scared ways before this. But he had no sooner laughed at her than he found himself busy—to use Watton's word—in 'stroking' and making it up to her, so tender and clinging was the girl's whole nature, so golden was her hair, so white her skin!

'Isn't it the division news she is expecting?'

'Yes—but don't look so unhappy! She will bear up —even if they are beaten. And they will be beaten. Fontenoy's hopes have been going down. The Government will get through this clause at all events—by a shave.'

'What a fuss everybody is making about this Bill!'

'Well, you don't root up whole industries without a
fuss. But, certainly, Maxwell has roused the country
finely.'

'*She* will break down if it goes on,' said Lady Madeleine in a melancholy voice.

Naseby laughed.

'Not at all! Lady Maxwell was made for war—she
thrives on it. Don't you, too, enjoy it?'

'I don't know,' said the girl, drearily. 'I don't know
what I was made for.'

And over her feather fan her wide eyes travelled to
the distant ogress figure of her mother, sitting majestical
in black wig and diamonds beside the Russian Ambas-
sador. Naseby's also travelled thither—unwillingly.
It was a disagreeable fact that Lady Kent had begun to
be very amiable to him of late.

Lady Madeleine's remark made him silent a moment.
Then he looked at her oddly.

'I am going to offend you,' he said deliberately.
'I am going to tell you that you were made to wear white
satin and pearls, and to look as you look this evening.'

The girl flushed hotly.

'I knew you despised women,' she said, in a strained
voice, staring back at him reproachfully. During her
months of distress and humiliation she had found her
only comfort in 'movements' and 'causes'—in the moral
aspirations generally—so far as her mother would allow
her to have anything to do with them. She had tried,
for instance, to work with Marcella Maxwell—to understand her.

But Naseby held his ground.

'Do I despise women because I think they make the
grace and poetry of the world?' he asked her. 'And,
mind you, I don't draw any lines. Let them be county
councillors and guardians, and inspectors, and queens as

much as they like. I'm very docile. I vote for them.
I do as I'm told.'

' Only, you don't think that *I* can do anything useful !

'I don't think you're cut out for a " platform woman,"
if that's what you mean,' he said, laughing—' even Lady
Maxwell isn't. And if she was, she wouldn't count.
The women who matter just now—and you women are
getting a terrible amount of influence—more than you've
had any time this half-century—are the women who
sit at home in their drawing-rooms, wear beautiful gowns,
and attract the men who are governing the country to
come and see them.'

'Lady Maxwell doesn't sit at home and wear beautiful gowns !'

'I vow she does !' said Naseby, with spirit. 'I can
vouch for it. I was caught that way myself. Not that ·I
belong to the men who are governing the country. And
now she has roped me to her chariot for good and all.
Ah, Ancoats ! how do you do ? '

He got up to make room for the master of the house
as he spoke. But as he walked away he said to himself,
with a kind of delight: 'Good ! she didn't turn a hair.'

Lady Madeleine, indeed, received her former suitor
with a cool dignity that might have seemed impossible to
anyone so plaintively pretty. He lingered beside her,
twirling his carefully pointed moustache, that matched
the small Richelieu chin, and looking at her with a furtive
closeness from time to time.

'Well—so you have just come back from Paris ? '
she said, indifferently.

'Yes ; I stayed a day or two after my mother. One
didn't want to come back to this dull hole.'

'Did you see the new piece at the Français ? '

He made a face.

'Not I ! One couldn't be caught by such *vieux jeu*

B B

as that! There was a splendid woman in one of the *cafés
chantants*—but I suppose you don't go to *cafés chantants*?'

'No,' said Madeleine, eyeing him over her fan with a
composure that astonished herself. 'No, I don't go to
cafés chantants.'

Ancoats looked blank a moment, then resumed, with
fervour :

'This woman's divine—*épatante!* Then, at the Chat
Noir—but—ah! well, perhaps you don't go to the Chat
Noir?'   .

'No, I don't go to the Chat Noir.'

He fidgeted for a minute. She sat silent. Then he
said :

'There are some new French pictures in the next
room. Will you come and see them?'

'Thank you, I think I'll stay here,' she said coldly.

He lingered another second or two, then departed.
The girl drew a long breath, then instinctively turned
her white neck to see if Naseby had really left her.
Strange! He too, from far away, was looking round. In
another moment he was making his way slowly back to
her.

'Ah, there's Tressady! Now for news.'

The remark was Naseby's. He and Lady Madeleine
were, as it happened, inspecting the very French pictures
that the girl had just refused to look at in Ancoats's company.

But now they hurried back to the main drawing-room
where the Tressadys were already surrounded by an eager
crowd. ¨

'Eighteen majority,' Tressady was saying. 'The
Socialists saved it at the last moment, after growling and
threatening till nobody knew what was going to happen.
Forty Ministerialists walked out, twenty more, at least,

were away unpaired, and the Old Liberals voted against the Government to a man.'

'Oh ! they'll go—they'll go on the next clause,' said an elderly peer, whose ruddy face glowed with delight. 'Serve them right, too ! Maxwell's whole aim is revolution made easy. The most dangerous man we have had for years ! Looks so precious moderate, too, all the time. Tell me how did Slade vote after all ? '

And Tressady found himself buttonholed by one person after another ; pressed for the events and incidents of the evening : how this person had voted, how that ; how Ministers had taken it ; whether, after this Pyrrhic victory there was any chance of the Bill's withdrawal, or at least of some radical modification in the coming clauses. Almost everyone in the crowded room belonged, directly or indirectly, to the governing political class. Barely three people among them could have given a coherent account of the Bill itself. But to their fathers and brothers and cousins would belong the passing or the destroying of it. And in this country there is no game that amuses so large a number of intelligent people as the political game.

'I don't know why he should look so d——d excited over it,' said Lord Cathedine to Naseby in a contemptuous aside, with a motion of the head towards Tressady, showing pale and tall above the crowd. 'He seems to have voted straight this time, but he's as shaky as he can be. You never know what that kind of fellow will be up to. Ah, my lady ! and how are you ? '

He made a low bow, and Naseby, turning, saw young Lady Tressady advancing.

'Are you, too, talking politics ? ' said Letty with affected disgust, giving her hand to Cathedine and a smile to Naseby.

'We will now talk of nothing but your scarlet gown,' said Cathedine in her ear. 'Amazing ! '

'You like it?' she said, with nonchalant self-possession. 'It makes me look dreadfully wicked, I know.'
And she threw a complacent glance at a mirror near,
which showed her a gleam of white shoulders in a setting
of flame-coloured tulle.

'Well, you wouldn't wish to look good,' said Cathedine,
pulling his black moustache. 'Any fool can do that!'

'You cynic!' she said, laughing. 'Come and talk to
me over there. Have you got me my invitations?'

Cathedine followed, a disagreeable smile on his full
lips, and they settled themselves in a corner out of the
press. Nor were they disturbed by the sudden hush and
parting of the crowd when, five minutes later, amid a
general joyous excitement, Fontenoy walked in.

Mrs. Allison forgot her usual dignity, and hurried to
meet the leader as he came up to her, with his usual
flushed and haggard air.

'Magnificent!' she said tremulously. 'Now you are
going to win!'

He shook his head, and would hardly let himself be
congratulated by any of the admirers, men or women,
who pressed to shake hands with him. To most of them
he said, impatiently, that it was no good hallooing till one
was out of the wood, that for his own part he had expected more, and that the Government might very well
rally on the next clause. Then, when he had effectively
chilled the enthusiasm of the room, he drew his hostess
aside.

'Well, and are you happier?' he said to her in a low
voice, his whole expression changing.

'Oh, dear friend! don't think of me,' she said, putting
out a thin hand to him with a grateful gesture. 'Yes, the
boy has been very good—he gives me a great deal of his
time. But how can one *know*—how can one possibly
know?'

Her pale, small face contracted with a look of pain. Fontenoy, too, frowned as he looked across at Ancoats, who was leaning against the wall in an affected pose, and quoting bits from a new play to George Tressady.

After a pause, he said :

'I think if I were you I should cultivate Tressady. Ancoats likes him. It might be possible some time for you to work through him.'

The mother assented eagerly, then said, with a smile :

'But I gather you don't find him much to be depended on in the House?'

Fontenoy shrugged his shoulders.

'Lady Maxwell has bedevilled him somehow. You're responsible!'

'Poor Castle Luton! You must tell me how it and I can make up. But you don't mean that there is any thought of his going over?'

'His vote's all safe—I suppose. He would make too great a fool of himself if he failed us there. But he has lost all heart for the business. And Harding Watton tells me it's all her doing. She has been taking him about in the East End—getting her friends to show him round.'

'And *now* you are in the mood to put the women down—to show them their place?'

She looked at him with gentle humour—a very delicate high-bred figure, in her characteristic black-and-white. Fontenoy's whole aspect changed as he caught the reference to their own relation. The look of premature old age, of harsh fatigue, was for the moment effaced by something young and ardent as he bent towards her.

'No—I take the rough with the smooth. Lady Maxwell may do her worst. We have the countercharm.'

A flush showed itself in her lined cheek. She was

fourteen years older than he, and had refused a dozen
times to marry him. But she would have found it hard
to live without his devotion, and she had brought him
by now into such good order that she dared to let him
know it.

Half an hour later George and Letty mounted another
palatial staircase, and at the top of it Letty put on fresh
smiles for a new hostess. George, tired out with the
drama of the day, could hardly stifle his yawns; but
Letty had treated the notion of going home after one
party when they might, if they pleased, 'do' four, with
indignant amazement.

So here they were at the house of one of the greatest
of bankers, and George stalked through the rooms in
his wife's train, taking comparatively little part in the
political buzz all about him, and thinking mostly of a
hurried little talk with Mrs. Allison that had taken up
his last few minutes in her drawing-room. Poor thing!
But what could he do for her? The lad was as stage-
struck as ever—could barely talk sense on any other
subject, and not much on that.

But if he, owing to the clash of an inner struggle,
was weary of politics, the world in general could think
and speak of nothing else. The rooms were full of
politicians and their wives, of members just arrived from
the House, of Ministers smiling at each other with lifted
eyebrows, like boys escaped from a birching. A tempest
of talk surged through the rooms—talk concerned with
all manner of great issues, with the fate of a Government,
the rousing of a country, the fortunes of individual
statesmen. Through it all the little host himself, a small
fair-haired man, with the tired eyes and hot-house air of
the financier, walked about from group to group, gossiping over the incidents of the division, and now and then

taking up some new-comer to be introduced to his pretty and fashionable wife.

Somewhere in the din George stumbled across Lady Leven, who was talking merrily to young Bayle; and found her, notwithstanding, very ready to turn and chat with him.

'Of course we are all waiting for the Maxwells,' she said to him. 'Will they come, I wonder?'

'Why not?'

'Do people show on their way to disaster? I think I should stay at home if I were she.'

'Why, they have to hearten their friends!'

'No good,' said Betty, pursing her pretty lips; 'and they have fought so hard.'

'And may win yet,' said George, an odd sparkle in his eye, as he stood looking over his tiny companion to the door. 'Nobody is sure of anything, I can tell you.'

'I don't believe *you* care,' she said audaciously, shaking her golden head at him.

'Pray, why?'

'Oh! you don't seem at all desperate,' she said coolly. 'Perhaps you're like Frank—you think the other side make so much better points than you do. "If Dowson makes another speech," Frank said to me yesterday, "I vow I shall rat!" There's a way of talking of your own chiefs. Oh! I shall have to take him out of politics.'

And she unfurled her fan with a jerk half-melancholy, half-decided. Then, suddenly, a laugh flashed over her face; she raised herself eagerly on tiptoe.

'Ah! bravo!' she said. 'Here they are!'

George turned with the crowd, and saw them enter, Marcella first, in a blaze of diamonds; then the quiet face and square shoulders of her husband.

Nothing, he thought, could have been better than the manner in which both bore themselves as they passed

through the throng, answering the greetings of friend and
foe, and followed by the keen or hostile scrutiny of
hundreds. There was no bravado, no attempt to disguise the despondency that must naturally follow on a
division so threatening and in many ways so wounding.
Maxwell looked grey with fatigue and short nights,
while her black eyes passed wistfully from friend to friend,
and had never been more quick, more responsive. Their
cause was in danger; nevertheless, the impression on
Tressady's mind was of two people consciously in the
grip of forces infinitely greater than they—forces that
would hold on their path whatever befell their insignificant
mortal agents.

> I steadier step when I recall,
> Howe'er I slip, thou canst not fall.

So cries the thinker to his mistress, Truth. And in the
temper of that cry lies the secret of brave living. One
looker-on, at least—and that an opponent—recalled the
words as he watched Marcella and her husband taking
their way through the London crowd, amid the doubts of
their friends and the half-concealed triumph of their foes.

It seemed to him that he could have no chance of
speech with her. But presently, from the other side of the
room, he saw that she had recognised and was greeting
him, and, do what he would, he must needs make his way
to her.

She welcomed him with great friendliness, and without
a word of small reproach on the score of the weeks he had
let pass without coming to see her. They fell into talk
about the speeches of the evening. George thought he could
see that she, or Maxwell speaking through her, was dissatisfied with Dowson's conduct of the Bill in the House,
and chafing under the constitutional practice that made
it necessary to give him so large a share in the matter.

But she said nothing ungenerous; nor was there any bitterness towards the many false friends who had deserted them that night in the division-lobby. She spoke with eager hope of a series of speeches Maxwell was about to make in the North, and then she turned upon her companion.

'You haven't spoken since the second reading—on any of the fighting points, at least. I have been wondering what you thought of many things.'

George threw his head back against the wall beside her, and was silent a moment. At last he said, looking down upon her:

'Perhaps, very often I haven't known what to think.'

She started—reddened ever so little. 'Does that mean'—she hesitated for a phrase—'that you have moved at all on the main question?'

'No,' he said deliberately—'no! I think as I always did, that you are calling in law to do what law can't do. But perhaps I appreciate better than I once did what provokes you to it. It seems to me difficult now to meet the case your side is putting forward by a mere *non possumus*. One wants to stop the machine a bit and think it out. So much I admit.'

She met his smile with a curious, tremulous look. Instinctively he guessed that this partial triumph in him of her cause—of Maxwell's cause—had let flow some inner fount of feeling.

'If you only knew,' she said, 'how all this Parliamentary rush and clatter seem to me beside the mark. People talk to me of divisions and votes. I think all the time of persons I know—of faces of children—sick-beds, horrible rooms——'

She had turned her face from the crowd towards the open window, in whose recess they were standing. As she spoke they both fell back a little into comparative

solitude, and he drew her on to talk—trying in a young
eager way to make her rest in his kindness, to soothe her
weariness and disappointment. And as she spoke, he
clutched at the minutes; he threw more and more
sympathy at her feet to keep her talking, to enchain
her there beside him, in her lovely whiteness and grace.
And, mingled with it all, was the happy guess that she
liked to linger with him—that amid all this hard clamour
of public talk and judgment she felt him a friend in a
peculiar sense—a friend whose loyalty grew with misfortune. As for this wild-beast world, that was thwarting
and libelling her, he began to think of it with a blind,
up-swelling rage—a desire to fight and win for her—to
put down——　　　．

'Tressady, your wife sent me to find you. She wishes
to go home.'

The voice was Harding Watton's. That observant
young man advanced bowing, and holding out his hand
to Lady Maxwell.

When Marcella had drifted once more into the fast-
melting crowd, George found himself face to face with
Letty. She was very white, and stared at him with
wide, passionate eyes.

And on the way home George, with all his efforts, could
not keep the peace. Letty flung at him a number of bitter
and insulting things that he found very hard to bear.

'What do you want me to do?' he said to her at last,
impatiently. 'I have hardly spoken six sentences to
Lady Maxwell, since the meeting, till to-night—I suppose
because you wished it. But neither you nor anyone else
shall make me rude to her. Don't be such a fool, Letty!
Make friends with her, and you will be ashamed of saying
or even thinking such things.'

Whereat Letty burst into hysterical tears, and he
soon found himself involved in all the remorseful, in-

consequent speeches to which a man in such a plight feels himself driven. She allowed herself to be calmed, and they had a dreary making-up. When it was over, however, George was left with the uneasy conviction that he knew very little of his wife. She was not of a nature to let any slight to her go unpunished. What was she planning? What would she do?

CHAPTER XVII

'HULLO! Are you come back?'

The speaker was George Tressady. He was descending the steps of his club in Pall Mall, and found his arm caught by Naseby, who had just dismissed his hansom outside.

'I came back last night. Are you going homewards? I'll walk across the Square with you.'

The two men turned into St. James's Square, and Naseby resumed:

'Yes, we had a most lively campaign. Maxwell spoke better than I ever heard him.'

'The speeches have been excellent reading, too. And you had good meetings?'

'Splendid! The country is rallying, I can tell you. The North is now strong for Maxwell and the Bill—or seems to be.'

'Just as we are going to kick it out in the House! It's very queer—for no one could tell, a month ago, how the big towns were going. And it looked as though London even were deserting them.'

'A mere wave, I think. At least, I'll bet you anything they'll win this Stepney election. Shall we get the division on the hours clause to-morrow?'

'They say so.'

'If you know your own interests, you'll hurry up,' said Naseby, smiling. 'The country is going against you.'

'I imagine Fontenoy has got his eye on the country! He's been letting the Socialists talk nonsense till now to frighten the steady-going old fellows on the other side, or putting up our men to mark time. But I saw yesterday there was a change.'

'Between ourselves, hasn't he been talking a good deal of nonsense on his own account?'

Naseby threw a glance of laughing inquiry at his companion. George shrugged his shoulders in silence. It had become matter of public remark during the last few days that Fontenoy was beginning at last to show the strain of the combat—that his speeches were growing hysterical and his rule a tyranny. His most trusted followers were now to be heard grumbling in private over certain aspects of his bearing in the House. He had come into damaging collision with the Speaker on one or two occasions, and had made here and there a blunder in tactics which seemed to show a weakening of self-command. Tressady, indeed, knew enough to wonder that the man's nerve and coolness had maintained themselves in their fulness so long.

'So Maxwell took a party to the North?' said George, dropping the subject of Fontenoy.

'Lady Maxwell, of course—myself, Bennett, and Madeleine Penley. It was a pleasure to see Lady Maxwell. She has been dreadfully depressed in town lately. But those trade-union meetings in Lancashire and Yorkshire were magnificent enough to cheer anyone up.'

George shook his head.

'I expect they come too late to save the Bill.'

'I daresay. Well, one can't help being tremendously sorry for her. I thought her looking quite thin and ill over it. It makes one doubt about women in politics! Maxwell will take it a deal more calmly, unless one misunderstands his cool ways. But I shouldn't wonder if *she* had a breakdown.'

George made no reply. Naseby talked a little more about Maxwell and the tour, the critical side of him gaining upon the sympathetic with every sentence. At the corner of King Street he stopped.

'I must go back to the club. By the way, have you heard anything of Ancoats lately?'

George made a face.

'I saw him in a hansom last night, late, crossing Regent Circus with a young woman—*the* young woman, to the best of my belief.'

In the few moments' chat that followed Tressady found that Naseby, like Fontenoy, regarded him as the new friend who might be able to do something for a wild fellow, now that mother and old friends were alike put aside and ignored. But, as he rather impatiently declared—and was glad to declare—such a view was mere nonsense. He had tried, for the mother's sake, and could do nothing. As for him, he believed the thing was very much a piece of *blague*——

'Which won't prevent it from taking him to the devil,' said Naseby, coolly; 'and his mother, by all accounts, will die of it. I'm sorry for her. He seems to think tremendous things of you. I thought you might, perhaps, have knocked it out of him.'

George shook his head again, and they parted.

In truth, Tressady was not particularly flattered by Ancoats's fancy for him. He did not care enough about the lad in return. Yet, in response to one or two outbreaks of talk on Ancoats's part—talks full of a stagey railing at convention—he had tried, for the mother's sake, to lecture the boy a little—to get in a word or two that might strike home. But Ancoats had merely stared a moment out of his greenish eyes, had shaken his queer

mane of hair, as an animal shakes off the hand that curbs
it, had changed the subject at once, and departed. Tressady had seen very little of him since.

And had not, in truth, taken it to heart. He had
neither time nor mind to think about Ancoats. Now, as
he walked home to dinner, he put the subject from him
impatiently. His own moral predicament absorbed him
—this weird, silent way in which the whole political scene
was changing in aspect and composition under his eyes,
was grouping itself for him round one figure—one face.

Had he any beliefs left about the Bill itself? He hardly
knew. In truth it was not his reason that was leading
him. It now was little more than a passionate boyish
longing to wrench himself free from this odious task of
hurting and defeating Marcella Maxwell. The long process
of political argument was perhaps tending every day to the
loosening and detaching of those easy convictions of a
young Chauvinism, that had drawn him originally to
Fontenoy's side. Intellectually he was all adrift. At the
same time he confessed to himself, with perfect frankness,
that he could and would have served Fontenoy happily
enough, but for another influence—another voice.

Yet his old loyalty to Fontenoy tugged sorely at his
will. And with this loyalty of course was bound up the
whole question of his own personal honour and fidelity—
his pledges to his constituents and his party.

Was there no rational and legitimate way out? He
pondered the political situation as he walked along with
great coolness and precision. When the division on the
hours clause was over the main struggle on the Bill, as
he had all along maintained, would be also at an end. If
the Government carried the clause—and the probability
still was that they would carry it by a handful of votes
—the two great novelties of the Bill would have been
affirmed by the House. The homework in the scheduled

trades would have been driven by law into inspected workshops, and the male workers in these same trades would have been brought under the time-restrictions of the Factory Acts.

Compared to these two great reforms, or revolutions, the remaining clause—the landlords clause—touched, as he had already said to Fontenoy, questions of secondary rank, of mere machinery. Might not a man thereupon— might not he, George Tressady—review and reconsider his whole position?

He had told Fontenoy that his vote was safe; but must that pledge extend to more than the vital stuff, the main proposals of the Bill? The hours clause?—yes. But after it?

Fontenoy, no doubt, would carry on the fight to the bitter end, counting on a final and hard-wrung victory. The sanguine confidence which had possessed him about the time of the second reading was gone. He did not, Tressady knew, reckon with any certainty on turning out the Government in this coming division. The miser-able majority with which they had carried the workshops clause would fall again—it would hardly be altogether effaced. That final wiping-out would come—if indeed it were attained—in the last contest of all, to which Fon-tenoy was already heartening and urging on his followers.

Fontenoy's position, of course, in the matter was clear. It was that of the leader and the irreconcilable.

But for the private member, who had seen cause to modify some of his opinions during the course of debate, who had voted loyally with his party up till now—might not the division on the hours clause be said to mark a new stage in the Bill—a stage which restored him his freedom?

The House would have pronounced on the main points of the Bill; the country was rallying in a remark-able and unexpected way to the Government—might it not be fairly argued that the war had been carried far enough ?

He already, indeed, saw signs of that backing down of opposition which he had prophesied to Fontenoy. The key to the whole matter lay, he believed, in the hands of the Old Liberals, that remnant of a once great host, who were now charging the Conservative Government with new and damaging concessions to the Socialist tyranny. These men kept a watchful eye on the country ; they had maintained all along that the country had not spoken. George had already perceived a certain weakening among them. And now, this campaign of Maxwell's, this new enthusiasm in the industrial North—no doubt they would have their effect.

He hurried on, closely weighing the whole matter, the prey to a strange and mingled excitement.

Meanwhile the streets through which he walked had the empty, listless air which marks a stage from which the actors have departed. It was nearing the middle of August, and society had fled.

All the same, as he reflected with a relief which was not without its sting, he and Letty would not be alone at dinner. Some political friends were coming, stranded, like themselves, in this West End, which had by now covered up its furniture and shut its shutters.

What a number of smart invitations had been showering upon them during the last weeks of the season, and were now still pursuing them, for the country house autumn ! The expansion of their social circle had of late often filled George with astonishment. No doubt, he said to himself—though with a curious doubtfulness—Letty was very successful ; still, the recent rush of attentions from big people, who had taken no notice of them on their marriage, was rather puzzling. It had affected her so far more than himself. For he had been hard pressed by

Parliament and the strike, and she had gone about a good deal alone—appearing, indeed, to prefer it.

'Come out with me on the Terrace,' said Marcella to Betty Leven; 'I had rather not wait here. Aldous, will you take us through?'

She and Betty were standing in the inner lobby of the House of Commons. The division had just been called and the galleries cleared. Members were still crowding into the House from the Library, the Terrace, and the smoking-rooms; and all the approaches to the Chamber itself were filled with a throng about equally divided between the eagerness of victory and the anxieties of defeat.

Maxwell took the ladies to the Terrace, and left them there, while he himself went back to the House. Marcella took a seat by the parapet, leant both hands upon it, and looked absently at the river and the clouds. It was a cloudy August night, with a broken, fleecy sky, and gusts of hot wind from the river. A few figures and groups were moving about the Terrace in the flickering light and shade—waiting like themselves.

'Will you be very sad if it goes wrongly?' said Betty, in a low voice, as she took her friend's hand in hers.

'Yes—' said Marcella, simply. Then, after a pause, she added, 'It will be all the harder after this time in the North. Everything will have come too late.'

There was a silence; then Betty said, not without sheepishness, 'Frank's all right.'

Marcella smiled. She knew that little Betty had been much troubled by Frank's tempers of late, and had been haunted by some quite serious qualms about his loyalty to Maxwell and the Bill. Marcella had never shared them. Frank Leven had not grit enough to make a scandal and desert a chief. But Betty's ambition had forced the boy into a life that was not his; had divided him from the streams and fields, from the country gentleman's duties and pleasures, that were his natural sphere. In this hot town game of politics, this contest of brains and ambitions, he was out of place—was, in fact, wasting both time and capacity. Betty would have to give way, or the comedy of a lovers' quarrel might grow to something ill-matched with the young grace and mirth of such a pair of handsome children.

Marcella meant to tell her friend all this in due time. Now she could only wait in silence, listening for every sound, Betty's soft fingers clasping her own, the wind as it blew from the bridge cooling her hot brow.

' Here they are ! ' said Betty.

They turned to the open doorway of the House. A rush of feet and voices approached, and the various groups on the Terrace hurried to meet it.

'Just saved ! By George, what a squeak ! ' said a man's voice in the distance; and at the same moment Maxwell touched his wife on the shoulder.

' A majority of ten ! Nobody knew how it had gone till the last moment.'

She put up her face to him, leaning against him.

' I suppose it means we can't pull through ? ' He bent to her.

' I should think so. Darling, don't take it to heart so much ! '

In the darkness he felt the touch of her lips on his hand. Then she turned, with a white cheek and smiling mouth, to meet the greetings and rueful congratulations of the friends that were crowding about them.

The Terrace was soon a moving mass of people, eagerly discussing the details of the division. The lamps, blown a little by the wind, threw uncertain lights on faces and figures, as they passed and repassed between the mass of building on the one hand and the wavering darkness of the river on the other. To Marcella, as she stood talking to person after person—talking she hardly knew what—the whole scene was a dim bewilderment, whence emerged from time to time faces or movements of special significance.

Now it was Dowson, the Home Secretary, advancing to greet her, with his grey shaven face, eyelids somewhat drooped, and the cool, ambiguous look of one not quite certain of his reception. He had been for long a close ally of Maxwell's. Marcella had thought him a true friend. But certainly, in his conduct of the Bill of late there had been a good deal to suggest the attitude of a man determined to secure himself a retreat, and uncertain how far to risk his personal fortunes on a doubtful issue. So that she found herself talking to him with a new formality, in the tone of those who have been friends, yet begin to foresee the time when they may be antagonists.

Or, again, it was Fontenoy—Fontenoy's great head and overhanging brows, thrown suddenly into light against the windy dusk. He was walking with a young viscount whose curls, clothes, and shoulders were alike unapproachable by the ordinary man. This youth could not forbear an exultant twitching of the lip as he passed the Maxwells. Fontenoy ceremoniously took off his hat. Marcella had a momentary impression of the passionate, bull-like force of the man, before he disappeared into the crowd. His eye had wavered as it met hers. Out of courtesy to the woman he had tried not to *look* his triumph.

And now it was quite another face—thin, delicately marked, a noticeable chin, an outstretched hand.

She was astonished by her own feeling of pleasure.

'Tell me,' she said quickly, as she moved eagerly forward—'tell me! is it about what you expected?'

They turned towards the river. George Tressady hung over the wall beside her.

'Yes. I thought it might be anything from eight to twenty.'

'I suppose Lord Fontenoy now thinks the end quite certain.'

'He may. But the end is not certain!'

'But what can prevent it! The despairing thing for us is, that if the country had been roused earlier, everything might have been different. But now the House——'

'Has got out of hand? It may be; but I find a great many people affected by Lord Maxwell's speeches in the North, and his reception there. To-day's result was inevitable, but, if I'm not mistaken, we shall now see a number of new combinations.'

The sensitive face became in a moment all intelligence. She played the politician, and cross-examined him. He hesitated. What he was doing was already a treachery. But he only hesitated to give way. They lingered by the wall together, discussing possibilities and persons; and when Maxwell at last turned from his own conversations to suggest to his wife that it was time to go home, she came forward with a mien of animation that surprised him. He greeted Tressady with friendliness, and then, as though a thought had struck him, suddenly drew the young man aside.

'Ancoats, of course,' said George to himself; and Ancoats it was.

Maxwell, without preliminaries, and taking his companion's knowledge of the story for granted—no doubt on Fontenoy's information—said a few words about the renewal of the difficulty. Did he not think it had all begun again? Yes, George had some reason to think so. 'If you can do anything for us——'

' Of course ! but what can I do ? As we all know, Ancoats does not sit still to be scolded.'

Their colloquy lasted only a minute or two ; yet when it was over, and the Maxwells had gone, George was left with a vivid impression of the great man's quiet strength and magnanimity.   No one could have guessed from his anxious and well-considered talk on this private matter that he was in the very heat of a political struggle that must affect all his own fortunes.   Tressady had been accustomed to spend his wit on the heavier sides of Maxwell's character.   To-night, he said to himself, half in a passion, grudging the confession, that it was not wonderful she loved him !

She ! The remembrance of how her whole nature had brightened from its cloud as he drew out for her his own forecast of what might still happen ; the sweet confidence and charm that she had shown him ; the intimacy of the tone she had allowed between them ; the mingling all through of a delicate abstinence from anything touching on his own personal position, with an unspoken recognition of it—the impulse of a generosity that could not help rewarding what seemed to it the yielding of an adversary ; these things filled him with a delicious pleasure as he walked home.   In a hundred directions— political, social, spiritual—the old horizons of the mind seemed to be lightening and expanding.   The cynical, indifferent temper of his youth was breaking down ; the whole man was more intelligent, capable, tender.   Yet what sadness and restlessness of soul as soon as the brief moment of joy had come and gone !

A few afternoons of Supply encroached upon the eight days that still remained before the last clause of the Bill came to a division.   But the whole eight days, neverthe- less, were filled with the new permutations and combinations which Tressady had foreseen. The Government carried the Stepney election, and in other quarters the effects of the speechmaking in the North began to be visible. Rumours of the syndicate already formed to take over large numbers of workshops in both the Jewish and Gentile quarters of the East End, and of the hours and wages that were likely to obtain in the new factories, were driving a considerable mass of working-class opinion, which had hitherto held aloof, straight for the Government, and splitting up much of that which had been purely hostile.

Nevertheless, the situation in the House itself was hardly changing with the change in the country. The Socialist members very soon developed the proposal to make the landlords responsible for the carrying-out of the new Act into a furious general attack on the landlords of London. Their diatribes kept up the terrors which had already cost the Government so many men. It was not possible, not seemly, to yield, as Maxwell was yielding, all along the line to these fellows!

But the Old Liberals, or the New Whigs, as George had expected, were restless. They felt the country, and they had no affection for landlords as such. Did a man arise who could give them a lead, there was no saying how soon they might not break away from the Fontenoy combination. Fontenoy felt it, and prowled among them like a Satan, urging them to complete their deed, to give the *coup de grâce*.

On the Wednesday afternoon before the Friday on which he thought the final vote would be taken, George let himself into his own house about six o'clock, thankful to feel that he had a quiet evening before him. He had been wandering about the House of Commons and its appurtenances all day, holding colloquies with this person and that, unable to see his way—to come to any decision.

And, as was now usual, he and Fontenoy had been engaged in steering out of each other's way as much as possible.

As he went upstairs he noticed a letter lying on the step. He took it up, and found an open note, which he read, at first without thinking of it:

'My dear Lady,—Chatsworth can't be done. I have thrown my flies with great skill, but—no go! I don't seem to have influence enough in that quarter. But I have various other plans on hand. You shall have a jolly autumn, if I can manage it. There are some Scotch invitations I can certainly get you—and I should like to show you the ways of those parts. By the way, I hope your husband shoots decently. People are very particular. And you really must consult me about your gowns—I'm deuced clever at that sort of thing! I shall come to-morrow, when I have packed off my family to the country. Don't know why God made families!

'Yours always,
'CATHEDINE.'

'George! is that you?' cried Letty from above him, in a voice half-angry, half-hesitating; 'and—and—that's my note. Please give it me at once.'

He finished it under her eyes, then handed it to her with formal courtesy. They walked into the drawing-room, and George shut the door. He was very pale, and Letty quailed a little.

'So Cathedine has been introducing us into society,' he said, 'and advising you as to your gowns. Was that—quite necessary—do you think?'

'It's very simple what he has been doing,' was her angry reply. 'You never take any pains to make life amusing to me, so I must look elsewhere, if I want society—that's all.'

'And it never occurs to you that you are thereby incurring an unseemly obligation to a man whom I dislike, whom I have warned you against, who bears everywhere an evil name? You think I am likely to enjoy—to put up with, even—the position of being asked on sufferance—as your appendage—provided I " shoot decently " ? '

His tone of scorn, his slight figure, imperiously drawn up, sent her a challenge, which she answered with sullen haste.

'That's all nonsense, of course! And he wouldn't be rude to you if you weren't always rude to him.'

' Rude to him ! ' He smiled. 'But now, let us get to the bottom of this thing. Did Cathedine get us the cards for Clarence House—and that Goodwood invitation ? '

Letty made no answer. She stared at him defiantly, twisting and untwisting the ribbons of her blue dress.

George reddened hotly. His personal pride in matters of social manners was one of his strongest characteristics.

' Let me beg you, at any rate, to write and tell Lord Cathedine that we will not trouble him for any more of these kind offices. And, moreover, I shall not go to any of these houses in the autumn unless I am quite certain he has had nothing to do with it.'

'I have accepted,' said Letty, breathing hard.

'I cannot help that. You should have been frank with me. I am not going to do what would destroy my own self-respect.'

' No—you prefer making love to Lady Maxwell ! '

He looked steadily a moment at her pallor and her furious eyes. Then he said, in another tone :

' Letty, does it ever occur to you that we have not been married yet five months ? Are our relations to each other to go on for ever like this ? I think we might make something better of them,'

'That's your look-out. But as to these invitations,
I have accepted them, and I shall go.'

'I don't think you will. You would find it wouldn't
do. Anyway, Cathedine must be written to.'

'I shall do nothing of the kind!' she cried.

'Then I shall write myself.'

She rose, quivering with passion, supporting herself
on the arm of her chair.

'If you do, I will find some way of punishing you for
it. Oh, if I had never made myself miserable by
marrying you!'

Their eyes met. Then he said:

'I think I had better go and dine at the club. We
are hardly fit to be together.'

'Go, for Heaven's sake!' she said, with a disdainful
gesture.

Outside the door he paused a moment, head bent,
hands clenched. Then a wild, passionate look overspread
his young face. 'It is her evening,' he said to himself.
'Letty turns me out. I will go.'

Meanwhile Letty stood where he had left her till
she had heard the street-door close. The typical, significant sound knelled to her heart. She began to
walk tempestuously up and down, crying with excitement.

Time passed on. The August evening closed in; and
in this deserted London nobody came to see her. She
dined alone, and afterwards spent what seemed to her interminable hours pacing the drawing-room and meditating.
At last there was a pause in the rush of selfish or jealous
feeling which had been pulsing through her for weeks
past, dictating all her actions, fevering all her thoughts.
And there is nothing so desolate as such a pause, to such
a nature. For it means reflection; it means putting one's
life away from one, and looking at it as a whole. And to

the Lettys of this world there is no process more abhor-
rent—none they will spend more energy in escaping.

It was inexplicable, intolerable that she should be so
unhappy. What was it that tortured her so—hatred
of Marcella Maxwell, or pain that she had lost her husband? But she had never imagined herself in love with
him when she married him. He had never obtained
from her before a tenth part of the thought she had
bestowed upon him during the past six weeks. During
all the time that she had been flirting with Cathedine, and
recklessly placing herself in his power by the favours she
asked of him, she saw now, with a kind of amazement,
that she had been thinking constantly of George, determined to impress him with her social success, to force
him to admire her and think much of her.

Cathedine? Had he any real attraction for her?
Why, she was afraid of him, she knew him to be coarse
and brutal, even while she played with him and sent him
on her errands. When she compared him with George
—even George as she had just seen him in this last odious
scene—she felt the tears of anger and despair rising.

But to be forced to dismiss him at George's word, to
submit in this matter of the invitations, to let herself be
trampled on, while George gave all his homage, all his
best mind, to Lady Maxwell—something scorching flew
through her veins as she thought of it. Never! never!
She would find, she had already thought of, a startling
way of avenging herself.

Late at night George came home. She had locked
her door, and he turned into his dressing-room. When
the house was quiet again, she pressed her face into the
pillows, and wept till she was amazed at her own pain,
and must needs turn her rage upon herself.

When Tressady arrived at the house in Mile End

Road he found the pretty, bare room where Marcella held her gatherings full of guests. The East End had not ' gone out of town.' The two little workhouse girls, in the whitest of caps and aprons, were carrying round trays of coffee and cakes ; and beyond the open window was a tiny garden, backed by a huge Board School and some tall warehouses, yet as pleasant within its own small space as a fountain and flowers, constantly replenished from Maxwell Court, could make it.

Amid the medley of workmen, union officials, and members of Parliament that the room contained, George was set first of all to talk to a young schoolmaster or two, but he had never felt so little able to adjust his mind to strangers. The thought of his home miseries burnt within him. When could he get his turn with her? He was thirsty for the sound of her voice, the kindness of her eyes.

She had received him with unusual warmth, and an eagerness of look that seemed to show she had at least as much to say to him as he to her. And at last his turn came. She took some of her guests into the garden. George followed, and they found themselves side by side. He noticed that she was very pale. Yet how was it that fatigue and anxiety instead of marring her physical charm, only increased it? This thin black dress in which the tall figure moved so finely, the black lace folded in a fashion all her own about her neck and breast, the waving lines of hair above the delicate stateliness of the brow—those slight tragic hollows in cheek and temple with their tale of spirit and passionate feeling, and all the ebb and flow of noble life—he had never felt her so rare, so adorable.

' Well! what do you think of it all to-day? Are you still inclined to prophesy?' she asked him, smiling.

' I might be—if I saw any chance of the man you want. But he doesn't seem to be forthcoming, and——'

'And to-morrow is the end!'

'The Government has quite made up its mind not to take defeat—not to accept modifications?'

She shook her head.

They were standing at the end of the garden, looking into the brightly lit windows of the Board School, where evening-classes were going on. She gave a long sigh.

'As for us personally, we can only be thankful to have it over. Neither of us could have borne it much longer. I suppose, when the crisis is all over, we shall go away for a long time.'

By 'the crisis' she meant, of course, the resignation of Ministers and a change of Government. So that a few days hence she would be no longer within his reach at all. Maxwell, once out of office, would, no doubt, for a long while to come prefer to spend the greater part of his time in Brookshire, away from politics. A sudden sharp perception woke in Tressady of what it would mean to him to find himself in a world where, on going out of a morning, it would be no longer possible to come across her.

At last she broke the silence.

'How little I really thought, in spite of all one's anxiety, that Lord Fontenoy was going to win! He has played his cards amazingly well.'

George took no notice. Thoughts were whirling in his brain.

'What would you say to me, I wonder,' he said at last, 'if *I* were to try the part?'

He spoke in a bantering tone, poking at the black London earth with his stick.

'What part?'

'Well, it seems to me I might put the case. One wants to argue the thing in a common-sense way. I don't

feel towards this clause as I did towards the others.   I
know a good many men don't.'

He turned to her with a light composure.

She stared in bewilderment.

'I don't understand.'

'Well ; why shouldn't one put the case ?   We have
always counted on the hostility of the country.   But the
country seems to be coming round.   Some of us now feel
the Bill should have its chance—we are inclined to let
Ministers take the responsibility.   But, gracious Heavens !
—to suppose the House would pay any attention to me ! '

He took up a stone and jerked it over the wall.   She
did not speak for a moment.   At last she said,

'It would be a grave thing for *you* to do.'

He turned, and their eyes met, hers full of emotion,
and his hesitating and reflective.   Then he laughed, his
pride stung a little by her expression.

' You think I should do myself more harm, than good
to anybody else ? '

' No.—Only it would be serious,' she repeated after a
pause.

Instantly he dropped the subject as far as his own
action was concerned.   He led her back into discussion
of other people, and of the situation in general.

Then suddenly, as they talked, a host of thoughts
fled cloud-like, rising and melting, through Marcella's
memory.   She remembered with what prestige—considering his youth and inexperience—he · had entered
Parliament, the impression made by the short and
brilliant campaign of his election.   Now, since the real
struggle of the session had begun, his energies seemed
to have been unaccountably in abeyance, and eclipse.
People, she noticed, had ceased to talk of him.   But
supposing, after all, there had been a crisis of mind and
conviction underlying it ?—supposing that now, at the last

moment, in a situation that cried out for a leader, something should suddenly release his powers and gifts to do
their proper work——

It vexed her to realise her own excitement, together
with an odd shrinking and reluctance that seemed to be
fighting with it. All in a moment, to Tressady's astonishment, she recalled the conversation to the point where it
had turned aside.

' And you think—you *really* think '— her voice had a
nervous appealing note—' that even at this eleventh hour
—No, I don't understand!—I *can't* understand!—why,
or how you should still think it possible to change things
enough ! '

He felt a sting of pleasure, and the passing sense of
hurt pride was soothed. At least he had conquered her
attention, her curiosity !

' I am sure that anything might still happen,' he said
stubbornly.

' Well, only let it be settled ! ' she said, trying to speak
lightly, ' else there will be nothing left of some of us.'

She raised her hand, and pushed back her hair with a
childish gesture of weariness, that was quite unconscious,
and therefore touching.

As she spoke, indeed, the thought of a strong man
harassed with overwork, and patiently preparing to lay
down his baffled task, and all his cherished hopes, captured
her mind, brought a quick rush of tears even to her eyes.
Tressady looked at her ; he saw the moisture in the eyes,
the reddening of the cheek, the effort for self-control.

' Why do you let yourself feel it so much?' he said
resentfully ; ' it is not natural, nor right.'

' That's our old quarrel, isn't it?' she answered,
smiling.

He was staring at the ground again, poking with his
stick.

'There are so many things one *must* feel,' he said in
a bitter low voice; 'one may as well try to take politics
calmly.'

She looked down upon him, understanding, but not
knowing how to meet him, how to express herself. His
words and manner were a confession of personal grief—
almost an appeal to her—the first he had ever made.
Yet how to touch the subject of his marriage! She
shrank from it painfully. What ominous, disagreeable
things she had heard lately of the young Lady Tressady
from people she trusted! Why, oh! why had he ruined
his own life in such a way!

And with the yearning towards all suffering which
was natural to her, there mingled so much else—inevitable
softness and gratitude for that homage towards herself,
which had begun to touch and challenge all the loving,
responsive impulse which was at the root of her character
—an eager wish to put out a hand and guide him—all
tending to shape in her this new longing to rouse him to
some critical and courageous action—action which should
give him at least the joy that men get from the strenuous
use of natural powers, from the realisation of themselves.
And through it all the most divinely selfish blindness to
the real truth of the situation! Yet she tried not to
think of Maxwell—she wished to think only of and for
her friend.

After his last words they stood side by side in silence
for a few moments. But the expression of her eyes, of
her attitude, was all sympathy. He must needs feel that
she cared, she understood, that his life, his pain, his story
mattered to her. At last she said, turning her face away
from him, and from the few people who had not yet
left the garden to go and listen to some music that
was going on in the drawing-room:

'Sometimes, the best way to forget one's own troubles

—don't you think ?—is to put something else first for a time—perhaps in your case, the public life and service. Mightn't it be ?   Suppose you thought it all really out, what you have been saying to me—gave yourself up to it—and then *determined*.   Perhaps afterwards——'

She paused—overcome with doubt, even shyness— and very pale too, as she turned to him again.   But so beautiful ! The very perplexity which spoke in the gently quivering face as it met his, made her lovelier in his eyes.   It seemed to strike down some of the barrier between them, to present her to him as weaker, more approachable.

But after waiting a moment, he gave a little harsh laugh.

' Afterwards, when one has somehow settled other people's affairs, one might see straighter in one's own ? Is that what you mean ? '

' I meant,' she said, speaking with difficulty, ' what I have often found—myself—that it helps one, sometimes, to throw oneself altogether into something outside one's own life, in a large disinterested way.   Afterwards, one comes back to one's own puzzles—with a fresh strength and hope.'

' Hope ! ' he said despondently, with a quick lifting of the shoulders.   Then, in another tone—

' So that's your advice to me—to take this thing seriously—to take myself seriously—to think it out ? '

' Yes, yes,' she said eagerly ; ' don't trifle with it—with what you might think and do—till it is too late to think and do anything.'

Suddenly it flashed across them both how far they had travelled since their first meeting in the spring.   Her mind filled with a kind of dread, an uneasy sense of responsibility—then with a tremulous consciousness of power.   It was as though she felt something fluttering like a bird in her hands. And all the time there echoed through her memory a voice speaking in a moonlit garden —'You know—you don't mind my saying it?—nobody is ever converted—politically—nowadays.'

No, but there may be honest advance and change— why not? And if she had influenced him—was it not Maxwell's work and thought that had spoken through her?

'Well, anyway,' said Tressady's voice beside her, 'whatever happens—you'll believe——'

'That you won't help to give us the *coup de grâce* un- less you must?' she said, half-laughing, yet with manifest emotion. 'Anyway, I should have believed that.'

'And you really care so much?' he asked her again, looking at her, wondering.

She suddenly dropped her head upon her hands. They were alone now in the moonlit garden, and she was leaning over the low wall that divided them from the school enclosure. But before he could say anything— before he could even move closer to her—she had raised her face again, and drawn her hand rapidly across her eyes.

'I suppose one is tired and foolish after all these weeks,' she said, with a breaking voice—'I apologise. You see when one comes to see everything through another's eyes—to live in another's life——'

He felt a sudden stab, then a leap of joy—hungry, desolate joy—that she should thus admit him to the very sanctuary of her heart—let him touch the 'very pulse of the machine.' At the same moment that it revealed the eternal gulf between them, it gave him a delicious pas- sionate sense of intimacy—of privilege.

'You have—a marvellous idea of marriage,' he said, under his breath, as he moved slowly beside her towards the house.

She made no answer. In another minute she was talking to him of indifferent things, and immediately afterwards he found himself parted from her in the crowd of the drawing-room.

When the party dispersed, and he was walking alone towards Aldgate through the night, he could do nothing but repeat to himself fragments of what she had said to him—lost all the time in a miserable yearning memory of her eyes and voice.

His mind was made up. And as he lay sleepless and solitary through the night, he scarcely thought any more of the strait to which his married life had come. Forty-eight hours hence he should have time for that. For the present he had only to 'think out' how it might be possible for him to turn doubt and turmoil into victory, and lay the crown of it at Marcella Maxwell's feet.

Meanwhile Marcella, on her return to St. James's Square, put her hands on Maxwell's shoulders, and said to him, in a voice unlike herself: 'Sir George Tressady was at the party to-night. I *think* he may be going to throw Lord Fontenoy over. Don't be surprised if he speaks in that sense to-morrow.'

Maxwell looked extraordinarily perturbed.

'I hope he will do nothing of the kind,' he said, with decision. 'It will do him enormous harm. All the conviction he has ever shown has been the other way. It will be thought to be a mere piece of caprice and indiscipline.'

Marcella said nothing. She walked away from him, her hands clasped behind her, her soft skirt trailing—a pale muse of meditation—meditation in which for once she did not invite him to share.

'Tressady, by all that's wonderful!' said a member of

Fontenoy's party to his neighbour. 'What's *he* got to say?'

The man addressed bent forward, with his hands on his knees, to look eagerly at the speaker.

'I knew there was something up,' he said. 'Every time I have come across Tressady to-day he has been deep with one or other of those fellows'—he jerked his head towards the Liberal benches. 'I saw him button-holing Green in the Library, then with Speedwell on the Terrace. And just look at their benches! They're as thick as bees! Yes, by George! there *is* something up.'

His young sportsman's face flushed with excitement, and he tried hard through the intervening heads to get a glimpse of Fontenoy. But nothing was to be seen of the leader but a hat jammed down over the eyes, a square chin, and a pair of folded arms.

The House, indeed, throughout the day had worn an aspect which, to the experienced observer—to the smooth-faced Home Secretary, for instance, watching the progress of this last critical division—meant that everything was possible, the unexpected above all. Rumours gathered and died away. Men might be seen talking with un-accustomed comrades; and those who were generally most frank had become discreet. It was known that Fontenoy's anxiety had been growing rapidly; and it was noticed that he and the young viscount who acted as the Whip of the party had kept an extraordinarily sharp watch on all their own men through the dinner-hour.

Fontenoy himself had spoken before dinner, throwing scorn upon the clause, as the ill-conceived finish of an impossible Bill. So the landlords were to be made the executants, the police, of this precious Act? Every man who let out a tenement-house in workmen's dwellings was to be haled before the law and punished if a tailor on his premises did his work at home, if a widow took in shirtmaking to keep her children. Pass, for the justice or the expediency of such a law in itself. But who but a madman ever supposed you could get it carried out! What if the landlords refused or neglected their part? *Quis custodiet?* And was Parliament going to make itself ridiculous by setting up a law which, were it a thousand times desirable, you simply could not enforce?

The speech was delivered with amazing energy. It abounded in savage epigram and personality; and a month before it would have had great effect. Every Englishman has an instinctive hatred of paper reforms.

During the dinner hour Tressady met Fontenoy in the Lobby, and suddenly stopped to speak. The young man was deeply flushed and holding himself stiffly erect. 'If you want me,' he said, 'you will find me in the Library. I don't want to spring anything upon you. You shall know all I know.'

'Thank you,' said the other, with slow bitterness— 'but we can look after ourselves. I think you and I understood each other this morning.'

The two men parted abruptly. Tressady walked on, stung and excited afresh by the memory of the hateful half-hour he had spent that morning in Fontenoy's library. For after all, when once he had come to his decision, he had tried to behave with frankness, with consideration.

Fontenoy hurried on to look for the young viscount with the curls and shoulders, and the two men stood about the inner lobby together, Fontenoy sombrely watching everybody who came out or in.

It was about ten o'clock when Tressady caught the Speaker's eye. He rose in a crowded House, a House conscious not only that the division shortly to be taken would decide the fate of a Government, but vaguely aware, besides, that something else was involved—one of those personal incidents that may at any moment make the dullest piece of routine dramatic, or rise into history by the juxtaposition of some great occasion.

The House had not yet made up its opinion about him as a speaker. He had done well; then, not so well. And, moreover, it was so long since he had taken any part in debate that the House had had time to forget whatever qualities he might once have shown.

His bearing and voice won him a first point. For youth, well-bred and well-equipped, the English House of Commons has always shown a peculiar indulgence. Then members began to bend eagerly forward, to crane necks, to put hands to ears. The Treasury Bench was seen to be listening as one man.

Before the speech was over many of those present had already recognised in it a political event of the first order. The speaker had traced with great frankness his own relation to the Bill—from an opinion which was but a prejudice, to a submission which was still half-repugnance. He drew attention to the remarkable and growing move-ment in support of the Maxwell policy which was now spreading throughout the country, after a period of cool-ness and suspended judgment; he pointed to the probable ease with which, as it was now seen, the 'harassed trades' would adapt themselves to the new law; he showed that the House, in at least three critical divisions, and under circumstances of enormous difficulty, had still affirmed the Bill; that the country, during the progress of the measure, had rallied unmistakably to the Govern-ment, and that all that remained was a question of machinery. That being so, he—and, he believed, some others—had reconsidered their positions. Their electoral pledges, in their opinion, no longer held, though they would be ready at any moment to submit themselves to consequences, if consequences there were to be.

Then, taking up the special subject-matter of the clause, he threw himself upon his leader's speech with a nervous energy, an information, and a resource which held the House amazed. He tore to pieces Fontenoy's elaborate attack, showed what practical men thought of the clause, and with what careful reliance upon their opinion and their experience it had been framed; and, finally—with a reference, not lacking in a veiled passion that told upon the House, to those 'dim toiling thousands' whose lot, 'as it comes to work upon the mind, is daily perplexing if not transforming the thoughts and ideals of such men as I '—he, in the plainest terms, announced his intention of voting with the Government, and sat down, amid the usual mingled storm, in a shouting and excited House.

The next hour passed in a tumult. One speaker after another got up from the Liberal benches—burly manufacturers and men of business, who had so far held a strong post in the army of resistance—to tender their submission, to admit that the fight had gone far enough, that the country was against them, and that the Bill must be borne. What use, too, in turning out a Government which would either be sent back with redoubled strength or replaced by combinations that had no attractions whatever for men of moderate minds? Sadness reigned in the speeches of this Liberal remnant; nor could the House from time to time forbear to jeer them. But they made their purpose plain, and the Government Whip, standing near the door, gleefully struck off name after name from his Opposition list.

Then followed the usual struggle between the division that all men wanted and the speakers that no man could endure. But at last the bell was rung, the House cleared. As Tressady turned against the stream of his party,

Fontenoy, with a sarcastic smile, stood elaborately aside to let him pass.

'We shall soon know what you have cost us,' he said hoarsely in Tressady's ear; then, advancing a little towards the centre of the floor, he looked up markedly and deliberately at the Ladies' Gallery. Tressady made no reply. He held his fair head higher than usual as he passed on his unaccustomed way to the Aye Lobby. Many an eager eye strained back to see how many recruits would join him as he reached the Front Opposition Bench; many a Parliamentary Nestor watched the young man's progress with a keenness born of memory—memory that burnt anew with the battles of the past.

'Do you remember Chandos,' said one old man to another—'young Chandos, that went for Peel in '46 against his party? It was my first year in Parliament. I can see him now. He was something like this young fellow.'

'But *his* ratting changed nothing,' said his companion, with an uneasy laugh; and they both struggled forward among the Noes.

Twenty minutes later the tellers were at the table, and the moment that was to make or mar a great Ministry had come.

'Ayes, 306; Noes, 280. The Ayes have it!'

'By Jove, he's done it!—the Judas!' cried a young fellow, crimson with excitement, who was standing beside Fontenoy!

'Yes—he's done it!' said Fontenoy, with grim composure, though the hand that held his hat shook. 'The curtain may now fall.'

'Where is he?' shouted the hot bloods around him, hooting and groaning, as their eyes searched the House for the man who had thus, in an afternoon, pulled down and defeated all their hopes.

But Tressady was nowhere to be seen. He had left the House just as the great news, surging like a wave through Lobby and corridor, reached a group of people waiting in a Minister's private room—and Marcella Maxwell knew that all was won.

CHAPTER XVIII

'I SHALL go straight to Brook Street, and see if I can be a comfort to Letty,' said Mrs. Watton, with a tone and air, however, that seemed to class her rather with the Sons of Thunder than the Sons of Consolation.

She was standing on the steps of the Ladies' Gallery entrance to the House of Commons, and Harding, who had just called a cab for her, was beside her.

'Could you see from the Gallery whether George had left?'

'He was still there when I came down,' said Mrs. Watton, ungraciously, as though she grudged to talk of such a monster. 'I saw him near the door while they hooted him. But, anyway, I should go to Letty—I don't forget that I am her only relative in town.'

As a matter of fact, her eyes had played her false. But the wrath with which her large face and bonnet were shaking was cause enough for hallucinations.

'Then I'll go, too,' said Harding, who had been hesitating. 'No doubt Tressady'll stay for his thanks! But I daresay we sha'n't find Letty at home yet. I know she was to go to the Lucys' to-night.'

'Poor lamb!' said Mrs. Watton, throwing up her hands.

Harding laughed.

'Oh! Letty won't take it like a lamb—you'll see!'

'What can a woman do?' said his mother, scornfully.

' A decent woman, I mean, whom one can still have in one's house. All she can do is to cry, and take a district.'

When they reached Upper Brook Street, the butler reported that his mistress had just come in. He made, of course, no difficulty about admitting Lady Tressady's aunt, and Mrs. Watton sailed up to the drawing-room, followed by Harding, who carried his head poked forward, as was usual to him, an opera-hat under his arm, and an eyeglass swinging from a limp wrist.

As they entered the drawing-room door, Letty, in full evening-dress, was standing with her back to them. She had the last edition of an evening paper open before her, so that her small head and shoulders seemed buried in the sheet. And so eager was her attention to what she was reading that she had not heard their approach.

' Letty ! ' said Mrs. Watton.

Her niece turned with a violent start.

' My dear Letty ! ' The aunt approached, quivering with majestic sympathy, both hands outstretched.

Letty looked at her a moment, frowning ; then recoiled impatiently, without taking any notice of the hands.

' So I see George has spoken against his party. There has been a scene. What has happened ? What's the end ? '

' Only that the Government has won its clause,' said Harding, interposing his smooth falsetto—' won by a substantial majority, too. No chance of the Lords playing the fool ! '

' The Government has won ?—the Maxwells have won, that is—she has won ! ' said Letty, still frowning, her voice sharp and tingling.

' If you like to put it so,' said Harding, raising his shoulders. ' Yes, I should think that set's pretty jubilant to-night.'

' And you mean to say that George did and said

nothing to prepare you, my poor child?' cried Mrs. Watton, in her heaviest manner. She had picked up the newspaper, and was looking with disgust at the large headlines with which the hastily printed sheet strove to eke out the brevity of the few words in which it announced the speech of the evening : ' *Scene in the House of Commons— Break-down of the Resistance to the Bill—Sir George Tressady's Speech—Unexampled Excitement.*'

Letty breathed fast.

' He said something a day or two ago about a change, but of course I never believed—He has disgraced himself ! '

She began to pace stormily up and down the room, her white skirts floating behind her, her small hands pulling at her gloves. Harding Watton stood looking on in an attitude of concern, one pensive finger laid upon his lip.

' Well, my dear Letty,' said Mrs. Watton, impressively, as she laid down the newspaper, ' the only thing to be done is to take him away. Let people forget it—if they can. And let me tell you, for your comfort, that he is not the first man, by a long way, that woman has led astray— nor will he be the last.'

Letty's pale cheeks flamed into red. She stopped. She turned upon her comforter with eyes of hot resentment and dislike.

' And they dare to say that he did it for her ! What right has anybody to say it? '

Mrs. Watton stared. Harding slowly and compassionately shook his head.

' I am afraid the world dares to say a great many unpleasant things—don't you know? One has to put up with it. Lady Maxwell has a characteristic way of doing things. It's like a painter : one can't miss the touch.'

' No more than one can mistake a saying of Harding Watton's,' said a vibrating voice behind them.

And there in the open doorway stood Tressady, pale, spent, and hollow-eyed, yet none the less the roused master of the house, determined to assert himself against a couple of intruders.

Letty looked at him in silence, one foot beating the ground. Harding started, and turned aside to search for his opera-hat, which he had deposited upon the sofa. Mrs. Watton was quite unabashed.

'We did not expect you so soon,' she said, holding out a chilly hand. 'And I daresay you will misunderstand our being here. I cannot help that. It seemed to me my duty, as Letty's nearest relative in London, to come here and condole with her to-night on this deplorable event.'

'I don't know what you mean,' said Tressady, coolly, his hand on his side. 'Are you speaking of the division?'

Mrs. Watton threw up her hands and her eyebrows. Then, gathering up her dress, she marched across the room to Letty.

'Good-night, Letty. I should have been glad to have had a quiet talk with you, but as your husband's come in I shall go. Oh! I'm not the person to interfere between husband and wife. Get him to tell you, if you can, *why* he has disappointed the friends and supporters who got him into Parliament; why he has broken all his promises, and given everybody the right to pity his unfortunate young wife! Oh! don't alarm yourself, Sir George! I say my mind, but I'm going. I know very well that I am intruding. Good-night. Letty understands that she will always find sympathy in *my* house.'

And the fierce old lady swept to the door, holding the culprit with her eyes. Harding, too, stepped up to Letty, who was standing now by the mantelpiece, with her back to the room. He took the hand hanging by her side, and folded it ostentatiously in both of his.

'Good-night, dear little cousin,' he said, in his most affected voice. .'If you have any need of us, command us.'

'Are you going?' said Tressady. His brow was curiously wrinkled.

Harding made him a bow, and walked with rather sidling steps to the door. Tressady followed him to the landing, called to the butler, who was still up, and ceremoniously told him to get Mrs. Watton a cab. Then he walked back to the drawing-room, and shut the door behind him.

'Letty!'

His tone startled her. She looked round hastily.

'Letty! you were defending me as I came in.'

He was extraordinarily pale—his blue eyes flashed. Every trace of the hauteur with which he had treated the Wattons had disappeared.

Letty recovered herself in an instant. The moment he showed softness she became the tyrant.

'Don't come!—don't touch me!' she said passionately, putting out her hand as he approached her. 'If I defended you, it was just for decency's sake. You *have* disgraced us both. It is perfectly true what Aunt Watton says. I don't suppose we shall ever get over it. Oh! don't try to bully me'—for Tressady had turned away with an impatient groan. 'It's no use. I know you think me a little fool! *I'm* not one of your great political ladies, who pretend to know everything that they may keep men dangling after them. I don't pose and play the hypocrite, as some—some people do. But, all the same, I know that you have done for yourself, and that people will say the most disgraceful things. Of course they will! And you can't deny them—you know you can't. Why did you never tell me a thing? *Who* made you change over? Ah! you can't answer—or you won't!'

Tressady was walking up and down with folded arms. He paused at her challenge.

'Why didn't I tell you? Do you remember that I wanted to talk to you yesterday morning—that I suggested you should come and hear my speech—and you wouldn't have it? You didn't care about politics, you said, and weren't going to pretend.—What made me go over? Well —I changed my mind—to some extent,' he said slowly.

'To some extent?' She laughed scornfully, mimicking his voice. '*To some extent!* Are you going to try and make me believe there was nothing else?'

'No. As I walked home to-night I determined not to conceal the truth from you. Opinions counted for something. I voted—yes, taking all things together, I think it may be said that I voted honestly. But I should never have taken the part I did but——' he hesitated, then went on deliberately—'but that I had come to have a strong—wish—to give Lady Maxwell her heart's desire. She has been my friend. I repaid her what I could.'

Letty, half beside herself, flung at him a shower of taunts hysterical and hardly intelligible. He showed no emotion. 'Of course,' he said disdainfully, 'if you choose to repeat this to others you will do us both great damage. I suppose I can't help it. For anybody else in the world —for Mrs. Watton and her son, for instance—I have a perfectly good political defence, and I shall defend myself stoutly. I have no intention whatever of playing the penitent in public.'

And what, she asked him, striving with all her might to regain the self-command which could alone enable her to wound him, to get the mastery—what was to be her part in this little comedy? Did he expect *her* to put up with this charming situation—to take what Marcella Maxwell left?

'No,' he said abruptly. 'You have no right to reproach

me or her in any vulgar way. But I recognise that the situation is impossible. I shall probably leave Parliament and London.'

She stared at him in speechless passion, then suddenly gathered up her fan and gloves and fled past him.

He caught at her, and stopped her, holding her satin skirt.

'My poor child!' he cried in remorse; 'bear with me, Letty—and forgive me!'

'I hate you!' she said fiercely, 'and I will never forgive you!'

She wrenched her dress away; he heard her quick steps across the floor and up the stairs.

Tressady fell into a chair, broken with exhaustion. His day in the House of Commons alone would have tried any man's nervous strength; this final scene had left him in a state to shrink from another word, another sound.

He must have dozed as he sat there from pure fatigue, for he found himself waking suddenly, with a sense of chill, as the August dawn was penetrating the closed windows and curtains.

He sprang up, and pulled the curtains back with a stealthy hand, so as to make no noise. Then he opened the window and stepped out upon the balcony, into a misty haze of sun.

The morning air blew upon him, and he drew it in with delight. How blessed was the sun, and the silence of the streets, and the dappled sky there to the east, beyond the Square!

After those long hours of mental tension in the crowd and heat of the House of Commons, what joy! what physical relief! He caught eagerly at the sensation of bodily pleasure, driving away his cares, letting the morning freshness recall to him a hundred memories—the memories of a traveller who has seen much, and loved Nature more than man. Blue surfaces of rippling sea, cool steeps among the mountains, streams brawling over their stones, a thousand combinations of grass and trees and sun—these things thronged through his brain, evoked by the wandering airs of this pale London sunrise and the few dusty planes which he could see to his right, behind the Park railings. And, like heralds before the presence, these various images flitted, passed, drew to one side, while memory in trembling revealed at last the best she had—an English river flowing through June meadows under a heaven of flame, a woman with a child, the scents of grass and hawthorn, the plashing of water.

He hung over the balcony, dreaming.

But before long he roused himself, and went back into the house. The gaudy drawing-room looked singularly comfortless and untidy in the delicate purity of the morning light. The flowers Letty had worn in her dress the night before were scattered on the floor, and the evening paper lay on the chair, where she had flung it down.

He stood in the centre of the room, his head raised, listening. No sound. Surely she was asleep. In spite of all the violence she had shown in their after talk, the memory of her speech to Mrs. Watton lingered in the young fellow's mind. It astonished him to realise, as he stood there, in this morning silence, straining to hear if his wife were moving overhead, how, *pari passu* with the headlong progress of his act of homage to the one woman, certain sharp perceptions with regard to the other had been rising in his mind.

His life had been singularly lacking till now in any conscious moral strain. That a man's desires should outrun his conscience had always seemed to him, on the whole, the normal human state. But all sorts of new standards and ideals had begun to torment him since

E E

the beginning of his friendship with Marcella Maxwell,
and a hundred questions that had never yet troubled
him were even now pressing through his mind as to his
relations to his wife, and the inexorableness of his debt
towards her.

Moreover, he had hardly left the House of Commons
and its uproar—his veins were still throbbing with the
excitement of the division—when a voice said to him, ' This
is the end! You have had your "moment"—now leave
the stage before any mean anti-climax comes to spoil it
all. Go. Break your life across. Don't wait to be dismissed and shaken off—take her gratitude with you, and
go!'.

Ah! but not yet—not yet! He sat down before his
wife's little writing-table, and buried his face in his hands,
while his heart burnt with longing. One day—then he
would accept his fate, and try and mend both his own life
and Letty's.

Would it be generous to drop out of her ken at once,
leave the gift in her lap, and say nothing? Ah! but he
was not capable of it. His act must have its price. Just
one half-hour with her—face to face. Then, shut the
door—and, good-bye! What was there to fear? He
could control himself. But after all these weeks, after
their conversation of the night before, to go away without
a word would be discourteous—unkind even—almost a
confession to her of the whys and wherefores of what he
had done.

He had a book of hers which he had promised to
return. It was a precious little manuscript book, contain-
ing records written out by herself of lives she had known
among the poor. She prized it much, and had begged
him to keep it safe and return it.

He took it out of his pocket, looked at it, and put it
carefully back. In a few hours the little book should

pass him into her presence. The impulse that possessed him barred for the moment all remorse, all regret.

Then he looked for paper and pen and began to write.

He sat for some time, absorbed in his task, doing his very best with it. It was a letter to his constituents, and it seemed to him he must have been thinking of it in his sleep, so easily did the sentences run.

No doubt, ill-natured gossip of the Watton type would be humming and hissing round her name for the next few days. Well, let him write his letter as well as he could, and publish it as soon as possible! It took him about an hour and a half, and when he read it over it appeared to him the best piece of political statement he had yet achieved. Very likely it would make Fontenoy more savage still. But Fontenoy's tone and attitude in the House of Commons had been already decisive. The breach between them was complete.

He put the sheets down at last, groaning within himself. Fustian and emptiness! What would ever give him back his old self-confidence, the gay whole-hearted-ness with which he had entered Parliament? But the thing had to be done, and he had done it efficiently. Moreover, the brain-exercise had acted as a tonic; his tension of nerve had returned. He stood beside the window once more, looking out into a fast-awakening London with an absent and frowning eye. He was thinking out the next few hours.

A little after eight Letty was roused from a restless sleep by the sound of a closing door. She rang hastily, and Grier appeared.

'Who was that went out?'

'Sir George, my lady. He's just dressed and left word that he had gone to take a packet to the "Pall Mall" office. He said it must be there early, and he would breakfast at his club.'

Letty sat up in bed, and bade Grier draw the curtains, and be quick in bringing her what she wanted. The maid glanced inquisitively, first at her mistress's haggard looks, then at the writing-table, as she passed it on her way to draw the blinds. The table was littered with writing-materials; some torn sheets had been transferred to the waste-paper basket, and a sealed letter was lying, address downwards, on the blotting-book. Letty, however, did not encourage her to talk. Indeed, she found herself sent away, and her mistress dressed without her.

Half an hour later Letty in her hat and cape slipped out of her room. She looked over the banisters into the hall. No one was to be seen, and she ran downstairs to the hall-door, which closed softly behind her. Five minutes later a latch-key turned quietly in the lock, and Letty reappeared. She went rapidly up to her room, a pale, angry ghost, glancing from side to side.

'Is Lady Maxwell at home?'

The butler glanced doubtfully at the inquirer.

'Sir George Tressady, I believe, sir? I will go and ask, if you will kindly wait a moment. Her ladyship does not generally see visitors in the morning.'

'Tell her, please, that I have brought a parcel to return to her.'

The butler retired, and shortly appeared at the corner of the stairs beckoning to the visitor. George mounted.

They passed through the outer drawing-room, and the servant drew aside the curtain of the inner room. Was it February again? The scent of hyacinth and narcissus seemed to be floating round him.

There was a hasty movement, and a tall figure came with a springing step to meet him.

'Sir George! How kind of you to come! I wish Maxwell were in. He would have enjoyed a chat with you so much. But Lord Ardagh sent him a note at breakfast-time, and he has just gone over to Downing Street. Hallin, move your puzzle a little, and make a way for Sir George to pass. Will you sit there?'

Hallin sprang up readily enough at the sight of his friend Sir George, put a fat hand into his, and then gave his puzzle-map of Europe a vigorous push to one side that drove Crete helplessly into the arms of the United Kingdom.

'Oh! what a muddle!' cried his mother, laughing, and standing to look at the disarray. 'You must try, Hallin, and see if you can straighten it out—as Sir George straightened out father's Bill for him last night.'

She turned to him; but the softness of her eyes was curiously veiled. It struck George at once that she was not at her ease—that there had been embarrassment in her very greeting of him.

They began to talk of the debate. She asked him minutely about the progress of the combination that had defeated Fontenoy. They discussed this or that man's attitude, or they compared the details of the division with those of the divisions which had gone before.

All through it seemed to Tressady that the person sitting in his chair and talking politics was a kind of automaton, with which the real George Tressady had very little to do. The automaton wore a grey summer suit, and seemed to be talking shrewdly enough, though with occasional lapses and languors. The real Tressady sat by, and noted what passed. '*How pale she is! She is not really happy—or triumphant. How she avoids all personal talk—nothing to be said, or hardly, of my part in it—my effort. Ah! she praises my speech, but with no warmth— I see! she would rather not owe such a debt to me. Her mind is troubled—perhaps Maxwell ?—or some vile talk ?'*

Meanwhile, all that Marcella perceived was that the man beside her became gradually more restless and more silent. She sat near him, with Hallin at her feet, her beautiful head held a little stiffly, her eyes at once kind and reserved. Nothing could have been simpler than her cool grey dress, her quiet attitude. Yet it seemed to him he had never felt her dignity so much—a moral dignity, infinitely subtle and exquisite, which breathed not only from her face and movements, but from the room about her—the room which held the pictures she loved, the books she read, the great pots of wild flowers or branching green it was her joy to set like jewels in its shady corners. He looked round it from time to time. It had for him the associations and the scents of a shrine, and he would never see it again! His heart swelled within him. The strange double sense died away.

Presently, Hallin, having put his puzzle safely into its box, ran off to his lessons. His mother looked after him wistfully. And he had no sooner shut the door than Tressady bent forward. 'You see—I thought it out!'

'Yes indeed!' she said, 'and to some purpose.'

But her voice was uncertain, and veiled like her eyes. Something in her reluctance to meet him, to talk it over, both alarmed and stung him. What was wrong? Had she any grievance against him? Had he so played his part as to offend her in any way? He searched his memory anxiously, his self-control, that he had been so sure of, failing him fast.

'It was a strange finish to the session—wasn't it?' he said, looking at her. 'We didn't think it would end so, when we first began to argue. What a queer game it all is! Well, my turn of it will have been exciting enough—though short. I can't say, however, that I shall much regret putting down the cards. I ought never to have taken a hand.'

She turned to him, in flushed dismay.

'You *are* thinking of leaving Parliament? But why —*why* should you?'

'Oh yes!—I am quite clear about that,' he said deliberately. 'It was not yesterday only. I am of no use in Parliament. And the only use it has been to me, is to show me—that—well!—that I have no party really, and no convictions. London has been a great mistake. I must get out of it—if only—lest my private life should drift on a rock and go to pieces. So far as I know it has brought me one joy only, one happiness only—to know you!'

He turned very pale. The hand that was lying on her lap suddenly shook. She raised it hastily, took some flowers out of a jar of poppies and grass that was standing near, and nervously put them back again. Then she said, gently, almost timidly—

'I owe a great deal to your friendship. My mind— please believe it—is full of thanks. I lay awake last night, thinking of all the thousands of people that speech of yours would save—all the lives that hang upon it.'

'I never thought of them at all,' he said abruptly. His heart seemed to be beating in his throat.

She shrank a little. Evidently her presence of mind failed her, and he took advantage.

'I never thought of them,' he repeated, 'or, at least, they weighed with me as nothing compared with another motive. As for the thing itself, by the time yesterday arrived I had given up my judgment to yours—I had simply come to think that what you wished was good. A force I no longer questioned drove me on to help you to your end. That was the whole secret of last night. The rest was only means to a goal.'

But he paused. He saw that she was trembling—that the tears were in her eyes.

'I have been afraid,' she said, trying hard for composure—'it has been weighing upon me all through these hours—that—I had been putting a claim—a claim of my own forward.' It seemed hardly possible for her to find the words. 'And I have been realising the issues for *you*, feeling bitterly that I had done a great wrong—if it were not a matter of conviction—in—in wringing so much from a friend. This morning everything—the victory, the joy of seeing hard work bear fruit—it has all been blurred to me.'

He gazed at her a moment—fixing every feature, every line upon his memory.

'Don't let it be,' he said quietly, at last. 'I have had my great moment. It does not fall to many to feel as I felt for about an hour last night. I had seen you in trouble and anxiety for many weeks. I was able to brush them away, to give you relief and joy—at least, I thought I was'—he drew himself up with a half-impatient smile. 'Sometimes I suspected that—that your kindness might be troubled about me; but I said to myself, "that will pass away, and the solid thing—the fact—will remain. She longed for this particular thing. She shall have it. And if the truth is as she supposes it —why not?—there are good men and keen brains with her—what has been done will go on gladdening and satisfying her year by year. As for me, I shall have acknowledged, shall have repaid——"'

He hesitated—paused—looked up.

A sudden terror seized her—her lips parted.

'Don't—don't say these things!' she said, imploring, lifting her hand. It was like a child flinching from a punishment.

He smiled unsteadily, trying to master himself, to find a way through the tumult of feeling.

'Won't you listen to me?' he said, at last; 'I sha'n't ever trouble you again.'

She could make no reply. Intolerable gratitude and pain held her, and he went on speaking, gazing straight into her shrinking face.

'It seems to me,' he said slowly, 'the people who grow up in the dry and mean habit of mind that I grew up in, break through in all sorts of different ways. Art and religion—I suppose they change and broaden a man. I don't know. I am not an artist—and religion talks to me of something I don't understand. To me, to know you has broken down the walls, opened the windows. It always used to come natural to me—well! to think little of people, to look for the mean, ugly things in them, especially in women. The only people I admired were men of action—soldiers, administrators; and it often seemed to me that women hampered and belittled them. I said to myself, one mustn't let women count for too much in one's life. And the idea of women troubling their heads with politics, or social difficulties, half amused, half disgusted me. At the same time I was all with Fontenoy in hating the usual philanthropic talk about the poor. It seemed to be leading us to mischief—I thought the greater part of it insincere. Then I came to know you.—And, after all, it seemed a woman could talk of public things, and still be real— the humanity didn't rub off, the colour stood! It was easy, of course, to say that you had a personal motive—other people said it, and I should have liked to echo it. But from the beginning I knew that didn't explain it. All the women '—he checked himself—'most of the women I had ever known judged everything by some petty personal standard. They talked magnificently, perhaps, but there was always something selfish and greedy at bottom. Well, I was always looking for it in you! Then instead—suddenly—I found myself anxious lest what I said should displease or hurt you—lest you should refuse to be my friend. I longed, desperately, to make you understand me—and then, after our talks, I hated myself for posing, and going further than was sincere. It was so strange to me not to be scoffing and despising.'

Marcella woke from her trance of pain—looked at him with amazement. But the sight of him—a man, with the perspiration on his brow, struggling now to tell the bare truth about himself and his plight—silenced her. She hung towards him again, as pale as he, bearing what fate had sent her.

'And ever since that day,' he went on, putting his hand over his eyes, 'when you walked home with me along the river, to be with you, to watch you, to puzzle over you, has built up a new self in me, that strains against and tears the old one. So these things— these heavenly, exquisite things that some men talk of— this sympathy, and purity, and sweetness—were true! They were true because you existed—because I had come to know something of your nature—had come to realise what it might be—for a man to have the right—— '

He broke off, and buried his face in his hands, murmuring incoherent things. Marcella rose hurriedly, then stood motionless, her head turned from him, that she might not hear. She felt herself stifled with rising tears. Once or twice she began to speak, and the words died away again. At last she said, bending towards him:

'I have done very ill—very, *very* ill. I have been

thinking all through of my personal want—of personal victory.'

He shook his head, protesting. And she hardly knew how to go on. But suddenly the word of nature, of truth, came ; though in the speaking it startled them both.

'Sir George!'—she put out her hand timidly and touched him—'may I tell you what I am thinking of? Not of you, nor of me—of another person altogether!'

He looked up.

'My wife?' he said, almost in his usual voice.

She said nothing; she was struggling with herself. He got up abruptly, walked to the open window, stood there a few seconds, and came back.

'It has to be all thought out again,' he said, looking at her appealingly. 'I must go away perhaps—and realise—what can be done. I took marriage as carelessly as I took everything else. I must try and do better with it.'

A sudden perception leapt in Marcella, revealing strange worlds. How she could have hated—with what fierceness, what flame!—the woman who taught ideal truths to Maxwell! She thought of the little self-complacent being in the white satin wedding-dress, that had sat beside her at Castle Luton—thought of her with overwhelming soreness and pain. Stepping quickly, her tears driven back, she went across the room to Tressady.

'I don't know what to say,' she began, stopping suddenly beside him, and leaning her hand for support on a table, while her head drooped. 'I have been very selfish—very blind. But—mayn't it be the beginning—of something quite—quite—different? I was thinking only of Maxwell—or myself. But I ought to have thought of you—of my friend. I ought to have seen—but oh! how *could* I!' She broke off, wrestling with this amazing difficulty of choosing, amid all the thoughts that thronged to her lips, something that might be said—and if said, might heal. But before he could interrupt her, she went on—'The harm was, in acting all through—by myself—as if only you and I, and Maxwell's work—were concerned. If I had made you known to *him*—if I had remembered—had thought——'

But she stopped again, in a kind of bewilderment. In truth she did not yet understand what had happened to her—how it could have happened to her—to *her*, whose life, soul, and body, to the red ripe of its inmost heart, was all Maxwell's, his possession, his chattel.

Tressady looked at her with a little sad smile.

'It was your unconsciousness,' he said, in a low trembling voice, 'of what you are—and have—that was so beautiful.'

Somehow the words recalled her natural dignity, her noble pride as Maxwell's wife. She stood erect, composure and self-command returning. She was not her own, to humble herself as she pleased.

'We must never talk to each other like this again,' she said gently, after a little pause. 'We must try and understand each other—the *real* things in each other's lives.—Don't lay a great remorse on me, Sir George!—don't spoil your future, and your wife's—don't give up Parliament! You have great, great gifts! All this will seem just a passing misunderstanding—both to you—and me—bye and bye. We shall learn to be—real friends—you and I—together?'

She looked at him appealing—her face one prayer.

But he, flushing, shook his head.

'I must not come into your world,' he said huskily. 'I must go.'

The wave of grief rolled upon her again. She turned away, looking across the room with wide, dim eyes, as though asking for some help that did not come.

Tressady walked quickly back to the chair where he had been sitting, and took up his hat and gloves. Suddenly, as he looked back to her, he struck one of the gloves across his hand.

'What a *coward*—what a mean, whining wretch I was to come to you this morning! I said to myself—like a hypocrite—that I could come—and go—without a word. My God—if I had!'—the low, hoarse voice became a cry of pain—'I might still have taken some joy——'

He wrestled with himself.

'It was mad selfishness,' he said at last, recovering himself by a fierce effort. 'Mad it must have been—or I could never have come here to give you pain. Some demon drove me. Oh, forgive me!—forgive me! Good-bye! I shall bless you while I live. But you—you must never think of me, never speak of me—again.'

She felt his grasp upon her fingers. He stooped, passionately kissed her hand and a fold of her dress. She rose hurriedly; but the door had closed upon him before she had found her voice or choked down the sob in her throat.

She could only drop back into her chair, weeping silently, her face hidden in her hands.

A few minutes passed. There was a step outside. She sprang up and listened, ready to fly to the window and hide herself among the curtains. Then the colour flooded into her cheek. She waited. Maxwell came in. He, too, looked disturbed, and as he entered the room he thrust a letter into his pocket, almost with violence. But when his eyes fell on his wife a pang seized him. He hurried to her, and she leant against him, saying in a sobbing voice:

'George Tressady has been here. I seem to have done him a wrong—and his wife. I am not fit to help you, Aldous. I do such rushing, blind, foolish things—and all that one hoped and worked for turns to mere selfishness and misery. Whom shall I hurt next? You, perhaps— *you !* '

And she clung to him in despair.

A few minutes later the husband and wife were in conference together, Marcella sitting, Maxwell standing beside her. Marcella's tears had ceased ; but never had Maxwell seen her so overwhelmed, so sad, and he felt half ashamed of his own burning irritation and annoyance with the whole matter.

Clearly, what he had dimly foreseen on the night of her return from the Mile End meeting had happened. This young man, ill-balanced, ill-mated, yet full of a sensitive ability and perception, had fallen in love with her; and Maxwell owed his political salvation to his wife's charm.

The more he loved her, the more odious the situation was to him. That any rational being should have even the shred of an excuse for regarding her as the political coquette, using her beauty for a personal end, affected him as a kind of sacrilege, and made him rage inwardly. Nevertheless, the idea struck him—struck and kindled him all at once—that the very perfectness of this tie that bound them together weakened her somewhat as a woman in her dealing with the outside world. It withdrew from her some of a woman's ordinary intuitions with regard to the men around her. The heart had no wants, and therefore no fears. To any man she liked she was always ready, as she came to know him, to show her true self with a freedom and loveliness that were like the freedom and loveliness of a noble child. To have supposed that such a man could have any feelings towards her other than those she gave to her friends would have seemed to her a piece of ill-bred vanity.

Such contingencies lay outside her ken ; she would have brushed them away with a laughing contempt had they been presented to her. Her life was at once too happy and too busy for such things. How could anyone fall in love with Aldous's wife ? Why should they ?—if one was to ask the simplest question of all.

Yet Maxwell, as he stood looking down upon her, conscious of a certain letter in his inner pocket, felt with growing yet most unwilling determination that he must somehow try and make her turn her eyes upon this dingy world and see it as it is.

For it was not the case merely of a spiritual drama in which a few souls, all equally sincere and void of offence, were concerned. That, in Maxwell's eyes, would have been already disagreeable and tragic enough. But here was this keen, spiteful crowd of London society watching for what it might devour—those hateful newspapers !—not to speak of the ordinary fool of everyday life.

There had not been wanting a number of small signs and warnings. The whole course of the previous day's debate, the hour of Tressady's speech, while Maxwell sat listening in the Speaker's Gallery overhead, had been for him—for her, too—poisoned by a growing uneasiness, a growing distaste for the triumph laid at their feet. She had come down to him from the Ladies' Gallery pale and nervous, shrinking almost from the grasp of his hand.

' What will happen ? Has he made his position in Parliament impossible ? ' she had said to him as they stood together for a moment in the Home Secretary's room ; and he understood, of course, that she was speaking of Tressady. In the throng that presently overwhelmed them he had no time to answer her ; but he believed that she, too, had been conscious of the peculiar note in some of the congratulations showered upon them on their way through the crowded corridors and lobbies. On the steps of St. Stephen's entrance an old white-haired gentleman, the friend and connection of Maxwell's father, had clapped the successful Minister on the back, with a laughing word in his ear : ' Upon my word, Aldous, your beautiful lady is a wife to conjure with ! I hear she has done the whole thing—educated the young man, brought him to his bearings, spoilt all Fontenoy's plans, broken up the group, in fact. Glorious ! ' and the old man looked with eyes half-sarcastic, half-admiring at the form of Lady Maxwell standing beside the carriage-door.

' I imagine the group has broken itself up,' said Maxwell, shortly, shaking off his tormentor. But as he glanced back from the carriage-window to the crowded doorway, and the faces looking after them, the thought of the talk that was probably passing amid the throng set every nerve on edge.

Meanwhile she sat beside him, unconsciously a little more stately than usual, but curiously silent—till at last, as they were nearing Trafalgar Square, she threw out her hand to him, almost timidly :

' You *do* rejoice ? '

' I do,' he said, with a long breath, pressing the hand. ' I suppose nothing ever happens as one has foreseen it. How strange, when one looks back to that Sunday ! '

She made no reply, and since then Tressady's name had been hardly mentioned between them. They had discussed every speech but his—even when the morning papers came, reflecting the astonishment and excitement of the public. The pang in Marcella's mind was—' Aldous thinks I asked a personal favour—*Did* I ? ' And memory would fall back into anxious recapitulation of the scene with Tressady. Had she indeed pressed her influence with him too much—taken advantage of his Parliamentary youth and inexperience. In the hours of the night that followed the division, merely to ask the question tormented a conscience as proud as it was delicate.

And now!—this visit—this incredible declaration—this eagerness for his reward! Maxwell's contempt and indignation were rising fast. Mere chivalry, mere decent manners even, he thought, might have deterred a man from such an act. Meanwhile, in rapid flashes of thought he began to debate with himself how he should use this letter in his pocket—this besmirching, degrading letter.

But Marcella had much more to say. Presently she roused herself from her trance and looked at her husband.

'Aldous!'—She touched him on the arm, and he turned to her gravely—'There was one moment at Mile End, when—when I did play upon his pity—his friendship. He came down to Mile End on Thursday night. I told you. I saw he was unhappy—unhappy at home. He wanted sympathy desperately. I gave it him. Then I urged him to throw himself into his public work—to think out this vote he was to give. Oh! I don't know! —I don't know—' she broke off, in a depressed voice, shaking her head slowly—'I believe I threw myself upon his feelings—I felt that he was very sympathetic, that I had a power over him—it was a kind of bribery.'

Her brow drooped under his eye.

'I believe you are quite unjust to yourself,' he said unwillingly. 'Of course, if any man chooses to misinterpret a confidence——'

'No,' she said steadily. 'I knew. It was quite different from any other time. I remember how uncomfortable I felt afterwards. I did try to influence him—just through being a woman. There!—it is quite true.'

He could not withdraw his eyes from hers—from the mingling of pride, humility, passion, under the dark lashes.

F F

'And if you did, do you suppose that *I* can blame you?' he said slowly.

He saw that she was holding an inquisition in her own heart, and looking to him as judge. How could he judge?—whatever there might be to judge. He adored her.

For the moment she did not answer him. She clasped her hands round her knees, thinking aloud.

'From the beginning, I remember I thought of him as somebody quite new and fresh to what he was doing— somebody who would certainly be influenced—who ought to be influenced. And then '—she raised her eyes again, half shrinking—'there was the feeling, I suppose, of personal antagonism to Lord Fontenoy! One could not be sorry to detach one of his chief men. Besides, after Castle Luton, George Tressady was so attractive! You did not know him, Aldous; but to talk to him stirred all one's energies; it was a perpetual battle,—one took it up again and again, enjoying it always. As we got deeper in the fight I tried never to think of him as a member of Parliament—often I stopped myself from saying things that might have persuaded him, as far as the House was concerned. And yet, of course '—her face, in its nobility, took a curious look of hardness— 'I *did* know all the time that he was coming to think more and more of me—to depend on me. He disliked me at first—afterwards he seemed to avoid me— then I felt a change. Now I see I thought of him all along just in one capacity—in relation to what I wanted —whether I tried to persuade him or no. And all the time——'

A cloud of pain effaced the frown. She leant her head against her husband's arm.

'Aldous!'—her voice was low and miserable—'what can his wife have felt towards me? I never thought of her after Castle Luton—she seemed to me such a

vulgar, common little being.   Surely, surely!—if they
are so unhappy, it can't be—*my* doing ; there was cause
enough——'

Nothing could have been more piteous than the tone.
It was laden with the remorse that only such a nature
could feel for such a cause.   Maxwell's hand touched
her head tenderly.   A variety of expressions crossed his
face, then a sharp flash of decision.

'Dear ! I think you ought to know—she has written
to me.'

Marcella sprang up.   Face and neck flushed crimson.
She threw him an uncertain look, the nostrils quivering.

'Will you show me the letter ?'

He hesitated.   On his first reading of it he had
vowed to himself that she should never see it.   But since
her confessions had begun to make the matter clearer to
him a moral weight had pressed upon him.   She must
realise her power, her responsibility !   Moreover, they
two, with conscience and good sense to guide them, had
got to find a way out of this matter.   He did not feel that
he could hide the letter from her if there was to be common action and common understanding.

So he gave it to her.

She read it pacing up and down, unconscious sounds
of pain and protest forcing themselves to her lips from
time to time, which made it very difficult for him to
stand quietly where he was.   On that effusion of gall
and bitterness poor Letty had spent her sleepless night.
Every charge that malice could bring, every distortion
that jealousy could apply to the simplest incident, every
insinuation that, judged by her own standard, had
seemed to her most likely to work upon a husband—Letty
had crowded them all into the mean, ill-written letter—
the letter of a shopgirl trying to rescue her young man
from the clutches of a rival.

But every sentence in it was a stab to Marcella. When she had finished it she stood with it in her hand beside her writing-table, looking absently through the window, pale, and deep in thought. Maxwell watched her.

When her moment of consideration broke, her look swept round to him.

' I shall go to her,' she said simply. ' I must see her ! '

Maxwell pondered.

' I think,' he said reluctantly, ' she would only repulse and insult you.'

' Then it must be borne. It cannot end so.'

She walked up to him and let him draw his arm about her. They stood in silence for a minute or two. When she raised her head again, her eyes sought his beseechingly.

' Aldous, help me ! If we cannot repair this mischief— you and I—what are we worth ? I will tell you my plan—'

There was a sound at the door. Husband and wife moved away from each other as the butler entered.

' My Lord, Mrs. Allison and Lord Fontenoy are in the library. They asked me to say that they wish to consult your Lordship on something very urgent. I told them I thought your Lordship was engaged, but I would come and see.'

Marcella and Maxwell looked at each other. Ancoats ! No doubt the catastrophe so long staved off had at last arrived. Maxwell's stifled exclamation was the groan of the overworked man who hardly knows how to find mind enough for another anxiety. But a new and sudden light shone in his wife's face. She turned to the servant almost with eagerness :

' Please tell Mrs. Allison and Lord Fontenoy to come up.'

CHAPTER XIX

THE door opened silently, and there came in a figure that for a moment was hardly recognised by either Maxwell or his wife. Shrunken, pale, and grief-stricken, Ancoats' poor mother entered, her eye seeking eagerly for Maxwell, perceiving nothing else. She was in black, her veil hurriedly thrown back, and the features beneath it were all blurred by distress and fatigue.

Marcella hurried to her. Mrs. Allison took her hand in both her own with the soft, appealing motion habitual to her, then said hastily, still looking at Maxwell:

'Maxwell, the boy has gone. He left me two days ago. This morning, in my trouble, I sent for Lord Fontenoy, my kind, kind friend. And he persuaded me to come to you at once. I begged him to come too——'

She glanced timidly from one to the other, implying many things.

But even with this preface, Maxwell's greeting of his defeated antagonist was ceremony itself. The natural instinct of such a man is to mask victory in courtesy. But a paragraph that morning in Fontenoy's paper—a paragraph that he happened to have seen in Lord Ardagh's room—had appealed to another natural instinct, stronger and more primitive. It amazed him that even this emergency and Mrs. Allison's persuasions could have brought the owner of the paper within his doors on this particular morning.

Fontenoy, immersed in the correspondence of the morning, had not yet chanced to see the paragraph, which was Harding Watton's. Yet, if he had, he could not have shown a more haughty and embarrassed bearing. He was there under a compulsion he did not know how to resist, a compulsion of tears and grief; but the instinct for manners, which so often upon occasion serves the man of illustrious family, as well, almost, as good feeling or education may serve another, had been for the time weakened in him by the violences and exhaustion of the political struggle, and he did not feel certain that he could trust himself. He was smarting still through every nerve, and the greeting especially that Maxwell's tall wife extended to him was gall and bitterness. She meanwhile, as she advanced towards him, was mostly struck with the perfection of his morning dress. The ultra-correctness and strict fashion that he affected in these matters, were generally a surprise to those who knew him only by reputation.

After five minutes' question and answer the Maxwells understood something of the situation. A servant of Ancoats's had been induced to disclose what he knew. There could be no question that the young fellow had gone off to Normandy, where he possessed a chalet close to Trouville, in the expectation that his fair lady would immediately join him there. She had not yet started. So much Fontenoy had already ascertained. But she had thrown up a recent engagement within the last few days, and before Ancoats's flight all Fontenoy's information had pointed to the likelihood of a *coup* of some sort. As for the boy himself, he had left his mother at Castle Luton, three days before, on the pretext of a Scotch visit, and had instead taken the evening train to Paris, leaving a letter for his mother in which the influence of certain modern French novels of the psychological kind could perhaps be detected. ' The call of the heart that drives me from you,' wrote this incredible young man, 'is something independent of myself. I wring my hands, but I follow where it leads. Love has its crimes—that I admit —but they are the only road to experience. And experience is all I care to live for! At any rate, I cannot accept the limits that you, mother, would impose upon me. Each of us must be content to recognise the other's personality. I have tried to reconcile you to an affection that must be content to be irregular. You repel it and me, under the influence of a bigotry in which I have ceased to believe. Suffer me, then, to act for myself in this respect. At any time that you like to call upon me I will be your dutiful son, so long as this matter is not mentioned between us. And let me implore you not to bring in third persons. They have already done mischief enough. Against them I should know how to protect myself.'

Maxwell returned the letter with a disgust he could hardly repress. Everything in it seemed to him as pinchbeck as the passion itself. Mrs. Allison took it with the same miserable look, which had in it, Marcella noticed, a certain strange sternness, as of some frail creature nerving itself to desperate things.

'Now what shall we do?' said Maxwell, abruptly.

Fontenoy moved forward. 'I presume you still command the same persons you set in motion before? Can you get at them to-day?'

Maxwell pondered. 'Yes, the clergyman. The solicitor-brother is too far away. Your idea is to stop the girl from crossing?'

'If it were still possible.' Fontenoy dropped his voice, and his gesture induced Maxwell to follow him to the recess of a distant window.

'The chief difficulty, perhaps,' said Fontenoy, resuming, 'concerns the lad himself. His mother, you will understand, cannot run any risk of being brought in contact with that woman. Nor is she physically fit

for the voyage; but some one must go, if only to content
her. There has been some wild talk of suicide,
apparently—mere bombast, of course, like so much of it,
but she has been alarmed.'

'Do you propose, then, to go yourself?'

'I am of no use,' said Fontenoy, decisively.

Maxwell had cause to know that the statement was
true, and did not press him. They fell into a rapid
consultation.

Meanwhile, Marcella had drawn Mrs. Allison to the
sofa beside her, and was attempting a futile task of
comfort. Mrs. Allison answered in monosyllables,
glancing hither and thither. At last she said in a low,
swift voice, as though addressing herself, rather than her
companion, 'If all fails, I have made up my mind. I
shall leave his house. I can take nothing more from him.'

Marcella started. 'But that would deprive you of all
chance, all hope of influencing him,' she said, her eager,
tender look searching the other woman's face.

'No; it would be my duty,' said Mrs. Allison, simply,
crossing her hands upon her lap. Her delicate blue
eyes, swollen with weeping, the white hair, of which a
lock had escaped from its usual quiet braids and hung
over her blanched cheeks, her look at once saintly and
indomitable—every detail of her changed aspect made a
chill and penetrating impression. Marcella began to
understand what the Christian might do, though the
mother should die of it.

Meanwhile she watched the two men at the other side
of the room, with a manifest eagerness for their return.
Presently, indeed, she half rose and called—

'Aldous!'

Lord Maxwell turned.

'Are you thinking of some one who might go to
Trouville?' she asked him.

'Yes, but we can hit on no one,' he replied in perplexity.

She moved towards him, bearing herself with a peculiar erectness and dignity.

'Would it be possible to ask Sir George Tressady to go?' she said quietly.

Maxwell looked at her open-mouthed for an instant. Fontenoy, behind him, threw a sudden, searching glance at the beautiful figure in grey.

'We all know,' she said, turning back to the mother, 'that Ancoats likes Sir George?'

Mrs. Allison shrank a little from the clear look. Fontenoy's rage of defeat, however modified in her presence, had nevertheless expressed itself to her in phrases and allusions that had both perplexed and troubled her. *Had* Marcella indeed made use of her beauty to decoy a weak youth from his allegiance? And now she spoke his name so simply.

But the momentary wonder died from the poor mother's mind.

'I remember,' she said sadly—'I remember he once spoke to me very kindly about my son.'

'And he thought kindly,' said Marcella, rapidly; 'he is kind at heart. Aldous! if Cousin Charlotte consents, why not at least put the case to him? He knows everything. He might undertake what we want, for her sake—for all our sakes—and it might succeed.'

The swift yet calm decision of her manner completed Maxwell's bewilderment.

His eyes sought hers, while the others waited, conscious, somehow, of a dramatic moment. Fontenoy's flash of malicious curiosity made him even forget, while it lasted, the little tragic figure on the sofa.

'What do you say, Cousin Charlotte?' said Maxwell at last.

His voice was dry and business-like. Only the wife
who watched him perceived the silent dignity with which
he had accepted her appeal.

He went to sit beside Mrs. Allison, stooping over her,
while they talked in a low key. Very soon she had caught
at Marcella's suggestion, with an energy of despair.

'But how can we find him?' she said at last, looking
helplessly round the room, at the very chair, among others,
where Tressady had just been sitting.

Maxwell felt the humour of the situation without
relishing it.

'Either at his own house,' he said shortly, 'or the
House of Commons.'

'He may have left town this morning. Lord Fontenoy
thought'—she looked timidly at her companion—'that he
would be sure to go and explain himself to his constituents at once.'

'Well, we can find out. If you give me instructions
—if you are sure this is what you want—we will find out
at once. Are you sure?'

'I can think of nothing better,' she said, with a piteous
gesture. 'And if he goes, I have only one message to
give him. Ancoats knows that I have exhausted every
argument, every entreaty. Now let him tell my son'—her
voice grew firm, in spite of her look of anguish—'that if he
insists on surrendering himself to a life of sin I can bear
him company no more. I shall leave his house, and go
somewhere by myself, to pray for him.'

Maxwell tried to soothe her, and there was some half-
whispered talk between them, she quietly wiping away
her tears from time to time.

Meanwhile, Marcella and Fontenoy sat together a
little way off, he at first watching Mrs. Allison, she
silent, and making no attempt to play the hostess.
Gradually, however, the sense of her presence beside

him, the memory of Tressady's speech, of the scene in
the House of the night before, began to work in his veins
with a pricking, exciting power. His family was famous
for a certain drastic way with women; his father, the
now old and half-insane Marquis, had parted from his
mother while Fontenoy was still a child, after scenes
that would have disgraced an inn parlour. Fontenoy
himself, in his reckless youth, had simply avoided the
whole sex, so far as its reputable members were concerned; till one woman by sympathy, by flattery perhaps,
by the strange mingling in herself of iron and gentleness,
had tamed him. But there were brutal instincts in his
blood, and he became conscious of them as he sat beside
Marcella Maxwell.

Suddenly he broke out, bending forward, one hand on
his knee, the other nervously adjusting the eyeglass
without which he was practically blind.

'I imagine your side had foreseen last night better
than we had?'

She drew herself together instantly.

'One can hardly say. It was evident, wasn't it, that
the House as a whole was surprised? Certainly no one
could have foreseen the numbers.'

She met his look straight, her white hand playing with
Mrs. Allison's card.

'Oh! a slide of that kind once begun goes like the
wind,' said Fontenoy. 'Well, and are you pleased with
your Bill—not afraid of your promises—of all the Edens
you have held out?'

The smile that he attempted roused such ogreish
associations in Marcella, she must needs say something
to give colour to the half-desperate laugh that caught
her.

'Did you suppose we should be already *en pénitence?*'
she asked him.

The man's wrath overcame him. So England—all
the serious forces of the country—were to be more and
more henceforward at the mercy of this kind of thing!
He had begun the struggle with a scornful disbelief in
current gossip. He—politically and morally the creation
of a woman—had yet not been able to bring himself to fear
a woman. And now he sat there, fiercely saying to himself
that this woman, playing the old game under new names,
had undone him.

'Ah! I see,' he said. 'You are of the mind of the
Oxford don—never regret, never retract, never apologise?'

The small, reddish eyes, like needle-points, fixed the
face before him. She looked up, her beautiful lips parting. She felt the insult—marvelled at it! On such an
errand, in her own house! Scorn was almost lost in
astonishment.

'A quotation which nobody gets right—isn't it so?'
she said calmly. 'If a wise man said it, I suppose he
meant, "Don't explain yourself to the wrong people,"
which is good advice, don't you think?'

She rose as she spoke, and moved away from him, that
she might listen to what her husband was saying.
Fontenoy was left to reflect on the folly of a man who,
being driven to ask a kindness of his enemy, cannot keep
his temper in the enemy's house. Yet his temper had
been freshly tried since he entered it. The whole suggestion of Tressady's embassy was to himself galling in
the extreme. 'There is a meaning in it,' he thought;
'of course she thinks it will save appearances!' There
was no extravagance, no calumny, that this cold critic of
other men's fervours was not for the moment ready to
believe.

Nevertheless, as he threw himself back in his chair,
and his eye caught Mrs. Allison's bent figure on the other
side of the room, he knew that he must needs submit—he

did submit—to anything that could give that torn heart ease. Of his two passions, one, the passion for politics, seemed for the moment to have lost itself in disgust and disappointment; to the other he clung but the more strongly. Once or twice in her talk with Maxwell, Mrs. Allison raised her gentle eyes and looked across to Fontenoy. 'Are you there, my friend?' the glance seemed to say, and a thrill spread itself through the man's rugged being. Ah, well! the follies of this young scapegrace must wear themselves out in time, and either he would marry and so free his mother, or he would so outrage her conscience that she would separate herself from him. Then would come other people's rewards.

Presently, indeed, Mrs. Allison rose from her seat and advanced to him with hurried steps.

'We have settled it, I think; Maxwell will do all he can. It seems hard to trust so much to a stranger like Sir George Tressady, but if he will go—if Ancoats likes him? We must do the best, mustn't we?'

She raised to him her delicate, small face, in a most winning dependence. Fontenoy did not even attempt resistance.

'Certainly—it is not a chance to lose. May I suggest also'—he looked at Maxwell—'that there is no time to lose?'

'Give me ten minutes, and I am off,' said Maxwell, hurriedly carrying a bundle of unopened letters to a distance. He looked through them, to see if anything especially urgent required him to give instructions to his secretary before leaving the house.

'Shall I take you home?' said Fontenoy to Mrs. Allison.

She drew her thick veil round her head and face, and said some tremulous words, which unconsciously deepened the gloom on Fontenoy's face. Apparently they were to the effect that before going home she

wished to see the Anglican priest in whom she especially
confided, a certain Father White, who was to all intents
and purposes her director.   For in his courtship of this
woman of fifty, with her curious distinction and her
ethereal charm, which years seemed only to increase,
Fontenoy had not one rival, but two—her son and her
religion.

Fontenoy's fingers barely touched those of Maxwell
and his wife.   As he closed the door behind Mrs.
Allison, leaving the two together, he said to himself
contemptuously that he pitied the husband.

When the latch had settled, Maxwell threw down his
letters and crossed the room to his wife.

'I only half understood you,' he said, a flush rising
in his face.   'You really mean that we, on this day of all
days—that I—am to personally ask this kindness of
George Tressady?'

'I do!' she cried, but without attempting any caress.
'If I could only go and ask it myself!'

'That would be impossible!' he said quickly.

'Then you, dear husband—dear love!—go and ask
it for me!   Must we not—oh! do see it as I do!—must
we not somehow make it possible to be friends again, to
wipe out that—that half-hour once for all?'—she threw
out her hand in an impetuous gesture.   'If you go, he
will feel that is what we mean—he will understand us at
once—there is nothing vile in him—nothing!   Dear, he
never said a word to me I could resent till this morning.
And, alack, alack! was it somehow my fault?'   She
dropped her face a moment on the back of the chair
she held.   'How I am to play my own part—well! I
must think.   But I cannot have such a thing on my
heart, Aldous—I cannot!'

He was silent a moment; then he said:

'Let me understand, at least, what it is precisely that

we are doing. Is the idea that it should be made possible for us all to meet again as though nothing had happened ? '

She shrank a moment from the man's common sense; then replied, controlling herself :

' Only not to leave the open sore—to help him to forget ! He must know—he does know '—she held herself proudly—'that I have no secrets from you. So that when the time comes for remembering, for thinking it over, he will shrink from you, or hate you. Whereas, what I want '—her eyes filled with tears—' is that he should *know* you—only that ! I ought to have brought it about long ago.'

' Are you forgetting that I owe him this morning my political existence ? '

The voice betrayed the inner passion.

' He would be the last person to remember it ! ' she cried. ' Why not take it quite, quite simply ?—behave so as to say to him, without words, " Be our friend—join with us in putting out of sight what hurts us no less than you to think of. Shut the door upon the old room—pass with us into a new ! "—oh ! if I could explain ! '

She hid her face in her hands again.

' I understand,' he said, after a long pause. ' It is very like you. I am not quite sure it is very wise. These things, to my mind, are best left to end themselves. But I promised Mrs. Allison ; and what you ask, dear, you shall have. So be it.'

She lifted her head hastily, and was dismayed by the signs of agitation in him as he turned away. She pursued him timidly, laying her hand on his arm.

' And then——'

Her voice sank to its most pleading note. He caught her hand ; but she withdrew herself in haste.

' And then,' she went on, struggling for a smile—' then

you and I have things to settle. Do you think I don't know that I have made all your work, and all your triumph, gall and bitterness to you—do you think I don't know?'

She gazed at him with a passionate intensity through her tears, yet by her gesture forbidding him to come near her. What man would not have endured such discomforts a thousand times for such a look?

He stooped to her.

' We are to talk that out, then, when I come back?— Please give these letters to Saunders—there is nothing of importance. I will go first to Tressady's house.'

Maxwell drove away through the sultry streets, his mind running on his task. It seemed to him that politics had never put him to anything so hard. But he began to plan it with his usual care and precision. The butler who opened the door of the Upper Brook Street house could only say that his master was not at home.

' Shall I find him, do you imagine, at the House of Commons ? '

The butler could not say. But Lady Tressady was in, though just on the point of going out. Should he inquire?

But the visitor made it plain that he had no intention of disturbing Lady Tressady, and would find out for himself. He left his card in the butler's hands.

' Who was that, Kenrick ? ' said a sharp voice behind the man as the hansom drove away. Letty Tressady, elaborately dressed, with a huge white hat and lace parasol, was standing on the stairs, her pale face peering out of the shadows. The butler handed her the card, and, telling him to get her a cab at once, she ran up again to the drawing-room.

Meanwhile Maxwell sped on towards Westminster,

frowning over his problem. As he drove down White-hall the sun brightened to a naked midday heat, throwing its cloak of mists behind it. The gilding on the Clock Tower sparkled in the light; even the dusty, airless street, with its withered planes, was on a sudden flooded with gaiety. Two or three official or Parliamentary acquaint-ances saluted the successful Minister as he passed; and each was conscious of a certain impatience with the gravity of the well-known face. That a great man should not be content to look victory, as well as win it, seemed a kind of hypocrisy.

In the House of Commons, a few last votes and other oddments of the now dying session were being pushed through to an accompaniment of empty benches. Tressady was not there, nor in the Library. Maxwell made his way to the upper Lobby, where writing-tables and materials are provided in the window-recesses for the use of members.

He had hardly entered the Lobby before he caught sight at its farther end of the long straight chin and fair head of the man he was in quest of. And almost at the same moment, Tressady, who was sitting writing amid a pile of letters and papers, lifted his eyes and saw Lord Maxwell approaching.

He started, then half rose, scattering his papers. Maxwell bowed as he neared the table, then stopped beside it, without offering his hand.

' I fear I may be disturbing you,' he said, with simple but cold courtesy. ' The fact is I have come down here on an urgent matter, which may perhaps be my excuse. Could you give me twenty minutes, in my room ? '

' By all means,' said Tressady. He tried to put his papers together, but to his own infinite annoyance his hand shook. He seemed hardly to know what to do with them.

' Do not let me hurry you,' said Maxwell, in the same manner. ' Will you follow me at your leisure ? '

G G

'I will follow you immediately,' said Tressady; 'as soon as I have put these under lock and key.'

His visitor departed. Tressady remained standing a moment by the table, his blue eyes, unusually wide open, fixed absently on the river, a dark red flush overspreading the face. Then he rapidly threw his papers together into a black bag that stood near, and walked with them to his locker in the wall.

For an hour after he left Marcella Maxwell he had wandered blindly up and down the Green Park; at the end of it a sudden impulse had driven him to the House, as his best refuge both from Letty and himself. There he found waiting for him a number of letters, and a sheaf of telegrams besides from his constituency, with which he had just begun to grapple when Maxwell interrupted him. Some hours of hard writing and thinking might, he thought, bring him by reaction to some notion of what to do with the next days and nights—how to take up the business of his private life again.

Now, as he withdrew his key from the lock, in a corridor almost empty of inhabitants, abstraction seized him once more. He leant against the wall a moment, with his hands in his pockets, seeing her face—the tears on her cheek—feeling the texture of her dress against his lips. Barely two hours ago! No doubt she had confided all to Maxwell in the interval. The young fellow burnt with mingled rage and shame. This interview with the husband seemed to transform it all to vaudeville, if not to farce. How was he to get through it with any dignity and self-command? Moreover, a passionate resentment towards Maxwell developed itself. His telling of his secret had been no matter for a common scandal, a vulgar jealousy. *She* knew that—she could not have so misrepresented him. A sense of the situation to which he had brought himself on all sides made his pride feel itself in the grip of something that asked his submission. Yet why, and to whom?

He walked along through the interminable corridors towards Maxwell's room in the House of Lords, a prey to what afterwards seemed to him the meanest moment of his life. Little knowing the pledges that a woman had given for him, he did say to himself that Maxwell owed him much—that he was not called upon to bear everything from a man he had given back to power. And all the time his thoughts built a thorn-hedge about her face, her pity. Let him see them no more, not even in the mirror of the mind. Great Heaven! what harm could such as he do to her?

By the time he reached Maxwell's door he seemed to himself as hard and cool as usual. As he entered, the Minister was standing by an oriel window, overlooking the river, turning over the contents of a despatch-box that had just been brought him. He advanced at once; and Tressady noticed that he had already dismissed his secretary.

'Will you sit by the window?' said Maxwell. 'The day promises to be extraordinarily hot.'

Tressady took the seat assigned him. Maxwell's grey eye ran over the young man's figure and bearing. Then he bent forward from a chair on the other side of a small writing-table.

'You will probably have guessed the reason of my intrusion upon you—you and I have already discussed this troublesome affair—and the kind manner in which you treated our anxieties then——'

'Ancoats!' exclaimed Tressady, with a start he could not control. 'You wish to consult me about Ancoats?'

A flash of wonder crossed the other's mind. 'He imagined——' Instinctively Maxwell's opening mildness stiffened into a colder dignity.

'I fear we may be making an altogether improper claim upon you,' he said quietly; 'but this morning, about an hour ago, Ancoats's mother came to us with the news that he had left her two days ago, and was now discovered to be at Trouville, where he has a chalet, waiting for this girl, of whom we all know, to join him. You will imagine Mrs. Allison's despair. The entanglement is in itself bad enough. But she—I think you know it—is no ordinary woman, nor can she bring any of the common philosophy of life to bear upon this matter. It seems to be sapping her very springs of existence, and the impression she left upon myself—and upon Lady Maxwell'—he said the words slowly—'was one of the deepest pity and sorrow. As you also know, I believe, I have till now been able to bring some restraining influence to bear upon the girl, who is of course not a girl, but a very much married woman, with a husband always threatening to turn up and avenge himself upon her. There is a good man, one of those High Church clergymen who interest themselves specially in the stage, who has helped us many times already. I have telegraphed to him, and expect him here before long. We know that she has not yet left London, and it may be possible again, at the eleventh hour, to stop her. But that——'

'Is not enough,' said Tressady, quickly, raising his head. 'You want some one to grapple with Ancoats?'

Face and voice were those of another man—attentive, normal, sympathetic. Maxwell observed him keenly.

'We want some one to go to Ancoats; to represent to him his mother's determination to leave him for good if this disgraceful affair goes on; to break the shock of the girl's non-arrival to him, if, indeed, we succeed in stopping her; and to watch him for a day or two, in case there should be anything in the miserable talk of suicide with which he seems to have been threatening his mother.'

'Oh! Suicide! Ancoats!' said Tressady, throwing back his head.

'We rate him, apparently, much the same,' said Maxwell, drily. 'But it is not to be wondered at that the mother should be differently affected. She sent you '— the speaker paused a moment—'what seemed to me a touching message.'

Tressady bent forward.

' " Tell him that I have no claim upon him—that I am ashamed to ask this of him. But he once said some kind words to me about my son, and I know that Ancoats desired his friendship. His help *might* save us. I can say no more." '

Tressady looked up quickly, reddening involuntarily.

' Was Fontenoy there ?—did he agree ? '

' Fontenoy agreed,' said Maxwell, in the same measured voice. ' In fact, you grasp our petition. To speak frankly, my wife suggested it, and I was deputed to bear it to you. But I need not say that we are quite prepared to find that you are not able to do what we have ventured to ask of you, or that your engagements will not permit it.'

A strange gulp rose in Tressady's throat. He understood—oh! he understood her—perfectly.

He leant back in his chair, looking through the open window to the Thames. A breeze had risen and was breaking up the thunderous sky into gay spaces of white and blue. The river was surging and boiling under the tide, and strings of barges were mounting with the mounting water, slipping fast along the Terrace wall. The fronts of the various buildings opposite rose in shadow against the dazzling blue and silver of the water. Here over the river, even for this jaded London, summer was still fresh ; every mast and spar, every track of boat or steamer in the burst of light, struck the eye with sharpness and delight.

Each line and hue printed itself on Tressady's brain. Then he turned slowly to his companion. Maxwell sat patiently waiting for his reply; and for the first time Tressady received, as it were, a full impression of a personality he had till now either ignored or disliked. In youth Maxwell had never passed for a handsome man. But middle life and noble habit were every year giving increased accent and spiritual energy to the youth's pleasant features; and Nature as she silvered the brown hair, and drove deep the lines of thought and experience, was bringing more than she took away. A quiet, modest fellow Maxwell would be to the end; not witty; not brilliant; more and more content to bear the yoke of the great commonplaces of life as subtlety and knowledge grew; saying nothing of spiritual things, only living them —yet a man, it seemed, on whom England would more and more lay the burden of her fortunes.

Tressady gazed at him, shaken with new reverences, new compunctions. Maxwell's eyes were drawn to his— mild, penetrating eyes, in which for an instant Tressady seemed to read what no words would ever say to him. Then he sprang up.

'There is an afternoon train put on this month. I can catch it. Tell me, if you can, a few more details.'

Maxwell took out a half-sheet of notes from his pocket, and the two men, standing together beside the table, went with care into a few matters it was well for Tressady to know. Tressady threw a quick intelligence into his questions that inevitably recalled to Maxwell the cut-and-thrust of his speech on the preceding evening; nor behind his rapid discussion of a vulgar business did the constrained emotion of his manner escape his companion.

At last all was settled. At the last moment an uneasy question rose in Maxwell's mind. 'Ought *we*, at such a crisis, to be sending him away from his wife?' But he could not bring himself to put it, even lightly, into words, and as it happened Tressady did not leave him in doubt.

'I am glad you caught me,' he said nervously, in what seemed an awkward pause, while he looked for his hat, forgetting where he had put it. 'I was intending to leave London to-night. But my business can very well wait till next week. Now I think I have every- thing.'

He gathered up a new Guide-Chaix that Maxwell had put into his hand, saw that the half-sheet of notes was safely stowed into his pocket-book, and took up his hat and stick. As he spoke, Maxwell had remembered the situation and Mrs. Allison's remark. No doubt Tressady had proposed to go north that night on a mission of explana- tion to his Market Malford constituents, and it struck one of the most scrupulous of men with an additional pang, that he should be thus helping to put private motives in the way of public duty. But what was done was done. And it seemed impossible that either should speak a word of politics.

'I ought to say,' said Tressady, pausing once more as they moved together towards the door, 'that I have not ultimately much hope for Mrs. Allison. If this entanglement is put aside, there will be something else. Trouville itself, in August, I should imagine, is a place of *bonnes fortunes* for the man who wants them, and Ancoats's mind runs to such things.'

He spoke with a curious eagerness, like one who pleads that his good will shall not be judged by mere failure or success.

Maxwell raised his shoulders.

'Nothing that can happen will in the least affect our gratitude to *you*,' he said gravely.

'Gratitude!' muttered the young man under his breath. His lip trembled. He looked uncertainly at his companion. Maxwell did not offer his hand, yet as he opened the door for his visitor there was a quiet cordiality and kindness in his manner that made his renewed words of thanks sound like a strange music in Tressady's ears.

When the Minister was once more alone he walked back to the window, and stood looking down thoughtfully on the gay pageant of the river. She was right—she was always right. There was nothing vile in that young fellow, and his face had a look of suffering it pained Maxwell to remember. Why had he personally not come to know him better? 'I think too little of men, too much of machinery,' he said to himself, despondently; 'unconsciously I leave the dealing with human beings far too often to her, and then I wonder that a man sees and feels her as she is!'

Yet as he stood there in the sunshine a feeling of moral relief stole upon him, the feeling that rewards a man who has tried to deal greatly with some common and personal strait. Some day, not yet, he would make Tressady his friend. He calmly felt it to be within his power.

Unless the wife!—He threw up his hand, and turned back to his writing-table. What was to be done with that letter? Had Tressady any knowledge of it? Maxwell could not conceive it possible that he had. But, no doubt, it would come to his knowledge, as well as Maxwell's reply.

For he meant to reply, and as he glanced at the clock on his table he saw that he had just half an hour before his clergyman-visitor arrived. Instantly, in his methodical way, he sat down to his task, labouring it, however, with toil and difficulty, when it was once begun.

The few words he ultimately wrote ran as follows:

'Dear Lady Tressady,—Your letter was a great surprise and a great pain to me. I believe you will recognise before long that you wrote it under a delusion, and that you have said in it both unkind and unjust things of one who is totally incapable of wronging you or anyone else. My wife read your letter, for she and I have no secrets. She will try and see you at once, and I trust you will not refuse to see her. She will prove to you, I think, that you have been giving yourself quite needless torture, for which she has no responsibility, but for which she is none the less sorrowful and distressed.

'I have treated your letter in this way because it is impossible to ignore the pain and trouble which drove you to write. I need not say that if it became necessary for me to write or act in another way, I should think only of my wife. But I will trust to the effect upon you of her own words and character ; and I cannot believe that you will misconstrue the generosity that prompts her to go to you.

'Is it not possible, also, that your misunderstanding of your husband may be in its own way as grave as your misunderstanding of Lady Maxwell ? Forgive an intrusive question, and believe me,

' Yours faithfully,
' MAXWELL.'

He read it anxiously over and over, then took a hasty copy of it, and finally sealed and sent it. He was but half satisfied with it. How was one to write such a letter without argument or recrimination? The poor thing had a vulgar, spiteful, little soul ; that was clear from her outpouring. It was also clear that she was miserable ; nor could Maxwell disguise from himself that in a sense she had ample cause. From that hard fact, with all its repellent and unpalatable consequences, a weaker man would by now have let his mind escape, would at any rate have begun to minimise and make light of George Tressady's act of the morning. In Maxwell, on the contrary, after a first movement of passionate resentment which had nothing whatever in common with ordinary jealousy, that act was now generating a compelling and beneficent force, that made for healing and reparation. Marcella had foreseen it, and in her pain and penitence had given the impulse. For all things are possible to a perfect affection, working through a nature at once healthy and strong.

Yet when Maxwell was once more established in his room at the Privy Council, overwhelmed with letters, interviews, and all the routine of official business, those who had to do with him noticed an unusual restlessness in their even-tempered chief. In truth, whenever his work left him free for a moment, all sorts of questions would start up in his mind: 'Is she there? Is that woman hurting and insulting her? Can I do nothing? My love! my poor love!'

But Marcella's plans so far had not prospered.

When George Tressady, after hastily despatching his most urgent business at the House, drove up to his own door in the afternoon just in time to put his things together and catch a newly-put-on dining-train to Paris, he found the house deserted. The butler reminded him that Letty, accompanied by Miss Tulloch, had gone to Hampton Court to join a river party for the day. George remembered; he hated the people she was to be with, and instinct told him that Cathedine would be there.

A rush of miserable worry overcame him. Ought he to be leaving her?

Then, in the darkness of the hall, he caught sight of

a card lying on the table. *Her card !* Amazement made
him almost dizzy, while the man at his arm explained.

' Her ladyship called just after luncheon. She thought
she would have found my lady in—before she went out.
But her ladyship is coming again, probably this evening,
as she wished to see Lady Tressady particularly.'

Tressady gave the man directions to pack for him
immediately, then took the card into his study, and stood
looking at it in a tumult of feeling. Ah ! let him begone
—out of her way ! Oh, heavenly goodness and compassion ! It seemed to him already that an angel had
trodden this dark house, and that another air breathed
in it.

That was his first thought. Then the rush of sore
longing, of unbearable self-contempt stirred all his worse
self to life again. Had she not better after all have left
him and Letty alone ! What did such lives as theirs
matter to her ?

He ran upstairs to make his last preparations, wrote
a few lines to Letty describing Mrs. Allison's plight and
the errand on which he was bound, and in half an
hour was at Charing Cross.

CHAPTER XX

' Did you ring, my lady ? '

'Yes.   Kenrick, if Lady Maxwell calls to see me
to-night, you will say, please, that I am particularly
engaged, and unable to receive anyone.'

Letty Tressady had just come in from her river party.
Dressed in a delicate gown of lace and pale green
chiffon, she was standing beside her writing-table with
Lady Maxwell's card in her hand.   Kenrick had given
it to her on her arrival, together with the message which
had accompanied it, and she had taken a few minutes to
think it over.   As she gave the man his order, the energy
of the small figure, as it half turned towards the door,
the brightness of the eyes under the white veil she had
just thrown back, no less than the emphasis of her tone,
awakened in the butler the clear perception that neither
the expected visit nor his mistress's directions were to
be taken as ordinary affairs.   After he left the drawing-
room, Grier passed him on the stairs.   He gave her a
slight signal, and the two retired to some nether region
to discuss the secrets of their employers.

Meanwhile Letty, having turned on the electric light
in the room, walked to the window and set it half open
behind the curtain.   In that way she would hear the
carriage approaching.   It was between eight and nine
o'clock.   No doubt Lady Maxwell would drive round
after dinner.

Then, still holding the card lightly in her hand, she threw herself on the sofa. She was tired, but so excited that she could not rest—first, by the memory of the day that had just passed; still more by the thought of the rebuff she was about to administer to the great lady who had affronted her. No doubt her letter had done its work. The remembrance of it filled her with an uneasy joy. Did George know of it by now? She did not care. Lady Maxwell, of course, was coming to try and appease her, to hush it up. There had been a scene, it was to be supposed, between her and her stiff husband. Letty gloated over the dream of it. Tears, humiliation, reproaches, she meted them all out in plenty to the woman she hated. Nor would things end there. Why, London was full of gossip! Harding's paragraph—for of course it was Harding's—had secured that. How clever of him! Not a name!—not a thing that could be taken hold of! —yet so clear. Well!—if she, Letty, was to be trampled on and set aside, at any rate other people should suffer too.

So George had gone off to France, leaving her alone, without 'Good-bye.' She did not believe a word of his excuse; and, if it were true, it was only another outrage that he should have thought twice of such a matter at such a crisis. But it was probably a mere device of his and *hers*—she would find out for what.

Her state of tension was too great to allow her to stay in the same place for more than a few minutes. She got up, and went to the glass before the mantelpiece. Taking out the pins that held her large Gainsborough hat, she arranged her hair with her hands, putting the curls of the fringe in their right place, fastening up some stray ends. She had given orders, as we have seen, to admit no one, and was presumably going to bed. Nevertheless, her behaviour was instinctively the behaviour of one who expects a guest.

When, more or less to her satisfaction, she had restored the symmetry of the little curled and crimped head, she took her face between her hands, and stared at her own reflection. Memories of the party she had just left, of the hot river, the slowly-filling locks, the revelry, the champagne, danced in her mind, especially of a certain walk through a wood. She defiantly watched the face in the glass grow red, the eyelids quiver. Then, like the tremor from some volcanic fire far within, a shudder ran through her. She dropped her head on her hands. She hated—*hated* him! Was it to-morrow evening she had told him he might come? She would go down to Ferth.

Wheels in the quiet street! Letty flew to the window like an excited child, her green and white twinkling through the room.

A brougham, and a tall figure in black stepping slowly out of it. Letty sheltered herself behind a curtain, held her breath, and listened.

Presently her lower lip dropped a little. What was Kenrick about? The front door had closed, and Lady Maxwell had not re-entered her carriage.

She opened the drawing-room door with care, and was stooping over the banisters when she saw Kenrick on the stairs. He seemed to be coming from the direction of George's study.

'What have you been doing?' she asked him in a hard under-voice, looking at him angrily. 'I told you not to let Lady Maxwell in.'

'I told her, my lady, that you were engaged and could see no one. Then her ladyship asked if she might write a few lines to you and send them up, asking when you would be able to see her. So I showed her into Sir George's study, my lady, and she is writing at Sir George's desk.'

'You should have done nothing of the sort,' said Letty, sharply. 'What is that letter?'

She took it from his hand before the butler, somewhat bewildered by the responsibilities of his position, could explain that he had just found it in the letter-box, where it might have been lying some little time, as he had heard no knock.

She let him go downstairs again, to await Lady Maxwell's exit, and herself ran back to read her letter, her heart beating, for the address of the sender was on the envelope.

When she had finished she threw it down, half suffocating.

'So I am to be lectured and preached to besides. Good Heavens! In his lofty manner, I suppose, that people talk of. Prig—odious, insufferable prig! So I have mistaken George, have I? My own husband! And insulted her—*her!* And she is actually downstairs, writing to me, in my own house!'

She locked her hands, and began stormily to pace the room again. The image of her rival, only a few feet from her, bending over George's table, worked in her with poisonous force. Suddenly she swept to the bell and rang it. A door opened downstairs. She ran to the landing.

'Kenrick!'

'Yes, my lady.' She heard a pause, and the soft rustle of a dress.

'Tell Lady Maxwell, please'—she struggled hard for the right, the dignified tone—'that if it is not too late for her to stay, I am now able to see her.'

She hurried back into the drawing-room and waited. *Would* she come? Letty's whole being was now throbbing with one mad desire. If Kenrick let her go!

But steps approached; the door was thrown open.

Marcella Maxwell came in timidly, very pale, the

dark eyes shrinking from the sudden light of the drawing-room. She was bare-headed, and wore a long cloak of black lace over her white evening dress. Letty's flash of thought as she saw her was twofold : first, hatred of her beauty, then triumph in the evident nervousness with which her visitor approached her.

Without making the slightest change of position, the mistress of the house spoke first.

' Will you please tell me,' she said, in her sharpest, thinnest voice, ' to what I owe the honour of this visit? '

Marcella paused half-way towards her hostess.

' I read your letter to my husband,' she said quietly, though her voice shook, ' and I thought you would hardly refuse to let me speak to you about it.'

' Then perhaps you will sit down,' said Letty in the same voice ; and she seated herself.

If she had wished to heighten the effect of her reception by these small discourtesies she did not succeed. Rather, Marcella's self-possession returned under them. She looked round simply for a chair, brought one forward within speaking distance of her companion, moving once more, in her thin, tall grace, with all that unconscious dignity Letty had so often envied and admired from a distance.

But neither dignity nor grace made any bar to the emotion that filled her. She bent forward, clasping her hands on her knee.

' Your letter to my husband made me so unhappy —that I could not help coming,' she said, in a tone that was all entreaty, all humbleness. ' Not—of course—that it seemed to either of us a true or just account of what had happened '—she drew herself up gently—' but it made me realise—though indeed I had realised it before I read it—that in my friendship with your husband I had been forgetting—forgetting those things—one ought to remem-

ber most. You will let me put things, won't you, in
my own way, as they seem to me ? At Castle Luton Sir
George attracted me very much. The pleasure of talking
to him there first made me wish to try and alter some of
his views—to bring him across my poor people—to introduce him to our friends. Then, somehow, a special bond
grew up between him and me with regard to this particular struggle in which my husband and I '—she
dropped her eyes that she might not see Letty's heated
face—' have been so keenly interested. But what I ought
to have felt—from the very first—was, that there could be,
there ought to have been, something else added. Married
people '—she spoke hurriedly, her breath rising and
falling—' are not two, but one—and my first step should
have been to come—and—and ask you to let me know
you too—to find out what your feelings were, whether
you wished for a friendship—that—that I had perhaps
no right to offer to Sir George alone. I have been
looking into my own heart '—her voice trembled again
—' and I see that fault, that great fault. To be excluded
myself from any strong friendship my husband might
make, would be agony to me ! ' The frank, sudden passion of her lifted eyes sent a thrill even through Letty's
fierce and hardly-kept silence. ' And that I wanted to
say to you, first of all. I wronged my own conception of
what marriage should be, and you were quite, quite right
to be angry ! '

' Well, I think it's quite clear, isn't it, that you forgot
from the beginning George had a wife ? ' cried Letty
in her most insulting voice. ' That certainly can't be
denied. Anybody could see that at Castle Luton ! '

Marcella looked at her in perplexity. What could
suggest to her how to say the right word, touch the right
chord ? Would she be able to do more than satisfy her
own conscience and then go, leaving this strange little

fury to make what use she pleased of her visit and her avowals?

She shaded her eyes with her hand a moment, thinking. Then she said :

'Perhaps it is of no use for me to ask you to remember how full our minds—my husband's and mine—have been of one subject—one set of ideas. But, if I am not keeping you too long, I should like to give you an account, from my point of view, of the friendship between Sir George and myself. I think I can remember every talk of ours, from our first meeting in the hospital down to—down to this morning.'

'This morning!' cried Letty, springing up. 'This *morning!* He went to you to-day?'

The little face convulsed with passion raised an intolerable distress in Marcella.

'Yes, he came to see me,' she said, her dark eyes, full of pain, full, too, once more, of entreaty, fixed upon her interrogator. 'But do let me tell you! I never saw any one in deeper trouble—trouble about you—trouble about himself.'

Letty burst into a wild laugh.

'Of course! No doubt he went to complain of me—that I flirted—that I ill-treated his mother—that I spent too much money—and a lot of other pleasant little things. Oh! I can imagine it perfectly. Besides that, I suppose he went to be thanked. Well, he deserved *that.* He has thrown away his career to please you; so if you didn't thank him, you ought! Everybody says his position in Parliament now isn't worth a straw—that he must resign —which is delightful, of course, for his wife. And I saw it all from the beginning—I understood exactly what you *wanted* to do at Castle Luton—only I couldn't believe then—I was only six weeks married——'

A wave of excitement and self-pity swept over her. She broke off with a sob.

Marcella's heart was wrung. She knew nothing of the real Letty Tressady. It was the wife as such, slighted and set aside, that appealed to the imagination, the remorse of this happy, this beloved woman. She rose quickly, she held out her hands, looking down upon the little venomous creature who had been pouring these insults upon her.

'Don't—*don't* believe such things,' she said, with sobbing breath. 'I never wronged you consciously for a moment. Can't you believe that Sir George and I became friends because we cared for the same kind of questions; because I—I was full of my husband's work and everything that concerned it; because I liked to talk about it, to win him friends. If it had ever entered my mind that such a thing could pain and hurt you——'

'Where have you sent him to-day?' cried Letty, peremptorily, interrupting her, while she drew her handkerchief fiercely across her eyes.

Instantly, Marcella was conscious of the difficulty of explaining her own impulse and Maxwell's action!

'Sir George told me,' she said, faltering, 'that he must go away from London immediately, to think out some trouble that was oppressing him. Only a few minutes after he left our house we heard from Mrs. Allison that she was in great distress about her son. She came, in fact, to beg us to help her find him. I won't go into the story, of course; I am sure you know it. My husband and I talked it over. It occurred to us that if Maxwell went to him—to Sir George—and asked him to do us and her this great kindness of going to Ancoats and trying to bring him back to his mother, it would put everything on a different footing. Maxwell would get to know him, —as I had got to know him. One would find a way—to silence the foolish, unjust things—that have been said—I suppose—I don't know——'

She paused, confused by the difficulties in her path, her cheeks hot and flushed. But the heart knew its own innocence. She recovered herself; she came nearer.

'—If only—at the same time—I could make you realise how truly—how bitterly—I had felt for any pain you might have suffered—if I could persuade you to look at it all—your husband's conduct and mine—in its true light, and to believe that he cares—he *must* care—for nothing in the world so much as his home—as you and your happiness!'

The nobleness of the speaker, the futility of the speech, were about equally balanced! Candour was impossible, if only for kindness' sake. And the story, so told, was not only unconvincing, it was hardly intelligible even, to Letty. For the two personalities moved in different worlds, and what had seemed to the woman who was all delicate impulse and romance the natural and right course, merely excited in Letty, and not without reason, fresh suspicion and offence. If words had been all, Marcella had gained nothing.

But a strange tumult was rising in Letty's breast. There was something in this mingling of self-abasement with an extraordinary moral richness and dignity, in these eyes, these hands that would have so gladly caught and clasped her own, which began almost to intimidate her. She broke out again, so as to hold her own bewilderment at bay :

'What right had you to send him away—to plan anything for *my* husband without my consent? Oh, of course you put it very finely; I dare say you know about all sorts of things *I* don't know about; I'm not clever; I don't talk politics. But I don't quite see the good of it, if it's only to take husbands away from their wives. All the same, I'm not a hypocrite, and I don't mean to pretend I'm a meek saint. Far from it. I've no doubt that George thinks he's been perfectly justified from the beginning, and that I have brought everything upon myself. Well! I don't care to argue about it. Don't imagine, please, that I have been playing the deserted wife all the time. If people injure me, it's not my way to hold my tongue, and I imagine that, after all, I do understand my own husband, in spite of Lord Maxwell's kind remarks!' She pointed scornfully to Maxwell's letter on the table. 'But as soon as I saw that nothing I said mattered to George, and that his whole mind was taken up with your society, why, of course I took my own measures! There are other men in the world—and one of them happens to amuse me particularly at this moment. It's your doing and George's, you see, if he doesn't like it!'

Marcella recoiled in sudden horror, staring at her companion with wide, startled eyes. Letty braved her defiantly, her dry lips drawn into a miserable smile. She stood, looking very small and elegant, beside her writing-table, her hand, blazing with rings, resting lightly upon it, the little, hot, withered face alone betraying the nerve tension behind.

The situation lasted a few seconds, then with a quick step Marcella hurried to a chair on the farther side of the room, sank into it, and covered her face with her hands.

Letty's heart seemed to dip, as it were, into an abyss. But there was a frenzied triumph in the spectacle of Marcella's grief and tears.

Marcella Maxwell—thus silenced, thus subdued! The famous name, with all that it had stood for in Letty's mind, of things to be envied and desired, echoed in her ear, delighted her revenge. She struggled to maintain her attitude.

'I don't know why what I said should make you so unhappy,' she said coldly, after a pause.

Marcella did not reply. Presently Letty saw that

she was resting her cheek on her hand and gazing before her into vacancy. At last she turned round, and Letty could satisfy herself that in truth her eyes were wet.

'Is there no one,' asked the full, tremulous voice, ' whom you care for, whom you would send for now to advise and help you?'

'Thank you!' said Letty calmly, leaning against the little writing-table, and beating the ground slightly with her foot. 'I don't want them. And I don't know why you should trouble yourself about it.'

But for the first time, and against its owner's will, the hard tone wavered.

Marcella rose impetuously again, and came towards her.

'When one thinks of all the long years of married life,' she said, still trembling, ' of the children that may come——'

Letty lifted her eyebrows.

'If one happened to wish for them. But I don't happen to wish for them, never did. I dare say it sounds horrid. Anyway, one needn't take that into consideration.'

'And your husband? Your husband, who must be miserable, whose great gifts will be all spoiled unless you will somehow give up your anger and make peace. And instead of that, you are only thinking of revenging yourself, of making more ruin and pain. It breaks one's heart! And it would need such a *little* effort on your part, only a few words written or spoken, to bring him back, to end all this unhappiness!'

'Oh! George can take care of himself,' said Letty, provokingly; 'so can I. Besides, you have sent him away.'

Marcella looked at her in despair. Then silently she turned away, and Letty saw that she was searching for some gloves and a handkerchief she had been carrying in her hand when she came in.

Letty watched her take them up, then said suddenly, ' Are you going away ? '

' It is best, I think. I can do nothing.'

' I wish I knew why you came to see me at all ! They say, of course, you are very much in love with Lord Maxwell. Perhaps—that made you sorry for me ? '

Marcella's pride leapt at the mention by those lips of her own married life. Then she drove her pride down.

' You have put it better than I have been able to do, all the time.' Her mouth parted in a slight, sad smile— ' Good-night.'

Letty took no notice. She sat down on the arm of a chair near her. Her eyes suddenly blazed, her face grew dead-white.

' Well, if you want to know——' she said—' no, don't go—I don't mean to let you go just yet—I *am* about the most miserable wretch going ! There, you may take it or leave it ; it's true. I don't suppose I cared much about George when I married him ; plenty of girls don't. But as soon as he began to care about *you*—just contrariness, I suppose—I began to feel that I could kill anybody that took him from me, and kill myself afterwards ! Oh, good gracious ! there was plenty of reason for his getting tired of me. I'm not the sort of person to let anyone get the whip-hand of me, and I *would* spend his money as I liked, and I *would* ask the persons I chose to the house ; and, above all, I wasn't going to be pestered with looking after and giving up to his *dreadful* mother, who made my life a burden to me. Oh ! why do you look so white ? Well, I dare say it does sound atrocious. I don't care. Perhaps you'll be still more horrified when you know that they came round this afternoon, when I was out and George was gone, to tell me that Lady

Tressady was frightfully ill—dying, I think my maid said. And I haven't given it another thought since—not one—till now '—she struck one hand against the other— 'because directly afterwards the butler told me of your visit this afternoon, and that you were coming again— and I wasn't going to think of anything else in the world but you, and George. No, don't look like that, don't come near me—I'm not mad. I assure you I'm not mad! But that's all by the way. What was I saying? Oh! that George had cause enough to stop caring about me. Of course he had; but if he's lost to me—I shall give him a good deal more cause before we've done. That other man—you know him—Cathedine —gave me a kiss this afternoon, when we were in a wood together '—the same involuntary shudder overtook her, while she still held her companion at arm's length. 'Oh, he is a brute—a *brute!* But what do I care what happens to me? It's so strange I don't—rather credit- able, I think—for after all I like parties, and being asked about. But now George hates me—and let you send him away from me—why, of course, it's all simple enough! I—Don't—don't come. I shall never, never forgive—it's just being tired——'

But Marcella sprang forward. Mercifully, there is a limit to nerve endurance, and Letty in her raving had overpassed it. She sank gasping on a sofa, still putting out her hand as though to protect herself. But Marcella knelt beside her, the tears running down her cheeks. She put her arms—arms formed for tenderness, for motherliness —round the girl's slight frame. 'Don't—don't re- pulse me,' she said, with trembling lips, and suddenly Letty yielded. She found herself sobbing in Lady Maxwell's embrace, while all the healing, all the remorse, all the comfort that self-abandonment and pity can pour out on such a plight as hers, descended upon her from

Marcella's clinging touch, her hurried, fragmentary words. Assurances that all could be made right—entreaties for gentleness and patience—revelations of her own inmost heart as a wife, far too sacred for the ears of Letty Tressady—little phrases and snatches of autobiography steeped in an exquisite experience : the nature Letty had rained her blows upon, kept nothing back, gave her all its best. How irrelevant much of it was!—chequered throughout by those oblivions, and optimisms, and foolish hopes by which such a nature as Marcella's protects itself from the hard facts of the world. By the time she had ranged through every note of entreaty and consolation, Marcella had almost persuaded herself and Letty that George Tressady had never said a word to her beyond the commonplaces of an ordinary friendship; she had passionately determined that this blurred and spoiled marriage could and should be mended, and that it lay with her to do it ; and in the spirit of her audacious youth she had taken upon herself the burden of Letty's character and fate, vowing herself to a moral mission, to a long patience. The quality of her own nature, perhaps, made her bear Letty's violences and frenzies more patiently than would have been possible to a woman of another type; generous remorse and regret, combined with her ignorance of Letty's history and the details of Letty's life, led her even to look upon these violences as the effects of love perverted—the anguish of a jealous heart. Imagination, keen and loving, drew the situation for her in rapid strokes, draped Letty in the subtleties and powers of her own heart, and made forbearance easy.

As for Letty, her whole being surrendered itself to a mere ebb and flow of sensations. That she had been able thus to break down the barriers of Marcella's stateliness filled her all through, in her passion as in her yielding, with a kind of exultation. A vision of a tall

figure in a white and silver dress, sitting stiff and unapproachable beside her in the Castle Luton drawing-
room, fled through her mind now and then, only to make
the wonder of this pleading voice, these confidences, this
pity, the more wonderful. But there was more than this,
and better than this. Strange up-wellings of feelings
long trampled on and suppressed—momentary awaken-
ings of conscience, of repentance, of regret—sharp
realisations of an envy that was no longer ignoble but
moral, softer thoughts of George, the suffocating, unwilling
recognition of what love meant in another woman's life
—these messengers and forerunners of diviner things
passed and repassed through the spaces of Letty's soul
as she lay white and passive under Marcella's yearning
look. There was a marvellous relief besides, much of
it a physical relief, in this mere silence, this mere ceasing
from angry railing and offence.

Marcella was still sitting beside her, holding her
hands, and talking in the same low voice, when suddenly
the loud sound of a bell clanged through the house.
Letty sprang up, white and startled.

'What can it be? It's past ten o'clock. It can't be
a telegram.'

Then a guilty remembrance struck her. She hurried
to the door as Kenrick entered.

'Lady Tressady's maid would like to see you, my
lady. They want Sir George's address. The doctors
think she will hardly live over to-morrow.'

And behind Kenrick, Justine, the French maid, pushed
her way in, weeping and exclaiming. Lady Tressady, it
seemed, had been in frightful pain all the afternoon.
She was now easier for the moment, though dangerously
exhausted. But if the heart attacks returned during the
next twenty-four hours, nothing could save her. The
probability was that they would return, and she was

asking piteously for her son, who had seen her, Justine believed, the day before these seizures began, just before his departure for Paris, and had written. 'Et la pauvre âme!' cried the Frenchwoman at last, not caring what she said to this amazing daughter-in-law, 'elle est là toujours, quand les douleurs s'apaisent un peu, écoutant, espérant—et personne ne vient—*personne !* Voulez-vous bien, madame, me dire où on peut trouver Sir George?'

'Poste Restante, Trouville,' said Letty, sullenly. 'It is the only address that I know of.'

But she stood there irresolute and frowning, while the French girl, hardly able to contain herself, stared at the disfigured face, demanding by her quick-breathing silence, by her whole attitude, something else, something more than Sir George's address.

Meanwhile Marcella waited in the background, obliged to hear what passed, and struck with amazement. It is perhaps truer of the moral world than the social that one half of it never conceives how the other half lives. George Tressady's mother—alone—dying—in her son's absence—and Letty Tressady knew nothing of her illness till it had become a question of life and death, and had then actually refused to go—forgotten the summons even !

When Letty, feverish and bewildered, turned back to the companion whose heart had been poured out before her during this past hour of high emotion, she saw a new expression in Lady Maxwell's eyes from which she shrank.

'Ought I to go?' she said fretfully, almost like a peevish child, putting her hand to her brow.

'My carriage is downstairs,' said Marcella, quickly. 'I can take you there at once. Is there a nurse?' she asked, turning to the maid.

Oh, yes; there was an excellent nurse, just installed, or Justine could not have left her mistress; and the doctor close by could be got at a moment's notice. But the poor lady wanted her son, or at least some one of the family—Justine bit her lip, and threw a nervous side glance at Letty—and it went to the heart to see her. The girl found relief in describing her mistress's state to this grave and friendly lady, and showed more feeling and sincerity in speaking of it than might have been expected from her affected dress and manner.

Meanwhile Letty seemed to be wandering aimlessly about the room. Marcella went up to her.

' Your hat is here, on this chair. I have a shawl in the carriage. Won't you come at once, and leave word to your maid to bring after you what you want? Then I can go on, if you wish it, and send your telegram to Sir George.'

' But you wanted him to do something?' said Letty, looking at her uncertainly.

' Mothers come first, I think!' said Marcella, with a smile of wonder. 'It is best to write it before we go. Will you tell me what to say?'

She went to the writing-table, and had to write the telegram with small help from Letty, who in her dazed, miserable soul was still fighting some demonic resistance or other to the step asked of her. Instinctively and gradually, however, Marcella took command of her. A few quiet words to Justine sent her to make arrangements with Grier. Then Letty found a cloak that had been sent for being drawn round her shoulders, and was coaxed to put on her hat. In another minute she was in the Maxwells' brougham, with her hand clasped in Marcella's.

'They will want me to sit up,' she said, dashing an irrelevant tear from her eyes, as they drove away. ' I am so tired—and I hate illness!'

'Very likely they won't let you see her to-night. But you will be there if the illness comes on again. You would feel it terribly if—if she died all alone, with Sir George away.'

'Died!' Letty repeated, half angrily. 'But that would be so horrible—what could I do?'

Marcella looked at her with a strange smile.

'Only be kind; only forget everything but her!'

The softness of her voice had yet a severity beneath it that Letty felt, but had no spirit to resent. Rather it awakened an uneasy and painful sense that, after all, it was not she who had come off conqueror in this great encounter. The incidents of the last half-hour seemed in some curious way to have reversed their positions. Letty, smarting, realised that her relation to George's dying mother had revealed her to Lady Maxwell far more than any wild and half-sincere confessions could have done. Her vanity felt a deep inner wound, yet of a new sort. At any rate, Marcella's self-abasement was over, and Letty instinctively realised that she would never see it again, while at the same time a new and clinging need had arisen in herself. The very neighbourhood of the personality beside her had begun to thrill and subjugate her. She had been conscious enough before—enviously, hatefully, conscious—of all the attributes and possessions that made Maxwell's wife a great person in the world of London. What was stealing upon her now was glamour and rank and influence of another kind.

Not unmixed, no doubt, with more mundane thoughts! No ordinary preacher, no middle-class eloquence perhaps would have sufficed—nothing less dramatic and distinguished than the scene which had actually passed, than a Marcella at her feet. Well! there are many modes and grades of conversion. Whether by what was worst in her, or what was best; whether the same weaknesses of character that had originally inflamed her had now helped to subdue her or no, what matter? So much

stood—that one short hour had been enough to draw this
vain, selfish nature within a moral grasp she was never
again to shake off.

Meanwhile, as they drove towards Warwick Square
Marcella's only thought was how to hand her over safe
to her husband. A sense of agonised responsibility
awoke in the elder woman at the thought of Cathedine.
But no more emotion—only common sense and gentleness.

As they neared Warwick Square, Letty withdrew her
hand.

'I don't suppose you will ever want to see me again,'
she said huskily, turning her head away.

'Do you think that very possible between two people
who have gone through such a time as you and I have?'
said Marcella, pale, but smiling. 'When may I come to
see you to-morrow? I shall send to inquire, of course,
very early.'

Some thought made Letty's breath come quickly.
'Will you come in the afternoon—about four?' she said
hastily. 'I suppose I shall be here.' They were just
stopping at the door in Warwick Square. 'You said you
would tell me——'

'I have a great deal to tell you. . . . I will come, then,
and see if you can be spared. . . . Good-night. I trust
she will be better! I will go on and send the telegram.'

Letty felt her hand gravely pressed, the footman
helped her out, and in another minute she was mounting
the stairs leading to Lady Tressady's room, having sent
a servant on before her to warn the nurse of her arrival.

The nurse came out, finger on lip. She was very
glad to see Lady Tressady, but the doctor had left word
that nothing whatever was to be allowed to disturb or
excite his patient. Of course, if the attack returned——
But just now there was hope. Only it was so difficult

to keep her quiet. Instead of trying to sleep, she was now asking for Justine, declaring that Justine must read French novels aloud to her, and bring out two of her evening dresses, that she might decide on some alteration in the trimmings. 'I daren't fight with her,' said the nurse, evidently in much perplexity. 'But if she only raises herself in bed she may kill herself.'

She hurried back to her patient, promising to inform the daughter-in-law at once if there was a change for the worse, and Letty, infinitely relieved, made her way to the spare room of the house, where Grier was already unpacking for her.

After a hasty undressing she threw herself into bed, longing for sleep. But from a short nightmare dream she woke up with a start. Where was she? In her mother-in-law's house—she could actually hear the shrill affected voice laughing and talking in the room next door —and brought there by Marcella Maxwell! The strangeness of these two facts kept her tossing restlessly from side to side. And where was George? Just arrived at Paris, perhaps. She thought of the glare and noise of the Gare du Nord—she heard his cab rattling over the long stone-paved street outside. In the darkness she felt a miserable sinking of heart at the thought of his going with every minute farther, farther away from her. Would he ever forgive her that letter to Lord Maxwell, when he knew of it? Did she want him to forgive her?

A mood that was at once soft and desolate stole upon her, and made her cry a little. It sprang, perhaps, from a sense of the many barriers she had heaped up between herself and happiness. The waves of feeling, half self-assertive, half repentant, ebbed and flowed. One moment she yearned for the hour when Marcella was to come to her; the next, she hated the notion of it. So between dream and misery, amid a maze of thought without a clue, Letty's night passed away. By the time the morning dawned, the sharp conviction had shaped itself within her that she had grown older, that life had passed into another stage, and could never again be as it had been the day before. Two emotions, at least, or excitements, had emerged from all the rest and filled her mind—the memory of the scene with Marcella—and the thought of George's return.

PART III

CHAPTER XXI

' MY dear, you don't mean to say you have had her here for ten days ? '

The speaker was Betty Leven, who had just arrived at Maxwell Court, and was sitting with her hostess under the cedars in front of the magnificent Caroline mansion, which it was the never-ending task of Marcella's life to bring somehow into a democratic scheme of things.

A still September afternoon, lightly charged with autumn mists, lay gently on the hollows of the park. Betty was in her liveliest mood and her gayest dress. Her hat, a marvel in poppies, was perched high upon no less ingenious waves and frettings of hair. Her straw-coloured gown, which was only simple for the untrained eye, gave added youth even to her childish figure ; and her very feet, clothed in the smallest and most preposterous of shoes, had something merry and provocative about them, as they lay crossed upon the wooden footstool Marcella had pushed towards her.

The remark just quoted followed upon one made by her hostess, to the effect that Lady Tressady would be down to tea shortly.

'Now, Betty,' said Marcella, seriously, though she laughed, ' I meant to have a few words with you on this

I I

subject first thing—let's have them.   Do you want to be
very kind to me, or do you ever want me to be very nice
to you?'

Betty considered.

'You can't do half as much for me now as you once
could, now that Frank's going to leave Parliament,' she
remarked, with as much worldly wisdom as her face
allowed. 'Nevertheless, the quality of my nature is
such that, sometimes, I might even be nice to you for
nothing. But information before benevolence—why have
you got her here?'

'Because she was fagged and unhappy in London,
and her husband had gone to take his mother abroad,
after first doing Maxwell a great kindness,' said Marcella
—not, however, without embarrassment, as Betty saw—
'and I want you to be kind to her.'

'Reasons one and two no reasons at all,' said Betty,
meditating; 'and the third wants examining. You mean
that George Tressady went after Ancoats?'

Marcella raised her shoulders, and was silent.

'If you are going to be stuffy and mysterious,' said
Betty with vivacity, 'you know what sort of a hedgehog
I can be. How can you expect me to be nice to Letty
Tressady unless you make it worth my while?'

'Betty, you infant!   Well, then, he did go after
Ancoats—got him safely away from Trouville, brought
him to Paris to join Mrs. Allison, and, in general, has
laid us all under very great obligations. Meanwhile, she
was very much tired out with nursing her mother-in-
law——'

'Oh, and such a mother-in-law — such a jewel!'
ejaculated Betty.

'And I brought her down here to rest, till he should
come back from Wildheim and take her home. He will
probably be here to-night.'

The speaker reddened unconsciously during her story, a fact not lost on Betty.

'Well, I knew most of that before,' said Betty, quietly. 'And what sort of a time have you been having this ten days?'

'I have been very glad to have her here,' came the quick reply. 'I ought to have known her long ago.'

Betty looked at the speaker with a half-incredulous smile.

'You have been "collecting" her, I suppose, as Hallin collects grasses. Of course, what I pine to know is what sort of a time *she's* had. You're not the easiest person in the world to get on with, my lady.'

'I know that,' said Marcella, sighing; 'but I don't think she has been unhappy.'

Betty's green eyes opened suddenly to the light.

'Are you ever going to tell me the truth? Have you got her under your thumb? Does she adore you?'

'Betty, don't be an idiot!'

'I expect she does,' said Betty, thoughtfully, a myriad thoughts and conjectures passing through her quick brain as she studied her friend's face and attitude. 'I see exactly what fate is going to happen to you in middle life. Women couldn't get on with you when you were a girl—you didn't like them, nor they you; and now everywhere I hear the young women beginning to talk about you, especially the young married women; and in a few years you will have them all about you like a cluster of doves, cooing and confessing, and making your life a burden to you.'

'Well, suppose you begin?' said Marcella, with meaning. 'I'm quite ready. How are Frank's spirits since the great decision?'

'Frank's spirits?' said Betty. She leisurely took off her glove. 'Frank's spirits, my dear, if you wish to

know, are simply an affront to his wife. My ruined
ambitions appear to affect him as Parrish's food does
the baby. I prophesy he will have gained a stone by
Christmas.'

For the great step had been taken. Betty had given
way, and Frank was to escape from politics. For three
years Betty had held him to his task—had written his
speeches, formed his opinions, and done her very best to
train him for a statesman. But the young man had in
truth no opinions, save indeed whatever might be involved
in the constant opinion that Heaven had intended him
for a country gentleman and a sportsman, and for nothing
else. And at last a mixture of revolt and melancholy
had served his purpose. Betty was subdued; the
Chiltern Hundreds were in sight. The young wife, with
many sighs, had laid down all dreams of a husband on
the front bench. But—in compensation—she had regained her lover, and the honeymoon shone once more.

'Frank came to see me yesterday,' said Marcella,
smiling.

Betty sprang forward.

'What did he say? Didn't he tell you I was an
angel? Now there's a bargain! Repeat to me every
single word he said, and I will devote myself, body and
bones, to Letty Tressady.'

'Hush!' said Marcella, laying two fingers on the
pretty mouth. 'Here she comes.'

Letty Tressady, in fact, had just emerged from a side
door of the house, and was slowly approaching the two
friends on the terrace. Lady Leven's discerning eye ran
over the advancing figure. Marcella heard her make
some exclamation under her breath. Then she rose with
little, hurrying steps, and went to greet the new-comer
with a charming ease and kindness.

Letty responded rather nervously. Marcella looked

up with a smile, and pointed to a low chair, which Letty
took with a certain stiffness. It was evident to Marcella
that she was afraid of Lady Leven, who had, indeed, shown
a marked indifference to her society at Castle Luton.

But Betty was disarmed. The 'minx' had lost her
colour, and, for the moment, her prettiness. She looked
depressed, and talked little. As to her relation to Marcella
Betty's inquisitive brain indulged itself in a score of
conjectures. 'How like her!' she thought to herself,
'to forget the wife's existence to begin with, and then to
make love to her by way of warding off the husband!'

Meanwhile, aloud, Lady Leven professed herself exceedingly dissatisfied with the entertainment provided for
her. Where were the gentlemen? What was the good of
one putting on one's best frock to come down to a Maxwell
Court Saturday to find only a ' hen tea-party' at the end?
Marcella protested that there were only too many men
somewhere on the premises already, and more—with
their wives—were arriving by the next train. But Maxwell had taken off such as had already appeared for a
long cross-country walk.

Betty demanded the names, and Marcella gave them
obediently. Betty perceived at once that the party was
the party of a political chief obliged to do his duty. She
allowed herself a good many shrugs of her small
shoulders. 'Oh, Mrs. Lexham—very charming, of course
—but what's the good of being friends with a person who
has five hundred people in London that call her Nelly?
Lady *Wendover* ? I ought to have had notice. A good
mother? I should think she is! That's the whole point
against her. She always gives you the idea of having
reared fifteen out of a possible twelve. To see her
beaming on her offspring makes me positively ashamed
of being in the same business myself. Don't you agree,
Lady Tressady ? '

But Letty, whose chief joy a month before would have been to dart in on such a list with little pecking proofs of acquaintance, was leaning back listlessly in her chair, and could only summon a forced smile for answer.

'And Sir George, too, is coming to-night, isn't he?' said Lady Leven.

'Yes, I expect my husband to-night,' said Letty, coldly, without looking at her questioner. Betty glanced quickly at the expression of the eyes which were bent upon the farther reaches of the park; then, to Letty's astonishment, she bent forward impulsively and laid her little hand on Lady Tressady's arm.

'Do you mind telling me,' she said in a loud whisper, with a glance over her shoulder, ' your candid opinion of *her* as a country lady?'

Letty, taken aback, turned and laughed uneasily ; but Betty went rattling on. 'Have you found out that she treats her servants like hospital nurses ; that they go off and on duty at stated hours ; that she has workshops and art schools for them in the back premises ; and that the first footman has just produced a cantata which has been sent in to the committee of the Worcester Festival (Be quiet, Marcella ; if it isn't that, it's something near it) ; that she teaches the stable boys and the laundry maids old English dances, and the *pas de quatre* once a fortnight, and acts showman to her own pictures for the benefit of the neighbourhood once a week? I came once to see how she did it, but I found her and the Gairsley ironmonger measuring the ears of the Holbeins—it seems you can't know anything about pictures now unless you have measured all the ears and the little fingers, which I hope you know ; I didn't!—so I fled, as she hadn't a word to throw to me, even as one of the public. Then perhaps you don't know that she has invented a whole, new, and original system of game-preserving—she and Frank fight over it by the hour—that she has upset all the wage arrangements of the county—that, perhaps, you do know, for it got into the papers—and a hundred other trifles. Has she revealed these things?'

Letty looked in perplexity from Betty's face, full of sweetness and mirth, to Marcella's.

' She hasn't talked about them,' she said, hesitating. ' Of course, I haven't understood a good many things that are done here——'

' Don't try,' said Marcella, first laughing and then sighing.

Nothing appeased, Lady Leven chattered away, while Letty watched her hostess in silence. She had come down to the Court gloating somewhat, in spite of her very real unhappiness, over the prospect of the riches and magnificence she was to find there. And to discover that wealth might be merely the source of one long moral wrestle to the people who possessed it, burdening them with all sorts of problems and remorses that others escaped, had been a strange and, on the whole, jarring experience to her. Of course there must be rich and poor; of course there must be servants and masters. Marcella's rebellion against the barriers of life had been a sort of fatigue and offence to Letty ever since she had been made to feel it. And daily contact with the simple, and even Spartan, ways of living that prevailed—for the owners of it, at least—in the vast house, with the overflowing energy and humanity that often made its mistress a restless companion, and led her into a fair percentage of mistakes—had roused a score of half-scornful protests in the small, shrewd mind of her guest. Nevertheless, when Marcella was kind, when she put Letty on the sofa, insisting that she was tired, and anxiously accusing herself of some lack of consideration or other; when she took her to her room at night,

seeing to every comfort, and taking thought for luxuries
that in her heart she despised; or when, very rarely,
and turning rather pale, she said a few words—sweet,
hopeful, encouraging—about George's return; then Letty
was conscious of a strange leap of something till then
unknown, something that made her want to sob, that
seemed to open to her a new room in the House of
Life. Marcella had not kissed her since the day of their
great scene; they had been 'Lady Maxwell' and 'Lady
Tressady' to each other all the time, and Letty had but
realised her own insolences and audacities the more, as
gradually the spiritual dignity of the woman she had
raved at came home to her. But sometimes when Marcella stood beside her, unconscious, talking pleasantly of
London folk or Ancoats, or trying to inform herself as to
Letty's life at Ferth, a half-desolate intuition would flash
across the younger woman of what it might be to be
admitted to the intimate friendship of such a nature, to
feel those long, slender arms pressed about her once more,
not in pity or remonstrance, as of one trying to exorcise
an evil spirit, but in mere love, as of one asking as well
as giving. The tender and adoring friendship of women
for women, which has become so marked a feature of our
self-realising generation, had passed Letty by. She had
never known it. Now, in these unforeseen circumstances,
she seemed to be trembling within reach of its emotion;
divining it, desiring it, yet forced onward to the question,
'What is there in me that may claim it?'

Marcella, indeed, after their first stormy interview, had
once more returned to the subject of it. She had told
the story of her friendship with George Tressady, very
gently and plainly, in a further conversation, held
between them at the elder Lady Tressady's house during
that odd lady's very odd convalescence; till, indeed, she
reached the last scene. She could not bring herself to

deliver the truth of that. Nor was it necessary. Letty's jealousy had guessed it near enough long ago. But when all else was told, Letty had been conscious at first of a half-sore resentment that there was so little to tell. In her secret soul she knew very well what had been the effect on George. Her husband's mind had been gradually absorbed by another ideal in which she had no part ; nor could she deny that he had suffered miserably. The memory of his face as he asked her to ' forgive him ' when she fled past him on that last wretched night was enough. But suffered for what? A few talks about politics, a few visits to poor people, an office of kindness after a street accident that any stranger must have rendered, a few meetings in the House and elsewhere !

Letty's vanity was stabbed anew by the fact that Lady Maxwell's offence was so small. It gave her a kind of measure of her own hold upon her husband.

Once, indeed, Marcella's voice and colour had wavered when she made herself describe how, on the Mile End evening, she had been conscious of pressing the personal influence to gain the political end. But good heavens ! —Letty hardly understood what the speaker's evident compunction was about. Why, it was all for Maxwell ! What had she thought of all through but Maxwell? Letty's humiliation grew as she understood, and as in the quiet of Maxwell Court she saw the husband and wife together.

Her anger and resentment might very well only have transferred themselves the more hotly to George. But this new moral influence upon her had a kind of paralysing effect. The incidents of the weeks before the crisis excited in her now a sick, shamed feeling whenever she thought of them. For contact with people on a wholly different plane of conduct, if such persons as Letty can once be brought to submit to it, will often produce effects,

especially on women, like those one sees produced every
day by the clash of two standards of manners. It means
simply the recognition that one is unfit to be of certain
company; and perhaps there are few moral ferments
more penetrating. Probably Letty would have gone to
her grave knowing nothing of it, but for the accident
which had opened to her the inmost heart of a woman
with whom, once known, not even her vanity dared
measure itself.

George and she had already met since the day when
he had gone off to Paris in search of Ancoats. The
telegram sent to him by Marcella on the night of his
mother's violent illness had, indeed, been recalled next
day. Lady Tressady, following the idiosyncrasies of
her disease, sprang from death to life—and life of the
sprightliest kind—in the course of a few hours. The
battered, grey-haired woman—so old, do what she would,
under the betraying hand of physical decay!—no sooner
heard that George had been sent for than she at once
and peremptorily telegraphed to him herself to stay
away.. 'I'm not dead yet,' she wrote to him afterwards,
'in spite of all the fuss they've made with me. I was
simply ashamed to own such a cadaverous-looking wretch
as you were when you came here last, and if you take
my advice you'll stay at Trouville with Lord Ancoats and
amuse yourself. As to that young man, of course it's no
good, and his mother's a great fool to suppose that you
or anybody else can prevent his enjoying himself. But
these High Church women are so extraordinary.'

Letty, indeed, remembering her mother-in-law's old
ways, and finding them little changed as far as she herself
was concerned, was puzzled and astonished by the new
relations between mother and son, On the smallest
excuse or none, Lady Tressady, a year before, would
have been ready to fetch him back from farthest Ind

without the least scruple. Now, however, she thought of him, or for him, incessantly. And one day Letty actually found her crying over an official intimation from the lawyer concerned that another instalment of the Shapetsky debt would be due within a month. But she angrily dried her tears at sight of Letty, and Letty said nothing.

George, however, came back within about ten days of his departure, having apparently done what he was commissioned to do, though Letty took so little interest in the Ancoats affair that she barely read those portions of his letters in which he described the course of it. His letters, indeed, with the exception of a few ambiguous words here and there, dealt entirely with Trouville, Ancoats, or the ups and downs of public opinion on the subject of his action and speech in the House. Letty could only gather from a stray phrase or two that he enjoyed nothing; but evidently he could not yet bring himself to speak of what had happened.

When he did come back, the husband and wife saw very little of each other. It was more convenient that he should stay in Upper Brook Street while she remained at her mother-in-law's; and altogether he was hardly three days in London. He rushed up to Market Malford to deliver his promised speech to his constituents, and immediately afterwards, on the urgent advice of the doctors, he went off to Wildheim with his mother and the elderly cousin whose aid he had already invoked. Before he went, he formally thanked his wife—who hardly spoke to him unless she was obliged—for her attention to his mother, and then lingered a little, looking no less 'cadaverous,' certainly, than when he had gone away, and apparently desiring to say more.

' I suppose I shall be away about a fortnight,' he said at last, ' if one is to settle her comfortably. You haven't told me yet what you would like to do. Couldn't you get Miss Tulloch to go down with you to Ferth, or would you go to your people for a fortnight?'

He was longing to ask her what had come of that promised visit of Lady Maxwell's. But neither by letter nor by word of mouth had Letty as yet said a word of it. And he did not know how to open the subject. During the time that he was with his wife and mother, nothing was seen of Marcella in Warwick Square, and an interview that he was to have had with Maxwell, by way of supplement to his numerous letters, had to be postponed because of over-crowded days on both sides. So that he was still in the dark.

Letty at first made no answer to his rather lame proposals for her benefit. But just as he was turning away with a look of added worry, she said :

'I don't want to go home, thank you, and I still less want to go to Ferth.'

'But you can't stay in London. There isn't a soul in town ; and it would be too dull for you.'

He gazed at her in perplexity, praying, however, that he might not provoke a scene, for the carriage that was to take him and his mother to the station was almost at the door.

Letty rose slowly, and folded up some embroidery she had been playing with. Then she took a note from her work-basket, and laid it on the table.

'You may read that if you like. That's where I'm going.'

And she quickly went out of the room.

George read the note. His face flushed, and he hurriedly busied himself with some of his preparations for departure. When his wife came into the room again he went up to her.

'You could have done nothing so likely to save us both,' he said huskily, and then could think of nothing more to say. He drew her to him as though to kiss her, but a blind movement of the old rage with him or circumstance leapt in her, and she pulled herself away. The thought of that particular moment had done more perhaps than anything else to thin and whiten her since she had been at Maxwell Court.

And now he would be here to-night. She knew both from her host himself and from George's letters that Lord Maxwell had specially written to him begging him to come to the Court on his return, in order to join his wife and also to give that oral report of his mission for which there had been no time on his first reappearance. Maxwell had spoken to her of his wish to see her husband, without a tone or a word that could suggest anything but the natural friendliness and goodwill of the man who has accepted a signal service from his junior. But Letty avoided Maxwell when she could; nor would he willingly have been left alone with this thin, sharp-faced girl whose letter to him had been like the drawing of an ugly veil from nameless and incredible things. He was sorry for her; but in his strong, deep nature he felt a repulsion for her he could not explain; and to watch Marcella with her amazed him.

Immediately after tea, Lady Leven's complaints of her entertainment became absurd. Guests poured in from the afternoon train, and a variety of men, her husband foremost among them, were soon at her disposal, asking nothing better than to amuse her.

Letty Tressady meanwhile looked on for a time at the brilliant crowd about her on the terrace, with a dull sense of being forgotten and of no account. She said to herself sullenly that of course no one would want to talk to her; it was not her circle, and she had even few acquaintances among them.

Then, to her astonishment, she began to find herself
the object of an evident curiosity and interest to many
people among the throng. She divined that her name
was being handed from one to the other, and she soon
perceived that Marcella had been asked to introduce to
her this person and that, several of them men and
women whose kindness, a few weeks before, would have
flattered her social ambitions to the highest point.
Colour and nerve returned, and she found herself sitting
up, forgetting her headache, and talking fast.

'I am delighted to have this opportunity of telling
you, Lady Tressady, how much I admired your husband's
great speech,' said the deep and unctuous voice of the
grey-haired Solicitor-General as he sank into a chair
beside her. 'It was not only that it gave us our Bill, it
gave the House of Commons a new speaker. Manner,
voice, matter—all of it excellent! I hope there'll be no
nonsense about his giving up his seat. Don't you let
him! He will find his feet and his right place before
long, and you'll be uncommonly proud of him before
you've done.'

'Lady Tressady, I'm afraid you've forgotten me,' said
a plaintive voice; and, on turning, Letty saw the red-
haired Lady Madeleine asking with smiles to be remembered. 'Do you know, I was lucky enough to get into
the House on the great day? What a scene it was!
You were there, of course?'

When Letty unwillingly said 'No,' there was a little
chorus of astonishment.

'Well, take my advice, my dear lady,' said the
Solicitor-General, speaking with lazy patronage somewhere from the depths of comfort—he was accustomed
to use these paternal modes of speech to young women—
'don't you miss your husband's speeches. We can't do
without our domestic critics. But for the bad quarters

of an hour that lady over there has given me, I should be nowhere.'

And he nodded complacently towards the wife as stout as himself, who was sitting a few yards away. She, hearing her name, nodded back, with smiles aside to the bystanders. Most of the spectators, however, were already acquainted with a conjugal pose which was generally believed to be not according to facts, and no one took the cue.

Then presently Mr. Bennett—the workmen's member from the North—was at Letty's elbow saying the most cordial things of the absent George. Bayle, too, the most immaculate and exclusive of private secretaries, who was at the Court on a wedding visit with a new wife, chose to remember Lady Tressady's existence for the first time for many months, and to bestow some of his carefully adapted conversation upon her. While, last of all, Edward Watton came up to her with a cousinly kindness she had scarcely yet received from him, and, drawing a chair beside her, overflowed with talk about George, and the Bill, and the state of things at Market Malford. In fact, it was soon clear even to Letty's bewildered sense that till her husband should arrive she was perhaps, for the moment, the person of most interest to this brilliant and representative gathering of a victorious party.

Meanwhile she was made constantly aware that her hostess remembered her. Once, as Marcella passed her, after introducing some one to her, Letty felt a hand gently laid on her shoulder and then withdrawn. Strange waves of emotion ran through the girl's senses. When would George be here? About seven, she thought, when they would all have gone up to dress. He would have arrived from Wildheim in the morning, and was to spend the day doing business in town.

CHAPTER XXII

LETTY was lying on a sofa in her bedroom. Her maid
was to come to her shortly, and she was impatiently
listening to every sound that approached or passed her
door. The great clock in the distant hall struck seven,
and it seemed to her intolerably long before she heard
movements in the passage, and then Maxwell's voice
outside.

'Here is your room, Sir George. I hope you don't
mind a few ghosts! It is one of the oldest bits of the
house.'

Letty sprang up. She heard the shutting of the passage door, then immediately afterwards the door from the
dressing-room opened, and George came through.

'Well!' she said, staring at him, her face flushing;
'surely you are very late?'

He came up to her, and put his arms round her, while
she stood passive. 'Not so very,' he said, and she
could hear that his voice was unsteady. 'How are you?
Give me a kiss, little woman—be a little glad to see me!'

He looked down upon her wistfully. On the journey
he had been conscious of great weariness of mind and
body, a longing to escape from struggle, to give and receive the balm of kind looks and soft words. He had
come back full of repentance towards her, if she had only
known, full too of a natural young longing for peace and
good times.

She let him kiss her, but as he stooped to her it

suddenly struck her that she had never seen him look so white and worn. Still; after all this holiday-making! Why? For love of a woman who never gave him a thought, except of pity. Bitterness possessed her. She turned away indifferently.

'Well, you'll only just have time to dress. Is some one unpacking for you?'

He looked at her.

'Is that all you have to say?'

She threw back her head and was silent.

'I was very glad to come back to you,' he said, with a sigh, 'though I—I wish it were anywhere else than here. But, all things considered, I did not see how to refuse. And you have been here the whole fortnight?'

'Yes.'

'Have you'—he hesitated—'have you seen a great deal of Lady Maxwell?'

'Well, I suppose I have—in her own house.' Then she broke out, her heart leaping visibly under her light dressing-gown. 'I don't blame *her* any more, if you want to know that; she doesn't think of anyone in the world but him.'

The gesture of her hand seemed to pursue the voice that had been just speaking in the corridor.

He smiled.

'Well, at least I'm glad you've come to see that!' he said quietly. 'And is that all?'

He had walked away from her, but at his renewed question he turned back quickly, his hands in his pockets. Something in the look of him gave her a moment of pleasure, a throb of possession. But she showed nothing of it.

'No, it's not all'—her pale blue eyes pierced him. 'Why did you go and see her that morning, and why have you never told me since?'

He started, and shrugged his shoulders.

'If you have been seeing much of her,' he replied, after a pause, 'you probably know as much as I could tell you.'

'No,' she said steadily; 'she has told me much about everything—but that.'

He walked restlessly about for a few seconds, then returned, holding out his hands.

'Well, my dear, I said some mad and miserable things. They are as dead now as if they had never been spoken. And they were not love-making—they were crying for the moon. Take me, and forget them. I am an unsatisfactory sort of fellow, but I will do the best I can.'

'Wait a bit,' she said, retreating, and speaking with a hard incisiveness. 'There are plenty of things you don't know. Perhaps you don't know, for instance, that I wrote to Lord Maxwell? I sat up writing it that night—he got it the same morning you saw her.'

'You wrote to Maxwell!' he said in amazement—then, under his breath—'to complain of her. My God!'

He walked away again, trying to control himself.

'You didn't suppose,' she said huskily, 'I was going to sit down calmly under your neglect of me? I might have been silly in not—not seeing what kind of a woman she was; that's different—besides, of course she ought to have thought more about me. But *that's* not all!'

Her hand shook as she stood leaning on the sofa. George turned, and looked at her attentively.

'The day you left I went to Hampton Court with the Lucys. Cathedine was there. Of course I flirted with him all the time, and as we were going through a wood near the river he said abominable things to me, and kissed me.'

Her brows were drawn defiantly. Her eyes seemed to be riveted to his. He was silent a moment, the colour dyeing his pale face deep. Then she heard his long breath.

'Well, we seem to be about quits,' he said, in a bitter voice. 'Have you seen him since?'

'No. That's Grier knocking—you'd better go and dress.'

He paused irresolutely. But Letty said, 'Come in,' and he retreated into his dressing-room.

Husband and wife hurried down together, without another word to each other. When George at last found himself at table between Lady Leven and Mr. Bayle's new and lively wife, he had never been so grateful before to the ease of women's tongues. In his mental and physical fatigue, he could scarcely bear even to let himself feel the strangeness of his presence in this room—at her table, in Maxwell's splendid house. *Not* to feel!—somehow to recover his old balance and coolness—that was the cry of the inner man.

But the situation conquered him. *Why* was he here? It was barely a month since in her London drawing-room he had found words for an emotion, a confession it now burnt him to remember. And here he was, breaking bread with her and Maxwell, a few weeks afterwards, as though nothing lay between them but a political incident. Oh! the smallness, the triviality of our modern life!

Was it only four weeks, or nearly? What he had suffered in that time! An instant's shudder ran through him, during an interval, while Betty's unwilling occupation with her left-hand neighbour left memory its chance. All the flitting scenes of the past month, Ancoats's half-vicious absurdities, the humours of the Trouville beach, the waves of its grey sea, his mother's whims and plaints, the crowd and heat of the little German watering-place where he had left her—was it he, George Tressady, that had been really wrestling with these things and persons, walking among them, or beside them? It seemed hardly credible. What was real, what remained, was merely the thought of some hours of solitude, beside the Norman sea, or among the great beech-woods that swept down the hills about Bad Wildheim. Those hours—they only—had stung, had penetrated, had found the shrinking core of the soul.

What in truth was it that had happened to him? After weeks of a growing madness he had finally lost his self-command, had spoken passionately, as only love speaks, to a married woman, who had no thought for any man in the world but her husband, a woman who had immediately—so he had always read the riddle of Maxwell's behaviour—reported every incident of his conversation with her to the husband, and had then tried her best, with an exquisite kindness and compunction, to undo the mischief her own charm had caused. For that effort, in the first instance, George, under the shock of his act and her pain, had been, at intervals, speechlessly grateful to her; all his energies had gone into pitiful, eager response. Now, her attempt, and Maxwell's share in it, seemed to have laid him under a weight he could no longer bear. His acceptance of Maxwell's invitation had finally exhausted his power of playing the superhuman part to which she had invited him. He wished with all his heart he had not accepted it! From the moment of her greeting—with its mixture of shrinking and sweetness—he had realised the folly, the humiliation even, of his presence in her house. He could not rise—it was monstrous, ludicrous almost, that she should wish it—to what she seemed to ask of him.

What had he been in love with? He looked at her once or twice in bewilderment. Had not she herself, her dazzling, unconscious purity, debarred him always from the ordinary hopes and desires of the sensual man? His very thought had moved in awe of her, had knelt before her. Throughout there had been this half-bitter glorying in the strangeness of his own case. The common judgment, in its common vileness, mattered nothing to him. He had been in love with love, with grace, with tenderness, with delight. He had seen, too late, a vision of the *best*; had realised what things of enchantment life contains for the few, for the chosen—what woman at her richest can be to man. And there had been a cry of personal longing—personal anguish.

Well!—it was all done with. As for friendship, it was impossible, grotesque. Let him go home, appease Letty, and mend his life. He constantly realised now, with the same surprise, as on the night before his confession, the emergence within himself, independent as it were of his ordinary will, and parallel with the voice of passion or grief, of some new moral imperative. Half scornfully he discerned in his own nature the sort of paste that a man inherits from generations of decent dull forefathers who have kept the law as they understood it. He was conscious of the same 'ought' vibrating through the moral sense as had governed their narrower lives and minds. It is the presence or the absence indeed of this dumb compelling power that in moments of crisis differentiates one man from another. He felt it; wondered perhaps that he should feel it; but knew, nevertheless, that he should obey it. Yes, let him go home, make his wife forgive him, rear his children—he trusted to God there would be children!—and tame his soul. How strange to feel this tempest sweeping through him, this iron stiffening of the whole being, amid this scene, in this room, within a few feet of that magic, that voice——

'Thank goodness I have got rid of my man at last!'

said Betty's laughing whisper in his ear. 'Three successive packs of hounds have I followed from their cradles to their graves. Make it up to me, Sir George, at once! Tell me everything I want to know!'

George turned to her smiling.

'About Ancoats?'

'Of course. Now don't be discreet!—I know too much already. How did he receive you?'

George laughed—not noticing that, instead of laughing with him, little Betty was staring at him open-eyed over her fan.

'To begin with, he invited me to fight—coffee and pistols before eight, on the following morning, in the garden of his chalet, which would not have been at all a bad place, for he is magnificently installed. I came from his enemies, he said. They had prevented the woman he loved from joining him, and covered him with ridicule. As their representative I ought to be prepared to face the consequences like a man. All this time he was storming up and down, in a marvellous blue embroidered smoking suit——'

'Of course, to go with the hair,' put in Betty.

'I said I thought he'd better give me some dinner before we talked it out. Then he looked embarrassed, and said there were friends coming. I replied, "*Tant mieux.*" He inquired fiercely whether it was the part of a gentleman to thrust himself where he wasn't wanted. I kept my temper, and said I was too famished to consider. Then he haughtily left the room, and presently a servant came and asked for my luggage, which I had left at the station, and showed me a bedroom. Ancoats, however, appeared again to invite me to withdraw, and to suggest the names of two seconds who would, he assured me, be delighted to act for me. I pointed out to him that I was unpacked, and that to turn me out dinnerless would be simply barbarous. Then, after fidgeting about a little, he burst out laughing in an odd way, and said, " Very well— only, mind, I didn't ask you." Sure enough, of course, I found a party.'

George paused.

' You needn't tell me much about the party,' said Betty, nervously, ' unless it's necessary.'

' Well, it wasn't a very reputable affair, and two young women were present.'

' No need to talk about the young women,' said Betty, hastily.

George bowed submission.

' I only mentioned them because they are rather neces- sary to the story. Anyway, by the time the company was settled Ancoats suddenly threw off his embarrassment, and, with some defiant looks at me, behaved himself, I imagine, much as he would have done without me. When all the guests were gone, I asked him whether he was going to keep up the farce of a *grande passion* any more. He got in a rage and vowed that if " she " had come, of course all those creatures, male and female, would be packed off. I didn't suppose that he would allow the woman he loved to come within a mile of them ? I shrugged my shoulders and declined to suppose any- thing about his love affairs, which seemed to me too complicated. Then, of course, I had to come to plain speaking, and bring in his mother.

' That she should have produced such a being ! ' cried Betty ; ' that he should have any right in her at all ! '

' That she should keep such a heart for him ! ' said George, raising his eyebrows. ' He turned rather white, I was relieved to see, when I told him from her that she would leave his house if the London affair went on. Well, we walked up and down in his garden, smoking, the greater part of the night, till I could have dropped with fatigue. Every now and then Ancoats would make a dash for the brandy and soda on the verandah ; and in between I had to listen to tirades against marriage, English prudery, and English women—quotations from Gautier and Renan—and heaven knows what. At last, when we were both worn out, he suddenly stood still and delivered his ultimatum. " Look here—if you think I've no grievances, you're much mistaken. Go back and tell my mother that if she'll marry Fontenoy straight away I'll give up Marguerite ! " I said I would deliver no such impertinence. "Very well," he said ; "then I will. Tell her I shall be in Paris next week, and ask her to meet me there. When are you going ? " " Well," I said, rather taken aback, " there is such an institution as the post. Now I've come so far, suppose you show me Trouville for a few days ? " . He muttered something or other, and we went to bed. Afterwards, he behaved to me quite charmingly, would not let me go, and I ended by leaving him at the door of an hotel in Paris where he was to meet his mother. But on the subject of Fontenoy it is an *idée fixe.* He chafes under the whole position, and will yield nothing to a man who, as he conceives, has ne *locus standi.* But if his pride were no longer annoyed by its being said that his mother had sacrificed her own happiness to him, and if the situation were defined, I *think* he might be more amenable. I think they might marry him.'

'That's how the man puts it ! ' said Betty, tightening her lip. 'Of course *any* marriage is desirable for *any* woman ! '

'I was thinking of Mrs. Allison,' said George, defensively. 'One can't think of a Lady Ancoats till she exists.'

'*Merci !* Never mind. Don't apologise for the masculine view. It has to be taken with the rest of you. Do you understand that matrimony is in the air here to-night? Have you been talking to Lady Madeleine?'

'No, not yet. But how handsome she's grown! I see Naseby's not far off.'

George turned smiling to his companion. But, as he did so, again, something cold and lifeless in his own face and in the expression underlying the smile pricked little Betty painfully. Marcella had made her no confidences, but there had been much gossip, and Letty Tressady's mere presence at the Court set the intimate friend guessing very near the truth.

She did her best to chatter on, so as to keep him at least superficially amused. But both became more and more conscious of two figures, and two figures only, at the crowded table—Letty Tressady, who was listening absently to Edward Watton with oppressed and indrawn eyes, and Lady Maxwell.

George, indeed, watched his wife constantly. He hungered to know more of that first scene between her and Lady Maxwell, or he thought with bitter repulsion of the letter she had confessed to him. Had he known of it,— in spite of that strange, that compelling letter of Maxwell's, so reticent, and yet in truth so plain—he could hardly have come as a guest to Maxwell's house. As for her revelations about Cathedine, he felt little resentment or excitement. For the future a noxious brute had to be kept in order—that was all. It was his own fault, he supposed, much more than hers. The inward voice, as before, was clear enough. 'I must just take her home and be good to her. *She* shirked nothing —now, no doubt, she expects me to do my part.'

'Do you notice those jewels that Lady Maxwell is wearing to-night?' said Betty at last, unable to keep away from the name.

'I imagine they are a famous set?'

'They belonged to Marie Antoinette. At last Maxwell has made her have them cleaned and reset. What
a pity to have such desperate scruples as she has about
all your pretty things!'

'Must diamonds and rubies, then, perish out of the
world?' he asked her, absently, letting his eyes rest again
upon the beautiful head and neck.

Betty made some flippant rejoinder, but as she watched
him she was not gay.

George had had but a few words with his hostess
before dinner, and afterwards a short conversation was
all that either claimed. She had hoped and planned so
much! On the stage of imagination—before he came—
she had seen his coming so often. All was to be forgotten and forgiven, and this difficult visit was to lead,
naturally and without recall, to another and happier relation. And now that he was here she felt herself tongue-
tied, moving near him in a dumb distress. Both realised
the pressure of the same necessities, the same ineluct-
able facts; and tacitly, they met and answered each
other, in the common avoidance of a companionship
which could after all avail nothing. Once or twice, as
they stood together after dinner, he noticed amid her
gracious kindness, her inquiries after Mrs. Allison or
his mother, the search her eyes made for Letty, and
presently she began to talk with nervous, almost appealing, emphasis — with a marked significance and
intensity indeed—of Letty's fatigue after her nursing,
and the need she had for complete change and rest.
George found himself half-resenting the implications of
her manner, as the sentences flowed on. He felt her
love of influence, and was not without a hidden sarcasm.
In spite of his passionate gratitude to her, he must needs

ask himself, did she suppose that a man or a marriage was to be re-made in a month, even by her plastic fingers ? Women envisaged these things so easily, so childishly, almost.

When he moved away, a number of men who had already been talking to him after dinner, and some of the most agreeable women of the party besides, closed about him, making him, as it were, the centre of a conversation which was concerned almost entirely with the personalities and chances of the political moment. He was scarcely less astonished than Letty had been by his own position amongst the guests gathered under Maxwell's roof. Never had he been treated with so much sympathy, so much deference even. Clearly, if he willed it so, what had seemed the dislocation might only be the better beginning of a career. Nonsense ! He meant to throw it all up as soon as Parliament met again in February. The state of his money affairs alone determined that. The strike was going from bad to worse. He must go home and look after his own business. It was a folly ever to have attempted political life. Meanwhile he felt the stimulus of his reception in a company which included some of the keenest brains in England. It appealed to his intelligence and virility, and they responded. Letty once, glancing at him, saw that he was talking briskly, and said to herself, with contradictory bitterness, that he was looking as well as ever, and was going, she supposed, to behave as if nothing had happened.

' What is the matter with you to-night, my lady ? ' said Naseby, taking a seat beside his hostess. ' May I be impertinent and guess ?—you don't like your gems ? Lady Leven has been telling me tales about them. They are the most magnificent things I ever saw. I condole with you.'

She turned rather listlessly to meet his bantering look.

' " Come you in friendship, or come you in war? " ' she said. ' I have no fight in me. But I have a great many things to say to you.'

He reddened for an instant, then recovered himself.

' So have I to you,' he said briskly. ' In the first place, I have some fresh news from Mile End.'

She half laughed, as who should say, ' You put me off,' then surrendered herself with eagerness to the pleasure of his report. At the moment of his approach, under pretence of talking to an elderly cousin of Maxwell's, she had been lost in such an abstraction of powerless pity for George Tressady—whose fair head, somehow, never escaped her, wherever it moved—that she had hardly been able to bear with her guests or the burden of the evening.

But Naseby roused her. And, indeed, his story so far was one to set the blood throbbing in the veins of a creature who, on one side pure woman, was on the other half-poet, half-reformer. Since the passage of the Max- well Bill, indeed, Naseby and a few friends of his, some ' gilded youths ' like himself, together with some trade- union officials of a long experience, had done wonders. They had been planning out the industrial reorganisation of a whole district, through its two staple trades, with the enthusiastic co-operation of the workpeople themselves ; and the result so far struck the imagination. Everywhere the old workshops were to be bought up, improved, or closed ; everywhere factories in which life might be decent, and work more than tolerable, were to be set up ; everywhere the prospective shortening of hours and the doing away with the most melancholy of the home trades was working already like the incoming of a great slowly- surging tide, raising a whole population on its breast to another level of well-being and of hope.

Most of what had been done or designed was of course already well known to Maxwell's wife; she had indeed given substantial help to Naseby throughout. But Naseby had some fresh advances to report since she was last in East London, and she drank them in with an eagerness, which somehow assuaged a hidden smart; while he wondered a little perhaps in his philosopher's soul at the woman of our English day, with her compunctions and altruisms, her entanglement with the old scheme of things, her pining for a new. It had often seemed to him that to be a Nihilist nurse among a Russian peasantry would be an infinitely easier task than to reconcile the social remorses and compassions that tore his companion's mind with the social pageant in which her life, do what she would, must needs be lived. He knew that, intellectually, she no more than Maxwell saw any way out of unequal place, unequal spending, unequal recompense, if civilisation were to be held together; but he perceived that morally she suffered. Why? Because she and not some one else had been chosen to rule the palace and wear the gems that yet must be? In the end, Naseby could but shrug his shoulders over it. Yet even his sceptical temper made no question of sincerity.

When all his budget was out, and her comments made, she leant back a little in her chair, studying him. A smile came to play about her lips.

' What do you want to say to me?' he asked her quickly.

She looked round her to see that they were not over-heard.

' When did you see Madeleine last?'

' At her brother's house, a fortnight ago.'

' Was she nice to you?'

He bit his lip, and drew his brows a little together, under her scrutiny.

'Do you imagine I am going to be cross-examined like this?'

'Yes—reply!'

'Well, I don't know what her conception of "niceness" may be; it didn't fit mine. She had got it into her head that I "pitied" her, which seemed to be a crime. I didn't see how to disprove it, so I came away.'

He spoke with a dry lightness, but she perceived anxiety and unrest under his tone. She bent forward.

'Do you know where Madeleine is now?'

'Not in the least.'

'In the Long Gallery. I sent her there.'

'Upon my word!' he said, after a pause. 'Do you want to rule us all?' His cheek had flushed again; his look was half rebellious.

A flash of pain struck through her brightness.

'No, no!' she said, protesting. 'But I know—you don't!'

He rose deliberately, and bowed with the air of obeying her commands. Then suddenly he bent down to her.

'I knew perfectly well that she was in the Long Gallery! But I also knew that Mrs. Bayle had chosen to join her there. The coast, you may perceive, is now clear.'

He walked away. Marcella looked round, and saw an elegant little bride, Mr. Bayle's new wife, rustling into the room again. She leant back in her chair, half laughing, yet her eyes were wet. The new joy brought a certain ease to old regrets. Only that word 'rule' rankled a little.

Yet the old regrets were all sharp and active again. It seemed to be impossible now to talk with George Tressady, to make any real breach in the barrier between them; but how impossible also not to think of him!—of the young fellow, who had given Maxwell his reward, and said to herself such sad, such agitating things! She did think of him. Her heart ached to serve him. The situation made a new and a very troubling appeal to her womanhood.

The night was warm and still, and the windows were open to it as they had been on that May night at Castle Luton. Maxwell came to look for Tressady, and took him out upon a flagged terrace that ran the length of the house.

They talked first of the Ancoats incident, George supplementing his letters by some little verbal pictures of Ancoats's life and surroundings that made Maxwell laugh grimly from time to time. As to Mrs. Allison, Maxwell reported that Ancoats seemed to have gained his point. There was talk of the marriage coming off some time in the winter.

'Well, Fontenoy has earned his prize,' said George.

'There are more than twelve years between them. But she seems to be one of the women who don't age. I have seen her go through griefs that would kill most women ; and it has been like the passage of a storm over a flower.'

'Religion, I suppose, carried to that point, protects one a good deal,' said George, not, in truth, feeling much interest in the matter or in Mrs. Allison now that his task was done.

'And especially religion of the type that allows you to give your soul into some one else's keeping. There is no such anodyne,' said Maxwell, musing. 'I have often noticed how Catholic women keep their youth and softness. But now, do allow me a few words about yourself. Is what I hear about your withdrawal from Parliament irrevocable ? '

George's reply led to a discussion in which Maxwell without any attempt at party proselytism, endeavoured to combat all that he could understand of the young man's twofold disgust, disgust with his own random convictions no less than with the working of the party machine.

'Where do I belong?' he said. 'I don't know myself. I ought never to have gone in. Anyway, I had better stand aside for a time.'

'But evidently the Malford people want to keep you.'

'Well, and of course I shall consult their convenience as much as I can,' said George, unwillingly, but would say no more.

Nothing, indeed, could be more flattering, more healing, than all that was implied in Maxwell's earnestness, in the peculiar sympathy and kindness with which the elder man strove to win the younger's confidence; but George could not respond. His whole inner being was too sore; and his mind ran incomparably more upon the damnable letter that must be lying somewhere in the archives of the memory of the man talking to him, than upon his own political prospects. The conversation ended for Maxwell in mere awkwardness and disappointment—deep disappointment if the truth were known. Once roused, his idealism was little less stubborn, less wilful, than Marcella's.

When the ladies withdrew, a brilliant group of them stood for a moment on the first landing of the great oak staircase, lighting candles and chattering. Madeleine Penley took her candle absently from Marcella's hand, saying nothing. The girl's curious face under its crown of gold-red hair was transformed somehow to an extraordinary beauty. The frightened parting of the lips and lifting of the brows had become rather a look of exquisite surprise, as of one who knows at last 'the very heart of love.'

'I am coming to you, presently,' murmured Marcella, laying her cheek against the girl's.

'Oh, *do* come!' said Madeleine, with a great breath, and she walked away, unsteadily, by herself, into the darkness of the tapestried passage, her white dress floating behind her.

Marcella looked after her, then turned with shining eyes to Letty Tressady. Her expression changed.

'I am afraid your headache has been very bad all the evening,' she said penitently. 'Do let me come and look after you.'

She went with Letty to her room, and put her into a chair beside the wood fire, that even on this warm night was not unwelcome in the huge place. Letty, indeed, shivered a little as she bent towards it.

'Must you go so early?' said Marcella, hanging over her. 'I heard Sir George speak of the ten o'clock train.'

'Oh, yes,' said Letty, 'that will be best.'

She stared into the fire without speaking. Marcella knelt down beside her.

'You won't hate me any more?' she said, in a low, pleading voice, taking two cold hands in her own.

Letty looked up.

'I should like,' she said, speaking with difficulty, 'if you cared—to see you sometimes.'

'Only tell me when,' said Marcella, laying her lips lightly on the hands, 'and I will come.' Then she hesitated. 'Oh, do believe,' she broke out at last, but still in the same low voice, 'that all can be healed! Only show him love—forget everything else—and happiness must come. Marriage is so difficult—such an art—even for the happiest people, one has to learn it afresh day by day.'

Letty's tired eyes wavered under the other's look.

'I can't understand it like that,' she said. Then she

L L

moved restlessly in her chair. 'Ferth is a terrible place! I wonder how I shall bear it!'

An hour later Marcella left Madeleine Penley and went back to her own room. The smile and flush with which she had received the girl's last happy kisses disappeared as she walked along the corridor. Her head drooped, her arms hung listlessly beside her.

Maxwell found her in her own little sitting-room almost in the dark. He sat down by her and took her hand.

'You couldn't make any impression on him as to Parliament?' she asked him, almost whispering.

'No. He persists that he must go. I think his private circumstances at Ferth have a great deal to do with it.'

She shook her head. She turned away from him, took up a paper-knife, and let it fall on the table beside her. He thought that she must have been in tears, before he found her, and he saw that she could find no words in which to express herself. Lifting her hand to his lips, he held it there, silently, with a touch all tenderness.

'Oh, why am I so happy!' she broke out at last, with a sob, almost drawing her hand away. 'Such a life as mine seems to absorb and batten upon other people's dues—to grow rich by robbing their joy, joy that should feed hundreds and comes all to me! And that besides I should actually bruise and hurt——'

Her voice failed her.

'Fate has a way of being tolerably even, at last,' said Maxwell, slowly, after a pause. 'As to Tressady, no one can say what will come of it. He has strange stuff in him—fine stuff I think. He will pull himself together. And for the wife—probably, already he owes you much!

I saw her look at you to-night—once as you touched her
shoulder.   Dear!—what spells have you been using?'

'Oh! I will do all I can—all I can!' Marcella repeated in a low passionate voice, as one who makes a
vow to her own heart.

'But after to-morrow he will not willingly come
across us again,' said Maxwell, quietly.   'That I saw.'   '

She gave a sad and wordless assent.

CHAPTER XXIII

LETTY TRESSADY sat beside the doorway of one of the small red-brick houses that make up the village of Ferth. It was a rainy October afternoon, and through the door she could see the black main street—houses and road alike bedabbled in wet and mire. At one point in the street her eye caught a small standing crowd of women and children, most of them with tattered shawls thrown over their heads to protect them from the weather. She knew what it meant. They were waiting for the daily opening of the soup kitchen, started in the third week of the great strike by the Baptist minister, who, in the language of the Tory paper, was 'among the worst fire-brands of the district.' There was another soup kitchen farther down, to which George had begun to subscribe immediately on his return to the place. She had thought it a foolish act on his part thus to help his own men to fight him the better. But—now, as she watched the miserable crowd outside the Baptist chapel, she felt the teasing pressure of those new puzzles of her married life which had so far done little else, it seemed, than take away her gaiety and her power of amusing herself.

Near her sat an oldish woman with an almost tooth-less mouth, who was chattering to her in a tone that Letty knew to be three parts hypocritical.

'Well, the treüth is the men is that fool'ardy when they gets a thing into their yeds, there's no taakin wi un. There's plenty as dōne like the strike, my lady, but they dursent say so—they'd be afeard o losin the skin off their backs, for soom o them lads o Bewick's is a routin rough lot as dōnc keer what they doos to a mon, an yo canna cxspeck a quiet body to stan up agen em. Now, my son, ee comes in at neet all slamp and downcast, an I says to im, "Is there noa news yet o the Jint Committee, John?" I ses to un. "Noa, mither," ee says, "they're just keepin ov it on." An ee do seem so down'earted when ee sees the poor soart ov a supper as is aw I can gic un to is stomach. Now, *I'm* wun o thoase as *wants* nuthin. The doctor ses, "Yo've got no blude in yer, Missus 'Ammersley, what ull yer ave?" An I says, "*Nuthin!*" It's sūn cut, an it's sūn cooked, *nuthin!* Noa, I've niver bin on t' parish—an I *might*—times. An I don't old wi strikes. Lor, it is a poor pleace, is ours—ain't it?—an nobbut a bit o bread an drippin for supper.'

The old woman threw her eyes round her kitchen, bringing them back slyly to Letty's face. Letty ended by leaving some money with her, and walking away as dissatisfied with her own charity as she was with its recipient. Perhaps this old body was the only person in the village who would have begged of 'Tressady's wife' at this particular moment. Letty, moreover, had some reason to believe that her son was one of the roughest of Bewick's bodyguard; while the old woman was certainly no worse off than any of her neighbours.

Outside, she was disturbed to find as she walked home, that the street was full of people, in spite of the rain—of gaunt men and pinched women, who threw her hostile and sidelong glances as she passed. She hurried through them. How was it that she knew nothing of them—except, perhaps, of the few toadies and parasites among them? How was one to penetrate into this ugly,

incomprehensible world of ' the people ' ? The mere idea
of trying to do so filled her with distaste and *ennui*. She
was afraid of them. She wished she had not stayed so
long with that old gossip, Mrs. Hammersley, and that there
were not so many yards of dark road between her and
her own gate. Where was George? She knew that he
had gone up to the pits that afternoon to consult his
manager about some defect in the pumping arrangements.
She wished she had secured his escort for the walk home.

But before she left the village she paused irresolutely,
then turned down a side street, and went to see Mary
Batchelor, George's old nurse, the mother who had lost
her only son in his prime.

When, a few minutes later, she came up the lane, she
was flatly conscious of having done a virtuous thing—
several virtuous things—that afternoon, but certainly
without any pleasure in them. She did not get on with
Mary, nor Mary with her. The tragic absorption of the
mother—little abated since the spring—in her dead boy
seemed somehow to strike Letty dumb. She felt pity, but
yet the whole emotion was beyond her, and she shrank
from it. As for Mary, she had so far received Lady
Tressady's visits with a kind of dull surprise, always
repeated and not flattering. Letty believed that, in her
inmost heart, the broken woman was offended each time
that it was not George who came. Moreover, though she
never said a word of it to Tressady's wife, she was known
to be passionately on the side of the strikers, and her
manner gave the impression that she did not want to be
talking with their oppressors. Perhaps it was this feeling
that had reconciled her to the loutish lad who lived with
her, and had been twice ' run in ' by the police for stone-
throwing at non-union men since the beginning of the
strike. At any rate, she took a great deal more notice of
him than she had done.

No—they were not very satisfactory, these attempts of Letty's in the village. She thought of them with a kind of inner exasperation as she walked home. She had been going to a few old and sick people, and trying to ignore the strike. But at bottom she felt an angry resentment towards these loafing, troublesome fellows, who filled the village street when they ought to have been down in the pits—who were starving their own children no less than disturbing and curtailing the incomes of their betters. Did they suppose that people were going to run pits for them for nothing? Their drink and their religion seemed to her equally hideous. She hated the two Dissenting ministers of the place only less than Valentine Bewick himself, and delighted to pass their wives with her head high in air.

With these general feelings towards the population in her mind, why these efforts at consolation and almsgiving? Well, the poor old people were not responsible; but she did not see that any good had come of it. She had said nothing about her visits to George, nor did she suppose that he had noticed them. He had been so incessantly busy since their arrival with conferences and committees that she had seen very little of him. It was generally believed that the strike was nearing its end, and that the men were exhausted; but she did not think that George was very hopeful yet.

Presently, as she neared a dark slope of road, bordered with trees on one side and the high ' bank ' of the main pit on the other, her thoughts turned back to their natural and abiding subject—herself. Oh, the dulness of life at Ferth during the last three weeks! She thought of her amusements in town, of the country houses where they might now be staying but for George's pride, of Cathedine, even; and a rush of revolt and self-pity filled her mind. George always away, nothing to do in the ugly

house, and Lady Tressady coming directly—she said to
herself, suffocating, her small hands stiffening, that she
felt fit to kill herself.

Half-way down the slope she heard steps behind her
in the gathering darkness, and at the same moment
something struck her violently on the shoulder. She
cried out, and clutched at some wooden railings along the
road for support, as the lump of ' dirt' from the bank
which had been flung at her dropped beside her.

' Letty, is that you?' shouted a voice from the direction of the village—her husband's voice. She heard
running. In a few seconds George had reached her and
was holding her.

' What is it struck you? I see! Cowards! *damned*
cowards! Has it broken your arm? Try and move it.'

Sick with pain she tried to obey him. ' No,' she said
faintly; ' it is not broken—I think not.'

' Good!' he cried, rejoicing; ' probably only a bad
bruise. The brute mercifully picked up nothing very
hard '—and he pushed the lump with his foot. ' Take
my scarf, dear; let me sling it. Ah!—what was that?
Letty! can you be brave—can you let me go one minute?
I shan't be out of your sight.'

And he pointed excitedly to a dark spot moving among
the bushes along the lower edge of the ' bank.'

Letty nodded. ' I can stay here.'

George leapt the palings and ran. The dark spot ran
too, but in queer leaps and bounds. There was the sound
of a scuffle, then George returned, dragging some thing or
some one behind him.

' I knew it,' he said, panting, as he came within
earshot of his wife; ' it was that young ruffian, Mary
Batchelor's grandson! Now you stand still, will you?
I could hold two of the likes of you with one hand.
Madan!'

He had but just parted from his manager on the path which led sideways up the 'bank,' and waited anxiously to see if his voice would reach the Scotchman's ears. But no one replied. He shouted again; then he put two fingers in his mouth and whistled loudly towards the pit, holding the struggling lad all the time.

At the same moment a couple of heavily built men, evidently colliers, came down the road from the village. George at once called to them from across the palings.

'Here, you there! this young rascal has been throwing a lump of dirt at Lady Tressady, and has hit her badly on the arm. Will you two just walk him up to the police-station for me, while I take my wife home?'

The two men stopped and stared at the lady by the railings and at Sir George holding the boy, whose white but grinning face was just visible in the growing dusk.

'Noa,' said one of them at last, 'it's noa business ov ourn—is it, Bill?'

'Noa,' said the other stolidly; and on they tramped.

'Oh, you heroes!' George flung after them. 'Attacking a woman in the dark is about what you understand!
—Madan!'

He whistled again, and this time there was a hurrying from overhead.

'Sir George!'

'Come down here, will you, at once!'

In a few more minutes the boy was being marched up the road to the police-station in charge of the strong-wristed Scotch manager, and George was free to attend to Letty.

He adjusted a sling very fairly, then made her cling to him with her sound arm; and they were soon inside their own gates.

'You can't climb this hill,' he said to her anxiously. 'Rest at the lodge, and let me go for the brougham.'

'I can walk perfectly well—and it will be much quicker.'

Involuntarily, he was surprised to find her rather belittling than exaggerating the ill. As they climbed on in the dark, he helping her as much as he could, both could not but think of another accident and another victim. Letty found herself imagining again and again what the scene with Lady Maxwell, after the East-End meeting, might have been like; while, as for him, a face drew itself upon the rainy dusk, which the will seemed powerless to blot out. It was a curious and unwelcome coincidence. His secret sense of it made him the more restlessly kind.

'What were you in the village for?' he asked, bending to her; 'I did not know you had anything to do there!'

'I had been to see old Bessie Hammersley and Mrs. Batchelor,' she said, in a tone that tried to be stiff or indifferent. 'Bessie begged, as usual.'

'That was very good of you. Have you been doing visiting, then, during all these days I have been away?'

'Yes—a few people.'

George groaned.

'What's the use of it—or of anything? They hate us, and we them. This strike begins to eat into my very being. And the men will be beaten soon, and the feeling towards the employers will be worse than ever.'

'You are sure they will be beaten?'

'Before Christmas, any way. I daresay there will be some bad times first. To think a woman even can't walk these roads without danger of ill-treatment! How is one to have any dealings with the brutes, or any peace with them?' ·

His rage and bitterness made her somehow feel her bruises less. She even looked up in protest.

'Well, it was only a boy, and you used to think he wasn't all there.'

'Oh! all there!' said George scornfully. 'There'd be half of them in Bedlam if one had to make that excuse for them. There isn't a day passes without some devilry against the non-union men somewhere. It was only this morning I heard of two men being driven into a reservoir near Rilston, and stoned in the water.'

'Perhaps we should do the same,' she said unwillingly.

'Lean on me more heavily—we shall soon be there. You think we should be brutes too? Probably. We seem to be all brutes for each other—that's the charming way this competitive world is managed. So you have been looking after some of the old people, have you? You must have had a dull time of it this last three weeks —don't think I don't know that!'

He spoke with emotion. He thought he felt her grasp waver a little on his arm, but she did not speak.

'Suppose—when this business was over—I were to cut the whole concern—let the pits and the house, and go right away? I daresay I could.'

'Could you?' she said eagerly.

'We shouldn't get so much money, you know, as in the best years. But then it would be certain. What would you say to a thousand a year less?' he asked her, trying to speak lightly.

'Well, it doesn't seem easy to get on with what we have—even if we had it,' she said sharply.

He understood the reference to his mother's debts, and was silent.

But evidently the recollection, once introduced, generated the usual heat and irritation in her, for, as they neared the front door, she suddenly said, with an acerbity he had not heard for some weeks:

'Of course, to have a country house, and not to be able to spend a farthing upon it—to ask your friends, or have anything decent—is enough to make anyone sick of it.

And, above all, when we needn't have been here at all
this October——'

She stopped, shrinking from the rest of the sentence,
but not before he had time to think, ' She say *that !*—
monstrous ! '

Aloud he coldly replied :

' It is difficult to see where I could have been but
here, this October.'

Then the door opened, and the light showed her to
him pale, with lips tight pressed from the pain of her
injury. Instantly he forgot everything but his natural
pity and chivalry towards women. He led her in, and
half carried her upstairs. A little later she was resting
on her bed, and he had done everything he could for her
till the doctor should come. She seemed to have passed
into an eclipse of temper or moodiness, and he got little
gratitude.

The evening post brought her a letter which he took
up to her himself. He knew the clear, rapid hand, and
he knew, too, that Letty had received many such during
the preceding month. He stood beside her a moment,
almost on the point of asking her to let him see it. But
the words died on his lips. And, perceiving that she would
not read it while he was there, he went away again.

When he returned, carrying a new book and asking if
he should read to her, he found her lying with her check
on her hand, staring into the fire, and so white and
miserable that his heart sank. Had he married her, a
girl of twenty-four, only to destroy her chance of happiness altogether ? A kind of terror seized him. He had
been 'good to her,' so far as she and his business had
allowed him, since their return ; there had been very little
outward jarring; but no one knew better than he that
there had not been one truly frank or reconciling moment.
His own inner life during these weeks had passed in one

obscure continuous struggle—a sort of dull fever of the soul. And she had simply held herself aloof from him.

He knelt down beside her, and laid his face against hers.

'Don't look so unhappy!' he said in a whisper, caressing her free hand. She did not answer or make any response till, as he got up again in a kind of despair as to what to do or say next, she hastily asked:

'Has the constable been up here to see you?'

He looked at her in surprise.

'Yes. It is all arranged. The lad will be brought up before the magistrates on Thursday.'

She fidgeted, then said abruptly:

'I should like him to be let off.'

He hesitated.

'That's very nice of you, but it wouldn't be very good for the district.'

She did not press the matter, but as he moved away she said fretfully:

'I wish you'd read to me. The pain's horrid.'

Thankful, in his remorse, to do anything for her, he tried to amuse and distract her as he best could. But in the middle of a magazine story she interrupted him:

'Isn't it the day after to-morrow your mother's coming?'

'According to her letter this morning.' He put down the book. 'But I don't think you'll be at all fit to look after her. Shall I write to-night and suggest that she stays in London a little?'

'No. I shall be all right, the doctor says. I want to tell Esther'—Esther was the housemaid—'not to get the Blue Room ready for her. I looked in to-day, and it seemed damp. The back room over the dining-room is smaller, but it's much warmer.'

She turned to look at him with a rather flushed face.

'You know best,' he said, smiling. 'I am sure it will be all right. But I sha'n't let her come unless you are better.'

He went on reading till it grew late, and it seemed to him she was dropping off to sleep. He was stealing off by way of the large dressing-room near by, where he had been installed since their return, when she said faintly, 'Good-night!'

He returned, and felt the drawing of her hot hand. He stooped and kissed her. Then she turned away from him, and seemed to go instantly to sleep.

He went downstairs to his library, and gathered about him some documents he had brought back from the last meeting of the masters' committee, which had to be read. But in reality he spent an hour of random thought. When would she herself tell him anything of her relations to Lady Maxwell, of the nature and causes of that strange subjection which, as he saw quite plainly, had been brought about? She must know that he pined to know; yet she held her secret only the more jealously, no doubt to punish him.

He thought of her visits to the village, half humorously, half sadly; then of her speech about the Blue Room and his mother. They seemed to him signs of some influence at work.

But at last he turned back to his papers with a long impatient sigh. The clear pessimism with which he was wont to see facts that concerned himself maintained that all the surrounding circumstance of the case was as untoward as it could be—this dull house, a troubled district, his money affairs, the perpetual burden of his mother, Letty's own thirst for pleasure, and the dying down in himself of the feelings that might once—possibly—have made up to her for a good deal. The feelings might be simulated. Was the woman likely to be deceived? That she was capable of the fiercest jealousy had been made abundantly plain; and such a temper once roused would find a hundred new provocations, day by day, in the acts and doings of a husband who had ceased to be a lover.

Two days later Lady Tressady arrived, with Justine, and her dogs, and all her paraphernalia. She declared herself better, but she was a mere shadow of the woman who had tormented George with her debts and affectations at Malford House a twelvemonth before. She took Ferth discontentedly, as usual, and was particularly cross with Letty's assignment to her of the back room, instead of the larger spare room to the front of the house.

'Damp?—nonsense!' she said to Justine, who was trying to soothe her on the night she arrived. 'I suppose Lady Tressady has some friend of her own coming to stay—that's, of *course*, what it is. *C'est parfaitement clair, je te dis—parfaitement!*'

The French maid reminded her that her daughter-in-law had said, on showing her the room, she had only to express a wish to change, and the arrangements should be altered at once.

'I daresay,' cried Lady Tressady. 'But I shall ask *no* favours of her—and that, of course, she knew.'

'But, miladi, I need only speak to the housemaid.'

'Thank you! Then afterwards, whenever I had a pain or a finger-ache, it would be, "I told you so!" No! she has managed it very cleverly—very cleverly indeed! —and I shall let it alone.'

Thenceforward, however, there were constant complaints of everything provided for her—room, food, the dulness of the place, the manners of her daughter-in-law. Whether it was that her illness had now reached a stage when the will could no longer fight against it, and its only effect was demoralising; or whether the strange flash of courage and natural affection struck from the volatile nature by the first threat of death could not in any case have maintained itself, it is hard to say. At any rate, George also found it hard to keep up his new and better ways with her. The fact was, he suffered through Letty. In a few days his sympathies were all with her, and to his amazement he perceived before long that, in spite of occasional sharp speeches and sulky moments that only an angel could have forborne, she was really more patient under his mother's idiosyncrasies than he was. Yet Lady Tressady, even now, was rarely unmanageable in his presence, and could still restrain herself if it was a question of his comfort and repose; whereas, it was clear that she felt a cat-like impulse to torment Letty whenever she saw her.

One recent habit, however, bore with special heaviness on himself. Oddly enough, it was a habit of religious discussion. Lady Tressady in health had never troubled herself in the least as to what the doctors of the soul might have to say, and had generally gaily professed herself a sceptic in religious matters, mostly, as George had often thought, for the sake of escaping all inconvenient restrictions—such as family prayers, or keeping Sunday, or observing Lent—which might have got in the way of her amusements.

But now, poor lady, she was all curiosity and anxiety about this strange other side of things, and inclined, too, to be rather proud of the originality of her inquiries on the subject. So that night after night she would keep George up, after an exhausting day, till the small hours, while she declared her own views 'on God, on Nature and on Human Life,' and endeavoured to extract his. This latter part of the exercise was indeed particularly attractive to her; no doubt because of its difficulty. George had been a singularly reserved person in these respects all his life, and had no mind now to play the part of a coal-seam for his mother to 'pike' at. But 'pike' she would incessantly.

'Now, George, look here! what do you *really* think about a future life? Now don't try and get out of it! And don't just talk nonsense to me because you think I'm ill. I'm not a baby—I really am not. Tell me—seriously—what you think. Do you honestly expect there *is* a future life?'

'I've told you before, mother, that I have no particular thoughts on that subject. It isn't in my line,' George would say, smiling profanely, but uneasily, and wondering how long this bout of it might be going to last.

'Don't be shocking, George! You *must* have some ideas about it. Now, don't hum and haw—just tell me what you think.' And she would lean forward, all urgency and expectation.

A pause, during which George could think only of the ghastly figure on the sofa. She sat upright, generally, against a prop of cushions, dressed in a white French tea-gown, slim enough to begin with, but far too large now for the shrunk form—a bright spot of rouge on either pinched cheek, and the dyed 'fringe' and 'coils' covering all the once shapely head. Meanwhile her hand would play impatiently on her knee. The hand was skin and bone ; and the rings with which it was laden would often slip off from it to the floor—a diversion of which George was always prompt to avail himself.

'Why don't you talk to Mr. Fearon, mother?' he would say gently at last. 'It's his business to discuss these things.'

'Talk to a clergyman! thank you! I hope I have more respect for my own intelligence. What can a priest do for you? What does he know more than anybody else? But I do want to know what my own son thinks. Now, George, just answer me. If there *is* a future life'

—she spread out her hand slowly on her lap—'what do you suppose your father's doing at this moment? That's a thing I often think of, George. I don't think I want a future life if it's to be just like the past. You know—you remember how he used to be—poking about the house, and going down to the pits, and—and—swearing at the servants, and having rows with me about the accounts—and all his dear dreadful little ways? Yet, what else in the world can you imagine him doing? As to singing hymns!'

She raised her hands expressively.

George laughed, and puffed away at his cigarette. But as he still said nothing Lady Tressady began to frown.

'That's the way you always get out of my questions,' she said fretfully; 'it's so provoking of you.'

'I've recommended you to the professional,' he said, patting her hand. 'What else could I do?'

Her thin cheek flamed.

'As if we couldn't be certain, anyway,' she cried, 'that the Christians don't know anything about it. As M. d'Estrelles used to say to me at Monte Carlo, if there's one thing clear, it is that we needn't bother ourselves with *their* doctrines!'

'Needn't we?' said George. Then he looked at her, smiling. 'And you think M. d'Estrelles was an authority?'

Odd recollections began to run through his mind of this elderly French admirer of his mother's, whom he had seen occasionally flitting about their London lodgings when, as a boy, he came up from Eton for his *exeat*.

'Oh! don't you scoff, George,' said his mother, angrily. 'M. d'Estrelles was a very clever man, though he did gamble like a fool. Everybody said his memory was marvellous. He used to quote me pages out of Voltaire and the rest of them on the nights when we walked up and down the gardens at Monte Carlo, after he'd cleared himself out. He always said he didn't see why these things should be kept from women—why men shouldn't tell women exactly what they think. And I know he'd been a Catholic in his youth, so he'd had experience of both. However, I don't care about M. d'Estrelles. I want your opinions. Now, George!'—her voice would begin to break—'how can you be so unkind? You might really compose my mind a little, as the doctors say!'

And through her incorrigible levity he would see for a moment the terror which always possessed her raise its head. Then it would be time for him to go and put his arm round her, and try and coax her to bed.

One night, after he had taken her upstairs, he came down so wearied and irritable that he put all his letters aside, and tried to forget himself in some miscellaneous reading.

His knowledge of literature was no more complete than his character. Certain modern English poets— Rossetti, Morris, Keats, and Shelley—he knew almost by heart. And in travels and biography—mostly of men of action—he had, at one time or another, read voraciously. But 'the classics he had not read,' as with most of us, would have made a list of lamentable length.

Since his return to Ferth, however, he had browsed a good deal among the books collected by his grandfather, mostly by way of distracting himself at night from the troubles and worries of the day.

On this particular night there were two books lying on his table. One was a volume of Madame de Sévigné, the other St. Augustine's 'Confessions.' He turned over first one, then the other.

'Au reste, ma fille, une de mes grandes envies, ce serait d'être dévote; je ne suis ni au Dieu, ni au Diable; cet état m'ennuie, quoique entre nous je le trouve le plus

naturel du monde. On n'est point au Diable parce qu'on
craint Dieu, et qu'au fond on a un principe de religion ;
on n'est point à Dieu aussi, parce que sa loi paroît dure,
et qu'on n'aime point à se détruire soi-même.'

'Admirable !' he thought to himself, '*admirable !*
We are all there—my mother and I—three parts of mankind.'

But on a page of the other book he had marked these
lines—for the beauty of them :

'Beatus qui amat te, et amicum in te, et inimicum
propter te. Solus enim nullum eorum amittit, cui omnes
in illo cari sunt qui non amittitur.'

He hung over the fire, pondering the two utterances.

'A marvellous music,' he thought of the last. 'But I
know no more what it means than I know what a
symphony of Brahms' means. Yet some say they know.
Perhaps of *her* it might be true.'

The weeks ran on. Outside, the strike was at its
worst, though George still believed the men would give
in before Christmas. There was hideous distress, and
some bad rioting in different parts of the country.
Various attempts had been made by the employers to use
and protect non-union labour, but the crop of outrage
they had produced had been too threatening : in spite of
the exasperation of the masters they had been perforce
let drop. The Press and the public were now intervening
in good earnest—'every fool thinks he can do our
business for us,' as George would put it bitterly to Letty.
Bewick was speaking up and down the district with a
superhuman energy, varied only by the drinking-bouts to
which he occasionally succumbed ; and George carried
a revolver with him when he went abroad.

The struggle wore him to death ; the melancholy of
his temperament had never been so marked. At the

same time Letty saw a doggedness in him, a toughness like Fontenoy's own, which astonished her. Two men seemed to be fighting in him. He would talk with perfect philosophy of the miners' point of view, and the physical-force sanction by which the lawless among them were determined to support it; but at the same time he belonged to the stiffest set among the masters.

Meanwhile, at home, friction and discomfort were constantly recurring. In the course of three or four weeks Lady Tressady had several attacks of illness, and it was evident that her weakness increased rapidly. And with the weakness, alas! the ugly incessant irritability, that dried up the tenderness of nurses, and made a battle-ground of the sick-room. Though, indeed, she could never be kept in her room; she resented being left a moment alone. She claimed, in spite of the anxieties of the moment, to be constantly amused; and though George could sometimes distract and quiet her, nothing that Letty did, or said, or wore was ever tolerable to a woman who merely saw in this youth beside her a bitter reminder of her own.

At last, one day early in November, came a worse turn than usual. The doctor was in the house most of the day, but George had gone off before the alarm to a place on the farther side of the county, and could not be got at till the evening.

He came in to find Letty waiting for him in the hall. There had been a rally; the doctor had gone his way marvelling, and it was thought there was no immediate danger.

'But oh, the pain!' said Letty under her breath, pressing her hands together, and shivering. Her eyes were red, her cheeks pale; he saw that she was on the point of exhaustion; and he guessed that she had never seen such a sight before.

He ran up to visit his mother, whom he found almost speechless from weakness, yet waiting, with evident signs of impatience and temper, for her evening food. And while he and Letty were at their melancholy dinner together, Justine came flying downstairs in tears. Miladi would not eat what had been taken to her. She was exciting herself; there would be another attack.

Husband and wife hurried from the room. In the hall they found the butler just receiving a parcel left by the railway delivery-cart.

George passed the box with an exclamation and a shudder. It bore a large label 'From Worth et Cie,' and was addressed to Lady Tressady. But Letty stopped short, with a sudden look of pleasure.

'You go to her. I will have this unpacked.'

He went up and coaxed his mother like a child to take her soup and champagne. And presently, just as she was revived enough to talk to him, Letty appeared. Her mother-in-law frowned, but Letty came gaily up to the bed.

'There is a parcel from Paris for you,' she said, smiling. 'I have had it opened. Would you like it brought in?'

Lady Tressady first whimpered, and said it should go back—what did a dying woman want with such things? —then demanded greedily to see it.

Letty brought it in herself. It was a new evening gown of the softest greens and shell-pinks, fit for a bride in her first season. To see the invalid, ashen-grey, stretching out her hand to finger it was almost more than George could stand. But Letty shook out the rustling thing, put on the skirt herself that Lady Tressady might see, and paraded up and down in it, praising every cut and turning with the most ingenious ardour.

'I sha'n't wear it, of course, till after Christmas,' said

Lady Tressady at last, still looking at it with half-shut covetous eyes. 'Isn't it *darling* the way the lace is put on! Put it away. George!—it's the *first* I've had from him this year.'

She looked up at him appealingly. He stooped and kissed her.

'I am so glad you like it, mother dear. Can't you sleep now?'

'Yes, I think so. Good-night. And good-night, Letty.'

Letty came, and Lady Tressady held her hand, while the blue eyes, still bearing the awful impress of suffering, stared at her oddly.

'It was nice of you to put it on, Letty. I didn't think you'd have done it. And I'm glad you think it's pretty. I wish you would have one made like it. Kiss me.'

Letty kissed her. Then George slipped his wife's arm in his, and they left the room together. Outside Letty turned suddenly white, and nearly fell. George put his arms round her, and carried her down to his study. He put her on the sofa, and watched her tenderly, rubbing the cold hands.

'How you *could*,' he said at last, in a low voice, when he saw that she was able to talk; 'how you *could!* I shall never forget that little scene.'

'You'd have done anything, if you'd seen her this morning,' she said with her eyes still closed.

He sat beside her, silent, thinking over the miseries of the last few weeks. The net result of them—he recognised it with a leap of surprise—seemed to have been the formation of a new and secret bond between himself and Letty. During all the time he had been preparing himself for the worst this strange thing had been going on. How had it been possible for her to be, comparatively, so forbearing? He could see nothing in his past knowledge of her to explain it.

He recalled the effort and gloom with which she had made her first preparations for Lady Tressady. Yet she had made them. Is there really some mystic power, as the Christians say, in every act of self-sacrifice, however imperfect—a power that represents at once the impelling and the rewarding God—that generates, moreover, from its own exercise, the force to repeat itself? Personally such a point of view meant little to him, nor did his mind dwell upon it long. All that he knew was that some angel had stirred the pool—that old wounds smarted less —that hope seemed more possible.

Letty knew quite well that he was watching her in a new way, that there was a new clinging in his touch. She, little more than he, understood what was happening to her. From time to time during these weeks of painful tension there had been hours of wild rebellion, when she had hated her surroundings, her mother-in-law, and her general ill-luck as fiercely as ever. Then there had followed strange appeasements, and inflowing calms —moments when she had been able somehow to express herself to one who cared to listen—who poured upon her in return a sympathy which braced while it healed.

Suddenly she opened her eyes.

'Do you want to hear about that first time when she came to see me?' she whispered, her look wavering under his.

He flushed and hesitated. Then he kissed her hand.

'No, not now. You are worn out. Another time. But I love you for thinking of telling me.'

A feeling of rest and well-being stole over her. Mercifully he made no protestations, and she asked for none, but there was a gentle moving of heart towards heart. And the memory of that hour, that night, made one of the chief barriers between her and despair in the time that followed.

Two days later a painless death, death in her sleep, overtook Lady Tressady. Her delicate face, restored to its true years, and framed in its natural grey hair, seemed for the first time beautiful to George when he saw her in her coffin. He could not remember admiring her, even when he was a boy, and she was reckoned among the handsomest women of her day. Parting with her was like the snapping of a strain that had pulled life out of its true bearings and proportions. An immense, inevitable relief followed. But after her death Letty never said a harsh word of her, and George had a queer humble feeling that after all he might be found to owe her much.

For as November and December passed away the relation between the husband and wife steadily settled and improved. 'We shall rub along,' George said to himself in his frank, secret thoughts—'in the end it will be much better perhaps than either of us could have hoped.' That no doubt was the utmost that could ever be said; but it was much.

The night after his mother's death, Letty abruptly, violently even, as though worked up to it by an inner excitement, told him the story of her wrestle with Marcella. Then, throwing some letters into his hand, she broke into sobbing and ran away from him. When he went to look for her his own eyes were wet. 'Who else could have done such a thing?' he said; and Letty made no protest.

The letters gave him food for thought for many a day afterwards. They were little less of a revelation to him than the motives and personality lying behind them had been to Letty. In spite of all that he had felt for the woman who had written them, they still roused in him a secret and abiding astonishment. We use the words 'spiritual,' 'poetic' in relation to human conduct; we talk as though all that the words meant were familiarly understood by us; and yet when the spiritual or the poetic comes actually to walk among us, slips into the forms and functions of our common life, we find it amazing, almost inhuman. It gives us some trouble to take it simply, to believe in it simply.

Yet nothing in truth could be a more inevitable outcome of character and circumstance than these letters of Marcella Maxwell to George Tressady's wife. Marcella had suffered under a strong natural remorse, and to free her heart from the load of it she had thrown herself into an effort of reconciliation and atonement with all the passion, the subtlety, and the resource of her temperament. She had now been wooing Letty Tressady for weeks, nor had the eager contriving ability she had been giving to the process missed its reward. Letty fresh from the new impressions made upon her by Marcella at home, and Marcella as a wife, by a beauty she could no longer hate, and a charm to which she had been forced to yield, had found herself amid the loneliness and dulness of Ferth gradually enveloped and possessed anew by the same influence, acting in ways that grew week by week more personal, and more subduing.

What to begin with could be more flattering either to heart or vanity than the persistence with which one of the most famous women of her time—watched, praised, copied, attacked, surrounded, as Letty knew her to be, from morning till night—had devoted herself first to the understanding, then to the capturing, of the smaller, narrower life. The reaction towards a natural reserve, a certain proud instinctive self-defence, which had governed Marcella's manner during a great part of Letty's visit to the Court had been in these letters deliberately broken down —at first with effort, then more and more frankly, more and more sweetly. Day after day, as Letty knew, Marcella had taken time from politics, from society, from her most cherished occupations, to write to this far-off girl, from whom she had nothing either to gain or to fear, who had no claims whatever on her friendship, had things gone normally, while thick about the opening of their relation to each other hung the memory of Letty's insults and Letty's violence.

·And the letters were written with such abandonment! As a rule Marcella was a hasty or impatient correspondent. She thought letters a waste of time; life was full enough without them. But here, with Letty, she lingered, she took pains. The mistress of Les Rochers writing to her absent, her exacting Pauline could hardly have been more eager to please. She talked—at leisure—of all that concerned her—husband, child, high politics, the persons she saw, the gaieties she bore with, the books she read, the schemes in which she was busied; then, with greater tenderness, greater minuteness, of the difficulties and tediums of Letty's life at Ferth, as they had been dismally drawn out for her in Letty's own letters. The animation, the eager kindness of it all went for much; the amazing self-surrender, self-offering, implied in every page, for much more.

Strange!—as he read the letters George felt his own heart beating. Were they in some hidden way meant for him too?—he seemed to hear in them a secret message—a woman's yearning, a woman's response.

At any rate, the loving reconciling effort had done its work. Letty could not be insensible to such a flattery, a compliment so unexpected, so bewildering—the heart of a Marcella Maxwell poured out to her for the taking. She neither felt it so profoundly nor so delicately as hundreds of other women could have felt it. Nevertheless the excitement of it had thrilled and broken up the hardnesses of her own nature. And with each yielding

on her part had come new capacity for yielding, new
emotions that amazed herself ; till she found herself, as it
were, groping in a strange world, clinging to Marcella's
hand, trying to express feelings that had never visited
her before, one moment proud of her new friend with a
pride half moral, half selfish, the next, ill at ease with her,
and through it all catching dimly the light of new ideals.

One day, as George walked into Letty's sitting-room,
to discuss some small business of the afternoon, he saw
on her writing-table that same photograph of Lady Maxwell and her boy, whereof an earlier copy had come to
such a tragic end in Letty's hands. He walked up to it
with an exclamation ; Letty was not in the room. Suddenly, however, she came in. He made no attempt
whatever to disguise that he had been looking at the
photograph ; he bent over it indeed a moment longer,
deliberately. Then, walking away to the window, he
began speaking of the matter which had brought him to
look for his wife. Letty answered absently. The colour
had rushed to her face. Her hands fidgeted with the
books and papers on her table, and her mind was full of
fevered remembrance.

Presently George, having settled the little point he
came to speak of, fell silent. But he still stood by the
window, looking out through the rain-splashed glass to
the wintry valley below with its chimneys and straggling
village. Letty, who was pretending to write a note, raised
her head, looked at him—the quick breath beating through
the parted lips, the blue eyes half wild, half miserable.
She was not nearly so pretty as she had been a year
before. George had often noticed it ; it made part of his
remorse. But the face was more troubling, infinitely
more human ; and, in truth, he knew it much better, was
more sensitively alive to it, so to speak, than he ever had
been in the days of their courtship.

Before he left the room he came back to her, put his arm round her shoulders and kissed her hair. She did not raise her head or say anything. But when he had gone she looked up with a sudden fierce sob, took the photograph from its place, and thrust it angrily into the drawer in front of her. Afterwards she sat for some minutes, motionless, with her handkerchief at her lips, trying to choke down the tears that had seized her. And last of all, with trembling fingers, she took out the picture again, wrapped it in some soft tissue paper that lay near, as though propitiating it, and once more put it out of sight.

What had made her first ask Marcella for it, and then place it on her table where George might, nay, must see it? Some vague wish, no doubt, to 'make up'; to punish herself, while touching him. But the recollection of him, bending over the picture, tortured her, gripped her at the heart for many a day afterwards. She let it be seen no more. Yet that week she wrote more fully, more incoherently, more piteously to Marcella than ever before. She talked, not without bitterness and injustice, of her bringing up, asked what she should read, spread out her puzzles with the poor, or with her household—half angrily, as though she were accusing some one. For the first time, as it were, she was seeking a teacher in the art of living. And though the tone was still querulous, she knew, and Marcella presently dared to guess, that the ugly house on the hill had in truth ceased to be in the least dull or burdensome to her. George went in and out of it. And for the woman that has come to hunger for her husband's step, there is no more *ennui*.

Letty indeed hardly knew the strength of her own position. The reading of Lady Maxwell's letters to his wife had cleared a number of relics and fragments from George's mind. The day of passion was done. Yes !—but to see her frequently, to be brought back into any of the old social or political relations to her and Maxwell, from this his pride shrank no less than his conscience. Yet there was a large party in his constituency, and belonging to it some of the men whose probity and intelligence he had come to rate most highly, who were pressing him hard not to resign in February, and, indeed, not to resign at all. The few public meetings he had so far addressed had been stormy indeed, but on the whole decidedly friendly to him, and it was urged that he must at least present himself for re-election, in which case his expenses should be borne, and he should be left as unpledged as possible. Since the passage of the Bill Fontenoy's reactionary movement had lost ground largely in the constituency; and the position of independent member with a general leaning to the Government was no doubt easily open to George Tressady.

But his whole soul shrank from such a renewal of the effort of politics—probably because of that something in him, that enfeebling, paralysing something, which in all directions made him really prefer the half to the whole, and see barriers in the way of all enthusiasms. Nevertheless, the arguments he had to meet, and the kind persuasions he had to rebut, made these weeks all the more trying to him.

The second week of December came, the beginning of the end so far as the strike was concerned. The men's resources were exhausted; the masters stood unbroken. They had met the men in a joint committee; but they had steadily refused arbitration from outside. At the beginning of this week, rioting broke out in a district where the Union had least strength, caused, no doubt, by the rage of impending failure. By the middle of the following week, men were going in here and there, and the stampede of defeat had begun.

George, passing through the pinched and lowering faces that lined the village, hated the triumph of his class. On the 21st, he rode over to a neighbouring town, where local committees, both of masters and men, were sitting, to see if there was any final news as to the pits of his own valley.

About eight o'clock in the evening Letty heard his horse's hoofs returning. She knew that he was accustomed to ride in the dark, but the rumours of violence and excitement that filled the air had unnerved her, and she had been listening to every sound for some time past.

When the door was opened she ran out.

'Yes, I'm late,' said George, in answer to her remonstrances; 'but it is all right—it was worth waiting for. The thing's over. Some of the men go down to-morrow week, and the rest as we can find room for them.'

'On the masters' terms?'

'Of course—or all but.'

She clapped her hands.

'Oh, for goodness' sake don't!' he said, as he hung up his hat, and she, supposing that he was irritable from over-fatigue, managed to overlook the sharpness of his tone.

Their Christmas passed in solitude. George, more and more painfully alive to the disadvantages of Ferth as the home of a young woman with a natural love of gaiety, had tried, in spite of their mourning, to persuade Letty to ask some friends to spend Christmas week with them. She had refused, however, and they were still alone when the end of the strike arrived.

The day before the men were to go back to work, George returned late from a last meeting of the employers.

Letty had begun dinner, and when he walked into the
dining-room she saw at once that some unusual excitement or strain had befallen him.

'Let me have some food!' was all he would say in
answer to her first questions, and she let him alone.
When the servants were gone he looked up.

'I have had a shindy with Bewick, dear—rather a
bad one. But that's all. I walked down to the
station with Ashton '—Ashton was a neighbouring magis-
trate and coal-owner—'and there we found Valentine
Bewick. Two or three friends were in charge of him,
and it has been given out lately that he has been suffering
from nervous breakdown, owing to his exertions. All that
I could see was that he was drunker than usual—no doubt
to drown defeat. Anyway, directly he saw me he made
a scene—foamed and shouted. According to him, I am
at the bottom of the men's defeat. It is all my wild-
beast delight in the sight of suffering—my love of " fatten-
ing on the misery of the collier "—my charming villanies
of all sorts—that are responsible for everything. Altogether he reached a fine flight! Then he got violent—
tried to get at me with his knobbed stick. Ashton and I,
and the men with him, succeeded in quelling him without bothering the police.—I don't think anything more
will come of it.'

And he stretched out his hand to some salted almonds,
helping himself with particular deliberation.

After dinner, however, he lay down on a sofa in
Letty's sitting-room, obliged to confess himself worn out.
She made him comfortable, and after she had given him
a cushion, she suddenly bent over him from behind and
kissed him.

'Come here!' he said, with a smile, throwing up his
hand to catch her. But, with an odd blush and conscious
look, she eluded him.

When, a little later, she came to sit by him with some needlework she found him restless and inclined to talk.

'I wonder if we are always to live in this state of war for one's bread and butter!' he said, impatiently throwing down a newspaper he had been reading. 'It doesn't tend to make life agreeable—does it? Yet what on earth——'

He threw back his head, with a stiff protesting air, staring across the room.

Letty had the sudden impression that he was not talking to her at all, but to some third person, unseen.

'*Either* capital gets its fair remuneration'—he went on in an argumentative voice—'and ability its fair wages —*or* the Marxian state, labour-notes, and the rest of it. There is no half-way house—absolutely none. As for me, I am not going to lend my capital for nothing—nor to give my superintendence for nothing. And I don't ask exorbitant pay for either. It is quite simple. My conscience is quite clear.'

'I should think so!' said Letty, resentfully. 'I wonder whether Marcella—is all for the men? She has never mentioned the strike in her letters.'

As the Christian name slipped out, she flushed, and he was conscious of a curious start. But the breaking through of a long reticence was deliberate on Letty's part.

'Very likely she is all for the men,' he said drily, after a pause. 'She never could take a strike calmly. Her instinct always was to catch hold of any stick that could beat the employers—Watton and I used often to tease her about it.'

He threw himself back against the sofa, with a little laugh that was musical in Letty's ear. It was the first time that Lady Maxwell's name had been mentioned between them in this trivial ordinary way. The young

N N

wife sat alert and straight at her work, her cheek still pink, her eyes bright.

But after a silence, George suddenly sprang up to pace the little room, letting drop every now and then some queer fragmentary saying about the strike and the men, which would make Letty glance at him in perplexity, needle and hand pausing.

'George, what is the matter with you?' she said at last, looking at him in some anxiety.

'Oh! nothing. I seem to be talking rot, don't I?— Darling, who's ill? I saw the old doctor on the road home, and he threw me a word as he passed about having been here—looked quite jolly over it! What's wrong—one of the servants?'

Letty put down her work upon her knee and her hands upon it. She grew red and pale; then she turned away from him, pressing her face into the back of her chair.

He flew to her, and she murmured in his ear.

What she said was by no means all sweetness. There was mingled with it much terror and some anger. Letty was not one of the women who take maternity as a matter of course.

But emotion and natural feeling had their way. George was dissolved in joy. He threw himself at her feet, resting his head against her knee.

'If he doesn't have your eyes and hair I'll disinherit him,' he said, with a gaiety which seemed to have effaced all his fatigue.

'I don't want him,' was her pettish reply; 'but if *she* has your chin, I'll put her out to nurse. Oh! how I hate the thought of it!' and she shuddered.

He caught her hand, comforting her. Then, putting up both his own, he drew her down to him.

'After all, little woman, it hasn't turned out so badly?' he said in her ear, with sad appeal. Their lips met, trembling. Suddenly Letty broke into passionate weeping. George sprang up, gathered her upon his knee, and they sat for long, in silence, clinging to each other.

At last Letty drew back from him, pushing a hand against his shoulder.

'You know—you didn't care a bit for me—when you married me,' she said, half bitter, half crying.

'Didn't I? And you?' he asked, raising his eyebrows.

'Oh! I don't remember!' she said hurriedly, and dropped her face on his coat again.

'Well, we are going to care for each other,' he said in a low voice, after a pause. 'That's what matters now, isn't it?'

She made no reply, but she put up a hand, and touched his face. He turned his lips to the hand and kissed it tenderly. There was a sore sad spot in each heart; and neither dared to look forward. But to-night there was a sense of belonging to each other in a new and sacred way, of being drawn apart, separated from the world, husband and wife, together. Through George's mind there wandered half-astonished thoughts about this strange compelling power of marriage,—the deep grip it makes on life—the almost mechanical way in which it bears down resistance, provided only that certain compunctions, certain scruples still remain for it to work on.

George slept lightly, being over-tired. All through the night the vision of the beaten men going down sullenly to their first shift seemed to hold him as though in a nightmare. It was a kind of moral nausea that oppressed him, affecting all his ideas of his own place and rights in a world of combat.

'I shall get over it,' he said to himself in a half-waking interval.   'There is no sense in it.'

Between seven and eight o'clock a sound startled him.   He found himself standing by his bed, struggling to wake and collect himself.

A sound that had shaken the house passed like a dull thud through the valley.   A horror seized him. He looked at Letty, who was fast asleep; then he walked noiselessly into his dressing-room, and began to hurry on his clothes.

Five minutes later he was running down the hill at his full speed.   It was bitterly cold and still; the first snow lay on the grass, and a raw grey veil hung over the hills.   As he came in sight of the distant pit-bank he saw a crowd of women swarming up it; a confused and hideous sound of crying and shrieking came to his ears; and at the same moment a boy, panting and dead-white, ran through the lodge-gates to meet him.

'Where is it, Sprowston?'

'Oh, sir, it's No. 2 pit.   The damp's comin up the upcast, and the cage is blown to pieces.   But the down shaft's all right, and Mr. Madan and Mr. Macgregor were starting down as I come away.   There was eighty-six men and boys went down first shift.'

George groaned, and rushed on.

CHAPTER XXIV

ENGLAND knows these scenes too well!

When Tressady, out of breath with running, reached the top of the bank, and threw a hurried look in front of him, his feeling was that he had seen everything before—the wintry dawn, the crowds of pale men and weeping women ranged on either hand, the police keeping the ground round the shafts clear for the mine officials—even the set white face of his manager, who, with Macgregor the fireman and two hewers, had just emerged from the cage that was waiting at the mouth of the downcast shaft.

As soon as Madan saw Tressady rounding the corner of the engine-house he hurried towards his employer.

'Have you been down yet?' Tressady cried to him.

'Just come up, sir. We got about fifty yards—air fairly good—then we found falls along the main intake. We got over three or four, till the damp rose on us too bad—we had a rough bit getting back. I thought you'd be here by now. Macgregor thinks from the direction in which things were lying that the blast had come from Holford's Heading or thereabouts.'

And the manager hastily opened a map of the colliery he was carrying in his hand against the wall of the engine-house, and pointed to the spot.

'How many men there?'

'About thirty-two in the workings round about—as near as I can reckon it.'

'Any sign of the rest? How many went down?'

'Eighty-six. A cageful of men and lads—just them from the shaft-bottom—got up immediately after the explosion. Since then, not a sound from anyone! The uptake shaft is chockfull of damp. Mitchell, in the fan-room, had to run for it at first, it was coming up so fast.'

'Good God!' said George under his breath; and the two men eyed each other painfully.

'Have you sent for the inspector?' said Tressady, after a moment.

'He ought to be here in five minutes now, sir.'

'Got some baulks together?'

'The men are piling them by the shaft at this moment.'

'Fan uninjured?'

'Yes, sir—and speed increased.'

Followed by Madan, Tressady walked up to the shaft, and himself questioned Macgregor and the two hewers.

Then he beckoned to Madan, and the two walked in close converse towards the lamphouse, discussing a plan of action. As they passed slowly along the bank the eyes of the miserable terror-stricken throng to either side followed every movement. But there was not a sound from anyone. Once Tressady looked up and caught the faces of some men near him—dark faces, charged with a meaning that seemed instantly to stiffen his own nerve for what he had to do.

'I give Dixon three more minutes,' he said, impatiently looking at his watch; 'then we go down without him.'

Dixon was the inspector. He was well known throughout the district, a plucky, wiry fellow, who was generally at the pit's mouth immediately after an accident, ready and keen to go with any rescue party on any errand, however dangerous—purely, as he himself declared, for professional and scientific reasons. In this case, he

lived only a mile away, on the farther side of the village,
so that Madan's messenger had not far to go.

As he spoke, George felt his arm clutched from behind. He turned, and saw Mary Batchelor, who had
come forward from a group of women.

'Sir George! Listen ere, Sir George.' Her lined face
and tear-blurred eyes worked with a passion of entreaty.
'The boy went down at five with the rest. Don't yer
bear im no malice. Ee's a poor sickly creetur, an the
Lord an't give im the full use of his wits.'

George smiled at the poor thing's madness, and
touched her kindly on the shoulder.

'Don't you trouble yourself, Mary; all that can be
done will be done—for everybody. We are only giving
Mr. Dixon another minute; then we go down. Look
here '—he drew her inside the door of the lamproom,
which happened to be close by, for an open-mouthed
group, eager to hear whatever he might be saying, had
begun to press about them. 'Can you take this message from me up to the house? There'll be no news here,
you know, for a long time, and I left Lady Tressady
asleep.'

He tore a half-sheet from the letter in his pocket,
scribbled a few words upon it, and put it into Mary's
hand.

The woman, with her shawl over her head, ran past
the lamphouse towards the entrance-gate as fast as her
age would let her, while George rejoined Madan.

'Ah, there he is!'

For the small, lean figure of the inspector was
already passing the gate.

Tressady hurried to meet him.

By the time the first questions and answers were over,
Tressady, looking round for Madan, saw that the manager
was speaking angrily to a tall man in a rough coat and

corduroy trousers who had entered the pit premises in
the wake of Mr. Dixon.

'You take yourself off, Mr. Bewick! You're not
wanted here.'

'Madan!' called Tressady, 'attend to Mr. Dixon,
please. I'll see to that man.'

And he walked up to Bewick, while the men standing
near crowded over the line they had been told to keep.

'What do you want?' he said, as he reached the new-
comer.

'I have come to offer myself for the rescue party.
I've been a working miner for years. I've had special
experience in accidents before. I can beat anybody here
in physical strength.'

As he spoke, the great heavily built fellow looked
round him, and a murmur of assenting applause came
from the bystanders.

Tressady studied him.

'Are you fit?' he said shortly.

Bewick flushed. Tressady's penetrating look forced
his own to meet it.

'As fit as you are,' was his haughty reply.

'Well'—said Tressady, slowly, 'we don't want to be
refusing strong men. If Madan 'll have you, you shall
come. Mind, we're all under his orders.'

He went to the manager, and said a word in his ear.
Madan, in response, vouchsafed neither look nor remark
to the man, whom he hated apparently more bitterly than
his employer did. But he made no further objection to
his joining the search party.

Presently all preparations were made. Picked bands
of firemen and timbermen descended first, with Madan
at their head. Then George, Mr. Dixon, a couple of
local doctors who had hurried up to offer their services,
and Bewick.

As they shot down into the darkness George was conscious of a strange exhilaration. Working on the indications given him by the first exploring party, his mind was alive with conjectures as to the cause of the accident, and with plans for dealing with the various obstacles that might occur. Never during these weeks of struggle and noise and objurgation had he felt so fit, so strenuous. At the bottom of the shaft he had even to remind himself, with a shudder, of the dead men who must be waiting for them in these black depths.

For some little distance from the shaft nothing was to be seen that spoke of an explosion. Some lamps in the porch of the shaft and along the main roadway were burning as usual, and the 'journey' of trucks, from which the 'hookers-on' and engine-men had escaped at the first sign of danger, was standing laden in the entrance of the mine. The door of the under-manager's cabin, near the base of the shaft, was open. Madan looked into the little den, where the lamp was still burning on the wall, and groaned. The young fellow who was generally to be found there was a great friend of his, and they attended the same chapel together. A little farther an open cupboard was noticed with a wisp of spun yarn hanging out from it—inflammable stuff, quite untouched. But about thirty yards farther they came upon the first signs of mischief. A heavy fall of roof had to be scrambled over, and beyond it afterdamp was clearly perceptible.

Here there was an exclamation from Bewick, who was to the front, and the first victim showed out of the dark in the pale glow-worm light of the lamps turned upon him. A man lay on his side, close against the wall, with an unlocked lamp in his hands, which were badly burnt. But no other part of him was burnt, and it was clear that he had died of afterdamp in trying to escape. He had

evidently come from one of the nearer work-places, and
fallen within a few yards of safety. The inspector pounced
upon the lamp at once, while the doctors knelt by the body.
But in itself the lamp told little. If it were the illegal
unlocking of a lamp that caused the disaster, neither this
lamp nor this man could be at fault; for he had died
clearly on the verge of the explosion area, and from the
after-effects of the calamity. But the inspector, who had
barely looked at the dead man, turned the lamp round
in his hands, dissatisfied.

'Bad pattern! bad pattern! If I had my way I'd
fine every manager whose lamps *could* be unlocked,' he
said to himself, but quite audibly.

'The fireman may have unlocked it, sir, to re-light
his own or some one else's,' said Madan, stiffly, put at
once on his defence.

'Oh! I know you're within your legal right, Mr.
Madan,' said the inspector briskly. '*I* haven't the making
of the laws.'

And he sat down on the floor, taking the lamp to
pieces, and bending his shrewd black-eyed face over it,
all the time that the doctors were examining its owner.
He was, perhaps, one of the most humane men in his
profession, but a long experience had led him to the
conclusion that in these emergencies the fragments of
a lamp, or a 'tamping,' or a 'shot,' matter more to the
community than dead men.

Meanwhile George crouched beside the doctors,
watching them. The owner of the lamp was a strong,
fair-haired young man, without a mark on him except
for the burning of the hands, the eyes quietly shut, the
face at peace. One of the colliers in the search party
had burst out crying when he saw him. The lad was his
nephew, and had been a favourite in the pit, partly
because of his prowess as a football-player. But the

young life had gone out irrevocably. The doctor shook his head as he lifted himself, and they left him there, in order not to waste any chance of getting out the living first.

Twenty yards farther on three more bodies were found, two oldish men and a boy, very little-burnt. They also had been killed in escaping, dragged down by the inexorable afterdamp.

A little beyond this group a fall of mingled stone and coal from the roof blocked the way so heavily that the hewers and timbermen had to be set to work to open out and shore up before a passage could be made. Meanwhile the air in the haulage road was clearing fast, and George could sit on a lump of stone and watch the dim light playing on the figures of the men at work. The blows struck echoed from floor to roof; the work of the bare arms and backs, as they swayed and jerked, woke a clamour in the mine. Were there any ears still to listen for them beyond that mass? He could scarcely keep a limb quiet, as he sat looking on, for impatience and excitement. Bewick meanwhile was wielding a pick with the rest, and George envied him the bodily skill and strength that, in spite of his irregular ways of life, were still left to him.

To restore the ventilation-current was their first object, and the foremost pick had no sooner gained the roadway on the other side than a strong movement of the air was perceptible. Madan's face cleared. The ventilation circuit between the downcast and upcast shafts must be already in some sort re-established. Let them only get a few more 'stoppings' and brattices put temporarily to rights, and the fan, working at its increased speed, would soon drive the renewed air-currents forward again, and make it possible to get all over the mine. The hole made was quickly enlarged, and the rescuers scrambled through.

But still fall after fall on the farther side delayed their progress, and the work of repairing the blown-out stoppings by such wood brattice as could be got at, was long and tedious. The rescuers toiled and sweated, pausing every now and then to draw upon the food and drink sent up from behind; and the hours flew unheeded. At last, upon the farther side of one of the worst of these falls— a loose mingled mass of rock and coal—they came on indications that showed them they had reached the centre and heart of the disaster. A door leading on the right to one of the side-roads of the pit known as Holford's Heading was blown outwards, and some trucks from the heading had been dashed across the main intake, and piled up in a huddled and broken mass against the farther wall. Just inside that door lay victim after victim, mostly on their faces, poor fellows! as they had come running out from their stalls at the noise of the explosion, only to meet the fiery blast that killed them. Two or three had been flung violently against the sides of the heading, and were left torn, with still bleeding wounds, as well as charred and blackened by the flame. Of sixteen men and boys that lay in this place of death, not one had survived to hear the stifled words—half groans, half sobs, of the comrades who had found them.

'But, thank God! no torture, no *thought*,' said George to himself as he went from face to face; 'an instant—a flash—then nothingness.'

Many of the men were well known to him. He had seen them last hanging about the village street, pale with famine—the hatred in their eyes pursuing him.

He knelt down an instant beside an elderly man whom he could remember since he was quite a boy—a weak-eyed, sallow fellow, much given to preaching—much given, too, it was said, to beating his wife and children, as the waves of excitement took him. Anyway, a fellow who could feel, whose nerves stung and tormented him, even in the courses of ordinary life. He lay with his eyes half open, the face terribly scorched, the hands clenched, as though he still fought with the death that had overcome him.

George covered the man's face with a handkerchief as the doctor left the body. '*He* suffered,' he said under his breath. The doctor heard him, and nodded sadly.

Hark! What was that? A cry—a faint cry!

'They're some of them alive in the end workings,' cried Madan, with a sob of joy. 'Come on, my lads! come on!'

And the party—all but Mr. Dixon—leaving the dead, pushed on through the foul atmosphere, over heaps of fallen stone and coal, in quest of the living.

'Leave me a man,' said Mr. Dixon, detaining the manager a moment. 'I stay here. You have enough with you. If I judge right, it all began here.'

A collier stayed with him, unwillingly, panting all the time under the emotion of the rescue the man imagined but was not to see.

For while the inspector measured and sketched, far up the heading, in some disused workings off a side-dip or roadway, Bewick was the first to come upon twenty-five men, eighteen of whom were conscious and uninjured. Two of them had strength enough, as they heard the footsteps and shouts approaching, to stagger out into the heading to meet their rescuers. One, a long, thin lad, came forward with leaps and gambols, in spite of his weakness, and fell almost at Tressady's feet. As he recognised the tall man standing above him, his bloodless mouth twitched into a broad grin.

'I say, give us a chance. Take me out—won't you?'

It was Mary Batchelor's grandson. In retribution
for the assault on Letty the lad had been sentenced to
three weeks' imprisonment, and George had not seen
him since. He stooped now, and poured some brandy
down the boy's throat. 'We'll get you out directly,' he
said, ' as soon as we've looked to the others.'

'There's some on em not worth takin out,' said the
boy, clinging to George's leg. 'They're dead. Take me
out first.' Then, with another grin, as George disengaged
himself, ' Some on em's prayin.'

Indeed, the first sight of that little group was a
strange and touching one. About a dozen men sat
huddled round one of their number, a Wesleyan class-
leader, who had been praying with them and reciting
passages from St. John. All of them, young or old, were
dazed and bent from the effects of afterdamp, and scarcely
one of them had strength to rise till they were helped to
their feet. Nevertheless, the cry which had been heard
by their rescuers had not been a cry for help, but the
voices of the little prayer-meeting raised feebly through
the darkness in the Old Hundredth.

A little distance from the prayer-meeting, the sceptics
of the party leant against the wall or lay along the floor,
unheeding; while seven men were unconscious, and
possibly dying. Two or three young fellows meanwhile,
who had been least touched by the afterdamp, had
' amused themselves,' as they said, by riding up and
down the neighbouring level on the ' jummer ' or coal-
truck of one of them.

'Weren't you afraid?' Tressady asked one of these,
turning a curious look at him, while the doctors were
examining the worst cases, and rough men were sobbing
and shaking each other's hands.

'Noa,' said the young hewer, his face, like something
cut out in yellowish wax, returning the light from

Tressady's lamp. 'Noa, theer was cumpany. Old Moses, there—ee saved us.'

Old Moses was the leader of the prayer-meeting. He was a fireman besides, who had been for twenty-six years in the mine. At the time of the explosion, it appeared, he had been in a working close to that door on the heading where death had done so ghastly and complete a work. But the flame in its caprice had passed him by, and he and another man had been able to struggle through the afterdamp back along the heading, just in time to stem the rush of men and boys from the workings at the farther end. These men were at the moment in a madness of terror, and ready even to plunge into the white death-mist advancing to meet them, obeying only the instinct of the trapped animal to 'get out.' But Moses was able to control them, to draw them back by degrees along the heading, till, in the distant workings where they were found, the air was more tolerable, and they could wait for rescue.

George was the first to help the old fireman to his feet. But instead of listening to any praises of his own conduct, he was no sooner clinging to Tressady's arm than he called to Madan :

'Mr. Madan, sir !'

'Ay, Moses.'

'Have ye heard aught of them in the West Heading yet ?'

'No, Moses; we must get these fellows out first. We'll go there next.'

'I left thirty men and boys there this morning at half-past six. It was fair thronged up with them.' The old man's voice shook.

Meanwhile Madan and the doctors were busy with the transport of the seven unconscious men, some of whom were already dying. Each of them had to be carried on his back by two men, and as soon as the sick procession was organised it was seen that only three of the search party were left free—Tressady, Bewick, and the Scotch fireman, Macgregor.

Up the level and along the heading, past the point where Dixon was still at work, over the minor falls that everywhere attested the range of the explosion, and through the pools of water that here and there gathered the drippings of the mine, the seven men were tenderly dragged or carried, till at last the party regained the main intake or roadway.

George turned to Madan.

'You will have your hands full with these poor fellows. Macgregor and I—Mr. Bewick, if he likes—will push on to the West Heading.'

Madan looked uneasy.

'You'd better go up, Sir George,' he said in a low voice, 'and let me go on. You don't know the signs of the roof as I do. Eight or nine hours after an explosion is the worst time for falls. Send down another shift, sir, as quick as you can.'

'Why should you risk more than I?' said George, quietly. 'Stop! What time is it?' He looked at his watch. Five o'clock—nearly nine hours since they descended! He might have guessed it at three, if he had been asked. Time in the midst of such an experience contracts to a pin's point. But the sight of the watch stirred a pang in him.

'Send word at once to Lady Tressady,' he said in Madan's ear, drawing the manager to one side. 'Tell her I have gone on a little farther, and may be another hour or two in getting back. If she is down at the bank, beg her from me to go home. Tell her the chances are that we may find the other men as safe as these.'

Madan acquiesced reluctantly. George then plundered

him of some dry biscuits—of some keys, moreover, that might be useful in opening one or two locked doors farther up the workings.

'Macgregor, you'll come?'

'Ay, Sir George.'

'You, Mr. Bewick?'

'Of course,' said Bewick, carelessly, throwing back his handsome head.

Some of the rescued men turned and looked hard at their agent and leader with their sunken eyes. Others took no notice. His prestige had been lost in defeat; and George had noticed that they avoided speech with him. No doubt this rescue party had presented itself to the agent as an opening he dare not neglect.

'Come on, then,' said George; and the three men turned back towards the interior of the pit.

Old Moses, from whose clutch George had just freed himself, stopped short and looked after them. Then he raised a hoarse voice:

'Be you going to the West Heading, Sir George?'

'Yes,' George flung back over his shoulder, already far away.

'The Lord go with yer, Sir George!'

No answer. The old man, breathing hard, caught hold of one of his stronger comrades and tottered on towards the shaft. Two or three of his fellows gathered round him. 'Ay,' said one of them, out of Madan's hearing, 'ee's been a-squeezing of us through the ground, ee ave, but ee's a plucky lot, is the boss.'

'They do say as Bewick slanged im fine at the station yesterday,' said another, hoarsely. 'Called im the devil untied, one man told me.'

The first speaker, still haggard and bowed from the poison in his blood, made no reply, and the movement of old Moses's lips, as he staggered forward, helped on by

o o

the two others, his head hanging on his breast, showed
that he was praying. · ·

Meanwhile George and his two companions pushed
cautiously on, Macgregor trying the roof with his lamp
from time to time for signs of fire-damp. Two seams of
coal were worked in the mine, one of which was 'fiery.'
No naked lights, therefore, were allowed, and all 'shots'
or charges for loosening the coal were electrically fired.

As they made their way, now walking, now scramb-
ling, they spoke sometimes of the possible cause of the
disaster : whereof Dixon, as they passed him, had bluntly
declined to say a word till his task was done. George,
by a kind of contradiction—his mind alive all the time
with feverish images of death and mutilation—fell into a
strain of caustic remark as to the obstinate disobedience
or carelessness of a certain type of miner—disobedience
which, in his own experience even, had already led to a
score of fatal accidents. Bewick, irritated apparently by
his tone, took up a provoking line of reply. Suppose a
miner, set to choose between the risk of bringing the coal-
roof down on his head for lack of a proper light to work
by, and the risk of 'being blown to hell' by the opening
of his lamp, did a mad thing sometimes, who were other
people that they should blame him? His large ox-like
eyes, clear in the light of his lamp, turned a scornful
defiance on his companion. 'Try it yourself, my fine gentleman '—that was what the expression of them meant.

' He doesn't only risk his own life,' said George, shortly.
' That's the answer.—I say, Macgregor, isn't this the door
to the Meadows Pit? If anything cut us off from the
shaft, and supposing we couldn't get round yet by the
return, we might have to try it, mightn't we ? '

Macgregor assented, and George as he passed stepped
up to the heavy wooden door, and tried one of the keys

he held, that he might be sure of opening it in case of
need.

The door had been unopened for long, and he shook
it backwards and forwards to make the key bite.

Meanwhile Macgregor had lingered a little behind,
while Bewick had walked on.   Suddenly, above the
rattle of the door a cracking noise was heard. A voice
of agony rang through the roadway.

'Run, Sir George! run!'

A rattle like thunder roared through the mine. It
was heard at the pithead, and the people crowded there
ran hither and thither in dismay, thinking it was another
explosion.

Hours passed.   At last in George's numbed brain
there was a faint stir of consciousness.   He opened his
eyes slowly.

Oh, horror! oh, cruelty! to come back from mer-
ciful nothingness and peace to this burning anguish,
not to be borne, of body and mind. 'I had died,' he
thought—'it was done with,' and a wild, impotent
rage, as against some brutality done him, surged through
him.

A little later he made a first slight movement, which
was answered at once by another movement on the part
of a man sitting near him.   The man bent over him in
the darkness and felt for his pulse.

'Bewick!'   The whisper was just perceptible.

'Yes, Sir George.'

'What has happened?   Where is Macgregor?   Give
me some brandy—there, in my inner pocket.'

'No; I have it. Can you swallow it? I have tried
several times before, but your mouth was set—it ran
down my fingers.'

'Give it me.'

Their fingers met, George feeling for the flask. As he moved his arm a groan of anguish broke from him.

'Drink it—if you possibly can.'

George put all the power of his being into the effort to swallow a few drops. Still the anguish! 'Oh God, my back! and the legs—paralysed!'

The words were only spoken in the brain, but it seemed to him that he cried them aloud. For a moment or two the mind swam again; then the brandy began to sting.

He slid down a hand slowly, defying the pain it caused him, to feel his right leg. The trouser round the thigh hung in ribbons, but the fragments lying on the flesh were caked and hard; and beneath him was a pool. His reason worked with difficulty, but clearly. 'Some bad injury to the thigh,' he thought. 'Much bleeding— probably the bleeding has dulled the worst pain. The back and shoulders burnt——'

Then, in the same hesitating, difficult way he managed to lift his hand to his head, which ached intolerably. The right temple and the hair upon it were also caked and wet.

He let his hand drop. 'How long have I——?' he thought. For already his revived consciousness could hardly maintain itself; something from the black tunnels of the mine seemed to be perpetually pressing out upon it, threatening to drown it like a flood.

'Bewick!'—he felt again with his hand—'where's Macgregor?'

A sob broke from the darkness beside him.

'Crushed in an instant. I heard one cry. Why not we, too?'

'It was such a bad fall?'

'The whole mine seemed to come down.' George felt the shudder of the huge frame. 'I escaped; you must have been caught by some of it. Macgregor was right underneath it. But there was an explosion besides.'

'Macgregor's lamp? Broken?' whispered George, after a pause.

'Possibly. It couldn't have been much, or we should have been killed instantly. I was only stunned—a bit scorched, too—not badly. You're the lucky one. I shall die by inches.'

'Cheer up!' said George, faintly. 'I can't last—but they'll find you.'

'What chance for either of us,' said Bewick, groaning. 'The return must be blocked, too, or they'd have got round to us by now.'

'How long——'

'God knows! To judge by the time I've been sitting — since I got you here—it's night long ago.'

'Since you got me here?' repeated George, with feeble interrogation.

'When I came to I was lying with my face in a dampish sort of hollow, and I suppose the afterdamp had lifted a bit, for I could raise my head. I felt you close by. Then I dragged myself on a bit, till I felt some brattice. I got past that, found a dip where the air was better, came back for you, and dragged you here. I thought you were dead at first; then I felt your heart. And since we got here I've found an air-pipe up here along the wall, and broken it.'

George was silent. But the better atmosphere was affecting him somewhat, and consciousness was becoming clearer. Only, what seemed to him a loud noise disturbed him—tortured the wound in his head. Then, gradually, as he bent his mind upon it, he made out what it was—a slow drip or trickle of water from the face of the wall. The contrast between his imagination and the reality supplied him with a kind of measure of the silence that enwrapped them—silence that seemed in itself a living thing, charged with the brooding vengeance of the earth upon the creatures that had been delving at her heart.

'Bewick!—that water—maddens me.' He moved his head miserably. 'Could you get some?. The brandy-flask has a cup.'

'There is a little pool by the brattice. I put my cap in as we got there, and dashed it over you. I'll go again.'

George heard the long limbs drag themselves painfully along. Then he lost count again of time, and all impressions on the ear, till he was roused by the water at his lips and a hand dashing some on his brow.

He drank greedily.

'Thanks! Put it by me—there; that's safe. Now, Bewick, I'm dying. Leave me. You can't do anything —and you—you might still try for it. There are one or two ways that might be worth trying. Take these keys. I could explain——'

But the little thread of life wavered terribly as he spoke. Bewick had to put his ear close to the scorched lips.

'No,' he said gloomily, 'I don't leave a man while there's any life in him. Besides, there's no chance—I don't know the mine.'

Suddenly, as though answering to the other's despair, a throb of such agony rose in George it seemed to rive body and soul asunder. His poor Letty!—his child that was to be!—his own energy of life, he had been so conscious of at the very moment of descending to this hideous death—all gone, all done!—his little moment of being torn from him by the inexorable force that restores nothing and explains nothing.

A picture flashed into his mind, an etching that he had seen in Paris in a shop window—had seen and pondered over. 'Entombed' was written underneath it, and it showed a solitary miner, on whom the awful trap has fallen, lifting his arms to his face in a last cry against the universe that has brought him into being, that has given him nerve and brain—for this!

Wherever he turned his eyes in the blackness he saw it—the lifted arms, the bare torso of the man, writhing under the agony of realisation—the tools, symbols of a life's toil, lying as they had dropped for ever from the hands that should work no more. It had sent a shudder through him, even amid the gaiety of a Paris street.

Then this first image was swept away by a second. It seemed to him that he was on the pit bank again. It was night, but the crowd was still there, and big fires lighted for warmth threw a glow upon the faces. There were stars, and a pale light of snow upon the hills. He looked into the engine-house. There she was—his poor Letty! Oh God! He tried to get through to her, to speak to her. Impossible!

A sound disturbed his dream.

His ear and brain struggled with it—trying to give it a name. A man's long, painful breaths—half sobs. Bewick, no doubt,—thinking of the woman he loved—of the poor emaciated soul George had seen him tending in the cottage garden on that April day.

He put out his hand and touched his companion.

'Don't despair,' he whispered; 'you will see her again. How strange—we two—we enemies—but this is the end. Tell me about her.'

'I took her from a ruffian who had nearly murdered her and the child,' said the hoarse voice after a pause. 'She was happy—in spite of the drink, in spite of everything—she would have been happy, till she died. To think of her alone is too cruel. If people turned their backs on her, I made up.'

' You will see her again,' George repeated, but hardly
knowing what the words were he said.

When he next spoke it was with an added strength
that astonished his companion.

'Bewick, promise me something. Take a message
from me to my wife. Come nearer.'

Then, as he felt his companion's breath on his cheek,
he roused himself to speak plainly :

'Tell her—my love—was all hers—that I thanked her
with my whole heart and soul for her love—that it was
very hard to leave her—and our child. Write the words
for her, Bewick. Tell her it was impossible for me to
write, but I dictated this.' He paused for a long time, then
resumed : 'And tell her, too—my last wish was—that
she should ask Lord and Lady Maxwell—can you hear
plainly ? '—he repeated the names—' to be her friends and
guardians. And bid her ask them—from me—not to for-
sake her. Have you understood ? Will you repeat it ? '

Bewick, in the mood of one humouring the whim of
the dying, repeated what had been said to him word by
word, his own sensuous nature swept the while by the
terrors of a death which seemed but one little step farther
from himself than from Tressady. Yet he did his best
to understand, and recollect ; and to the message so
printed on his shrinking brain a woman's misery owed
its only comfort in the days that followed.

' Thank you,' said Tressady, painfully listening for the
last word. ' Give me your hand. Good-bye. You and
I—The world's a queer place—I wish I'd turned you back
at the pit's mouth. I wanted to show I bore no malice.
Well—at least I know——'

The words broke off incoherently. Bewick caught
the word ' suffering,' and some phrase about ' the men,'
then Tressady's head slipped back against the wall, and
he spoke no more.

But the mind was active long afterwards. Again and again he seemed to himself standing in a bright light, alive and free. Innumerable illusions played about him. In one of the most persistent he was climbing the slope of a Swiss meadow in May. Oh! the scent of the narcissus, heavy still with the morning dew—the brush of the wet grass against his ankles—those yellow anemones shining there beneath the pines—the roar of the river in the gorge below—and beyond, far above, the grey peak, sharp and tall against that unmatched brilliance of the blue. In another he was riding alone in a gorge aflame with rhododendrons, and far down in the plain—the burnt-up Indian plain—some great fortified town, grave on its hill-top, broke the level lines—' A rose-red city, half as old as time.' Or, again, it was the sea in some glow of sunset, the white reflections of the sails slipping down and down through the translucent pinks and blues, till the eye lost itself in the infinity of shades and tints, which the breeze—oh the freshness of it !—was painting each moment anew at its caprice—painting and blotting, over and over again, as the water swung under the ship.

But all through these freaks of memory some strange thing seemed to have happened to him. He carried something in his arms—on his breast. The anguish of his inner pity for Letty, piercing through all else, expressed itself so.

But sometimes, as the brain grew momentarily clearer, he would wonder, almost in his old cynical way, at his own pity. She seemed to have come to love him. But was it not altogether for her good that his flawed, contradictory life should be cut violently from hers ? Could their marriage, ill-planted, ill-grown, have come in the end to any tolerable fruit ? His mind passed back, with bitterness, over the nine months of it ; not bitterness towards her—he seemed to be talking to her all the time, as she lay hidden on his shoulder—bitterness towards himself, towards the futility of his own life and efforts and desires.

But why his more than any other? The futility, the insignificance of all that man desires, all that waits on him—that old self-scorn, which began with the race, tormented him none the less, in dying, for the myriads it had haunted so before. An image of human fate, which had struck him in some book, recurred to him now—an image of daisied grass, alive one moment in the evening light—a quivering world of blades and dew, insects and petals, a forest of innumerable lines, crossed by the in-numerable movements of living things—the next with-drawn into the night, all silenced, all effaced.

So life. Except, perhaps, for pain! His own pain never ceased. The only eternity that seemed conceivable, therefore, was an eternity of pain. It had become to him the last reality. What a horrible quickening had over-taken him of that sense for misery, that intolerable compassion, which in life he had always held to be the death of a man's natural energy! Again and again, as consciousness still flickered in the clouding brain, it seemed to him that he heard voices and hammerings in the mine. And while he listened, from the eternal darkness about him, dim tragic forms would break, in a faltering procession—men or young boys, burnt and marred and slain like himself—turning to him faces he remembered. It was as though the scorn for pity he had once flung at Marcella Maxwell had been but the fruit of some obscure and shrinking foresight that he himself should die drowned and lost in pity; for as he waited for death his soul seemed to sink into the suffer-ing of the world, as a spent swimmer sinks into the wave.

One perception, indeed, that was not a perception

of pain, seemed to spring out of the very sense of utter rout, of helpless, infinite submission. The accusing looks of hungry men, the puzzles of his own wavering heart, all social qualms and compunctions—these things troubled him no more. In the wanderings of death he was not without the solemn sense that, after all, he, George Tressady, a man of no professions, and no enthusiasms, had yet paid his share and done his part.

Was there something in this thought that softened the dolorous way? Once—nearly at the last—he opened his eyes with a start.

'What is it? Something watches me. There is a sense of something that supports—that reconciles. If—*if*—how little would it all matter! *Oh! what is this that knows the road I came—the flame turned cloud, the cloud returned to flame—the lifted, shifted steeps, and all the way!*' His dying thought clung to words long familiar, as that of other men might have clung to a prayer. There was a momentary sense of ecstasy, of something ineffable.

And with that sense came a rending of all barriers, a breaking of long tension, a flooding of the soul with joy. Was it a passing under new laws, into a new spiritual polity? He knew not; but as he lifted his sightless eyes he saw the dark roadway of the mine expand, and a woman, stepping with an exquisite lightness and freedom, came towards him. Neither shrank nor hesitated. She hurried to him, knelt by him, and took his hands. He saw the sweetness in her dark eyes. '*Is it so bad, my friend? Have courage—the end is near.*' '*Care for her—and keep me, too, in your heart,*' he cried to her, piteously. She smiled. Then light—blinding, featureless light—poured over the vision, and George Tressady had ceased to live.